"RANNEY IS A RICH, RARE FIND!"

Judith Ivory

WORDS OF LOVE

Catherine Dunnan is devastated when her beloved goes off to war—and only his promise to write often can sustain her in her loneliness. And what letters they are, filled with heartfelt emotions that move her to respond in kind. But then the unthinkable occurs. He is cruelly lost to her, and his beautiful words of passion and devotion cease forever.

When Moncrief agreed to write warm and loving missives in a fellow officer's name, he never expected he'd become so enamored of the incomparable lady who answered them, a woman he has never met. Returning to England to assume the unexpected title of duke, Moncrief is irresistibly drawn to the beauty who has unwittingly won his heart. More than anything, he yearns to ease Catherine's sadness with his tender kisses. But once she learns his secret, will his love be spurned?

By Karen Ranney

KAREN RANNEY

Till Next We Meet

An Avon Romantic Treasure

AVON BOOKS
An Imprint of HarperCollinsPublishers

This is a work of fiction. Names, characters, places, and incidents are products of the author's imagination or are used fictitiously and are not to be construed as real. Any resemblance to actual events, locales, organizations, or persons, living or dead, is entirely coincidental.

AVON BOOKS
An Imprint of HarperCollins*Publishers*
10 East 53rd Street
New York, New York 10022-5299

Copyright © 2005 by Karen Ranney
ISBN: 0-06-075737-X
www.avonromance.com

First Avon Books paperback printing: May 2005

Avon Trademark Reg. U.S. Pat. Off. and in Other Countries, Marca Registrada, Hecho en U.S.A.
HarperCollins® is a registered trademark of HarperCollins Publishers Inc.

Printed in the U.S.A.

10 9 8 7 6 5 4 3 2 1

To Jerry

Prologue

Quebec, Canada
April 1761

    My dearest,

    The other day I saw a robin, a pretty little bird, surrounded by sparrows. I wondered why I felt such compassion for him and then realized he was alone of his kind. While the robin had a lovely plumage and was a more attractive bird, the sparrows were a community.

    How silly I am to envy the sparrows.

    Even being so busy with the renovations of Colstin Hall cannot stop my thoughts of you. Sometimes, I walk into the room I've prepared as your library, and close my eyes, wondering if I can conjure you there with my loneliness. Without

*much difficulty, I can see you at your desk, your
eyes impatient at the interruption and then welcoming to see me standing there. You put down
your quill and stand, greeting me with a smile. I
stretch out my hand and can almost feel your
touch on my fingers.*

Oh, if it could only be true, my dearest.

*I worry for you so, in the wilds of North Amer-
ica. I cannot think the winters there easily spent. I
ache in our chamber when the wind grows wild and
the storms come, thinking of you suffering in that
desolate place. I have procured a map, and marked
the continent in my mind, wondering where you are
in that vast and strange country.*

*Enough of that. I will be brave as the vicar has
counseled me to be. I confess, however, that at dusk
I thank the Almighty for the end of another day.
Each one gone is one less to endure until you return
home again.*

*The vicar has been by again today. He visits
overmuch, I think. He reminds me you are safe if I
pray, and so, my dearest, I spend my waking hours
in a daze of petitions to the Almighty even as I go
about my work. I think I must pray even in my sleep
since I awake and for a moment think you are here.*

*I hear stories in the market of the war and I am
torn between wishing to hear more and not wanting
to know anything in all. I can pretend, otherwise,
that you are in Edinburgh or conferring with relatives. But then, all too soon I remember how you
looked in your uniform, handsome and impatient to
serve with your regiment.*

*Keep yourself safe for me. Forbid yourself, I im-
plore you, the opportunity of being a hero. Tell*

yourself, instead, that you must return home, whole and safe, to me.

Your devoted wife,
Catherine

Moncrief carefully folded the letter and placed it on the stack with the others before placing a rolled-up blanket in Captain Harry Dunnan's trunk. There were pitifully few things he could return to the man's widow.

He wrapped the pipe in a jerkin and placed it on the bottom of the trunk. Harry rarely smoked it and when he did it was more to warm his hands than for the flavor of the tobacco. A few souvenirs from the Indians were next, then a book of poetry Dunnan had taken from a dead Frenchman. Moncrief wrapped the other man's brush and shaving gear in a shirt and wedged them into a corner.

He glanced at the collection of letters and debated returning them to the captain's wife. In actuality, Moncrief was the one responsible for hoarding these, even though they rightfully belonged to Dunnan. After a minute of thought, he left them where they were on the end of the bed.

Harry's wife had sent him a pillowcase, deftly embroidered with thistles and roses. Moncrief ran his fingers over the intricate needlework before placing it atop Dunnan's other belongings. The Scots broadsword was next, along with Harry's dirk. The last item to be packed was a scarlet vest and tunic, and black trousers, a match to the uniform in which Captain Dunnan had been buried.

All in all, few mementos to assuage a widow's grief.

Moncrief closed the trunk lid and locked it, placing the key on his desk alongside a piece of blank paper and a newly trimmed quill.

He would have to write one last letter. A last letter. How many times had he told himself that? Circumstance, however, had succeeded in doing what his will could not—ended his correspondence with Catherine Dunnan.

One day, more than a year ago, he'd received a letter from Captain Dunnan's wife inquiring as to her husband's health. She'd not heard from him since he'd left Scotland and was concerned.

As colonel of the regiment, it was occasionally his duty to prod his men into communicating with those they'd left behind, a chore he did not relish. Nor was this errand a particularly easy one.

"You should be glad of someone to write, Dunnan," he'd said. Moncrief's father deplored the task and his brother claimed no time for it. Once, there had been a woman who'd liked writing Moncrief well enough, until waiting for him had paled next to the flattery of another man.

Harry had been stretched out on his bed, still attired in his muddy uniform from that afternoon's maneuvers. He'd only grinned and reached inside his trunk and tossed his latest, unread, letter at Moncrief.

"Here, Colonel, you write her. She's forever prattling on of things that bore me. I only married her because she was an heiress, but a month of marriage was enough for me." He laughed. "Now she's all in a twitter about that house she's inherited. Damn shame she couldn't have gotten the money before I joined the regiment."

"The least you could do is ease her mind, Dunnan. Send her a letter."

"If I write her back, Colonel, she'll just expect another. Best not to write her at all."

Moncrief left the room, already framing the words he'd write to Catherine Dunnan.

Dear Madam,

Your husband is an unmitigated ass who indulges his baser appetites with any available woman. He gambles and, I suspect, cheats at it. He abuses his horses and is too intent on killing for my piece of mind. Have I mentioned that I consider him the most amoral man it has been my misfortune to meet?

When he reached his room, Moncrief realized that he still had Mrs. Dunnan's letter clutched in his hand. He tossed it aside only to find it on his table two days later, tucked beneath a map of the area.

He'd finally opened it, read the words she'd intended only for her husband to see.

That first letter he'd written to Catherine Dunnan had been one generated from pity and regret that Harry should have treated her so callously. Moncrief had written the news of the day and his thoughts on being stationed so far from home, both topics that Harry might have chosen had he the inclination or the character to write his wife.

Moncrief assuaged his guilt about signing Harry's name with the thought that he had only done so to reassure Mrs. Dunnan. She would be content now in the silence, knowing that Harry was safe and well.

However, she'd written back. Harry had opened the letter and read it briefly before giving it to him. "Do answer her about the blasted roof, won't you, Colonel? I haven't an iota of interest in it."

Thus, Moncrief's friendship with Catherine Dunnan had begun, turning to interest and possibly something deeper as the year had progressed. He was careful not to reveal to Harry how impatient he was to read her letters, even when his captain would sometimes receive two or three at a time only to ignore their arrival. Finally, Moncrief began to intercept them, ignoring the fact his behavior was morally wrong.

Each time a letter arrived, he vowed to turn it over to Harry. Each time he overheard Harry bragging about one of his conquests at the Officers' Mess, Moncrief decided that his behavior was not so reprehensible. He told himself that writing Catherine was not unlike putting his thoughts down in a journal. But no journal writer had ever waited so impatiently for a reply, or wondered what another person thought of his words.

Now Moncrief opened another of Catherine's letters, one dated at the beginning of their correspondence.

My dearest,

I sense a difference in you, a warming to me and our vows that had not been there before. I can only hope that the vicar was right, and my prayers have been answered. You have given me hope that our marriage is to be what I've so long wished of it, a joining of two hearts and minds as well as a union of the flesh.

Please do not think ill of me for my forthrightness in this matter. But I have been so lonely for you all these long days since your departure. I most heartily ask your forgiveness for anything I might have done or said that kept you from our bed. I long for you so.

I hold each one of your letters against my chest as if I can feel your heartbeat within the pages, your touch hidden in your words. They ease my loneliness a little, enough that I can bear the days and weeks until your next letter.

I anticipate your homecoming with every breath

*and with every beat of my heart. I pray that it will
be soon, but these prayers are silent, selfish ones,
not shared with the vicar.*

Moncrief should never have written her again. He told
himself that one misstep could cause her pain. If he com-
plimented her, she would expect kindness of Harry when
he returned home. If he praised her efforts at renovating
Colstin Hall, she would anticipate a similar response
from Harry in the flesh. If he shared too many of his
thoughts, she would come to know him better than she
did her own husband.

Their correspondence was a threat even as he found
solace in it. He could, without too much effort, pretend
that he was far away from this raw and empty place, and
back in Scotland. She was a neighbor, a relative, a friend,
someone to share the loneliness.

When had it become more?

Possibly when he'd begun to anticipate her letters,
when he'd returned to the old house that had become the
headquarters for the regiment and one of his first
thoughts was to write her.

More than once, he'd wanted to ask Captain Dunnan
about her appearance, if Catherine was a pretty woman,
but doing so had always struck him as inappropriate. Not
to mention that his curiosity would have amused Harry
and called attention to Moncrief's continuing correspondence with his wife.

Therefore, he'd consoled himself with his imagination,
creating an image that began to solidify as the months
passed. In his mind she was petite with blond hair and
blue eyes. Her voice was soft, her smile luminous. A
woman who intrigued even as she attracted.

Now his words would only bring her pain.

Moncrief stared at the blank paper for a few moments.

Determined, he finally picked up the quill and took a deep breath. Having thought the words through, he wrote them once, deliberately altering his handwriting so that Catherine wouldn't notice its similarity to the man's whom she'd been writing for more than a year. When he finished, he sealed the letter and placed it to one side.

He glanced up as the door opened. Peter, his aide, looked barely out of his boyhood, but this past year had schooled him in war.

"Is it ready, sir?" he asked, glancing down at the trunk.

Moncrief nodded. She would take each item out one by one, he suspected, and shed tears over the pipe and the uniform. She'd wonder at Harry's collection of feathers, and the missing letters. There would be no one to tell her that he'd kept all her correspondence. But neither would there be anyone to divulge the manner of Harry Dunnan's true death.

"He was a bounder, wasn't he, sir?" Peter's expression left no doubt in his mind as to his opinion of the deceased captain.

"Perhaps you judge him too harshly, Peter."

Peter looked dubious. But he said nothing else before grabbing one end of the trunk and hefting it on his shoulder.

Colonel Moncrief of the Lowland Scots Fusiliers pushed any lingering thoughts of Catherine Dunnan from his mind.

Yet he wasn't entirely surprised when she refused to vanish.

Chapter 1

Colstin Hall, Scotland
October 1761

Catherine Dunnan stood at the window and pushed it ajar, feeling the sudden tenseness in the woman behind her. She almost wanted to reassure the young maid that she had no intention of throwing herself to the ground, but that would have required speech, and conversation was simply beyond her at the moment.

So many things were difficult, like rising in the morning and washing her face and hands. She preferred to stay abed, preferably asleep, but the world seemed to think that she should be awake and alert. So, she occasionally left her bed in order not to further worry her servants.

In actuality, she didn't care if the day was advanced or early, if it rained or was filled with sunshine outside her window. It had been six months since the letter and the trunk had come, but it might have only been yesterday for the pain she felt.

The day was overcast, any sight of the sun obscured by a white sky. A dampness clung to the air, making the leaves curl on the branches of the trees outside her window. Fog hugged the ground, as if the clouds had fallen from the sky.

The world looked upside down.

Behind her the maid puttered, placing a luncheon tray on a small circular table, arranging silverware, all the while prattling on about the morning's events. A litter of kittens had been born in the barn, Cook's bones were aching, the footman had a rash, a squirrel was found dead below her window.

Taken individually, each event was miniscule, almost unimportant. But added together, it became a sure and certain progression, the transcribing of life itself.

Once she had been interested in what went on around her. Now, however, her existence had narrowed, become fixed and immutable. She breathed in and out, and that was the extent of her focus.

An ache lodged bone deep in her chest, as painful as a spear wound. Never easing nor ceasing, it remained a constant thing against which to measure her hours. She awoke and it was there. She lay on her bed and prayed for sleep and it kept a vigil within her, a succubus that fed on her despair.

Air brushed across her skin, making her shiver. A squirrel scampered up from the fog, leaping from one branch to another. Through it all, the maid chattered. Catherine neither wanted to see nor hear nor feel anything, but however much she wished it otherwise, she was still alive.

And the living endure.

If she could only die. How could God not answer a simple enough prayer?

The vicar said she was wrong to pray for such things.

God would see to it that she died when He was ready and not she. The vicar was obtrusive in his care for her, assiduous in a way that was grating. How did one tell a man of the cloth that he was an irritant?

"What time is it?"

"Two o'clock, madam," the maid answered, quick enough that she must have anticipated the question.

So, she had slept most of the day after all. She would spend the night in restless nightmares.

"You look pale, madam. Are you feeling well?"

Did it matter? She slept and dreamed and slept and dreamed and sometimes she awoke, sat up against the headboard feeling adrift in a mindless confusion. At times like those she took another draught of the laudanum and waited to sleep again.

"You should eat something, madam," the maid said, finally done with the chore of arranging dishes and cutlery.

Catherine didn't turn from her survey of the strange fog-laden countryside. "I'm not hungry," she said. How many times would she have to repeat those words until her staff learned from them?

"Cook said you didn't eat dinner last night or breakfast this morning. You should eat a bite or two. Just that, madam. Please."

The girl's name was Betty, and she was adept at her tasks. She was walking out with a footman, and had a sparkling laugh and a habit of covering her mouth with her hand to hide her bad teeth. She was deferential and pleasant enough in the *before* time. The *before* time—that achingly innocent period when life had been halcyon and beautiful, ripe with promise and heavy with anticipation. The *before* time, before the letter had come, before Harry's body had been returned in a pitch-soaked coffin, before the world became shadowed and black, wearing mourning as deep as night.

She'd confessed in one of her letters to him that she was afraid of the dark.

The shadows of darkness, he'd written in reply, *give an ominous appearance even to friendly things. Think, instead, of evening as a time of welcome rest, and darkness as the Almighty's way of forcing peace upon his creatures. The owl and the field mouse will be night's sentinels.*

She had held that letter to her chest, cherishing the near poetry of his words. That night she'd tested herself by standing in the hallway outside her chamber with no candle or lantern to light her way.

I cannot promise you, my dearest, she'd responded, *that I met the darkness with any degree of comfort, but my loathing of it has eased somewhat.*

The night held no terrors for her now. Instead, daylight tested her courage. Being awake was a measure of her bravery.

"I'm not hungry," she repeated, hoping that the girl would have sense enough to hear the resolve in her tone. Food sickened her. Sleep did as well, bringing nightmares that were torturously confusing and colored red and purple and blue, but even those visions were preferable to being awake.

"Glynneth made me promise," Betty said.

Catherine forced a smile to her face. "Tell her that you succeeded." Her companion would not hesitate in hiding behind another in order to accomplish her aims. In the *before* time, she would have saluted Glynneth's courage. Now the other woman's tenacity was an annoyance.

She managed to hold the smile in place as she walked to the door and stood beside it. Betty sighed, sketched a very pretty little curtsy, and clasped her hands in front of her starched apron.

"If you're sure, madam."

"Do not worry about me," Catherine said. "Leave the tray here, and I'll eat something in a little while."

Reassured, the maid left, and she was blessedly alone again. Catherine closed the door, leaning her forehead against it. Her staff wanted so much for things to be as they were, never realizing that the *before* time could never come again. Not until God made it May again.

She'd been so eager for the post, so innocently happy when Glynneth brought her mail. She'd been disappointed not to receive some word from Harry, but she'd never felt a sense of premonition at opening the letter from his colonel.

Madam Dunnan,

It is with deep regret that I inform you that your husband, Harold Allen Dunnan of the Lowland Scots Fusiliers was killed in a skirmish with French soldiers on April 18, in the year of our Lord 1761.

Your husband died with valor, madam. His entire service with the regiment was one of honor and dedication. His death will leave a void.

I was privileged to know your husband well, and counted him as friend. My sympathies are with you, madam, and with Harold's family. In times such as these, mere words seem futile.

While she was eagerly awaiting his letters, Harry was already dead.

For the sake of her staff, Catherine sat and poured herself some tea, nibbled at a roll. Two bites of the fish muddle and she could eat no more.

She turned and looked at the trunk, set as it was at the end of her bed. How alien the worn leather looked amid the femininity of her chamber. She should have, by rights, sent it to Harry's room. That's how their life was before he joined the regiment. Harry in one chamber and she in another.

Harry had been content with the arrangements, just as he had been content to live in her father's home. She had never anticipated that he might have chafed under the restrictions of marriage to her, enough to join a Highland regiment. But he had been so filled with enthusiasm that she'd done what other women had done since time—and war—began. She kissed him and stood and waved at him until he was out of sight. Only then did she cry.

Catherine went to the trunk and lifted the lid, taking a letter from it. His letters to her were precious things and she kept them here, along with all those personal possessions that had been returned to her.

Carefully, she unfolded the letter and began to read.

You asked me to speak more of my companions. Shall I tell you of Peter, the colonel's aide? He is barely a man, and so earnest that he makes me feel old in comparison. He's impatient to experience all that life would grant him. Given that he amazes me with his wisdom sometimes, he might be one of those people who seem to have been born old and wise.

We have sent most of the French back to France, a decision made by Major General Wolfe. Quebec is a pretty place, but it's evident that we are not welcome here. I would just as soon leave the city and return home.

Home. If he'd only returned home, her life would have been so different.

She moved to the bed, grateful for the fatigue that suddenly overwhelmed her, slowing her heart until it felt like a pendulum, ponderously marking the minutes.

The blanket was comforting, the white darkness behind her eyes a welcome sight. She curled beneath the sheets, still holding his letter.

Catherine composed a letter to him in her mind, a habit she'd begun six months ago. They were transitory missives, never committed to paper, and not for the knowledge of another soul. It eased her mind to think that somewhere Harry could read them.

> *I'm so lonely, my dearest. The days pass and you aren't here. The nights come and you are gone. There isn't a hint of your voice or your scent or your touch. Is there majesty in Heaven? Can you see the stars?*

Her tears were hot, scorching her cheeks. She shuddered as she wept, then held both hands against her mouth to silence her cries.

Months had passed, and it felt like only a day.

Dear God, please end this.

But God never did.

"Are you certain that you don't wish me to go with you, Colonel? I mean, Your Grace?"

Peter looked abashed at his mistake, just as he had every time he'd made it during the journey from America. It was an easy error—going from the rank of colonel to Duke of Lymond was a change that Moncrief himself had not adjusted to yet.

He clapped his former aide on the shoulder, a wordless acceptance of his unspoken apology.

The innkeeper looked on curiously, as did the tavern maid, who was refilling Peter's cup. Perhaps he and his aide warranted a closer second look, since both of them were attired in their uniforms.

Kirkulben was a pleasant village, larger than he expected, with two main roads that crossed each other to make an X. Huddled between them were a myriad of cottages, all of them charming and carefully kept. The two main streets boasted a variety of shops, and two inns. He and Peter had stayed at the Royal Heather, the larger of the two last night.

"I'll only be a short while," Moncrief said.

"All the same, sir, Your Grace, you shouldn't be traveling without an escort. You're a duke now."

"My father maintained a strict code of ducal behavior all his life, Peter. Are you certain he didn't hire you to mind my manners?"

Peter's cheeks flared with color. "I'm sorry, sir, I was only attempting to be of assistance."

Moncrief took pity on the young man, and told him a partial truth. "The journey home has left me with an intense desire for my own company."

As they'd crossed the North Atlantic, autumn squalls had made Peter and most of the other passengers ill. Moncrief had been grateful for his hearty constitution, an irony considering that he was on his way home because his brother had died unexpectedly of influenza, and he'd become the twelfth Duke of Lymond.

His regimental days were over. But before he took up the mantle of responsibility for Balidonough and its people, he planned to remain the colonel of the Lowland Scots Fusiliers for a few more hours.

Long enough to call upon the Widow Dunnan.

"If you're certain, sir. Your Grace."

Moncrief smiled. "I'm very certain, Peter. You'll perform those errands I gave you?"

The young man nodded.

In actuality, they were only a few hours away from Moncrief's home, and they had all the provisions they needed. The horses were newly acquired, and his civilian clothing lay in readiness for him. Peter was finding the inactivity of civilian life disconcerting after three years of regimental restriction. Therefore, Moncrief had given him a series of tasks to perform, such as purchasing a gift for Balidonough's housekeeper and procuring several nonessential but welcome items like bay-rum scented soap and new cravats.

A few minutes later, Moncrief left the inn, following the innkeeper's directions to Colstin Hall.

Even blindfolded he would have known he was home in Scotland. There was a hint of peat fires in the air, a dampness that was strangely Scottish. A fine mist had fallen earlier and now solidified into fog that clung to the ground.

Scotland was an old country; here there was history in the trees and rocks and soil. It was this sense of continuity, of age, that he'd missed the last fourteen years.

His horse, a recently purchased stallion with a penchant for tossing his head to the right, wasn't even winded before the house was visible. Moncrief halted and dismounted, and wrapped the reins around a rock. He climbed a few boulders until he had an unobstructed view of Colstin Hall, Catherine Dunnan's home.

A narrow road framed by tall oaks led to the square three-story red brick structure surrounded by outbuildings and an acreage that looked well maintained as farmland. Fog clung to the trunks of the trees and curled up to the base of the house, making it appear as if it floated, cloudlike, above the ground.

The impulse that had driven him here was foolish, perhaps, but he hadn't been able to forget her in all these months.

He reached inside his tunic and pulled out the letter that was appropriate to this day. The other letters remained in his dispatch case, a place that was safe from prying eyes.

> *My dearest,*
>
> *I've had the front steps rebuilt, and the plastering around the windows restored. Colstin Hall looks a bright and cheerful place, as if waiting for your arrival.*
>
> *In spring, the flowers line the lane, bobbing their heads in the breeze. In summer you can hear the buzzing of the bees as they flit back and forth from their hives to the fields. I confess that in winter, the aspect is not so pleasant, unless we have snow and it dusts the bare branches with a mantle of white. But autumn is my favorite time of year.*
>
> *Come home in autumn, when the trees are changing color and the leaves fall like a soft rain. There will be a cool breeze and the sky will be a brilliant blue as if to give us a last hint of clement weather. Come home in autumn, my dearest.*

Although the season was right, the sky was pale, not deeply blue. No breeze greeted him, only that eerie fog, as if he trespassed on an otherworldly place.

He didn't lie to himself—he wasn't here because he wanted to give his regards to Harry's widow. Although he'd expressed his regrets in person to relatives of other fallen comrades, this visit was different. He wanted to meet her, just once, then he could put Catherine Dunnan into a nice little box in his mind and forget her, a feat he'd not been able to accomplish for the past six months.

Perhaps in person she'd be different. In fact, she could possess little of the character of the woman he'd come to know from her words. She could very well be selfish and bitter and narrow of mind and spirit. She might be cruel to her servants. She could be a spendthrift or a miser, someone utterly forgettable.

He unfolded the letter and read the last part again.

I sat beside my bed this evening, my dearest, and said a prayer for you. May the wind blow a warm breeze, may the winter be temperate. May you be sustained with food of a goodly quality and amount. May your health be perfect. But most all, may the travails of war not touch you.

When I finished, I realized how selfish my prayer sounded, so I expanded it to include all of those in your troop of men. Yet I cannot help but hope, my dearest, that God senses my especial need for you and sends you home with all blessed haste.

What if she wasn't forgettable? What if she proved as fascinating in person as she did in her letters? He felt as if he knew her already, knew those traits of personality kept hidden from strangers.

She was impatient with religion, disliked the posturing of the vicar. *Why is it that those who adore God are both-ersome about it? Surely God does not insist upon such obnoxious devotion?* The vicar had called upon her that day and she'd been annoyed by him.

She loved the changing sky above Colstin Hall, and thunderstorms. He'd once teased her that a woman who was uneasy in the dark should not be so enamored of storms.

But they are two different things entirely, she'd an-swered. *A storm is God's way of showing his presence, while the dark is an absence of light. Does evil not hap-pen more in the darkness than in the midst of a storm?*

As the months passed, Moncrief discovered that the

emotions he felt for Catherine Dunnan were not simply those of compassion and pity. He wanted to ease her occasional fears with comforting words, praise her wit, admire her tenacity and sense of purpose, and overall indulge in a type of adultery of the mind.

He should have measured every sentence, every thought, hiding behind the personality and ultimately, the character of her husband. Instead, Moncrief had begun to reveal more and more about himself, thoughts that he'd never before shared. His duplicity was made easier not only by Harry's complicit agreement, but also by the fact she'd been married to Dunnan only a month before he was posted to North America.

"Long enough to realize I'd made a disastrous mistake," Dunnan said one day. "Never marry an heiress, Colonel. They want avowals of your eternal affection to compensate for the promise of their money."

But Moncrief had discovered that Catherine was modest about her status in life, barely mentioning the fortune she'd inherited and speaking more of the man whose death had made her wealthy.

I miss my father dearly, she'd written once. *He made me smile even in his letters, and it seems as if the world is a grayer place after his death. Sometimes, I feel him close to me, and strangely enough, it is when I'm writing you. I glance over my shoulder and think I see him standing there, smiling at me.*

What would her dead father think now?

Go home, Your Grace. This is not the place for you. This is still a place of mourning, for what might have been, for a future that can never be.

Something else he and Catherine shared.

His own dreams could never be realized. Now it was painful to recall his plans for a reunion with his father, his brother. His father would never stand at the great doorway of Balidonough to greet him. Colin would likewise be absent, only his memories, like ghosts, populating the home Moncrief had never thought to inherit.

He'd never given much thought to his future, being so concerned with simply surviving the present. The past weeks had forced him to think about the woman he'd marry, the children he'd sire, an obligation he owed to Balidonough and the dukedom. Need it be simply another responsibility, however? Merely a duty he performed as diligently as he had all the tasks of the last fourteen years?

Impatient with reverie and his own hesitation, the Duke of Lymond, clad still in his uniform as a colonel of the Lowland Scots Fusiliers, made his way back to his horse, mounted, and followed the road to Colstin Hall.

Chapter 2

"**S**he won't see you," the housemaid said, beginning to close the door in his face.

Moncrief slapped his palm against the wooden panel.

"I insist," Moncrief said, irritated with the housemaid's refusal to at least confer with her mistress.

"She's in mourning, sir, and doesn't see anyone. Except the vicar," she added as an afterthought.

"I served with her husband."

The maid hesitated. "I'll tell her, sir. But it's her decision." She looked him up and down, a glance not unlike his father's scornful appraisal when he was a boy. "I wouldn't hold out any hope. She doesn't see anyone."

She grudgingly showed him to a small parlor facing west. The room was warm despite the fact that no fire had been lit, and the fog still lay thick in the glen. Dust had accumulated on the tables beside the settee and on the mantel, lending an unused, even abandoned, air to the chamber.

He walked the perimeter of the room, his boots echoing on the planked floor. A sound from overhead made him glance toward the ceiling. Was she coming?

The gold piping around the stand-up collar chafed at him. No doubt it always had, but he'd just noticed it now because he was on edge. He'd thought about this moment for so long that it was normal for him to be uneasy about it.

He caught sight of himself in the glass door of the cabinet. Strictly speaking, he was no longer attached to the regiment, but for this visit, he'd donned the distinctive scarlet tunic and black trousers he'd worn for the last fourteen years.

The Lowland Scots Fusiliers was a regiment formed fifteen years ago, a year after the abortive rebellion with England. The younger sons of many a distinguished family had served as a Fusilier, no doubt as a way to prove their loyalty to the British crown. He'd entered the regiment because there was nothing else for him to do with his life.

He wondered what Catherine would think when viewing him for the first time. When he shaved, he considered his face, but only from a task standpoint—had he missed any whiskers? Now he surveyed himself closely.

His eyes were blue, but then he'd been told his mother's were the same shade. Over the last fourteen years, he'd lost the habit of smiling and now practiced at his reflection. A pleasant enough expression. His face was neither excessively long nor square, but average. His nose, however, was patrician-looking, which was an annoyance. His hair was black, tied at the back with a red ribbon. The Lowland Scots Fusiliers had a distinctive headpiece, made of fur, but his was currently tucked under his arm since it would have been rude to enter a home attired in headgear.

His black trousers were tucked into his boots, appropriate garments for riding. The boots themselves were highly polished, a chore he'd done himself this morning.

A ducal rank did not preclude him from personal responsibility. He'd startled Peter with that comment, and the recollection brought a smile to his face now.

There, that expression looked natural enough.

A sound made him turn. A woman stood in the open doorway. She was tall, and almost painfully thin. Her brown hair was tangled and hanging past her shoulders. Her complexion was waxen, her lips cracked and dry. A rumpled wrapper slipped from one shoulder even as she attempted to keep it closed with both hands. Someone—a maid?—had thought to try to cover her with a blanket, but as she entered the room it fell to the floor.

She approached him slowly, her bare feet scuffling on the wooden floor. Her brown eyes were bloodshot, fixed on him with a stare that unnerved him. Moncrief didn't move to close the door behind her, or to assist her to the settee.

Shock rendered him immobile.

"You knew him?" Even her voice was different from what he'd imagined. Lower, stronger, a husky contralto when he'd expected a faint soprano.

"I served with Captain Dunnan, madam." He bowed slightly. "Regrettably, I was the one who informed you of his death."

Her face changed and for a horrifying moment he was certain she was going to weep. Dear God.

"I came to offer my condolences," he added, hoping that conversation would keep her from collapsing into tears.

She looked dazed, as if she didn't know what to do next. Concerned, he offered her his arm, but she only blinked at him as if not understanding that gesture either. He gently placed her hand on his arm and walked her to the settee. Then, as if she were an elderly lady devoid of most of her senses, he helped her sit.

The wrapper parted, exposing her legs below the knees. He retrieved her blanket from the floor and placed it across her lap. As he moved to sit beside her, he glanced downward to see one bare foot, delicate and shapely, toes curling against the floor.

Any disappointment he felt about this meeting was suddenly pushed aside by a surge of compassion.

Her gaze didn't leave his, expectant and hopeful in a way that was oddly painful.

"Tell me about him," she said, so softly that it was barely more than a breath. "Tell me about Harry. Please."

Her eyes were brimming with unshed tears, her nose was pink, her lips trembled. He didn't remember ever seeing a creature so devastated by grief. He wanted to call for her slippers, tuck her into her bed, and comfort her with something warm to drink. Only then would he tell her that Harry Dunnan was not worth such agony of spirit. Instead, Moncrief stretched out his hand to her and she placed hers in his, the trust in her touch disarming him.

"Please," she whispered. She leaned her head against the wooden back of the settee as if the effort to sit upright was suddenly too much.

Moncrief squared his shoulders and searched his memory for good things to say about Captain Dunnan. Since the man gambled extensively, he owed money to nearly every man in the regiment. He was cruel to his horses, and recklessly brave, putting others needlessly in danger. Moncrief suspected that Harry also enjoyed killing. During the siege of Quebec, Dunnan had been a ferocious fighter, all too eager for combat.

No human being, however, was entirely without attributes.

"He was very personable," Moncrief finally said, relieved to have found something good to say. "And a good soldier as well."

She nodded, retrieving her hand. Intent on his words, she barely breathed.

"He was an excellent marksman."

She smiled, a wobbly expression, but a smile nonetheless, making him wonder if his words conjured up a pleasant memory.

Silence stretched between them as he searched his memory for something more to say about Harry. The clock in the hallway chimed the hour, urging him to leave. A movement made him glance in the direction of the window. The wind had picked up, banishing the fog and tossing the leaves from the branches of a nearby tree. The day was no longer eerie, simply one that foretold winter.

A maid came to the door bearing a tray. After looking at her mistress and receiving no acknowledgment of her presence, she entered the room and placed the tray not far from the settee. She glanced once in his direction, her lips curving into a smile. He nodded, grateful for her timely interruption and the fact that it might ease his leave-taking.

When she moved, a ray of sunlight illuminated the maid's blond hair, reminding him of his previous thoughts of Catherine. This fragile, almost gaunt, wraith beside him could not be the woman with whom he'd corresponded for a year. She wasn't even lucid.

"I've brought refreshments, mistress," the maid said, bobbing a curtsy. "Some sweet buns and tea."

"I think I hear his voice sometimes," Catherine said in response.

Startled, he looked at her. Her eyes were closed, her smile otherworldly.

The maid covered her mouth with her hand as if to hide her smile. She glanced at Catherine again, and this time her eyes were dancing as if she were amused at the sight of her mistress, dazed and confused.

"That will be all," he said in dismissal. The maid bobbed another curtsy and left the room, closing the door behind her.

From Catherine's appearance and manner it was clear that no one was caring for her, either ensuring that she ate or was attired correctly. Not one person had come to inquire as to this meeting, or stopped her from appearing before him dressed in such a manner.

He placed his hand over one of hers, feeling her tremble.

She looked up at him, pulled her hand free again, and reached slowly into the pocket of her wrapper, extricating a much-read, much-folded letter. He knew the script well enough, he'd penned the words himself. Immersed in his fascination for Catherine Dunnan, he'd not given any thought to the possibility that she would treasure his words as strongly as he had hers.

"I hear his voice in his letters. Shall I read it to you?"

He shook his head, but she ignored his wishes, unfolded the page, and began to read.

If you could but see the sky here. It seems a cleaner and fresher place, Catherine, yet manages to remind me of home. I half expect to see the gorse, or the eagles or witness the craggy face of Ben Nevis in the distance. There is no heather, and no brave little creeks that flow from the hills. Here, the land is raw and barely born. The men who make their mark upon it do so at their peril. Scotland seems to me to be a willing and complicit partner in survival, as if the land acknowledges that life itself is sometimes a difficult venture. This place, however, is an adversary.

We occasionally meet with some Jesuits. One of our Indian guides told me that a Jesuit priest is the worst of all aberrations. The Indians do not like a beard on a man's face. Nor do they approve of a bald head. Therefore, a Jesuit is two times a devil in their eyes.

Catherine smiled weakly at him, unaware of Moncrief's growing discomfort.

As a leader, he'd always cultivated a distance and aloofness from his men. He found it difficult to be friends with those he had to order into battle. His time in North America had been marked by an aloneness that he eased by writing Catherine, by pretending that she was his, that her troubles were his, that the way she began her letters— my dearest—was meant for him.

What an absolute idiot he'd been.

She pressed the letter against her chest with both hands and closed her eyes again. Slowly, she recited the rest of the letter, evidently having memorized its contents. The words were pedestrian, the missive nothing that should be enshrined in anyone's memory, but they evidently had become a lifeline to Catherine Dunnan, a connection to the husband she had adored.

What in the name of St. Agnes's Bell had he done?

I would think that the vicar calls upon you overmuch, and is too concerned with your welfare and not that of the rest of his parish. I would encourage him to do good works in other places, Catherine.

As for your maid, I agree with your decision to retire Dorcas and give her a small plot of land. Service of any sort for such a loyal and loving person should be rewarded.

"He was always like that," she said. "Always thinking of others before himself."

In actuality, Harry was nothing like that. Harry Dunnan cared little for anyone but Harry Dunnan.

"Does the vicar come by to see you often?" he asked, impatient with her recitation of Harry's virtues and wishing to change the subject.

The question surprised her enough that she opened her eyes and stared at him.

"Yes, almost every day. Why do you ask?"

"Are you that great a sinner?"

One single tear welled from her left eye and fell in a haphazard course to her chin. He wanted to reach out and brush it away with his thumb, but doing so would have been an intimate gesture. The world, and Catherine, saw them as strangers.

She shook her head, lowering her gaze to a spot on the floor. "It doesn't matter now," she said softly, still smoothing her hands across the pages of the letter. How many times had she read it? A hundred? A thousand?

"Have you kept all his letters?" He knew the answer before she gave him a look filled with remonstration, as if he trod over sacred ground with hobnailed boots, or whistled in a church.

"Of course," she said. "I know each of them as well as this one. They're all I have left of Harry, you see."

Uncomfortable, Moncrief stood and walked to the window. "Your husband has been dead for some months, madam."

"So everyone tells me."

He glanced back at her as she folded the letter with infinite tenderness and placed it back in her pocket.

"But I still hear him through his letters. They speak to me."

Bloodshot and teary, her brown eyes conveyed a pathos that rendered him ill at ease. He wanted to tell her that she should guard herself more closely. Loss, despair, loneliness all shone in her eyes so perfectly that she had no need of speech.

Her hand pressed against her pocket as if to reassure herself that Harry's letter was safe. "His words make him come alive. I read his letters, and I can see him here, as close as you are."

"I have another," he heard himself saying with a kind of horror. "I have another letter from Harry."

Her eyes widened as she sat up straight. "Have you truly?"

He nodded, committed now to the lie. "He wrote it before he died," Moncrief said. "He was thinking of you and wished to write you."

The disturbing fact was not that he could come up with a falsehood so quickly, but that he could fill in such detail without much thought. A few more minutes, and he could, no doubt, convince himself that he'd actually seen Dunnan write the blasted thing.

She glanced at his tunic, then at his hands, as if he held the letter there even now.

"Please, would you give it to me?"

"I didn't bring it," he said, his newly found powers of prevarication abruptly leaving him. "I've left it behind at the inn."

Catherine wavered as she stood. When he rose to assist her, she shook her head, refusing his assistance. How long had it been since she'd eaten? She shuffled to the other side of the room, and jerked once on a richly embroidered bellpull.

"I will summon one of my staff," she said, turning and facing him. "We can send him for the letter."

"There's no need for that," he said, coming to her side. "I will bring it tomorrow."

Her face fell. "Must you wait so long? Could you not return this evening?"

What idiocy had propelled him to tell her he had another letter from her husband? To ease the look in her eyes, no doubt, even though he doubted that one more letter from Harry would truly aid in that task.

"It would be impossible, I'm afraid."

"Then the morning?"

He bowed once to her, and she nodded again, the smile she gave him fleeting and quite obviously a dismissal.

Moncrief said his farewells and escaped the house with a feeling of reprieve.

Catherine entered her room and slowly closed the door behind her. Her heart was beating too fast, and her breath was too tight. She stretched out one hand to brace herself against the wall, hoping that the nausea would soon pass.

Dear God, grief was making her ill.

Your husband has been dead for some months, madam.

She rested her cheek against the wall, wishing away the words. Why did people think it necessary to remind her of Harry's death? Did they think she might forget it? Wake in the morning and stretch, greet the sun with a smile, uncaring that she was a widow?

What an arrogant man. His eyes had been too sharp, too watchful, as if he gauged her every movement. Dressed in his Lowland Scots Fusiliers uniform, he'd been an arresting sight, tall like Harry had been tall, but Harry had blond hair while this man's hair was black. Harry's eyes had been soft and brown, kind eyes. The colonel's had been blue and piercing.

She took a deep breath, looked at the distance from the door to the bed, and wondered if she could make it without falling. Her limbs felt weak, as if she'd been walking for days and days, yet all she'd done was climb the staircase. Slowly, with arms outstretched, fingers trailing along the wall, she crossed the room, reaching her bed with a sigh of relief. She lay, drawing up her legs and pulling the blanket over them.

"There you are," Glynneth said a few minutes later, shattering Catherine's descent into sleep. "Are you resting again?"

She nodded, keeping her eyes shut, wishing Glynneth away. But the other woman was tenacious in her care of her and refused to be banished.

Glynneth bustled to the side of the bed, and covered her properly with the blanket, plumped up her pillow. "Are you certain that you wish to sleep again so soon after waking?"

"I am so very tired."

"You should not be," Glynneth said, her voice sounding concerned. She reached over and smoothed the hair back from Catherine's temple. Her hand felt so warm, and Catherine was so cold. She clamped her teeth together to keep them from chattering.

"Tell me about your visitor." Glynneth pulled up a chair and sat beside the bed.

Catherine turned her head and opened her eyes.

Glynneth Rowan was her age, a gentlewoman who was more of a companion than a lady's maid. Catherine had hired her more than a year ago. At the time, Catherine had envied Glynneth her blond hair the color of gold, her smile revealing even white teeth, the bloom of color on her face, and especially the color of her eyes, a deep gray that reminded her of smoke. Glynneth was everything she was not, petite and dainty while Catherine occasionally felt gawky and awkward.

She'd come to rely on Glynneth too much this last year, but the other woman didn't seem to mind. Instead, she had taken on some of Catherine's duties and done them with a smile.

"He's come from Harry's regiment."

Glynneth nodded. "I saw him leave. He's a very impressive man in his uniform."

"You should have been here to meet him."

"I was with the vicar, as you well know. I would have changed places with you if I could."

Catherine sighed. She didn't have the energy to deal with the vicar. "What does he want now?"

"He is certain that the roof of the church is about to tumble down about his ears. I think that he has it in his mind to solicit more funds from you."

Catherine closed her eyes again. "He does every month, for one project or another. Give him what he wants."

Glynneth smoothed the blanket up to Catherine's chin.

"How do you do it, Glynneth? How do you go on, day after day? You've been a widow longer than I, you must know."

"One simply endures."

Catherine glanced at the other woman. "I'm tired of simply enduring. Does the pain get better in time?"

Glynneth looked away. "You have no choice but to go on, Catherine. That is all."

"It sounds so easy," Catherine said. "But it is so difficult."

"Were you able to eat any lunch?" Glynneth patted the blanket, smoothing it before tucking the ends beneath the mattress.

"A little," Catherine said, not confessing that the squirrels had eaten more than she had.

"If I send another tray up, will you try to eat something? Perhaps drink some tea?"

Glynneth stood and looked down at her, so long that Catherine glanced up in puzzlement.

"Don't look so angry, Glynneth, I'll try to eat something."

"Good." A moment later, she spoke again. "Did he say anything about your husband? Since he was from the same regiment?"

Catherine closed her eyes, unable to fight back the tender beckoning of sleep. "He said Harry was a fine man, Glynneth. He has a letter for me."

"From Harry?"

Glynneth sounded surprised. A last thought before sleep claimed Catherine again.

Chapter 3

"It's a pretty little place, sir," Peter said, as he and Moncrief approached Colstin Hall the next afternoon.

Moncrief nodded. Today there was no fog, and the winds were gentle, swaying the branches with their burden of dying leaves. Regardless of the pastoral beauty, he wanted to be gone from here as fast as possible. The afternoon was well advanced, and he couldn't help but wonder if the delay of their arrival was due more to his own reluctance than to the fact that the small wagon holding their trunks had lost a wheel.

A decision could have been made to allow the wagon driver to follow him to Balidonough at a more leisurely pace. But he'd delayed as well, and now, staring down at Colstin Hall, Moncrief realized why.

He didn't want to see Catherine Dunnan again.

"I'll stay here if you don't mind, sir. Your Grace." Peter took the reins of Moncrief's horse as he dismounted.

Moncrief smiled his agreement and made his way down the path to the front door, the letter in his pocket seeming to burn its way through the cloth to his very skin.

He'd returned to the inn thinking that this letter would be a good opportunity for a little truth. Perhaps Harry should say something of his life in this last missive to his wife, speak of all the women he'd bedded in America. Or mention his gambling habit, and the fact that he would have used Colstin Hall as a stake until Moncrief had stepped in and refused to allow any of his men to accept the property.

Catherine had, in her grief, made Harry a hero, while the truth was something else entirely.

Moncrief hadn't, after all, written a letter of that type. He wasn't certain that Catherine Dunnan was mentally stable enough to read it or accept the truth of it. Instead, he'd used the disappointment of the meeting with her, his fatigue, and his own feelings of uncertainty about the future as fuel for the words he wrote under Harry's name. He told her of his irritation with his post, hiding his emotions for his father and his brother but allowing them to emerge in the very real tale of men who had died in their last battle.

In the end, the letter revealed a man who cared for his men and for his wife, who longed for the life she promised. Moncrief sealed the document, feeling as if it were also a glorious monument to his ability to lie without compunction.

Perhaps he was Harry's match in lack of character.

Moncrief knocked on the door just as he had the day before, but this visit found him attired not in his regimentals but in a plain black suit of clothes, the richness of the fabric and the silk of his stock the only concessions to his newly inherited wealth and title.

The same young maid answered the door, but her greeting was anything but what he expected.

"Oh, please come, sir, we can't rouse the mistress!" Tears were streaming down her face. She pulled Moncrief into the house by the sleeve of his coat, then pointed up the stairs. "She won't wake up!"

He took the stairs two at a time.

At the end of the hall three women were standing, all of them gripping their aprons and sobbing. He pushed past them, and into the room.

A woman standing beside the bed turned and looked at him.

"Can you help her?"

She was a creature of loveliness, a vision of blond beauty, an angel standing there.

"Quickly. She's still breathing, but I fear the worst."

His glance caught the small brown bottle beside the bed. He strode to the table, pulled out the cork, and sniffed the contents. Laudanum, a tincture of opium, mixed with alcohol and other ingredients, one of which smelled like ginger. "How much of this has she taken?"

The angel shook her head. "I don't know."

Catherine's complexion was ashen, her lips nearly blue. He pressed his fingers against her neck to find a faint and thready pulse.

"My aide is in the lane," he told one of the women in the door. "Go and get him."

One disappeared to do his bidding, and he turned to the other two. "Fetch her bathtub and fill it with cold water. As cold as you can make it."

"Cold water, sir?" one of the women said.

"Yes, and now."

"Miss Glynneth?" The other woman waited until the angel nodded before doing his bidding.

The room was evidently the refuge of a wealthy woman. The bed itself was large, four heavily carved posts sitting at each corner. A vanity with curved legs and claw and ball feet sat on one wall. Next to it was a mahogany-and-marble table topped with a ewer and basin richly patterned with trailing pink roses. A wing back chair and ottoman, both upholstered in a deep burgundy, sat adjacent to the fire.

He sat on the edge of the mattress, and pulled Catherine to a sitting position. Her head lolled, but she didn't otherwise respond.

"We might be too late," he said.

"I pray not," the woman beside him said.

"Too much opium, and a patient simply doesn't wake up. One of my sergeants had a brother who was an opium eater. He simply slept to his death." Moncrief stood, removed his coat, and hung it on the back of the chair before returning to the bed.

"Sir?" He turned to see Peter enter the room, followed by two young men bearing a large copper bath.

They set it down before the fireplace, and began to fill it with the buckets of water being brought up by the three women.

"What can I do to help, Colonel?" Peter asked, after taking in the sight of the unconscious woman and the activity around the bath.

"Clear the room, Peter."

His aide nodded and proceeded to do just that.

Moncrief picked up Catherine and held her in his arms, watching as Peter herded the unwilling servants from the room.

"And me? I won't leave."

He turned to face Glynneth, realizing that he'd forgotten the other woman. Now her perfect face was marred by a scowl.

"I won't leave her."

"Then help me save her life," he said. Moncrief glanced at Peter, and blessed the younger man's perception. His former aide stepped out the door and closed it solidly behind him. He would stand guard until told otherwise.

Moncrief strode to the bath and dropped Catherine into the cold water.

She sank like a stone.

He bent down and pulled her up by her shoulders. She sucked in her breath sharply. Her eyelids fluttered but otherwise, she didn't respond.

He dropped her again.

"Are you trying to drown her?"

Ignoring the woman behind him, he pulled Catherine out of the water. This time, her lips trembled, and her hands made weak splashing movements in the water.

"Leave her alone!"

He felt a slap on his shoulder, but didn't turn. "I'm trying to wake her. Or do you want her to sleep to her death?"

"But she's not properly attired."

The woman might be blessed with beauty, but she was evidently devoid of sense. "You would have her die for the sake of propriety, madam?"

She didn't answer him, and his concentration returned to the woman he was trying to save. The water was icy, turning his own hands numb. The fire, while burning brightly, was not sufficient to warm the area where the bath was located. If the water and the cold didn't wake her, Moncrief wasn't certain anything would.

The third time he pulled her out of the water, her eyelids fluttered open.

"Cold."

A single word, it nevertheless induced a smile from him. "So is the grave, madam."

Once more she went under, and this time when he pulled her up, she slapped at him with her hands.

"Fight me, then," he said, pleased that she was showing some reaction.

She frowned, more expression that she'd shown since he'd found her.

"Let me up," she said, the words faint and barely audible above the splash of water. She was beginning to tremble, a good sign that her body was finally beginning to respond to the icy water.

"Bring me a towel," he said to the woman at his side. She rushed to the dresser, opened the bottom drawer, and returned to his side with a length of folded toweling.

He helped Catherine stand and wrapped the toweling around her. She sank against him as he pulled her from the tub, her forehead leaning against his chest. Although the water was frigid, she was colder.

"Next time you try to die, madam, you might try a faster method. Laudanum kills by inches."

She shook her head weakly from side to side. He scooped her up in his arms and carried her to the fireplace, standing her as close to the fire as he dared.

"Will she be all right?"

"I think so. She is waking." He turned to look at the woman who'd addressed him. "No thanks to you, madam. Or to anyone in this house. Has no one thought to discourage her use of laudanum? Or feed her? Or have you only allowed her to wallow in her grief?"

She frowned at him. "You judge easily that which you don't know, sir."

He'd been a commander of men for enough years that he was familiar with excuses. He didn't want to hear a litany of them now. Setting Catherine down in front of the fire, he peeled the damp towel from her.

"We need another towel."

"You should leave now. I can care for her."

"No. She would no doubt expire of consumption if I left her to your care."

He ignored her soft reply, concentrating on Catherine

instead. She was shaking in earnest, standing with her arms at her sides, her head down. Her hair was long, hanging in sodden ropes to her waist. Her nightgown was rendered almost transparent by the water, but he removed it nonetheless, peeling it from her as if it were a second skin.

A female hand clamped on his wrist as he grabbed the towel again.

"Your behavior is shocking, sir," Glynneth said. "She is naked, and you are a stranger."

"Then leave the room if my presence so distresses you."

"Mrs. Dunnan is not your responsibility."

Yes, she is. The words didn't stun him as much as the fact they came instantly to his mind. She had become his responsibility the moment he'd put pen to paper, from the second he'd answered the letter that had begun—*My dearest.*

"Do you want to destroy her reputation?"

The accusation was not without merit. The world did not know of their tenuous bond or his guilt. To this woman, to all of Catherine's servants, he was only a stranger, now engaged in behavior that would be scandalous under any circumstances.

But he could not let her die.

He shook his wrist free and began to rub Catherine dry with the towel, turning her closer to the fire when he'd finished with her back.

The Greeks believed that the epitome of beauty was the entire female figure. The sweep of the back, the arch of the neck, the curve of the hips, the long, sleek stretch of leg were as important as high conical breasts and rounded arms. A goddess could not have been as perfect as Catherine Dunnan. No statue could have been so gloriously carved. But she was nearly as cold as marble, and pale enough to mimic stone.

He concentrated on the droplets of water that followed the curves from her shoulders to her waist, then focused on her trembling, on the very sound of her breathing, ragged and rough.

The task of drying her front done, he began rubbing Catherine's hair. There were tangles in it, but he would deal with those later. For now, he was content that she was still shivering, and that the color of her face had gone from waxy pale to pink.

"Get her a dry nightgown," he said to the other woman. Instead of obeying him, however, she made a sound of disgust and left the room, slamming the door behind her.

Irritated, Moncrief went to the bureau and began opening drawers, finding what he sought in the middle one. He unfolded the gown and returned to where Catherine stood, docile and silent, in front of the fire.

A few minutes later he wondered how mothers ever dressed their children. There were too many limbs, and they were not as easily arranged as he thought. Then, again, he'd had more experience undressing a woman than dressing one. Finally, he was done, Catherine attired in a pale green gown adorned with embroidery at the neck. He wondered if she'd done the needlework herself.

Moncrief placed his hand on her cheek, feeling how cold she still was to the touch.

"We need to get you fed, Catherine. Soup, I think. Or a stew. Something hot, and something hot to drink as well."

Catherine shook her head from side to side.

"Laudanum takes away the appetite. You'll find that you feel better once you stop taking that poison."

"I don't," she said faintly.

"I shall not argue the point with you now. Instead, I suggest we begin walking."

He slid his arm around her back, draped her arm over

his shoulder, and began to walk. "You can't sleep yet. If you do, I'm not altogether certain you'll wake."

Her only response was slowly to place one foot in front of the other in an exaggerated attempt at walking. He kept their pace measured, but he was determined that she would survive.

"I . . . didn't . . . try . . . to . . . die," she said a half hour later.

"I would beg to differ, madam," he said. "You nearly succeeded."

She shook her head from side to side.

An hour later she spoke again, her voice a little stronger.

"How much longer?" she asked, allowing him to support her as they turned.

He stood in front of her and gently tilted her chin up until he could see her eyes. Patches of color dotted her cheeks, and the bluish tinge had left her lips. His knuckles brushed against her throat, measuring the warmth of her skin. Her eyes looked clearer, more lucid.

"How do you feel?"

"Alive. Tired."

He walked her back to the side of her bed and helped her sit. She folded her hands together and placed them on her lap. Her head was bent, her gaze on the floor. Her lack of will disturbed him, but she might well be of that nature. The woman he'd known from her letters could be a mirage, a myth she'd constructed on paper, just as he had hidden behind her husband's persona. Perhaps they were both frauds, after all.

She lifted her head and regarded him with dazed eyes. "I'm very tired."

"The effect of the laudanum."

She turned away from him and drew her legs up on the mattress. He leaned down and covered her with the blanket. She closed her eyes, effectively dismissing him.

"Are you still cold?"

"Yes."

He went to the trunk at the end of her bed, startled to realize that it was Harry's. He left it alone and went to the bureau and found another blanket. As he covered her with it, Catherine grabbed the edge and pulled it up to her neck, still not looking at him.

"Are you a physician?"

"I've saved a life or two," he admitted. "But I've no training in it."

She nodded once, as if satisfied by his answer.

He stood and watched her for a few moments, reassured when her breathing was more regular and even. Bending, he tested her pulse again, feeling it beat strongly beneath his fingertips.

Did she grieve so desperately for Harry that she'd chosen to die rather than live without him? The Harry he'd known had not been worth such desperate emotion. He glanced at the trunk and wished she'd not placed it there, almost like a shrine.

He wanted to bid this place farewell, return home to Balidonough, and take up his new role in life. But until he was certain of Catherine's health, both in body and spirit, he was chained to Colstin Hall as surely as if he were actually Harry Dunnan.

Raised voices interrupted Moncrief's thoughts. He heard Peter shout, and the next instant the bedroom door was flung open so strongly that it bounced against the adjoining wall.

"I'd not thought to believe my ears, but my eyes do not deceive me. I am witnessing sinners in the very act of sin."

Moncrief straightened and turned.

The man who stood in the doorway was dressed in somber black, the only ornamentation to his attire being a plain white cravat. His cheeks were round and red like apples, his warm brown eyes owlish behind wire-rim spectacles. His lips were small, delicately pink, and pursed in a disapproving moue.

"Have you no shame, sir, that you would bed a woman in full daylight? And with her servants listening? As vicar of these good people, I'd never thought to witness such a scene of vice and degradation."

"Nor have you now," Moncrief said calmly. If he was to be found in a woman's chamber for nefarious purposes, she damn well wouldn't be sleeping, a fact that evidently escaped the vicar.

He was a full head taller than the other man, a point that obviously disturbed the vicar, who drew himself up and stared at Moncrief. His spectacles slid down to the tip of his nose, somewhat lessening the impact of his imperious gaze.

"You would debate a man of God, sir?" His round face quivered with indignation. "And who might you be? Other than a sinner and reprobate?"

"The Duke of Lymond," Moncrief said, using his title for full effect.

He glanced around the room, at the milling people in the doorway. A small, humorless smile graced his lips as he inclined his head to the vicar.

Astonishment altered the vicar's face, turned his florid face pale. His lips nearly disappeared as he pursed them in dismay.

"Your Grace?" His bow was half-done, as if he decided upon the gesture and changed his mind in the execution of it. He held his flat black hat with one pudgy hand, but the other fluttered in the air in front of him. His gaze abruptly focused on the floor, then to the left, then to the right, and back at Moncrief again.

Twice he tried to speak, both times the sound emerging

as a croak. The third time he cleared his throat and smiled weakly.

"Then surely there's a reason for your presence in Mrs. Dunnan's chamber, Your Grace."

Moncrief had no intention of divulging to the vicar that Catherine had tried to end her life, so he fell back on the only other plausible excuse for his presence. "I knew her husband."

The vicar nodded. "Naturally, you came to Colstin Hall to give her your condolences. Of course."

The vicar turned to the servants still clustered in the doorway. "There is no shame here, no scandal. Only a generous man doing his duty."

Of course it helped that he was a duke, and had the income to accompany it. Moncrief couldn't help but wonder what cause he would be expected to contribute toward before this day was done.

He glanced toward Catherine. No one thought it strange that she remained asleep. She had turned so that her profile was visible. In repose her face had a youthful purity. No lingering sadness curved her lips, and her closed lids shielded eyes that had been filled with despair.

She remained alone, with no one at her side. Not one person questioned her health or inquired as to her well-being, an omission that disturbed him on a visceral level.

Only Glynneth had protested his presence. She now stood silent behind the vicar.

Colstin Hall was a prosperous and well-maintained home. The servants evidently ate well and no one appeared overburdened by their duties. Where, then, was their loyalty? People often behave by rote, following a leader's example. Who, in this group, was their leader? Glynneth? Did the servants emulate her behavior toward Catherine, a distance that he could both see and feel?

"Is she not well?" the vicar asked, as if he'd heard Moncrief's thoughts.

"No. But I expect her to recover."

"You tended to her yourself, Your Grace?" The other man smiled at him, the expression punching his little apple cheeks up higher on his face until he looked like a squirrel with a mouthful of nuts. "How very kind of you. But you needn't concern yourself further. There are plenty here who can care for her."

Were there? What would happen to Catherine after he left? Would she continue to grieve? Or would she simply succeed the next time she chose to take too much laudanum?

Moncrief looked at the young maid who'd opened the door to him. She glanced away. Glynneth remained behind the vicar, eyes downcast. The other servants were huddled in the doorway, their faces avid with curiosity rather than concern. The young maid, who'd been so amused in the parlor, simpered at him now. Not one of them looked as if they gave a flying farthing what happened to their mistress.

He wouldn't leave a sick puppy in their care.

"I will counsel her myself, Your Grace." The vicar caught his thumbs in his vest, rocked back on his heels, looking pleased and altogether too prosperous for a vicar. Were they not supposed to abjure wealth? This man looked as if he'd had too many meals, and even the quality of his clothing did not indicate penury. No doubt because of Catherine's generosity. "Despite her illness, she should not have entertained visitors in her chamber, a point I will make abundantly clear."

In those few minutes, Moncrief realized that it was not simply momentous events that had the power to alter his life. This moment, for example, strung out like beads of moisture on a spiderweb, so infinitesimal, had the effect of altering his entire future.

"That won't be necessary, vicar," Moncrief heard himself say. "I believe that it's necessary for Mrs. Dunnan and myself to be wed with all possible haste, both for the sake of her reputation and my peace of mind."

Chapter 4

*H*e was touching her, his fingers lightly stroking her breasts. Occasionally, the back of his thumb would touch a nipple, and he would teasingly move away. She wanted to urge him not to be so delicate with her. She wanted the feel of him, the touch of him everywhere on her body. She wanted to smell of him in the morning, and see places on her body that he had marked with the roughness of his passion.

She felt his hands slide from her midriff to her waist and below to her hips, then even lower, all the while stroking, then moving away just when her skin began to tingle. He turned her in front of the fire, and she wanted to reach out to him, place her hands on his shoulders, and lean into his kiss. The lassitude that swept over her was so delicious that she lost herself in it.

His fingers ran down her back, pressing against her shoulder blades and under her arms, teasing just where the swelling of her breasts began. Then each hand cupped

*her buttocks and moved beneath them, as if half-daring
to touch her intimately.*

*She wanted to demand that he kiss her, a command that
she intended to utter in a soft and languorous tone. The
words, however, were so difficult to speak that she remained silent and hoped that he had the ability to read
her mind instead.*

The dream was foggy, tattered remnants that Catherine
couldn't recall. All that was left was an aching feeling as
if she'd cried in her sleep.

She felt his foot against hers and smiled to herself.
Harry had evidently stayed with her the night before,
something that didn't happen often. She brushed the bottom of his heel with her toes as she slowly turned her
head.

Harry was dead.

Abruptly, her eyes opened and she stared into the face
of a stranger. She jerked back her foot and sat up, clutching the sheet. She scooted to the edge of the bed, ignoring
the sudden and overwhelming pounding in her head.
Should she scream or race for the door to the hall? The
decision was taken out of her hands when the stranger
gripped her shoulder.

She screamed.

He clamped his hand over her mouth. "For the love of
God, stop it," he said, looking for all the world as if he
had the right to be incensed. He released her just as
quickly, and she sank back against the headboard.

"Who are you?" she asked faintly. A drumbeat clung to
every word and hammered through her head. She crossed
her arms over her chest and was grateful to note that she
was at least dressed, even if only in a threadbare nightgown. Although one thin layer of linen could not be said
to be properly attired. "What are you doing in my bed?"

She half expected him to vaporize in the next instant, a

figment of her imagination. But surely if she had dreamed him, she might have dreamed someone more close in appearance to Harry. Her beloved had blond hair and pleasing features. This scowling stranger with his disheveled black hair and coarse night beard was almost frightening in appearance.

"Do you not remember anything of the night before?" His voice was gravelly, as if he'd spoken for a long time and was now hoarse with it.

He sat up, still scowling at her, and it was only then that she noticed he was barefoot but otherwise fully dressed.

"Who are you?" She slid one leg out of the bed. Where were her servants? At her scream they should have come running.

Had he murdered them all in their beds?

"I am your husband, madam, and I chose to sleep beside you because I was concerned that your sleep would be one of permanence."

She simply stared at him, certain that this was some kind of dream, perhaps one brought about by too much laudanum. She was asleep and wandering among the heather, scattering the tiny pink blossoms into the air, not sitting here with a fully dressed and grumpy-looking man who had just declared they were forever linked by bonds of matrimony. Even in her most horrendous nightmares, she had never dreamed of such a thing.

"Have you no curiosity about how such an event occurred?"

"Have I died, then?" she asked softly. "Is this God's punishment for my many sins? The vicar says that I should purge my soul. Is it too late?"

She looked around her and thought it strange that the room should appear so much like it always had. Except, of course, that the bath was in front of the fireplace, and there were several towels on the floor. She was never that messy.

The room was a distortion of her real world.

"Is this hell, then?"

He was standing now and coming around the end of the bed. Before she could move away, he'd bent over her, placing both hands on the headboard and leaning over her so closely that she couldn't focus on his face. Her vision blurred and she closed her eyes.

"I am your husband, madam, and you are very much alive."

"Are you God?" she asked. She clutched the sheet tightly beneath her chin and forced herself to keep her eyes closed.

"The laudanum is giving you delusions."

Finally, something that made sense.

"Is that what you are? A delusion?" Her thoughts were confused, no doubt because of the deepening pain above her eyes.

She felt his hands move and she opened her eyes to find him standing beside the bed. "I am not a delusion. My name is Moncrief, Duke of Lymond and you, madam, are my duchess."

"I'm afraid you must be mistaken," she said, certain that if she wasn't dreaming or dead, and her wits hadn't left her, then he must be a lunatic who had come in through her window during the night.

When he didn't respond, she forced a smile to her face. Wasn't it common wisdom that it was better to humor a madman? Still, she glanced toward the fireplace and the tools arranged there. Perhaps she could get to the fireplace and brandish some kind of weapon against him, something that would keep him at bay while she summoned help.

"How long have we been married, dear sir?" she asked sweetly, dropping her other leg off the bed.

One of his eyebrows arched as he regarded her.

"A long time? Or have we recently been wed? Please forgive me if I cannot remember. The excitement of our union has no doubt thrust the date completely from my mind."

He was still scowling at her, a look that didn't reassure her at all. But she was standing and despite the pain in her head, she raced for the fireplace, grabbed the poker, and pointed it at him with both hands. The pain was so bad above her left eye that she could barely see, but she managed, nonetheless, to note his sudden look.

"Have I managed to amuse you, sir?"

"Indeed."

She frowned at him, backed up to the door, opened it and shouted for Glynneth. Her companion did not appear, but one of the maids did. Before her startled eyes, Abigail curtsied, her round face turning pink.

"Summon the magistrate, Abigail," Catherine said. "And the vicar if you will. He has some knowledge of healing. Together, they can no doubt assist this man."

Abigail looked behind her to Moncrief and curtsied, again, before glancing at Catherine.

"It's all right, Abigail," Moncrief said. "Perhaps summoning the vicar would be a good idea, but I doubt we need the magistrate."

"Yes, Your Grace," Abigail said, curtseying for the third time. "Would you like your breakfast now?"

"In the dining room, I think."

Moncrief strode toward Catherine and lifted the poker from her hands. He walked back to the fireplace and deposited it in its holder before turning and surveying her once again.

"As fetching as that garment is, I doubt it's appropriate for breakfast. Have you a wrapper? Or better yet, would you care to change?"

"I don't know you," she said, moving to stand with her

back to the wall. "I am a widow. I am not prepared to wed again. Not ever."

"However, you are. Would you care to know how it was done? Or would you prefer to continue in your claim that it was not?"

She moved a few feet to the left until she came to her favorite chair. Slowly lowering herself into it, she placed her hands on the arms and put her knees together, ankle-bones aligned perfectly, both feet together—the proper comportment for a lady of breeding.

Only then did she force herself to look at him again. How could she possibly be married to this man?

"Then tell me."

He turned and leaned his hands against the mantel, bracing himself there as if summoning strength for this revelation.

"I know you didn't expect to awake being wed. However, I suspect you didn't intend to awake at all. It was my good fortune to come upon you before the laudanum had taken effect. I was able to save your life, a fact that you no doubt resent now."

She would have spoken, but he turned and held up his hand as if to silence her. So surprised was she at his arrogance that she remained silent. How dare he command her in her own home. In her very own room. With a shock she realized that if they were truly wed, it was no longer her house or her room or her fortune.

He strode toward her with such resolve that she sank back against the chair. She was no match for him in physical strength. But he surprised her by sitting on the ottoman in front of her and holding out his hands, palms up. She looked at them, uncertain what he wished. Did he want her to place her own hands on them?

Instead, she closed her eyes and leaned her head back against the chair.

"Catherine?" he asked softly. "Are you feeling unwell? I'm not surprised. You took a great deal of laudanum."

She shook her head, ever so gently so as not to encourage the pain to grow worse. Slowly and silently, she counted to ten. When she opened her eyes he would be gone, and she would be marveling at the strange and disconcerting dream she'd had. But before she even opened her eyes, he spoke again.

"Catherine?"

"I am asleep," she said, interrupting what he would have said. "I have not awakened yet. None of this has been true or real. I am in the throes of one of my nightmares. And this one has not even brought me Harry, but a stranger."

"Do you dream often of him?"

"Every night and every day. Sleep has become a refuge. A place to go when the pain of losing him becomes too great."

She opened her eyes slowly and looked at him. "I do not tell that to other people," she confessed. "But you are only a figment in my nightmare. So it's all right if I tell you anything. What a manly creature you are. I must have been very observant before my marriage to note such things about a man. Your chest is very broad, you know. You fill out your shirt quite well. But I do not think that your trousers should be quite so tight, and I'm a little ashamed of myself that I have conjured you up. Especially with such impressive attributes." She stared at the bulge between his legs. Even sitting, it could not be dismissed.

How odd that the pain in her head felt real, as did her unshed tears. And her stomach was announcing that it, too, was in rebellion with other parts of her body. If she kept her eyes closed she would awaken soon, and this would simply be one more hideous nightmare.

A few moments later, she opened her eyes again.

Moncrief's eyes were blue.

Harry's eyes had been a warm and comforting brown.

"I'm not in the throes of a nightmare, am I?"

"Unless you think marriage is a nightmare, madam." He sat back, withdrawing his hands and placing them on his knees.

"It was a blessing," she said softly. "Too short, but a blessing nevertheless."

She looked away, trying to distance herself from this man who had altered her life so quickly and without her knowledge.

"Tell me how we come to be wed, then. And please, no tales of laudanum. I take it only to sleep, nothing more."

"To sleep forever, perhaps."

She pushed the pain in her head back far enough to scowl at him. "I have never used it to excess, nor do I appreciate your accusing me of doing so."

"You were near death last night, madam, or do you not recall that, either?"

She didn't, but did he have to know? What insanity had brought about her assent? She would never love anyone but Harry. Never share, willingly, her body with another man.

"Tell me," she said, looking away.

He told her then, and when he was done, she didn't speak, didn't question. A few minutes earlier she'd thought him a lunatic. She was certain of it at this moment.

"The vicar married us in this room, with your servants as attendants and witnesses."

She looked down at her nightgown, threadbare and worn, it had once been one of her favorites before she'd gone into mourning. She'd not had the heart to dye the tiny little pink and yellow flowers embroidered on the yoke and cuffs.

"And I was in my nightgown? Any woman would be shamed to be wed in her nightgown."

"Most women would not have tried to end their lives."

"I did not," she said, turning and fixing on him a look of such irritation that surely he must see the truth in her eyes. "Why would I have done such a thing now? Why not when word came of Harry's death?"

"Grief is a cumulative thing. It doesn't necessarily grow easier to cope with a loss the greater the time that passes."

"And you have experience with such grief, my lord?"

"Your Grace is acceptable. Or husband, if you prefer."

"I think I'll call you Moncrief. It is your name, is it not?"

"And what shall I call you? Wife?"

"Catherine."

He nodded. "What is the last thing you do remember?"

She hadn't a clear memory of any of it, only disjointed shapes and feelings.

"Do you at least remember me? I came to see you the day before yesterday. Tuesday."

Which would mean that today was Thursday. She knew that much, but she didn't know him. So many days had passed one into the other, becoming a gray fog of her life. She could remember Harry's words so clearly that they rang like a clarion bell in her mind, but she couldn't remember Tuesday.

She looked down at her clenched hands on her lap, determined not to look at his face. How did she explain losing time?

"I don't remember meeting you. I can only take your word for it." She looked around the room before finding the courage to face him finally.

His eyes were somber and the expression on his face serious yet blessedly empty of ridicule or contempt.

"By the fact that you are in my bedchamber, I will also have to accept your word for the fact that we are somewhat acquainted."

He smiled then, and stood, striding across the room, his boots echoing against the wooden floor. She wanted to tell him to quiet his sounds, to muffle the noise of his presence in her chamber, but she kept silent. If Abigail knew, then the whole of Scotland had learned of their marriage.

"Meet with the vicar if you want proof."

He was too cold in his looks, too arrogant. His eyebrows were black slashes on his face, his eyes too intently blue. His looks were too arresting; a woman would have no comfort with this sort of man.

"I would like to speak to the vicar."

He nodded. Because he so easily agreed, she was beginning to believe they were actually married.

"Surely we can undo what was so quickly done. I am in no need of rescuing." At the moment, however, she was not feeling so confident. The room was beginning to spin around her, and the chamber abruptly felt entirely too warm.

He regarded her intently as if he knew how ill she suddenly felt.

"I'm fine," she said, forcing her voice to steady. "But I would appreciate it if you would assist me in undoing this marriage."

"You don't look strong enough to sit there, madam, let alone to concern yourself with something that cannot be undone."

His words only strengthened her resolve that he would not see her become ill. He had evidently witnessed enough of her humiliation.

"Please," she said, waving her hand at the door, "if you would simply send the vicar to me when he arrives. I'd like to hear that from his lips."

She closed her eyes and laid her head back against the chair, wishing that the chamber wasn't revolving around her. Or perhaps it was remaining in place, and she was the one spinning.

Moncrief didn't leave. Instead, he placed a cold compress on her forehead, then used another cloth dipped in water to gently wipe her face and her throat. She wanted to thank him or pull away from his ministrations, but she had no energy left to do either. All of her attention was directed at not becoming ferociously sick. The clink of china made her turn her head and open her eyes.

He had placed an empty bowl on the table beside her. "I think you're going to need that," he said. "In the meantime, I can summon one of the servants to prepare you something warm to drink."

"Not an oatmeal posset." Not this morning. Cook was forever sending up the drink for her. Now her stomach rolled just speaking of it.

On the other side of the room the window heralded another gray morning. In the distance, she could hear the sound of the stable doors being opened. A wagon was coming in from the field. Water was being drawn from the well. Life was going on as it did at Colstin Hall, as if the house were a living entity, separate and apart from its owner. All who worked here served the manse and not simply her.

If it had been another day, if it had been a normal day, she might call for breakfast now. She might have dressed and left her bedroom. She would have met with the vicar, of course, and Glynneth, arranging with her the chores of the week. Every season brought responsibilities. Life was on a schedule at Colstin Hall. But Harry's death had altered everything.

"Please leave me," she said.

Then he was gone, her nightmare or her husband, whichever was true.

She sat still, the chair surrounding her. The upholstery

was familiar, the shape of it known and remembered. She had sat there often, either engaged in sewing or reading, her fingers stroking over the rounded arms.

When she was certain Moncrief wasn't returning, Catherine stood and made her way to the trunk, arms wrapped around her aching stomach. Slowly, she opened the lid of Harry's trunk and selected one of his letters. She needed him close to her now more than she had at any other time. She returned to her chair to hear Moncrief speaking in the hallway.

"I'm afraid she's going to be ill," he said. "Which is just as well. The sooner she has the remainder of the poison out of her system, the better." There was a moment of silence, then he spoke again, "You won't be giving her any more of the laudanum?"

Glynneth answered, her voice filled with irritation. "I never gave it to her before; I won't give it to her now."

"Good, I'd hate to be made a widower a day after I've become a husband."

Catherine returned to the chair, pressed Harry's letter against her chest, and began to weep.

Chapter 5

Three days later they left Colstin Hall, their destination Balidonough, the Duke of Lymond's seat. Her servants would follow along with Moncrief's aide, their luggage, and those possessions Catherine wished to bring to her new home.

The dark clouds overhead were an omen as she walked to the carriage. The wind was blowing briskly, tossing her hair, chilling her skin, almost as if in punishment for leaving her home. She closed her eyes against the strength of it, felt the wind careen over her shoulders, around her folded arms, pressing her skirt against her legs.

A storm was coming, and the wind was its herald. When it moaned through the trees, she wondered if nature itself was chastising her. If so, then it was in good company.

Glynneth was angry with her. When hearing of Moncrief's plans to travel to Balidonough, she'd disappeared for a day, and when she returned, the only thing she'd said was that she had business to attend to before she left the area.

Nor was the vicar happy. He had been oddly distracted, wishing her well in her new home with an absent wave and a Bible quotation.

Those servants she'd chosen to take to Balidonough with her were acting distressed to be chosen, but the staff left behind at Colstin Hall were equally unhappy.

No one was pleased with her, including Moncrief, who entered the carriage and sat stonily silent opposite her. So much rancor in such an enclosed space did not bode well for the remainder of the journey.

Balidonough was only two hours away, close enough that intrigues of the Dukes of Lymond had come to her ears, but distant enough that she could ignore them if she chose.

As the carriage pulled away, Moncrief regarded the scenery, which was nothing to boast of, just the house, its environs, and a one-lane road. But it was her last glimpse of Colstin Hall and all its attendant memories. She had raced down that path beside the pines as a child, feeling joy and wonder, had stood in the gardens as a young woman, staring up at the stars and wondering if love came to all creatures as suddenly as it had to her. She had wandered there to stand beneath a tree in the fullness of a storm, and wept with the rain after Harry had died.

Now Catherine closed her eyes against her tears and leaned her head back against the upholstered seat.

"Are you feeling ill again?"

The concern in Moncrief's voice made her open her eyes and regard him.

"No," she said. "I'm not. I'm feeling very much better, thank you."

He nodded once at her answer, then went back to his contemplation of the view.

Although he was a stranger to her, they were bound by law, the only silken cord that linked them the vicar's words spoken on a night she could still not recall. But she remembered only too well her conversation with Thomas McLeod, the vicar, three days earlier.

"I can assure you, Catherine, that the wedding did take place, with the whole of your servants as witnesses."

His usual plump face had been narrowed in displeasure, and some censure.

"Surely I did not give my consent, vicar?"

"But you did. Granted, it was not in your usual voice, but you agreed. I thought myself that you were eager for the union."

"I cannot be married to him. I cannot. Can you not annul this wedding?"

"I can assure you, Catherine," he said stiffly, "that I cannot. His Grace assured me that he had spent the night with you in your bed. Can you deny that?"

No, she could not.

She knew very little about Moncrief. He was the new Duke of Lymond. His home was Balidonough. In three days, he had taken control of her home. Her servants deferred to him, even the vicar chose to meet with him rather than her. He'd supervised her diet, according to Glynneth, insisted upon tasting her meals, but he'd left her alone and chose to sleep in her father's room. This morning was the first time they'd been together since the day after their marriage.

How strange to know nothing about a husband.

"My companion does not like you," she said, goading him a bit, if the truth be told. He didn't answer, so she was emboldened even further. "Glynneth says you were rude to her."

This time, his gaze shot over to her, and she was nearly pinned to the bench by the intensity of it.

"I've no doubt that she said as much. She was lax in her duties. I have no patience with those who are lazy, then claim they were not."

"I have always found her to be very diligent."

"She did not seem to care that you were close to death, which was her first mistake. But then she left you alone with me, not the actions of a worthwhile companion."

She had no rejoinder to that.

"Tell me about our first meeting."

"You still do not remember?"

She shook her head.

"Perhaps you never will," he said. "Laudanum takes away memory."

She didn't wish to get into a discussion about her use of laudanum. It had never been as egregious as he thought. She'd always been very careful not to ingest too much. However, she couldn't explain the loss of memory of the night they wed, or the fact that she'd lost two whole days of recollections.

"I came to visit you," he said, bracing himself against the corner of the coach, one elbow on the windowsill. His thumb brushed against his bottom lip as he concentrated on the view. "I was a friend of Harry's."

"You never told me that before."

"Not that you remember."

She frowned at him, and then a second later smoothed out her expression.

"Did Harry ever speak of me?"

He closed his eyes and leaned back against the seat.

"Soldiers will always speak of those they love, those they left behind. Harry was no exception."

"What did he say?"

For a long moment, he didn't answer. Finally, he spoke. "He read your letters to me occasionally."

That was a surprise. Harry's letters were inviolate to

her, something that she would never share with another. She'd naturally thought he would regard them the same way. She felt a flush come to her cheeks and looked away.

"They were very beautiful letters, Catherine."

The warmth was spreading throughout her whole body. She concentrated on the shape of her nails. They had grown longer; she needed to attend to them. Perhaps buff them a little. The moons were a curious color, a pale lavender, as if her whole body had been in mourning.

She nodded and hoped he wouldn't continue. A shame suffused her, not because of what she had written to Harry, but because her words were not meant for any eyes but his.

He glanced at her. "It was a kindness he did, to share your letters. I did not have the volume of correspondence that Harry did. My father wrote me once before he died. My brother, however, was an abominable letter writer. I don't believe I ever received one from him."

"Were you very close?"

"Not truly," he answered. "Colin was twelve years older and couldn't be bothered with another younger brother."

Before she could ask, he answered her. "I had another brother. Dermott was five years older than I. He died when he was thirteen. An imbecilic accident taking a fence on an untried horse."

"You sound as if he deserved to die for his foolishness."

Once again, he pinned her with the intensity of his blue gaze. "There are causes and effects in life, Catherine."

How utterly arrogant he was.

"You must be pleased to become duke, then. With two older brothers, you must not have expected it."

His face looked created for arrogance. The shape of his nose, the arch of his cheekbones, the imperious, squared chin.

"No, I didn't expect it. But now that Colin has died, I have a responsibility, and duties to perform."

"Have you always been so noble?"

"Is it nobility to do the right thing?"

He had the disconcerting habit of asking her a question in response to her question. She switched the subject. "Do you not worry what your family will say when you return to Balidonough with a wife?"

"I have not seen Balidonough for over fourteen years. My family, such as it is, has had nothing to do with my life for all that time, I have no concerns what they might think now."

"Have you always been so autocratic?"

To her surprise, he smiled. "It isn't arrogance to know one's place. The last fourteen years have been spent earning my way in the world. Whatever accomplishments I've achieved have been of no interest to my family. My value to Balidonough is the fact that I have inherited the title. Everything I do from this moment on will be simply because I'm the twelfth Duke of Lymond."

"And what is my place?"

"The Duchess of Lymond," he said flatly.

"I am not related to the peerage, other than a third cousin who's an earl. But we've never met. My father was only a farmer. We might be considered minor gentry, if that."

"Is there reason for this litany of your genealogy?"

"I do not see how a duke can marry just anyone. Are you not considered a prince?"

"I am Moncrief," he said, as if that were that, as if no further explanation was necessary or even desired.

"Don't you care that I'm just a farmer's daughter?"

His smile was bright, revealing white, even teeth. "I doubt you could be called that, madam. Your father owned more land than anyone in the shire. Neither is Colstin Hall a humble cottage."

"He was a modest man, however, who enjoined me never to think myself better than anyone else."

"In that case, he would be disappointed, no doubt, to find you married to a duke."

"He would be surprised," she admitted.

"It seems to me that if I am required to attend flocks of sheep, being a farmer's daughter would be an asset and not a detriment. We have a great many sheep at Balidonough."

"Will you be serious, Moncrief?"

"If your father had been a brewer or a distiller, you might be looked upon with greater favor by those at Balidonough. We are known for our whiskey and our ale, you see."

"And you see nothing wrong with this union?"

"Should I?" His smile disappeared and in its place that curiously intent look. "If you are asking me if I am egalitarian, then the answer is no. I do not treat my aide as if he's my friend. I have no desire to become a confidant of the maids. The footmen will not be my companions."

"And your wife? How will you treat me?"

"Your behavior is the clue to that answer, madam."

"Why did you marry me, Moncrief?"

"Because you needed rescuing."

That answer was not one she expected and for a few moments she was nonplussed, incapable of responding.

She clenched her hands tighter. Nature came to her aid then. In a burst of fury, the storm opened up directly atop them. The noise was such that she would have had to shout to speak, which was just as well. She didn't know what to say to him.

According to Glynneth, she was very ill the night of her marriage and might conceivably have died. But the way Moncrief said the words, so nonchalantly and almost uncaring, made her feel that she was no more important than a dog he might have rescued on the side of the road, some poor creature that had gotten in the way of the carriage wheels.

Granted, her life was not what she would have chosen for herself, but there were good days along with the bad. Gradually, in time, she would have come to accept the fact that Harry was not returning. The image of him would have faded, along with the love she felt for him. In time, she would have become reconciled to her grief.

Time, however, had been taken from her, and so had the rightness of her mourning.

Instead, this man with his air of command and his insistence the she was in danger from herself had stepped in and altered her life completely.

Nor did anyone have one word to say to stop him.

For long moments they remained silent, each captured in their own thoughts. The day was a brisk one, and she was grateful for the blanket she placed over her knees.

Her first view of Balidonough was through a curtain of rain, her new home transformed to a watery painting of red brick set among the fading green of the grass. The castle sat perched on the highest hill in the area, overlooking the glen, a formidable reminder of Scotland's tumultuous history.

The Dukes of Lymond had held power in this part of Scotland for generations, and looking at their castle, Catherine knew why. No one would dare to invade such a place, or argue against its lord's dictates.

The structure was so large that it seemed to stretch across the horizon. On the corners of what looked to be a square courtyard, circular towers overlooked the hilly landscape. A river approached the castle and disappeared beneath the wall and into the very heart of Balidonough.

How could she be expected to be mistress of something like that?

They traveled for nearly a quarter hour down a gravel road, past closely cropped and manicured hills to Balidonough. In all that time, Moncrief said nothing, only stared impassively at the passing scenery. She had a strange and unwelcome thought that this homecoming might be difficult for him.

"This is the first time you've been home since your brother died, isn't it?"

For a moment, she didn't think he was going to answer her. Perhaps it might have been better if he hadn't. She wouldn't have noticed that his hand clenched on the edge of the window, or that in the faint light his face looked even sterner.

"I have not been back to Balidonough for fourteen years. My father was alive then, and so was Colin."

He turned back to the window again, and she was effectively dismissed, but he'd given her more information about himself than he probably knew.

"You didn't like your father, did you?"

His look of surprise was too quickly masked for her to be absolutely certain she'd witnessed it.

"Why would you say that?"

"When my father passed away, it was a time of sorrow for me. And I still cannot remember his passing without wishing he was here. Every time I look around Colstin Hall, I can imagine what he would say to my renovations of it."

"I doubt my father would have noticed something as plebeian as a new banister, or new kitchen quarters."

"Then he, too, was every inch the duke, was he not?"

He smiled, an expression that took her aback. He had a very charming smile, but she wished he would look as somber as he had an instant ago. Surprisingly, that man was more comfortable to be around than this more approachable one.

"Are you asking, in a roundabout way, if my father would have approved of you? Probably not. My father did not agree with most of what I did. However, over the years I lost the need for his approval."

"I am sorry you were estranged at his death."

"But we weren't. He and I had come to an agreement about our natures. We each understood the other. Simply because you're related to someone doesn't mean that you have to like him. You tolerate them, you accept."

She had a sudden feeling that this was very much as their marriage might be, with him tolerating and her accepting.

Catherine realized that up until now she'd been very successful at creating a world around her, peopled with those she loved, with her favorite things added for a little comfort. She ate what she wished and accepted calls from whom she wished, and arranged her life to suit her own comfort. Residing at Colstin Hall was like living inside a cocoon, one that had abruptly split open to reveal a new world, a new life, this new man.

All of which terrified her almost to tears.

Harry Dunnan was in hell, laughing at him, Moncrief was certain.

Dear God, why had he ever written her? Why had he ever shared his thoughts with this woman who now sat looking down at the floor as if pretending they weren't in the same carriage? Why had he ever become fascinated by her thoughts?

This marriage was doomed to perdition if he didn't divulge the truth. Yet he doubted she would believe him. Anything that made her beloved Harry less a hero in her eyes she'd immediately reject. Or perhaps she would believe him, and become a raging madwoman. Even worse, she might take another dose of laudanum in her grief.

"Have you lived all your life at Colstin Hall?" he asked her.

She glanced at him and nodded. "It was my father's home, and Harry came to live with us after our marriage."

The very last thing he wanted to do was continue to talk about the departed Harry Dunnan. But he found himself led into the conversation all the same. "Did Harry like Colstin Hall?"

She studied the window, seemingly intent on the curtain of rain. But he allowed the time to stretch between them, wondering if talking of Harry was painful for her.

"I think he was bored," she said, surprising him. "When my father offered to help him buy a commission, Harry didn't hesitate."

"But you didn't approve."

Her intense study of the rain ended, but now she regarded her clasped hands as if she had never before seen them. "I had only been wed a month. Of course I didn't want him to leave me. But sometimes a wife's opinion does not count for very much."

"I shall not leave you, Catherine," he said.

Her face abruptly paled.

He forced a smile to his face and wished he had something in his dispatch case to read or study, some complicated problem to occupy his mind, some puzzle that he might reason out, anything but contemplate how irrational this marriage was and how much a farce it was proving to be.

He wished he could write her again, tell her his thoughts in words. In his mind, he composed another letter to her.

There should be no secret thoughts that create chasms between us. But I felt closer to you in Quebec than I do now sitting with such a short distance between us. I want to know what you think but the domain of your thoughts is locked and forbidden me. I have seen your nakedness and touched you in gentleness for all that we're strangers.

Harry stands between us, incorporeal, but with as much substance as if he were still alive. I do not doubt that he would have only contempt for your misery, but that is not something I can tell you. Nor can I convince you of his perfidy without revealing my own.

If he had never written her, he would be spared this purgatory. But he would have never known her either. Only time would tell whether the one was worth the other.

I married you because you needed rescuing.

Or he did.

This woman spoke with such self-possession, but he sensed it was only surface deep. He suspected also, with an insight that disturbed him, that she was trembling, holding herself tight so that he could not witness her discomfiture.

The carriage slowed, and he hooked a finger behind the leather shade and watched as Balidonough loomed before them. Instantly, he was reminded of a scene from his childhood.

As a boy, excited about riding his new pony, he'd raced down the stairs to the courtyard, only to be stopped by his father.

"Restraint is what separates us from the masses," the tenth Duke of Lymond had said. "If you cannot master your own baser emotions, you will never be better than lowliest peasant."

Moncrief had learned, over the years, to mask his emotions, at least in front of his father. He was careful never to show excitement or sadness or any of the riotous feelings a boy would normally demonstrate. That training put him in good stead to be a commander of men, to lead them into battle and never show fear, to send them to their deaths and never reveal regret.

He was doubly glad of his learned restraint now as he entered the courtyard of Balidonough almost exactly fourteen years after he had left it, returning a more experienced man, a colonel of the Lowland Scots Fusiliers. Inside, however, he felt as if he were ten years old again.

Moncrief was conscious of the fact that Catherine was watching him carefully, a scrutiny he'd not expected.

He'd once expressed his grief about his father to her by hiding it behind a very real anguish about his men.

There are times when I see their fresh faces and want to warn them that youth is not a guarantee of old age. They think themselves immortal, because they don't feel their bones growing brittle or their muscles aching as they rise in the morning. They don't realize they can be as easily struck down by disease as by a musket ball, by a fallen tree as quickly as an unexpected flood.

I see them in their revelry and I want to congratulate them on their wisdom in celebrating every moment of life. But instead of becoming inebriated, I want them to see a sunset or love a woman, or experience life in the very fullness of it. I want each of them to become a father, to greet their own fathers again. Yet I know even as I watch them, that nothing can guarantee that any of them will remain alive for a fortnight or a month. And so I can't help but distance myself from them, knowing that I will be packing the trunks of those who do not survive and writing final words to a loved one.

He had the absurd desire to confide in her, to tell her that this homecoming was a difficult one for him, a confession he'd not even made to Peter. Instead, he remained silent, and composed himself to meet what was left of his family.

Chapter 6

The outer courtyard was enormous, but it only led to another wall, and a drawbridge over which the carriage thundered. Catherine could feel her heart booming in her chest, and wondered if she looked as afraid as she felt.

"Balidonough is said to rival Warwick, the great English castle," Moncrief said.

"Indeed." How odd that it was difficult to swallow. Or even to breathe.

"Originally, the castle was a motte-and-bailey structure, but generations of my ancestors have built up the place. I doubt that we'll ever need the defenses again, however." He smiled at her. "After all, the world is much more civilized."

"Which is why you've spent the last fourteen years of your life fighting wars."

His smile was an acknowledgment of her sarcasm.

Moncrief, annoying, was infinitely preferable to Moncrief, charming.

The carriage stopped midpoint between the inner wall and the imposing steps leading to the arched oak door. She felt as if they were entering a cathedral rather than simply a home, albeit one for the Duke of Lymond.

The storm had not abated, but he removed his coat and placed it over her head to protect her from the worst of the rain. They left the carriage and raced up the steps.

"Don't look so terrified."

"I have a reason," she said, wiping her face with the edge of his cloak. "I'm about to face your family."

He smiled once more, a less genial expression than one with a bit of wickedness to it. "So am I," he said. "And who it will be is a mystery to us both."

She sent him an irritated look. "What do you mean, a mystery?"

"I've been away from home for fourteen years, Catherine. I've no idea what collection of relatives my brother assembled. If he'd had children, I wouldn't be here now, but perhaps there is a bevy of aunts, uncles, cousins, and the like behind that door."

She had never considered that his welcome might be a strange one.

He gripped the round ring in the middle of one door, and released it. Could anyone hear its sound over the storm?

The woman who opened the door held herself straight and tall, her shoulders and lean body forming a perfect "T." Her face was lean and angular, with surprisingly full lips. Her brown hair had a few traces of gray, as if Nature had not quite decided if she was young or old, or teetering somewhere in between.

"Yes?" When she spoke, only the lower half of her face moved. Her eyes didn't blink, her eyebrows remained stationary, and not a hair on her head budged despite the increasing wind.

Moncrief moved to stand in front of Catherine as if to protect her from such a paltry welcome. Surely, the inhabitants of Balidonough knew he was coming.

"Hortensia?" he asked.

"Moncrief? Is it you?" She smiled, mobilizing her face into something warm and welcoming. She stood aside, the sweep of her arm toward the interior an awkward gesture, as if welcoming strangers was a foreign concept to her.

"We have been awaiting you, Juliana and I." She peered at Moncrief through the dimness.

He placed his hand on the small of Catherine's back and drew her forward. "My wife, Catherine."

"I'll tell Juliana that you've arrived," she said, turning. "In the meantime, please follow me."

Moncrief raised an eyebrow, but didn't respond.

"Who is she?" Catherine whispered.

"Juliana's sister. Juliana was Colin's wife. My sister-in-law." That was the extent of their conversation as they entered Balidonough and followed Hortensia.

The entrance hall was, even in the near darkness, magnificent. The tall ceiling culminated in a dome, and surrounding it were twelve colonnades each adorned at the top with acanthus scrolls and the heads of mythical creatures. The staircase was of walnut, each step cantilevered out from the wall, leaving the impression that it floated in midair. The balustrade was of iron, twisted into decorative shapes and supported by sculptures of scantily clad goddesses.

There were traces of wealth wherever she looked, putting to rest the thought that Moncrief might have married her for her fortune. The floors were inlaid with woods in contrasting colors. Those walls not adorned with gilded mahogany panels were frescoed with scenes of what looked to be Moncrief's family's heritage. Barrel-vaulted ceilings gave way to bare timber, then to plaster ceilings where narrow interlaced panels formed small frames for brightly colored paintings.

The wall coverings varied from large, beautifully rendered tapestries to watered silk or cut velvet, or damask. Once, she peeked into a room to find the walls decked with hand-colored, wood-block-printed paper.

At the end of several corridors were fitted cabinets that look oriental in design. Catherine would have liked to have admired their contents, but Hortensia looked back impatiently several times as if to hurry them on their way.

Catherine was overwhelmed by the sheer size of Balidonough. A small village could live comfortably within the castle's dimensions and rarely need to venture outside.

But Balidonough had an emptiness about it, a feeling of disuse. She had the novel thought that it felt as if the castle were waiting to come alive, as if it had been placed under a spell of enchantment. The corridors were cold, the smell one of mustiness, and the darkness the result of none of the sconces being lit. If she had truly been the chatelaine of Balidonough, she would have lit the rooms against the oncoming night, caused the fires to blaze in empty rooms, and perfumed the air with dried flowers.

But it seemed impossible that she might have the power to do any of this, even if she wished it. All she wanted at this moment was to be back at Colstin Hall, the time a week earlier, when all that she had to cope with was her grief.

Finally, Hortensia entered a large yet welcoming room where a paltry fire blazed in the fireplace. The wall paneling, moldings, and shutters were of a dark cherrywood, heavily carved with cherubs holding garlands. Tall floor-to-ceiling windows that would ordinarily dwarf a smaller room were well proportioned in this chamber.

In front of the fire were two heavily carved chairs that looked as if they had rested there for generations. A few stubby candles sat in holders, but none of the lanterns had been lit. Hortensia didn't offer Moncrief any refreshment. Nor did she ask about their journey. She simply showed them the room and vanished, leaving Moncrief and Catherine alone in the empty room.

"It's rather gloomy, isn't it?"

"It's a mausoleum," Moncrief answered. He walked to the windows draped in thick velvet. The storm had settled over them, darkening the sky and making it impossible to tell if it was night or day.

"Has Balidonough always been this way?"

He shrugged. "I don't remember, isn't that strange? When I think of Balidonough, I think of my father, and he was such a force that he made everything and everyone around him look smaller in comparison."

She thought he was the same, but didn't say it. He looked oddly at home in this room, despite the fact that he'd not been given a welcome befitting the twelfth Duke of Lymond. Not one servant appeared, and after a few moments, Catherine peered out the door. There were no candles lit in the corridors, and they were now black as pitch.

"Do you think our welcome is so paltry because of the storm?" she asked, struggling to find a reason why no one had come to see to their comfort.

The appearance of a woman in the doorway interrupted Moncrief's reply.

"Juliana." He left her side and went to greet his sister-in-law.

The Dowager Duchess of Lymond was wearing paint. Her complexion had been generously dabbed with some concoction that lightened it considerably, but the mixture didn't cover her face completely. Instead, it looked as if she were wearing a mask, one adorned with two large dots of pink on her cheeks, and lips that were painted in a permanent moue. Her eyebrows arched like flying birds over her forehead, giving her an expression of eternal surprise.

"Moncrief?" she asked, her voice high-pitched and scratchy. She frowned at Moncrief, then stretched out her hand. "Hortensia said it was you, but I cannot believe my eyes. You don't look a day older than when I last saw you."

In a gesture Catherine would not have expected of him, Moncrief took the woman's hand and kissed the air above it.

"And you as well," he said kindly. "I trust you're well, Juliana?"

"How kind of you to ask," she said, pulling her hand away and gliding to a nearby chair.

Juliana was shorter than her sister, with blond hair that was interspersed with white. Nevertheless, it was becoming, especially arranged as it was in a severe coronet at the back of her head. If one could ignore the bizarre application of her face paint, Juliana could be considered an attractive woman.

"I'd like you to meet my wife, Catherine."

The dowager duchess nodded. "Are you from North America as well?"

"No. My home is Colstin Hall, not far from here."

With that, Juliana ignored her, and turned her attention to Moncrief.

"Your servants?"

"They will be here shortly," Moncrief said.

"I'll have rooms prepared." Once more, Juliana glanced at Catherine, but the look was no warmer the second time. "And you, Moncrief? The ducal apartments?"

He smiled, the expression so unlike his normal one that

Catherine realized he played a part the equal of Juliana's. "Of course. I trust they're ready?"

Juliana's expression didn't change, but she looked as if she'd drawn up into herself, as if shivering at a frigid gust of wind. Catherine wasn't surprised. Not only was the atmosphere a chilly one, but the room itself was cold enough for her to see her breath.

"They have been readied since Colin's death six months ago. We have, of course, been expecting you." The inference being that Moncrief would not have voluntarily returned to Balidonough until he was made duke.

Juliana stood and made her way to the door. Although she hesitated for a moment, she didn't speak again. When she left, the room felt appreciably warmer, a comment Catherine didn't make to Moncrief.

Still, she couldn't help but wonder if there had been antipathy between them for a very long time, or if it had only been prompted by Moncrief's ascension to the title. If she had known him better, or longer, she might have asked. But his very manner did not encourage questions, so she remained silent.

A moment later, a young footman appeared at the door, dressed in livery that was too short in the sleeves and was missing a few buttons. His gloves were gray rather than white, and his neckcloth frayed at the edges.

However, he was tall, with intelligent eyes, and a ready smile. His shock of red hair stuck up this way and that, and as he bowed, he smoothed his hand over it as if to tame it.

"Your Grace, if you'll follow me."

They were led again through a labyrinth of corridors.

"I shall never be able to find my way," she said, as they turned left and encountered a winding newel stair before turning right again.

"I'll give you a ball of string," Moncrief said, "and you can use it to retrace your path."

Only once did she recognize where they were, and that was when they encountered the cantilevered stairs. They climbed them to the second floor while the footman waited above at the landing.

"Where is Barrows?" Moncrief asked at the top.

"He died, sir, a year this April."

"And you've had no replacement?"

"No, Your Grace. Her Grace didn't think we needed a majordomo."

"Mrs. McElwee? I trust she is still with us?"

"Well, not exactly, Your Grace," the footman said.

"What does 'not exactly' mean, exactly?"

"Mrs. McElwee broke her foot a few months ago, and she's gone to be with her sister. None of us think she's coming back, since she and Her Grace don't get along." The young man halted, his Adam's apple bobbing nervously in his throat. "Begging your pardon, Your Grace."

"What, exactly, do they disagree about?"

He looked panicked, and actually glanced from the left to the right as if seeking an escape route. But perched as they were at the top of the stairs, there was nowhere to go. Catherine could have told him that it was no use trying to escape. Moncrief had a way of obtaining what he wanted.

"Money, Your Grace," he finally said, as if realizing only the truth would do. "Mrs. McElwee called the duchess a harridan of a miser with no idea how to run a place like Balidonough."

She had never before seen Moncrief look so surprised. Catherine smothered her smile with some difficulty.

"Indeed," he said.

"Yes, Your Grace. Mrs. McElwee was wanting the maids to have new uniforms and her Grace refused. They even came to words about it, with Mrs. McElwee threatening never to speak to her again. It's how she broke her foot, you see."

Moncrief was leading the way down the corridor, the young footman following, warming up to his tale.

"How did she break her foot?" Catherine asked, curious.

The footman turned to look at her. "Well, Your Grace, it's after one of their rows, and Mrs. McElwee came into the servants' dining room and kicked the door shut. When she screamed a minute later, we knew it wasn't because of Her Grace."

Moncrief was at the doors at the end of the corridor, as if, in escaping the suddenly voluble footman, he could equally ignore the evident chaos at Balidonough.

"Thank you," Catherine said, fumbling for the young man's name.

"Wallace, Your Grace." He bowed again to her and once to Moncrief, who wasn't paying him the slightest attention. Evidently deciding that it was better to escape the new duke's notice than to garner it, the young footman bowed once more, turned around, and walked quickly away.

Moncrief flung open the double doors and walked inside. He strode to the windows and pulled back the curtains where the watery sunlight gave some illumination.

Catherine had never before seen a bedchamber of such proportions. She could have fit the entire first floor of Colstin Hall into it and still had room to spare.

On the opposite wall was a massive bed with one post at each corner hung with burgundy draperies matching those on the windows and puddled on the dark, heavily waxed, floor.

A tapestry on the wall behind the bed was of Helen of Troy watching Paris's departure. Another was of Achilles encamped before the city. But the greatest feature of the room was the height of the walls, and the life-sized portraits mounted there.

Each one of them looked arrogant, and each bore Moncrief's coloring and distinctive blue eyes.

"Will you be able to sleep with so many of your ancestors looking down upon you?" she asked.

Moncrief glanced around him. He might have been a portrait, himself, someone who had stepped down from a frame. "I think we'll do fine."

She glanced at him, but he was walking to the side of the bed, where he drew back the curtains.

"It doesn't seem an entirely comfortable room."

"It isn't meant to be, I think," he said, looking about him. "Dukes are born here, and die here as well. Momentous deeds of state are performed here, not the least of which is bedding reluctant heiresses."

She looked at him, eyes widening and knees suddenly weak.

"You needn't look so frightened, Catherine, I was talking of the past."

But she was an heiress and reluctant.

"Is my chamber similarly adorned? Filled with portraits of duchesses?"

"I haven't seen the Duchess's Chamber for years. I don't know."

She'd been so fascinated by Balidonough that she'd forgotten the essence of their arrival. She was his wife. Unwilling, but nonetheless a legal spouse when all she wished to be was herself. Was she supposed to forget Harry simply because Moncrief had arrived at her home one night and deemed her to be worthy of rescuing? How foolish a thought.

A door was set alongside one of the tapestries. She walked to it and placed her hand on the handle.

"Catherine?"

Did he realize how badly she wanted to escape?

The door was ornate, filled with delicate carvings of

leaves and flowers. She wondered how long it had taken the craftsman to create this one door. She concentrated on a particularly blowsy rose all the while hearing him walk toward her.

Please, do not touch me.

If he did, she would shatter like a porcelain statuette.

"Catherine?"

He was not going away. She knew, even without turning, that his face would be set in stern lines once again, every inch the duke.

"I am not prepared to share your bed, Moncrief." The words sounded as if they came from far away.

"And I am not prepared to have my estate revert to a distant relative. I must have an heir, Catherine."

How unemotional he sounded, how distant.

"I did not bear Harry a child."

"You were not married that long."

She traced one enormous blossom—a primrose?— fighting back the urge to flee. Where would she go?

"It's too soon."

When he didn't speak, she mustered her remaining courage and turned to face him.

"We've known each other less than a week," she said, raising her gaze to encounter the glittering brightness of his intense blue eyes. "Can you not give me some time?"

"How long would you consider sufficient, madam?" His lips only hinted at a smile; his eyes held absolutely no humor.

She hadn't expected him to ask her that. She fumbled for an answer, but evidently was not quick enough for him.

"I do not intend for this marriage to be a celibate one, Catherine. And if you intend for our familiarity to be based on years and years of companionship, then I must disagree."

"A month."

"Very well, a month. But you will sleep in my bed until then."

"Is that necessary? Harry and I did not even share a chamber."

For a long moment he simply looked at her, then the corner of his lip turned up in a half smile. "That is hardly a recommendation, madam. You'll sleep here."

He turned and without another word left the room, leaving the door open behind him. She wanted to slam it, but at the last moment held on to it so it barely made a whisper when it closed.

She leaned her forehead against the ornate carving of one panel, and urged her heart to slow its frenetic beating. Until he returned, she would have some privacy, some peace. There, she would take her comfort in minutes and hours.

Memories of the night of their marriage came back to her in flashes, almost dreamlike pieces of thought and memory. She sincerely hoped that some of those recollections were only sketchy pieces of a nightmare. Otherwise, she never wanted to remember all of it.

She thought at one point that she'd stood before Moncrief entirely naked, warmed by the fire and the curious lassitude that the drug had caused within her. She'd felt as if her body were detached from her mind, and she was free of any pain or uncertainty. She had not felt anything at all but those physical sensations. Gone was the overwhelming sense of loss that had accompanied so much of her waking hours.

Perhaps Moncrief had been right after all, and she had found too much solace in opium. She hated to think she'd been so weak.

She needed courage now, more than ever before. One day at a time, and if that were too much to face, one hour at a time.

Chapter 7

Moncrief left the room and retraced his steps down the hall, then the grand staircase.

There were probably servants still at Balidonough who dated from his youth, but he found it difficult to accept that Barrows was gone. The old man had mussed his hair, inspected his nails, and when he needed it, scolded him and sent him on his way. The cook had given him an extra scone when no one was looking, and he'd sought refuge in Mrs. McElwee's room more times than he cared to remember. The housekeeper would slip him a horehound candy and talk to him of silly things, and pretend not to see that he could barely sit, so bad was his latest beating.

He had easily set aside the trappings of his rank and his occupation, as if he simply took off the uniform and reverted to the man he'd always been.

The boy was dying a harder death than the colonel.

At the bottom of the stone steps, he turned left, down the servants' stair and into the large kitchens that served

Balidonough. As he had suspected, the footmen and two of his acquaintances, both attired in uniforms that should have been replaced years ago, sat at a large wooden table, tankards in each of their hands.

Balidonough might be in shambles, but they evidently still made good whiskey.

He frowned at them and braced both hands against the doorframe.

"Wallace."

At the sound of his name, the young man sprang to attention, nearly knocking over the bench in his hurry to stand. The other two were slower, but they stood as well. "Yes, Your Grace?"

"You said there is no majordomo at Balidonough, no one to oversee the male employees, correct?"

"That's correct, Your Grace. The duchess hasn't hired one yet."

He would have to talk to Juliana to obtain an answer to that riddle. In the meantime, however, he would establish his own chain of command.

"From this moment on, you are our majordomo, Wallace."

"Me, sir?" The young man looked terrified and amazed. Moncrief gave him a moment to decline the position and when he didn't, asked another question.

"Are there any other members of the family living at Balidonough?"

Wallace looked confused.

"Any aunts, cousins, uncles in residence?"

His face cleared, and he shook his head. "No, Your Grace. Only the duchess and her sister."

"The dowager duchess. My wife is now duchess."

Wallace ducked his head in an embarrassed nod. "Yes, Your Grace."

"I want the maids sent with some cleaning supplies

throughout Balidonough beginning tomorrow. I want it cleaned as if the king himself was to visit here."

"Yes, Your Grace."

"Oh, and Wallace," he said, turning to leave the room.

"Yes, Your Grace?"

"Do something with your hair. Slick it down or have it cut."

The young man who'd just been promoted to a position of unparalleled responsibility, clamped one hand over the top of his head and nodded. "Yes, Your Grace."

"Every great majordomo has to begin somewhere, Wallace. Move your belongings into the butler's quarters as well."

As he left the room, Moncrief had the distinct notion that he'd made at least one person at Balidonough ecstatic. However, he doubted his chances of continuing with that trend. His sister-in-law had made an effort of concealing her irritation at his presence, but he doubted that it would last long. Juliana had a way of grating on him like metal against metal. And his wife . . . well, Catherine was another story entirely.

By nightfall, the servants' coach had arrived, along with the wagon containing their trunks. Moncrief stood at the front of Balidonough watching the vehicles pull into position. A few moments later, the servants, including Peter, descended from the coach. The young man looked distinctly irritated.

"An eventful journey, Peter?"

"A crowded coach, Your Grace. And a great many women." He sent a disgusted look toward two of the maids, who giggled in response. Moncrief noticed that Glynneth ignored him and her traveling companions with the insouciance of royalty.

"She wasn't annoying, sir," Peter said, as if answering a question Moncrief hadn't voiced. "At least she didn't spend half the time giggling. Kept to herself, she did."

Moncrief didn't care if Glynneth had hung out the window singing riotous drinking songs, but he kept that thought to himself.

He pointed to Catherine's trunk. "Put that in the duke's apartments, Peter." He glanced at Harry's trunk and wondered if the damnable thing would haunt him for the rest of his life. "You might as well take that one, also. One of the footmen can show you where."

"Yes, Your Grace." After a pause, he spoke again. "Balidonough's a lot bigger than I expected."

"It was built for a dynasty." Now, however, it seemed empty. Time had not magnified the size of the castle in his mind. A hundred people could have lived comfortably within its walls. Evidently, however, the twenty-some-odd bedrooms were uninhabited, the various state rooms no doubt rarely used.

Moncrief turned and looked up at Balidonough, shadowed and looming against the fast-moving clouds of night. He'd never expected to stand here, heir to it and all its attendant responsibilities. But he had expected to return home. To be welcomed, perhaps, by his father, by Colin. They were both gone, and he was angry at them for dying. They had suddenly disappeared from his world, and all those months when he'd not known of his father's death, and that moment he'd been informed of Colin's, came at him now like attackers from the darkness.

The river was a ribbon of black. The orange disk of the moon slid into a pocket of clouds. It was not a serene night; it heralded troubled dreams, a tinge of tears on the back of the throat, a disturbing dream waiting for him to sleep.

He'd always thought there would be time to know Colin better, to mend the rift time and distance had accentuated. He'd thought of coming home, of discussing the memories they'd evoke by sharing a meal, talking over a glass of Balidonough whiskey. They'd get to know each other, become the friends they'd never truly been.

At an early age Moncrief had been branded a wastrel, a disgrace, someone who did not deserve to truly be a member of such an auspicious family. His sins? The fact he dared to disagree with his autocratic father or that he was different from his brothers. He challenged every dictate, every command.

But being a recalcitrant son had proven to be a blessing in disguise. He recognized insubordination when it came and knew full well how to handle it. The seeds of his promotion to colonel had been sown by the intractable youth he'd been. By refusing to back down, by standing up to his father, he'd developed a singular type of courage, and a sense of identity that had served him well as a man of war.

"Your Grace?"

Peter bowed before him, effectively ending his reverie. "Is there anything else you need, Your Grace?"

He shook his head. "No, Peter, after you've delivered the trunks, find your own room and get a good night's sleep. Tomorrow is soon enough to reconnoiter Balidonough."

Peter bowed again and was gone, Harry's trunk easily braced on one shoulder.

Moncrief walked down the gravel drive to the fountain and stood there, his hand braced against the stone. Once again he turned back to look at Balidonough. The night was full upon them, the moon now obscured by the fast-moving clouds. The rain had left puddles on the ground and a freshness to the air. The lowlands of Scotland had a pastoral beauty that never failed to calm him. Until now. Now his mind was too immersed in chaotic thoughts to allow scenery, however bucolic, to affect his mood.

Catherine stood when Peter knocked, and smiled as he entered the room bringing her trunks. He and a footman made a parade of it, until they were neatly stacked in the corner of the room. Tomorrow, she'd unpack and place her things around her, pretending that this was home.

The last of the trunks was Harry's, and she directed Peter to place it at the end of the bed. During the past few days at Colstin Hall, Catherine found Peter eager to serve with a pleasant disposition, and a ready smile.

A strange companion for Moncrief.

The day after their marriage, Peter had come to her room with her dinner tray, bowed low, and introduced himself. After she'd recovered from the surprise of his impromptu gesture, he'd done something even more startling. He'd straightened and faced her, his expression solemn and sober.

"Congratulations on your marriage, Your Grace," he'd said. "I hope you'll be very happy."

She'd only nodded to him, bemused.

Now she addressed a question to him. "Did you know my husband, Peter?"

"The duke, your grace? Yes, ma'am, I've been with him since North America," he said proudly.

"Not Moncrief," she said shaking her head. "Harry Dunnan."

Peter was too young to school his face like Moncrief. He was not a master of concealing his expressions quite yet. Therefore, she saw when his eyes changed and his face tightened.

"Did you not like my husband, Peter?"

"I didn't know him well, Your Grace."

"But you didn't like him," she said, certain of it.

"No, Your Grace," he said straightening. To his credit, he didn't look away, but directly at her. That was one thing he still had not lost, an almost painful honesty of youth. "I knew plenty of men who did like him though."

"But you weren't one of them."

He shook his head, but didn't volunteer any further information. She tried once more to elicit an answer from him. "Why didn't you like him, Peter?"

Peter looked away and then back to the fire as if its flames were intensely important. "He gambled a lot, Your Grace, and he wasn't good with horses. We lost a lot of them."

He bowed then and picked up the sling he had used to carry the trunk into the room.

"If that will be everything, Your Grace," he said, backing out the door as if afraid she would ask another question.

Even though she was certain he wanted to say more, she let him go.

"Thank you, Peter."

She stared at the closing door. A gambler? Harry? He never mentioned such a thing in his letters, and the few times he had mentioned his horses he had done so with fondness.

Catherine walked to the trunk and selected one of Harry's letters. She read the first sentence, and that's all that she needed to take her back to the time when she'd first received the letter. It was one of the first ones she'd received from him in North America. There had been something different about it, something unique about the way he had spoken to her, a warmth that she'd come to expect as their correspondence lengthened.

My dearest Catherine,

Quebec is a cold city, not only in temperature but in its people. They look at us as if we are invaders and we are in truth. The battle to reach here has been long and well fought on both sides. My French is not as good as it should be, perhaps, but is enough for me to understand the insults and invectives they hurl our way. But for all of the people who are unfriendly and ungovernable, there are those who are generally hospitable. Every week a few ladies stop by the garrison, bringing pies and tarts as a way of welcome. I think that women are the true peacekeepers.

You seem to have done yeoman's work on Colstin Hall. I enjoy listening to your comments about the builders, and your daily exploits bring me closer to home.

You have asked me about the other men in our regiment. On the whole we are simply military men, all given to dreams of glory from time to time. Most of us come from the south of Scotland, some near Glasgow. There are few of us Highland-born, but their speech is such that we often find it difficult to understand them. The colonel of our regiment is given to secluding himself from others. I think he is the loneliest of us all. But no more about him.

Tell me, what do you have planned for spring?

I wish I was there to help you, to take the burden off your shoulders. But I think there have always been separations of this sort. Men go to war and women remain behind. I cannot help but think that women have gotten the brunt of the burden. But if they had been like you, Catherine, those women would have survived and prospered, I am certain of it.

What would he think to see her now, so tired and frightened?

A month. Only a month. Simply a month. Thirty days. How was she to become acquainted with Moncrief in only a month? He looked at her oddly from time to time, and he was occasionally impatient and visibly irritated, but she didn't think he was unkind. Sending her Harry's trunk, for example, had been a gesture she hadn't expected of him.

She set aside Harry's letter and stared at the newly built fire. Moncrief wouldn't be an easy man to get to know. And to think, she had to share a bed with him. Tonight.

He gave the impression of needing no one, of requiring nothing, no praise, no recognition, no friendship. But she knew how foolish that was. Everyone needed someone, even a man as arrogant and aloof as the twelfth Duke of Lymond.

She walked to the window and stared outside, wishing that she could see where he'd gone. Perhaps if she studied him in silence, without him watching or knowing it, she would be closer to understanding the enigma that was Moncrief. Instead, this room faced a dormant garden, mulched for the winter.

This was to be her home. Perhaps she might be able to go back to Colstin Hall from time to time. But for the rest of her life she was to live here.

What did Moncrief think upon coming home?

She returned to Harry's trunk and selected another of the letters at random, returning to the bed. By the light of the lone candle she began to read. The letter was one she knew well, coming only weeks before word of Harry's death.

My dearest Catherine,

The days are long here, as if the sun is reluctant to say farewell. I am grateful to say that war seems behind us for a little while, and we have only the peace to administer. It is difficult for men who have been trained in combat to relish the absence of it, however, and even the most peace-loving man among us is occasionally restless.

I thank God for the respite in writing you. You are my release, dearest, and I am grateful for it. The other day I saw a lovely bonnet being worn by a lady on the street and my first thought was to find its replica and send it to you. But such things as bonnets do not travel in official dispatches, so let me satisfy myself with only thoughts of generosity.

Your ideas about the new crops seem well reasoned. I look forward to hearing tales of your harvest.

Thank you for the constancy of your letters. Thank you for the anticipation of them. Thank you for your words that buoy my own spirits.

I wish I could find a way to do so in kind, but even though the war seems to be winding down, our stay here does not. However, I cannot help but dream that I am at Colstin Hall, hand in hand with you, my dearest.

Catherine held the letter to her chest for several long moments, wondering how she could ever forget Harry. Slipping the letter below her pillow, she vowed that she would never do so.

Moncrief returned to the ducal chamber expecting the worst: a torrent of tears, perhaps, at the delivery of the sainted Harry's trunk or a wifely rebellion, with Catherine standing against the wall in fear and fright.

Thank God he was prepared.

Catherine was pulling down the covers of the bed when he entered the room. She was clad in a black nightgown, her breasts pressing against the material, the drape of the garment not quite hiding her curves.

"Is everything in your wardrobe black?"

"Of course, I'm a widow."

"Even your stays?"

She drew herself up, as if offended by the question. He wanted to tell her that the pillow she pulled off the bed and placed in front of her was no protection. He remembered only too well what she looked like naked.

Never before had he witnessed a body as beautiful as hers. The firelight had limned her figure with flashes of orange and red, making her skin look as if it were dusted by gold.

She had a long waist that flared to a slight curve of hips and long graceful legs. Her breasts were upturned and impudent, full and so perfectly round they looked crafted not by Nature but by a man's dreams. Her stomach was flat, the triangle of hair so perfect that it looked like an arrowhead.

Such beauty was so adequately covered by the ugly black mourning dress that he might have forgotten it had he not been celibate for so long. Or he might never be able to forget it, necessitating that he place that thought and memory in a closely guarded compartment labeled: Forbidden Thoughts.

She walked with grace, her body limber and lithe, but her head was always bent, her gaze on the ground. As if she possessed a dual nature, one sensuous, the other restrained.

"That is hardly a question you should be asking, Moncrief."

He was struck by the most unholy amusement at the moment. Here he was, the new Duke of Lymond, a black sheep turned gray by circumstance. In defiance of his father's dire predictions, he'd outlived battles, disease, and injury to find himself back at Balidonough.

If that were not enough of an irony, he'd returned with a woman who thought that it was more important to honor her widowhood than be a wife.

He had never been indiscriminate in matters of the flesh, but Moncrief couldn't help but wish, right at this moment, that he'd been more like Harry. If so, he wouldn't be feeling this surge of hunger for a woman who didn't even see him as a man. An obstruction to her grief, yes. An irritant, most certainly. A rescuer, grudgingly perhaps. But it was evident she didn't see him as a husband.

No doubt a lady's book existed somewhere that dictated the most proper and formal conversations for events such as these. An unwanted marriage? An inconvenient husband? Address the weather, ladies. Or perhaps remark upon the day, how lengthy it seems or conversely how short. Or to confound the issue completely, perhaps one might discuss with the new husband the assets of the old. Catherine had evidently read that chapter.

He much preferred that she talk about hats and gloves and intimate attire.

This was a night of celebration, a time to be thankful, an occasion to commemorate. Instead, his welcome tasted like ashes. His family was gone, as were the servants who had acted the part of parents for him. His wife was in love with another man.

"Take it off."

"I beg your pardon?"

"Take the blasted thing off, Catherine. This is a bed, not a bier."

She placed a palm against the base of her throat, a place he wanted to kiss. "I can't do that, Moncrief. I would be naked."

"You have my word, madam, that you will awaken as chaste as when you retire."

"I would prefer to keep my nightgown."

"And I would prefer that you rid yourself of it."

They stood staring at each other, and he had the feeling

that she might well be as stubborn as he, although more subtle in her obstinacy.

"If I find you a nightshirt, will you sleep in that?" he finally asked.

"Is it the garment you object to, Moncrief, or its color?"

"The color, madam."

"Then I will wear what you wish, but remember this: In my heart I mourn my husband."

"I am your husband."

He walked to where she stood, still clutching her pillow. He pulled it from her and threw it on the bed.

"Perhaps you're right, Catherine. Perhaps I've not acted in accordance with my role. If I were truly your husband," he said, tracing a delicate path under her chin with his forefinger, "I would touch you here." His finger stopped at the base of her neck. "Several times, I've seen you pull your cloak close to your throat as if it's a place of special sensitivity. If I were your husband, Catherine, I would kiss you right here, and feel you shiver."

He said nothing for a minute, and her eyes widened.

"Lovemaking is an art, some men say."

She closed her eyes.

"Perhaps it isn't as important to consummate this marriage as it is to bring you joy."

He brushed his finger against her bottom lip, and she jerked at the touch. "Do you feel pleasure making love, Catherine? A foolish question to ask one's wife, is it not? I should know by now, should have memorized the feel of your kiss, the soft touch of your hands on my body.

"Even in loneliness, one can find some comfort. Even as strangers, perhaps. But does your heart have to be occupied, or only your senses?"

"Moncrief."

"I like it when you call my name in such a tone. How

proper of you, Catherine. It makes me want to do something utterly wicked to shock you further."

She opened her eyes wider.

"I have to admit that I haven't forgotten what you looked like standing naked in front of me. You appear even in my dreams. Damn fevered things of late. Your skin is the color of cream, and your body is made for loving. Mourning should be a sin."

She shook her head. He bent forward and kissed her cheek, a soft and lingering—almost tender—kiss.

"Are you waiting for me, Catherine? Or will you remain, for all time, a vestal virgin for the late, eternally lamented Harry?"

He wondered if she willed herself not to move. He was not a wild animal waiting to pounce.

"What a waste," he said, turning away from her. "Keep your nightgown, Catherine, and your letters. I find I don't like being second best."

Chapter 8

Balidonough, evidently, came alive with the first traces of the sun. Moncrief awoke at dawn to the sounds of life beyond the velvet draperies of the bed: the splash of water from the stable trough, a few of the stableboys laughing with each other, a rooster's crow, and the sound of a heavily laden wagon, the wheels turning slowly on the graveled road.

He stretched slowly, feeling the empty spot beside him instantly.

Where was Catherine?

Moncrief sat up and pushed the bed hangings aside to find an empty room. Had she fled back to Colstin Hall? He'd been true to his word and had left her alone last night. She'd entered the bed like a martyr and lain there with her arms at her sides, her black nightgown more protection than any suit of armor.

He stood and walked across the room to a door that hid the water closet. Once his morning ablutions were complete, he dressed in a simple white shirt and black trousers, the better to oversee Balidonough. He pushed open the double doors to the balcony and stood surveying what was now his to command.

A kingdom, a castle easily the size of a small village.

Today he would be about the business of acquainting himself with Balidonough. He would meet with the steward, and a few of the tenant farmers. There would need to be some type of celebration to honor his wedding and ascension. *The duke is dead; long live the duke.* Transitions, however painful, needed to be marked and celebrated.

Moncrief left the duke's apartments, wondering where Catherine had gone. If he were an ardent bridegroom, he would know. If he were truly an ardent bridegroom, they'd still be abed. He'd have awakened her with a kiss, inquired about her well-being. Did you sleep well? Was the mattress to your liking? What can I bring to please you?

Anything but memories of Harry.

It felt wrong allowing her to mourn for a man who did not deserve her constancy and devotion. For a moment he allowed himself the mental image of retrieving Harry's trunk and placing it in the circular drive in front of Balidonough before setting it afire.

That first day at Colstin Hall he'd been shocked by Catherine's appearance and demeanor. She'd been a pitiful creature, one who had elicited his compassion. Despite her protests, Moncrief didn't believe that Catherine had been accidentally drugged. If she'd tried to end her life because of loneliness and grief, what would she do after learning the truth?

All he could do was be patient, not a character trait that came naturally to him.

The second floor was devoid of maids, but not so the first. A battalion of industrious young women all attired in the same light blue dress with blue aprons were scrubbing and polishing and dusting every conceivable piece of furniture, every ornament, panel and carving. Wallace had evidently taken his instructions to heart, because the footman-made-majordomo stood at the doorway alternately frowning and pointing, then looking earnestly up the stairs. When he spied Moncrief, his face altered, and in that instant, Moncrief could see what the young man would look like with a few years on him.

"Good morning, Wallace," he said. "I approve of your industriousness."

"Her Grace said that supervising the maids was usually a job for the housekeeper, but since she's new to the job, that I should handle the chores for today."

"The housekeeper? I thought we didn't have one."

"I believe Her Grace has already appointed someone for the post."

The sense of relief he felt was entirely unwarranted. Of course Catherine hadn't left him. "Where would my wife be now, Wallace?"

"She's in the kitchen, Your Grace, with Cook and the housekeeper."

Moncrief headed for the rear of the castle. A few of the large corridors that linked the various rooms were adorned with shields that men of the family had taken into battle. Once he'd been impressed by such a display; now it didn't interest him. Was it because he was tired of war itself? What was that biblical expression? Beating his sword into a plowshare? While he doubted that his regimental dress sword would be an adequate farming implement, he might well bury it somewhere on the estate, along with the memories of the battles he'd fought and the men he had killed.

Balidonough had been built in a time when protection was necessary. Three wells inside what was once the outer perimeter walls provided fresh drinking water.

Farm animals could be herded to a small enclosed corral, and a small garden to the rear of the main structure provided vegetables. Balidonough could withstand a siege of weeks, and had, more than once.

He passed the servant staircase and dipped below a low-hanging lintel. Last night he'd not noticed the disrepair in this, the oldest part of the castle. A few of the walls looked to need shoring up, and there were a few high windows that were cracked. But the air of disuse was everywhere at Balidonough, as if the castle had been neglected all these years.

The walls here were three feet thick and had been repaired at various times throughout the centuries. Sound did not carry well except where it echoed in isolated places such as the bottom of the staircase or the entrance to the pit dungeon.

He could shout at the top of his voice in this one location and no one would ever hear him, as if the stone itself absorbed noise. He rounded one wall and entered the kitchen, only to be immediately summoned by Catherine.

"Moncrief!" She motioned him closer with a wooden spoon. "Did you know, Moncrief? I have never heard of anything more ghastly in my life. Did you know?"

He kept himself from rearing back physically beneath the onslaught of her words. Planting his feet apart, he folded his arms and studied her. His wife was frowning at him, her face flushed. Catherine looked irritated and ready for battle.

Today, as usual, she was dressed in unrelieved black from head to toe, except for her blue apron.

"Could you not find a black apron to wear?"

She blinked at him, evidently startled by his remark.

"It's been long enough, Catherine, surely you can see yourself graduating to lavender. Or will you wear black for the remainder of your life?"

She folded her arms in a mirror image of his stance and glared at him. "Perhaps some other time we can discuss my wardrobe, Moncrief. At the moment, we have another, greater problem."

"And what would that be?"

"Do you know what Juliana is doing with the scraps from dinner?"

"Giving them to the poor? Feeding them to the pigs?"

"Either of which would be acceptable," Catherine said. "No, she is having Cook make them into another dish."

Cook curtsied. Not a good sign that the cook was tall and skinny. Did she not eat her own cooking?

"It's true, Your Grace. Her Grace does not like food left over. She thinks it's wasteful. So she has me scrape all the plates into a large pot, and I serve it the next day to the servants."

"I trust that wasn't what she's planned for tonight," Moncrief said, his stomach rolling.

"It is not, sir. But I have all the leftovers from dinner to feed staff this morning."

"That will not happen, Cook," Catherine said, turning to her. "I have never heard of such thriftiness in my life. Even at Colstin Hall, Moncrief, we never treated the servants like they were rutting pigs."

"Nor will we here," Moncrief said. "How many servants do we employ?"

Glynneth appeared, and he realized she'd been standing behind the curved wall. In her hand was a large book, and she glanced down at it before answering him. "One hundred seventeen, Your Grace, all in various functions. Fifty-seven house staff. The remaining servants either work in the fields or in the stables or outbuildings."

"Send the scraps to the farm, Cook," he said, before turning and leaving the room.

Catherine followed as he hoped she would.

He turned at the end of the corridor and faced her. "I take it you have appointed Glynneth as our new housekeeper?"

She frowned at him again. "I have. She had experience at Colstin Hall, and with a prior employer. Do you have any objections?"

He studied her for a moment. "I am willing to agree to your choice, if you are willing to concede one minor point to me."

She folded her arms again. "What would that be?"

"I am tired of your eternal black. Although the color suits you, I would much rather see you in some other shade."

She opened her mouth as if she started to say something, then thought better of it. He wanted to congratulate her on her restraint. The last thing he wanted to hear at this moment was Harry Dunnan's name.

"Do we have an agreement?"

"Yes, Moncrief, we have an agreement. But you are not to badger Glynneth. Allow her to do her job."

He smiled, and she no doubt took it as assent. In actuality, he was amused and pleased. Up until this moment, her speech had been carefully reserved. Today he'd heard a vestige of the woman he'd known from her letters.

He turned and walked away, only to stop when she called out his name. He glanced over his shoulder at her.

"Thank you," she said. The stones seem to absorb the sound, but he heard it nonetheless. He sent a smile in her direction and left her before he was tempted to do more.

His first meeting was with the farm manager, Munson. The man looked happy to see him, his face crinkling into a sunburst of wrinkles as he smiled. Munson was one of the few people he remembered from his youth. His clothing was worn but clean, his tall leather boots were scuffed but brushed. He looked exactly the same as he had fourteen years ago.

"Lot of changes here lately," Munson said around the stem of his pipe. "Don't think your father would've been happy with most of them. He was a man who understood that the land owns you more than you owning the land."

Moncrief had grown up with Munson's pronouncements, always dour and always profound.

They inspected the stables that housed thirty-six stalls for horses. Only three of them were occupied. The outbuildings were in need of repair. Doors were falling off their hinges, and roofs needed to be patched. At the end of the survey of the castle and its close environs, he turned to Munson.

"Why has everything gone to hell, Munson?"

The old man clamped his teeth around the pipe and stared at the ground. He created an arc with the toe of his boot and shoved his hands deep in his pockets.

Finally, he looked up again, took the pipe out of his mouth, and spat. "It wasn't me, Your Grace. It was her."

He jerked his chin toward Balidonough. "I thought your father was thrifty with a coin, but I've never yet seen a skinflint to beat her in the last six months. She begrudges the chickens their feed. She's fired half the farm workers, saying that we should keep most of the fields fallow. Where does she think she's going to get all the money to hoard? Balidonough isn't just a pretty place," he added in disgust. "The land needs to be farmed."

"The damage I've seen took longer than six months, Munson."

"Aye, that it did. Your brother had other things on his mind. Well, truth to tell, they both did, enough to beggar Balidonough."

Moncrief raised one eyebrow. "Jacobites?"

Munson nodded.

One thing from Moncrief's past hadn't changed. He'd always found it odd that as close in temperament as his brother and his father were, they'd disagreed on one fundamental point. His father had no love for those who'd instigated the rebellion while Colin had evidently drained Balidonough to support the Jacobite cause.

That would change today.

"I'm surprised the castle hasn't fallen down around our ears. The east wall needs shoring up and the chapel roof's sprung a leak. I've been trying to make do as I could, but I've been losing against the duchess. When I heard you were coming home, Your Grace, these old legs almost danced a jig." He puffed on his pipe some more, then smiled again. "You'll begging my pardon, Your Grace, but I've never been so glad to see anyone in my entire life."

What would his father think to know that Moncrief had returned after all these years, that the third son, wastrel and ruin, was now the twelfth Duke of Lymond? He could almost hear his father's voice echoing through time. *You will not fail, Moncrief. You will do your duty.*

What other choice had he? Balidonough was his birthright, the castle more than brick and mortar and stone. Instead it was a heritage, a past, and a future that he somehow needed to protect.

In the last fourteen years, he'd been faced with challenges, some of them meaning the difference between a man living or dying. At this moment, however, not only did he have the problem of Balidonough to solve, but he had a suspicion that Catherine would prove even more daunting a trial.

Why had he married her? A tiny voice, no doubt the voice of his conscience, knew full well why he had taken advantage of the situation. He had wanted with Catherine what they'd had during their correspondence, a melding of the minds, a union of thoughts and feelings that hinted at, then promised, more. But he was as far from that goal as he was of turning her thoughts from the damnable Harry Dunnan.

Perhaps he should write her again.

Dearest Catherine,

I am home again, in a place I dreamed of for so many years. And I've brought you here, a woman who confuses, irritates, and charms me.

You love with such fervor that I wonder if you will ever surrender Harry. Life is for the living, Catherine, and I wonder if time will teach you that essential lesson.

How do I battle a ghost, especially when that ghost is me?

Chapter 9

"**W**hy do I have to be introduced to a group of strangers?"

Catherine stared at herself in the mirror. Tonight they were hosting a dinner for Juliana's friends. A command performance, she had been told.

"They'll leave soon enough," Moncrief said, when he'd told her about the dinner plans. "They simply want to get a look at you and me."

"Is it absolutely necessary?"

He'd only smiled at her, in the same way the young maid who'd been assigned to her since Glynneth's promotion to housekeeper was now smiling: a patient, kindly smile one would give to the village idiot.

The young maid continued to arrange her hair in a style much more formal than anything she'd worn before. Her hair had been swept back, artfully arranged curls cascading down to rest at the back of her neck. Through it all, Mary had wound a lavender ribbon, which had been further adorned with small pearls.

Mary, who had been assigned to her in a promotion of sorts, had been with the staff for three years. She was a sweet thing with a milkmaid's spotted complexion and a regrettable shyness. Catherine wished she was more talkative, but she'd said hardly a word since being assigned to her. With Glynneth's elevation to housekeeper, the only person Catherine had to speak with was Moncrief.

Sometimes silence was wiser.

Tonight she was wearing lavender, a gown Balidonough's seamstress had constructed for her in the last week. It was a lovely creation, simple in design, with trailing sleeves and an underskirt of cream linen. She'd gone from black to lavender in deference to her arrangement with Moncrief.

"I feel woefully unprepared for tonight," she confessed to Mary.

"You look beautiful, however, Your Grace."

"You are very kind."

"It is not kindness, truly . . ." Mary's words trailed away.

Catherine looked up to find Moncrief standing in the doorway. She nodded to Mary, who put down the comb she was using, curtsied, and left the room, closing the door behind her.

Moncrief still didn't speak, and after a moment Catherine fumbled with the bows adorning the front of the gown.

"I've never seen you dressed in anything but black before," he said finally. "I thought the color suited you, but I was wrong."

She glanced up to meet his eyes in the mirror and looked away, uncomfortable with his steady gaze.

"Then I take it you don't disapprove?"

"On the contrary. You look lovely, but then, you always do."

Why did being around Moncrief always make her uncomfortable? Especially now? The décolletage of the dress had not been too low earlier, but now it felt as if the whole of her chest was exposed for his gaze. She glanced toward the door to the hall, wishing she could escape as quickly as Mary.

"Have the guests begun to arrive?" she asked, desperate to have him leave. Moncrief could simply enter a room and dominate it by his presence. No wonder the staff were spending most of their time bowing or curtsying around him.

"Not yet. Are you anticipating their arrival?"

"Dreading it, actually."

"You have no reason to do so. They've come to meet you."

"To gawk, you mean."

"Let them gawk. You're the Duchess of Lymond."

"Did your men always obey you?" she asked, wishing the question back the minute the words were out of her mouth.

"Why would you ask that?"

"I was thinking that most people at Balidonough seem to fear you."

He didn't say anything, and when she glanced he was smiling at her. The expression so startled her that she stared at him for a moment before looking away again.

"I think what you see is uncertainty, because people do not know if I'm more like my brothers or my father. My father ruled with a tyrannical hand while I suspect my brother didn't rule at all."

"Which are you?"

"Neither," he said shortly. "I am Moncrief."

He'd said that before, in just that tone of supreme confidence. She envied him that, and his fearlessness.

"Do you not care what other people think of you?"

"I have never found that it was an exercise much to my liking," he said. "Especially not since I am paying their wages."

"Do you not care what *I* think of you?"

"I am torn, Catherine, between giving you the truth and sweetening it for your benefit."

"By all means, Moncrief, give me the truth," she said when she found her voice.

"Very well. You will form your own opinion over my actions and my words. It would be best, therefore, if I simply act as myself."

Once again, he had the effect of transporting her from one emotion to the next, as if she were a runaway coach on a crooked road. She careened from confusion to irritation and back to confusion again.

"The people who are attending this dinner tonight are important in the neighborhood," he said.

She nodded, having been given the guest list by Juliana. Minor nobility, the religious leader of the community, a few widows, and three prosperous landowners and their families. More people then Catherine had entertained in all her years at Colstin Hall.

"I would appreciate it if they were left in ignorance of the nature of our marriage."

She turned on the bench and regarded him. Sitting with hands clasped and knees together, she hoped she looked the very picture of propriety. Her father had been a wealthy man and had sent her to a dame school, providing for her education as well as any parent, duke or farmer.

"Is their opinion important to you?"

"Not at all," he said. "However, I'm a private man and would prefer that the exact nature of my personal dealings be left that way."

She rearranged the comb on the top of the vanity with one finger, carefully not looking at him.

"Are you afraid of me, Catherine?"

"You've never before given me a reason to feel afraid, Moncrief."

"That's reassuring."

"You've allowed some of my staff to come with me from Colstin Hall, a concession that most men might not have made. You've allowed me Harry's trunk. The fact that you do not smile often does not take away from your cordiality. Instead, it's a personal characteristic, like your height. Your . . . largeness."

"I'm large?"

"Do you not think so? You tower over the footmen. Even Wallace has to look up at you."

"I sound like an amiable giant."

"I didn't mean it as an insult."

"Perhaps I should be grateful that your compliments are flavored with vinegar. I will forever be humbled by them."

Had she offended him?

Blessedly, he turned and left the room.

Then, just before he closed the door between their rooms, he hesitated, then strode across to room to stand directly in front of her. He stood so close that the skirts of her dress covered his boots.

She looked up at him, at the impossible height of him, irritated that he would stand so close that she would have to tilt her head backwards so far to see him.

"I neglected to give you this," he said, and held out his hand.

He was not yet done with surprises. Sitting on his palm with the arrogance of Moncrief himself, was an enormous ring. A brilliant cut sapphire, surrounded by rubies and emeralds, sat sparkling in a gold setting.

"What is it?" she asked, reaching out her fingers to touch it. But she didn't take it from him.

"An ancestral ring, given to the Duchess of Lymond at the occasion of her wedding." She still had not taken it from him, so he hooked one finger around it and held it out to her.

"Juliana could not have surrendered it without a struggle," she said.

His laughter startled her.

She looked up at him, thinking that she'd never heard Moncrief truly laugh before. The sound bemused her so much that she actually reached out and took the ring.

"It is a very gaudy piece, isn't it?" she asked, fixing her attention on the setting rather than Moncrief. All in all, the jewels were a less disturbing sight than Moncrief, amused.

"It has been in the family for generations, so I cannot claim any responsibility for the setting."

"Must I wear it?"

"Do possessions of any sort not impress you, Catherine?"

She thought about the question for a moment. "I don't think I've ever liked or disliked a person because of what they owned, Moncrief."

"But you aren't singularly impressed about Balidonough?"

"Balidonough? It's your home."

"And if I had brought you to a cottage, what would you have thought of me, then?"

"Nothing more or less than I do now. Are you Balidonough, Moncrief? Or are you yourself? You can say that you are duke, but who is the man?"

He studied her for a long moment, not the first time he had done so. She was uncomfortable, however, with this perusal, sensing that it went deeper than his normal examination. She wanted to ask him what he was thinking, but that was an intrusive and almost intimate question. Nor was she entirely certain she wanted to know. She had the impression that she had disappointed him in some way.

"It's a pity then, that I am not simply the colonel of the regiment since none of my possessions impress you."

"I didn't say they failed to impress me. Balidonough is a magnificent place. But should I judge you by a structure?"

"It might be easier," he said. "What other criteria would you judge me on?"

She sought kinder words this time. "Your honor. Your decency as a human being. Your generosity." She realized as she enumerated all the qualities upon which she might judge him, that he had been exemplary in all of them. Scooting to the end of the bench, she stood. At least this way he did not tower over her so much.

Catherine stretched out her hand to show that she slipped on the ring. Before she could withdraw it, he had captured her wrist. Gently he slipped the ring off her right hand. Giving her no chance to escape, he slid the gold band from her left hand and replaced it with the Lymond ring.

Then, before she could protest or even feel a surge of resentment, he turned her hand and bent his head and very gently kissed the center of her palm.

"There," he said. "Now you are my bride."

Not until he left the room did she realize that he'd not returned Harry's ring to her.

The rain had delayed the coach, which meant that Glynneth would have to explain away her tardy return to Balidonough. Even though Catherine was generous, almost foolishly so, she deserved an explanation.

My son was ill. What would Catherine say to that?

If they had still been at Colstin Hall, Glynneth might

have told her the truth. All Catherine would have probably done was turn over and go back to sleep, retreating to a drug-induced haze. Now? Glynneth didn't know what Catherine would say to learn that she had a child.

Moving to Balidonough had been a shock, but a good thing as it turned out. Not only was she closer to Robbie, but she had been promoted to housekeeper. A few years of stringent savings, and Glynneth might have enough money for a house for the two of them, someplace where she could actually live with her son instead of only paying a visit on every day off.

She had truly loved only two people in the world, and one of them was gone. A ghost companion, he felt even more real every time she took this journey, as if he sat beside her and watched their son. She could almost envision his proud glance, the words he'd never spoken. *Aren't we to be congratulated? Aren't we special and talented people?*

Only on the way back did the truth sink in again, and she realized the depth of her loneliness. The wheels of the coach seemed to repeat the same refrain. *He'll never come again, he'll never come again.*

Robbie was the other person who mattered to her, and she would do whatever was necessary to ensure his well-being. He was her child, her son, her bright and shining wonder that she had somehow brought into the world. Her pregnancy had been a disaster at the time, but now Robbie's presence was a deep and wondrous blessing.

As she did each time she came away from him, Glynneth vowed that her son would never suffer for the mistakes of his parents.

She'd been unable to avoid falling in love with a man with gleaming brown eyes and an easy smile. Her parents hadn't approved. Her father had considered her love a wastrel, a cad, someone he didn't want to marry his daughter. By the time she'd discovered she was with child, it was too late. Her sweetest, her dearest, her truest love had gone away.

Glynneth's mother had died not long after that, and everything about her life changed again. Her father, no doubt maddened with grief, had set her out, and she'd been forced to make her own way in the world. She had done so first as a scullery maid, working impossibly long hours in hideous conditions until she'd given birth. She had taken her mother's name, Rowan, in order not to further shame her father. Then, with her figure back, she moved on to being an upstairs maid, and from there she learned of a position at Colstin Hall.

Catherine had everything she hadn't, and at times it was hard to hide what she truly felt. The other woman would have them be friends, as if Glynneth could ever forget her place in life. Yet because of Catherine's generosity, she was now more than a simple servant, she was a housekeeper, an important and prestigious position.

She peeled back the leather shade and looked out. Nothing but rain.

The coach was always crowded, and this time was no exception. Her companions were an agreeable group. She recognized one woman from a previous trip, and they nodded to each other in perfect accord before Glynneth closed her eyes and leaned her head against the corner. The carriage was too uncomfortable for anyone ever to truly fall asleep, but by her pretense she walled herself off from her companions. They didn't talk to her, and she had more time to think of the visit just made.

Her son was growing, looking so much like his father that she wanted to hold him tight and never release him. When she did, he always wiggled away laughing, and she always chased him, his smile banishing her tears.

The McClarens had looked after him since Robbie was

a baby, their job as foster parents changing over the last two years to become something warmer. She still paid them for their care, but now they treated Robbie as if he were their own grandchild.

She opened her eyes as the coach slowed at the crossroads. In the distance she could see Balidonough. She straightened her shoulders and tidied her coat, thinking as she did that Fate had put her in the employ of a woman who genuinely cared about her, the one woman in the world she could easily hate.

How strange that Catherine should be wed, and to a duke. Glynneth disliked Moncrief and distrusted him, knowing that he felt the same about her. If anyone could discover her secrets, it would be Moncrief, and for that reason she was determined to avoid the man.

Chapter 10

The Great Hall still possessed its original dimensions, barrel-vaulted ceiling, and recessed panels. The ceiling was frescoed with dancing nymphlike cupids painted in the Raphael style. Thick blue draperies hung in swags from gold cornice boards mounted over the windows. A mirror twenty feet high and fifteen feet wide, topped with an enormous crest, stood at the end of the room. Along either side of the Hall sat a sideboard of marble and gold, topped with rare blue frosted glass from Persia. The wooden boards of the floor were polished to a high sheen, half-covered with a magnificent oriental rug in shades of blue and green. The receiving chairs were upholstered in dark blue silk, the mahogany wood of the arms and backs burnished with gold.

Two fireplaces with wide and deep marble mantels might have warmed the room had more than a puny fire been laid in one of them.

Only Juliana and her sister were in the Great Hall.

Catherine hesitated at the threshold, wishing she could be anywhere but here. But the last week had proven that this was no nightmare. She was at Balidonough, and it was to be her home, like it or not, for the remainder of her life.

With a great deal of reluctance, she entered the room.

"Good evening," Catherine said, nodding to both of them.

Hortensia managed a feeble smile while Juliana pointedly ignored her.

Rarely did the two women meet, but whenever their paths did accidentally cross, Juliana left no doubt of her impression of Catherine. Her aquiline nose would point into the air, and she would sniff as if she smelled something unpleasant.

However, in Catherine's experience, people were never completely bad or even completely annoying, even someone like Juliana. She no doubt had a great many virtues, one of which was the fact that she was unfailingly kind to her sister. The two of them were often seen together walking arm in arm in the dormant gardens.

Hortensia was less distant of the two. However, Hortensia had a great many maladies, none of which she was shy about sharing. This past week, she'd been in bed with an inflammation in the sinuses, made worse, she said, by the eternal dampness and dust that the maids, at Moncrief's and Wallace's behest, were stirring up. She also got hives from all manner of food, and was certain that her lungs were weak from a childhood illness.

All these complaints were transmitted to Catherine on the one occasion when she'd visited Hortensia in her chamber.

Catherine walked to the fireplace and stretched her hands out before the meager fire. Juliana might have been accustomed to the cold, but Catherine was not. At Colstin Hall, all the fireplaces had been used, and the atmosphere in the manor house was one of warmth and comfort. In this sprawling castle, few things were designed for its inhabitants' convenience, from the distance one had to travel from the ducal chambers to any of the public rooms, to the sheer number of people it took to keep the castle orderly.

Nor was there any privacy at Balidonough. Someone was always watching her, anticipating her wants or needs. Servants were as thick as flies, each of them wanting to assist her in some way. She was, like it or not, no longer the mistress of a small manor house. By her marriage, she'd become a much more rarefied creature, a duchess, a member of the nobility. Yet she'd never been trained for such a role and wasn't comfortable with it.

When she walked into the kitchen area of Balidonough, Cook and her helpers immediately stopped talking. Cook would sketch a curtsy, as would the scullery maids. None of the parlor maids would look directly at her when she addressed them. True, she managed to accomplish some tasks, but not as quickly as she would have liked, what with all that bowing and curtsying. Nor was there a spirit of camaraderie, since most of the people employed at Balidonough treated her as if she were queen.

The only people with whom she could communicate were Glynneth and Wallace. In the end, it was better to assign tasks and simply leave them to be done. The moment she left a room Catherine could almost hear an audible sigh of relief, the result being that she was left with too much time on her hands and entirely too much time to think.

The last few days had been illuminating to another degree. She had found that as time passed, her thought processes grew easier. She didn't have to struggle to concentrate, or even to remember things, a fact that made her wonder if Moncrief had been right after all. Had she become addicted to laudanum?

Moncrief was the one person who treated her as if she was simply Catherine. Each night they returned to their chamber, Moncrief leaving no doubt of his opinion of her nightgowns. But he left her alone, never touching her, except for those rare mornings when she awoke and they were nose to nose, both their heads resting on one pillow.

He slept in the nude. At night she accidentally occasionally moved closer to him in her sleep. When she awoke, she would move away slowly, withdrawing her knee from alongside his thigh, moving her hand from his chest or arm. He would always awaken, and simply smile at her, as if he felt her sudden fear and wanted to reassure her in some way.

Consequently, she'd taken to awakening much earlier than ever before and busying herself with exploring the great castle.

"You will not know any of the people here tonight," Juliana said abruptly.

Catherine turned her attention to her sister-in-law.

"There will be some dignitaries, some minor nobility. Most of them will be above you in birth, despite the fact that you wear the title of duchess. Breeding must be inherited and not simply conveyed by marriage."

She looked at Catherine's new dress as if she found the garment loathsome. She, herself, was dressed in a deep blue gown with an overskirt of silver gauze. Evidently, Juliana's thrift did not extend to her own wardrobe. Hortensia was as richly attired in a pale green, heavily embroidered dress that looked to be new.

"What Moncrief was thinking of when he married you, I have no idea. I would not have approved."

"Is it important that you do so?" Catherine asked, annoyed enough to speak up. "It is my impression that you had nothing to do with Moncrief for over fourteen years.

Why would you express an interest in his life now except for the fact that he is the new duke?"

Juliana looked incensed, twin spots of color appearing on her otherwise chalky face.

Catherine was saved from Juliana's rejoinder by Moncrief's appearance.

He raised one eyebrow questioningly at her, but she only shook her head.

"Are you well?" he asked, after he'd greeted the other women.

"Of course. We only left each other thirty minutes ago."

"A great deal can happen in that amount of time. Whole battles can be won or lost."

She smiled. "I am not at war with anyone."

"Are you certain of that?" He glanced at his sister-in-law, who had gone to stand by the window. "Juliana does not look like she's disposed to be your friend at the moment."

"Since I am not disposed to be hers either, Moncrief, it's a situation that should be left alone."

"If you're certain."

She nodded.

Wallace pulled open the wide double doors just then, standing aside and announcing the first of their guests in a voice that sounded too high and almost panicked. Catherine couldn't help but feel empathy for the young majordomo, especially when Juliana turned and skewered him with a frosty look. But Juliana's stares were no match for Moncrief's, and Wallace had evidently learned from experience with the new duke. His face simply became immobile.

Moncrief reached out and cupped her elbow in his palm. Even through the material of her dress she could feel the warmth of his hand, almost as if he claimed her with his touch.

As she was introduced to an endless stream of people, Catherine tried to ignore Juliana's narrow-eyed look. At one point the other woman crossed behind her back, and whispered, "Do not shame us," in a voice so low that only Catherine could hear.

She had attended a dame's school, and relied on her old teacher's adage: If in doubt, do nothing. She watched Hortensia surreptitiously if she was concerned how to greet a particular guest, and managed to make it through the introductions without a misstep.

Moncrief was a model of courteous, almost courtly, behavior. More than a few of the women guests were studying Moncrief with a lean and hungry look, like a cat just before it pounced on a fat bird.

When dinner was announced, he surrendered her to an older gentleman who'd been a friend of his father's, while he escorted Juliana into the dining room.

The King's Dining Hall was a large cavernous room with two fireplaces, one on each end. Heraldic banners hung from the ceiling, and broadswords and shields were aligned high on the walls. The floor, a rough stone, was uneven in places, and a gap between one wall and the ceiling made Catherine think that this part of the castle was the oldest.

Moncrief had, in defiance of propriety, insisted upon Catherine sitting to his right. In that position, she was relatively sheltered from the guests and protected from Juliana's barbs.

"It's a gloomy room," he said in an aside, as their guests were being seated.

"It needn't be. Balidonough is filled with treasures. If you lit the sconces on the walls, and placed a few tapestries in here, perhaps even laid some woven mats on the floor, the room could be beautiful."

She looked up at the walls, decorated with instruments

of war. "You might even wish to transport some of your ancestors from our bedchamber. They could look down on the table instead of us."

"Then do it. Make Balidonough as much a home as you did Colstin Hall."

"I doubt Juliana would approve. She's made no secret of her feelings about Glynneth's new post, not to mention the new uniforms I've ordered for the maids."

"You're the Duchess of Lymond. Not Juliana."

She didn't respond, uncertain exactly what to say.

"Money isn't an issue, despite Juliana's thrift. Despite any appearance to the contrary, the distillery is prosperous, and the dukedom is thriving."

"Then why . . ." She silenced herself before the question could be fully voiced.

"Has Juliana allowed Balidonough to fall into such disrepair? I'm not entirely certain."

"Still, to allow those Flemish tapestries to become moth-eaten is a sin."

His smile was almost too warm, as if he approved of her vehemence.

Moncrief gave the signal to Wallace, and the meal began. A parade of footmen entered through the rear door of the dining room, circled the table laden with items for the first course, a fish soup that was Cook's specialty. The huge tureen was crafted of white porcelain in the shape of a leaping fish, its tail near its head.

Once again, Moncrief nodded, and Wallace made a similar gesture. A dozen footmen, evidently newly trained in the task, began to serve their guests.

She glanced at Moncrief out of the corner of her eye, watching him as he commanded dinner with the same organization she imagined he had put to a military operation. She was certain it was a duty the Duchess of Lymond should have performed, but she was inexperienced in entertaining so many people. However, she made a point of studying him so that next time she would know how it was done.

Moncrief's dining companion was the wife of a Sinclair, a prosperous family who lived not far from Colstin Hall. She'd heard of the couple and their seven children but she'd never sat at table with them. The man at her right was an earl, a very pleasant companion who was more fascinated with his dinner than any conversation she might offer.

In fact, she couldn't help but wonder if Moncrief had deliberately placed him here since the man was portly and aged with a penchant for slurping his soup. By the time the beef was served he'd imbibed more than his share of wine and was dozing between courses.

She'd never before dined in such a setting, and she couldn't help but be a little bemused by it. The sheer size of the room was dwarfed by the fact that forty guests sat at the long mahogany table and each of them had a footman in new livery standing six feet behind him or her ready to serve at a moment's notice.

The room was getting warmer from the sheer press of people and all of the candles that had been lit against the evening. One of the youngest footman's duties was simply to remove a candle when it had burned out halfway and replace it with another.

Juliana had not, Catherine suspected, protested the expense of this dinner.

A tittering of laughter down at the end of the table made her concentrate upon her beef. In actuality, she wasn't hungry anymore, but she pushed the fork around her plate. She was growing increasingly uncomfortable, since several times she'd thought she heard her name, followed by a burst of laughter. More than a few of the guests had looked in her direction, then away.

Moncrief, however, was not making any attempts to hide his irritation. Twice, he'd allowed his fork to clank down on his plate, a rudeness that was accompanied by a frown toward Juliana.

Catherine reached over and placed her hand on his sleeve when he would have risen.

"Please," she said softly. His defense of her was admirable, but she truly didn't need it. "Do not say anything," she whispered to him.

He turned and looked her.

In her laudanum-induced world, she wouldn't have felt any fear at all staring directly at him. Now, however, it took a great deal of courage to do so. He was visibly angry. But as she watched, his look softened, as if he reminded himself that he was not, after all, angry at her.

"Juliana has been consistent in her dislike of me. I expect no less."

"While I do. You are my wife."

"As in you are my horse? Or you are my hound?" He could be the most annoying man.

He leaned back in his chair, both hands on the arms. Despite the indolent nature of his pose, she knew he wasn't relaxed. The muscle in his cheek flexed, and his lips bore a half smile that was more for their guests' benefit than hers.

She folded her hands on her lap and faced him.

Perhaps he was angry at her after all.

"What would you prefer that I do, Catherine?" he asked. "Allow my sister-in-law to say anything she wishes?"

"If necessary," Catherine said calmly. "Why should it matter what anyone says about me?" She picked up her wine and took a sip. "After all," she said, in a parody of his earlier declaration, "I'm Moncrief's wife."

"Yes," he said softly. "You are."

How strange that the comment sounded almost like a dare.

They had been at Balidonough only a week. The longer she knew him, the easier it was to understand why Moncrief had felt compelled to marry her. Never once had she seen him be unkind. Irritated, yes. Annoyed, of a certainty. Yet Moncrief possessed a core of honor, something so ingrained that it defined him. He'd thought she needed protection, and therefore had married her.

The thought was oddly disconcerting.

She concentrated on her dinner, but as the night wore on, it grew harder and harder for Catherine to view Juliana with any charity. The lower half of the table where she held court swept into laughter several times, and Catherine suspected it was at her expense.

Finally, Moncrief pushed back his chair and regarded Juliana with a look that could only be construed as murderous.

Catherine glanced at him out of the corner of her eye and immediately looked away, thanking Providence that such an expression was not directed at her.

"Madam," he said in a voice that could have carried to the other side of Balidonough so loud and commanding was it. "You will want to make your apologies to our guests."

Talk abruptly ceased. Every single pair of eyes turned in Moncrief's direction except for hers. After a glance down the table, Catherine kept her attention determinedly on the plate in front of her.

"What can you be saying, Moncrief? Of course I'm not leaving our guests."

"Madam," Moncrief repeated, "you will want to make your apologies now. Now," he repeated, as if there had been any doubt that she'd not heard him.

Juliana stood, her fingertips resting on the snowy white

linen as she glared at Moncrief. Wisely, however, she remained silent.

"If you wish to remain in this room, you will remember that my wife is to be addressed as Her Grace. Her rank is higher than yours. At no time, especially within my hearing, will you say anything less than favorable about her. Is that understood?"

The guests' heads turned as they regarded first Moncrief, then Juliana. The older woman looked as if she could cheerfully throttle Moncrief in plain view of forty people, but she raised her chin, her ghostly white face seeming even more pale, and nodded. Only that, but it seemed to satisfy Moncrief.

She sat amidst silence so thick that Catherine could feel it.

When Catherine glanced at Moncrief, he sat and smiled at her. "Try the beef, Catherine. I think you'll find it delicious."

The rest of the dinner was horridly uncomfortable. The guests rarely spoke, and Juliana said nothing at all. The occasional question Moncrief posed resulted in a monosyllabic reply from Mrs. Sinclair while the earl to her right had resumed his habit of dozing between courses.

Catherine was very conscious of Moncrief's mood. With every passing moment, he grew stiffer, almost as if he were freezing inside. He would raise his head from time to time and glare down the table. The guests grew even quieter. The soft murmurs of "Excuse me," "Pardon me," "Would you mind," faded away into silence.

She had never been so humiliated in her life.

Finally, Catherine stood, surprising Moncrief, her dinner companion, who was jolted awake, snorting, and the footman, who rushed to pull out her chair. She arranged her napkin on the table and forced herself to face the assembled guests.

"You'll have to excuse me."

She left the room, not even bothering to look back at Moncrief.

Catherine debated whether or not to return to their chamber, and decided against it. Instead, she went to the library, a place Moncrief had made his sanctuary and a room that would serve the purpose for her as well.

The library took up two floors of Balidonough. One of the newer sections of the castle complex, it was nestled next to the conservatory and boasted thousands of volumes. The room was constructed in a horseshoe shape, with the opening stretching out toward the mullioned windows and the view of the river flowing beneath the battlements. Light streamed into the room even on the dimmest of days, and at night she often found the oil sconces still lit as if in readiness for the duke's pleasure.

Like the entranceway, the library boasted at least a dozen statues, all standing on the edge of the second level, their solemn and classically lovely faces turned toward the bookshelves. Their diaphanous garments proved them to be female, with figures no mortal woman could hope to attain.

Several glass cases were arranged against the wall, each containing objects from the family's past. The buttons belonging to a famous ancestor were mounted alongside a broken sword, its blade remaining blood-encrusted all these years. But there were other, less martial, treasures. A fine Chinese porcelain bowl was a present from a Duke of Lymond to his bride, shipped from Portugal to Scotland, and wrapped in a spare pair of his woolen trews so that it wouldn't be broken on the journey. *The Booke of Common Praier* dating from 1550 encased in the glass display cabinet was a prized possession of a less warlike duke.

Catherine had been in the library often in the last week

when she could find nothing to do and time seemed to creep by on turtle feet. She always waited until the business of the estate took Moncrief from Balidonough before exploring the selection of volumes, some of which were old and evidently valuable.

Unlike the dining room, a fire was laid here, and it blazed brightly in anticipation of a reader's presence. She stood before the marble mantel and stretched her hands out to the flames, wondering how long until Moncrief followed her.

Less than five minutes.

The door opened and closed behind her. She sighed and turned, facing him.

"We've made a shambles of dinner, Moncrief," she said. "They'll be talking about this night for months."

"If not years. Are you truly concerned?"

She considered the matter for a moment. "I am a farmer's daughter, Moncrief, but that does not mean that I lack manners."

"You're a duchess now."

"Then what excuse shall we claim for the disaster of this evening? Temporary madness?"

He didn't answer her, only began to smile.

She truly couldn't understand him. When she was prepared for one emotion, he demonstrated another.

"Why are you so amused?"

"I like your temper. Today is the first time I've seen signs of it."

"Perhaps I was not irritated at you before."

"Or perhaps you were simply taking too much laudanum."

Catherine walked over to him, taking care to stop when a foot still separated them. She tilted back her head and wished he wasn't quite so tall before poking him in the chest with her finger.

"I would appreciate it, Moncrief," she said, enunciating her words very carefully so he couldn't mistake their meaning, "if you would cease mentioning that."

He only smiled, reached down, and wrapped his hand around her finger, then did something that startled her into silence. He kissed the tip of her finger, trapped as it was by his large hand. While she was still bemused at his actions, he kissed her nose.

A sound at the door made her glance in that direction. At least six women were crowded there, each of them watching them with various expressions on their faces.

"You have just given them something else to talk about," she whispered.

He glanced over his shoulder, his smile widening.

"Then shall we continue?"

In front of the women, he bent his head and kissed her lightly on the lips, the first such time he'd ever done so. Of course, he wanted pretense, a masquerade. He wanted the world to think they were happily married and that theirs was a love match.

His hands went to her shoulders, and he drew her to him, slowly so that she could pull away if she wanted. But, dear God, how wonderful it felt to be held. Just for a moment. Just for a second to feel the warmth of another person's flesh against her own.

She opened her mouth a little, and he deepened the kiss, and for a time, she forgot that it was pretense or that they were being observed. When he released her, she bent her head and tried to regain her composure, but it was difficult with her heart beating so hard and her breath feeling tight in her chest.

Finally, she stepped back. His smile had disappeared and in its place was that intent gaze of his. She didn't know what to say to him and as the moments passed, so did the opportunity.

She turned toward the door to find that their guests had left. In defiance of her upbringing and training, she disappeared as well, not to play the part of hostess, but to their chamber, where she sat for a long time with her fingers pressed against her lips.

Chapter 11

"I think it would take months to do a complete inventory of Balidonough," Glynneth said two weeks later.

Catherine nodded, looking at the chaos around them. Furniture was stacked from the floor to the rafters of the attic. "Dour thoughts will only make this job seem longer and more boring."

Glynneth gave her a quick look. Today Glynneth looked every bit the housekeeper, with her hair pinned up high and a set of keys dangling from a heavy chain at her waist.

"I do admit, however, that it looks like a daunting chore."

"Did they not throw anything away?"

"Not if Juliana had anything to say about it," Catherine said. "I think quite possibly that my sister-in-law is the most frugal woman it has ever been my misfortune to meet."

"What we need to do," Glynneth suggested, "is to have

some of the footmen take a few of the trunks downstairs, so we can, at least, have room to move around."

"You're right. We can't even navigate through here."

"What shall we do in the meantime?"

"There's always the keep," Catherine said.

They descended the stairs only to find themselves in another area of the castle, one unfamiliar to Catherine.

"It's the Picture Stairs," Glynneth said. "All we need to do is turn right and the corridor will lead to the Grand Staircase."

"Picture Stairs?"

"It leads to the gallery of ducal portraits."

"There are more?" Catherine asked.

Every night she faced the solemn faces of the previous dukes before falling asleep, and every night she pretended that it was not disturbing to be frowned upon—as if they, too, disapproved of her black nightgowns.

She had not been sleeping well of late, no doubt a result of her avoidance of laudanum. But she would not have confessed that to Moncrief any more than she would have sought a substitute for the drug. At least her dreams, when she finally did fall asleep, were not torturous things filled with bright bands of color and images that couldn't possibly be real.

"Did they have an artist on staff whose sole duty was to paint the Dukes of Lymond?"

Glynneth only smiled.

"I'd like to see this gallery."

At the top of the stairs, they turned left and walked some distance before the ceiling abruptly changed, towering to a high pitch above them. On one side was a wall of glass, twenty-some-odd windows whose mullioned panes were casting patterns on the dark wooden floor. Here, the maids had not, evidently, had a chance to clean, since the floor was gray with dust.

The walls were covered in a deep red silk that was faded in several places, especially where the sun struck it. But it was the other wall, the one facing the windows, that captured Catherine's attention. Massive frames of gilt surrounded what looked to be a chronological portrayal of Lymond dukes. Life-size paintings faced them, some with the subject turned toward them in a three-quarters pose, ermine slung over one shoulder, a pair of hunting dogs playing around his feet, others more formally posed.

Another portrait showed two boys, and she read from the tag affixed to the frame that it was Colin and Dermott, Moncrief's older brothers. They were both blond, each possessing a narrow face and sharp chin.

Another picture caught her eye and as she walked toward it, Catherine wondered if it was Moncrief. But then, she realized it couldn't be. This man was older, with a commanding presence evident even in a portrait. His hair was black with touches of gray at the temples, his eyes a brilliant blue. In his right hand he held what looked to be a scepter. His left hand was at his back, and he stood with feet firmly planted apart much like Moncrief often did, as if he were resting from standing at attention. In the background was a cathedral, painted as if obscured by fog. The expression on the subject's face was solemn, again a similarity to Moncrief. But amusement flashed in his dark blue eyes, as if he was privy to an eternal jest.

"Who is that?"

Glynneth bent forward and read from the plate. "The first Duke of Lymond. Conal."

"He looks like Moncrief," Catherine said. The same features, the same chin, squared and determined against the world. No doubt they shared the same temperament as well.

"I wonder why there's a cathedral in the painting?"

Catherine shook her head. She didn't know. Nor was she familiar with the scepter Conal held.

"Do you think he was a bishop?"

"Turned into a duke?" Catherine shrugged.

"Why isn't there a picture of Moncrief as a boy?"

"He was the third son and no doubt considered unimportant."

"Isn't it ironic that Fate delivered Moncrief up to be duke?" Glynneth asked.

Catherine went to stand in front of the picture of the two older boys. What was Moncrief doing in the weeks it took to paint this portrait? Had he been banished to the nursery? Had he even been born yet? The boys looked smug, well fed, and content with their life. They were both smiling, one sitting on a thronelike chair, the other on a footstool beside him. The older boy had his hand on the shoulder of the younger, making Catherine wonder if it was to assist him up or to keep him down.

Glynneth pointed out the portrait of Moncrief's father, and she could instantly see that his older sons resembled him. He had a narrow face with a pointed chin and a regrettably hooked nose that age had not softened. He didn't look like a pleasant man, but appearances were often deceiving. Next to him in line was Juliana's husband, Colin, all grown-up. While he had inherited his father's chin, his nose was blessedly not as hooked.

"He's an attractive man," Glynneth said.

"But don't you think he gives an impression of weakness, rather than strength?" Catherine tilted her head and stared at the painting from a different perspective.

One look at Moncrief, and one would have no reservations about forming an impression of him.

"Perhaps Moncrief will arrange to have his portrait painted now," Glynneth said.

"Perhaps. I've often wished I had a portrait of Harry."

In her mind, however, she would forever remember him, standing there smiling at her, the sun on his golden hair, his smile one of excitement for the future rather than sadness for their parting.

Glynneth said nothing, and Catherine glanced at her. "What about your husband, Glynneth? Do you have a miniature of him? Or a portrait?"

The other woman looked away, a small, reminiscent smile softening her face. "No, I have nothing."

For a moment, Catherine watched her friend, wondering what she'd said that was so amusing. But rather than questioning Glynneth, she turned and walked to the bank of windows. Stretching out before her were the grounds, manicured and beautifully laid out. Beyond the walls were undulating hills cut into square patches of farmland. Even now, after the crops had been harvested and the first frost already come and gone, she could see the pattern of the rows that would be hoed and tilled come spring. To the east was the river, where a slight haze rose from the water. To the west was a thick grove of trees. Perched solidly in the middle was Balidonough, like a jewel in a priceless setting.

She glanced down at a movement and saw Moncrief striding across the pale grass accompanied by another, older man.

What tasks had he done today? Another man might have rested, might have reassured himself that he was duke and others could perform the duties he'd set for them. Not Moncrief. He looked ready to work as always did, dressed in his black trousers and shiny black boots. Today he wore a greatcoat over his white shirt, the only concession to the blustery day. He wore no hat and occasionally speared his hand through his hair as if impatient with the wind's mussing of it.

Sometimes, like now, he would look around him as a

soldier might, as if not quite certain if an enemy lurked around the bush, a wall, or a tree. But his smile, when it came, tugged at her heart, especially as thoughts of him as a lonely young boy were still lodged in her mind.

Just then he looked up, and they exchanged a glance.

Ever since the formal dinner at Balidonough there had been a current between them, something Catherine told herself she didn't quite understand. In the last two weeks, she'd rarely seen him except at dinner. He attended those meals in the family dining room, and was present in that he communicated, shared ideas, and occasionally frowned Juliana into silence. At night she went to bed alone only to awaken the same way. An indentation on the pillow was the only sign that he'd come to bed at all.

She would be wise to be grateful for this new aloof Moncrief and not wonder where the other man had gone.

Only a week remained of her month, and she counseled herself that it would be better simply to give herself to him like a good wife. Once the deed was done, it would not have to be repeated more than a few times a month.

She didn't have a submissive nature. This marriage was not of her making or even her participation. Yet it was binding, and that's what chafed at her. Despite her wish or her will, Moncrief was her husband and would be until he died.

Go to him. After all, it hadn't been so difficult with Harry. But she had loved him, and the discomfort had been easily ignored over the pleasure of touching him and holding him for as long as he remained in her bed.

Go to him. End this. There were other things in life of much more importance. The inventory for one, or ensuring that Balidonough remained a heritage, or providing for the servants who depended upon the castle for their sustenance and livelihood.

Moncrief walked away with the older man, and she felt

released. But she still watched him for long moments, wondering if she had the courage to do what she dared.

She heard a noise behind her and turned and smiled at Glynneth.

"You wanted to visit the keep."

She scanned the horizon. The sunset was spectacular as it always was at Balidonough, as if God blessed the castle with particularly beautiful displays of His handiwork. "Some other day will suffice. Perhaps tomorrow."

"You promised me my day off."

Catherine nodded. "I did, didn't I? I'll investigate the keep on my own. And we'll finish the inventory as soon as Wallace has a few footmen move the furniture from the attic."

"Are you certain you don't wish to continue today?"

"No," Catherine said. "It's almost dark; there's little we could really accomplish."

"If you're certain."

In the blink of an eye, Glynneth had become the housekeeper again, and any warmth between them was stifled beneath her rigid demeanor.

"I'm very certain," Catherine said, becoming what she was as well, a reluctant duchess.

She retreated to the library, since Moncrief was still outside the castle. She closed the door behind her and stood listening to the sound of the wind careening around the windows. The room, for all its size, was a cozy one, encouraging the reader to sit in one of the overstuffed chairs or to perch on an upholstered bench and select a volume.

The setting sun was bathing the library in a brilliant yellow glow, a last farewell until dawn. But she took the precaution of lighting the branch of candles residing on the corner of the desk as well as an oil lamp. She left the candles lit on the desk but took the lamp with her as she climbed the winding stairs to the second level. Her fear of the dark had nearly been conquered, but she didn't want to be caught having to descend an iron staircase without some illumination.

She wanted to read something calming, a story that didn't involve loss or heartache, or even love. Nor was she in the mood for an adventure. Perhaps a book of poetry. Perhaps philosophy. Or a travel book.

In addition to rare books on metallurgy, and treatises on the properties of gold and silver, there were tomes here on religion, art, and astrology. Balidonough was rumored to boast one of the finest medieval libraries in the world simply because Dukes of Lymond had always been insatiably curious and were incapable of throwing out even a scrap of paper. She'd seen proof of it in an attic filled to the rafters with trunks of documents.

She stopped in front of the tall bookcases filled with volumes, but nothing caught her interest. Hortensia had mentioned a history of Balidonough, a volume that supposedly related the earliest history of the castle. All she really knew was that Moncrief's ancestors had ridden out from Balidonough on midnight raids. Those days were gone, however, ever since the family had discovered that distilling whiskey could provide more of a lucrative income than stealing cattle.

Between two tall bookcases was an alcove, housing a glass case. Mounted on the wall above it was the picture of a woman seated at a table, her chin propped on her hand. She was past the first blush of youth, but her face was kind, her eyes sparkling. She wore a wimple that fit snugly around her cheeks, the crisp white linen of it so perfectly portrayed that Catherine could see its texture.

Inside the glass case rested a single book. The volume was old, the leather cover cracked and worn, and deteriorating along the spine. Carefully, she lifted the top of the case, and opened the book. The words written on the fly-leaf were in another language, one she didn't understand. Disappointed, she opened the book in the middle, only to discover that it was a volume of illustrations.

Very graphic illustrations of naked men.

The first picture was of a young man, gloriously tumescent, standing with one hand on his hip and the other flat against his flank, a smile on his face and a gleam in his eyes as if he dared the artist to portray him in his erect state.

She slammed the cover shut and stood there staring at the painting above the case. The kindly older woman now seemed to have a mocking glint in her eyes as if she was well aware that Catherine was shocked.

Her hand was at her throat, her fingers feeling the rapid pulse at her neck. She stood there until she calmed, then glanced down at the book again. What kind of horror was this? Unseemly, and possibly even sinful, not the sort of book she would have expected in Balidonough's library.

Perhaps she had misunderstood. Perhaps she hadn't actually seen what she thought she had seen. Very slowly, she opened the cover of the book again and turned a page. No, the illustration was exactly the same. The young man was erect, his penis stiffly in front of him like a living lance. She felt the warmth race up her body but she could not force herself to look away.

A moment later, she turned the page. A thin vellum sheet separated it from the next drawing. Another man, older, with red hair not only on his head, but between his thighs as well, was pictured half-reclining on a bench with one leg drawn up, his wrist dangling on his knee. His other hand was wrapped around his engorged penis and he was staring directly at her as if he knew how utterly fascinated she was.

She'd never seen a naked man in such a condition. She

and Harry had only been married a month before he'd gone to join the regiment. And when he'd come to her bed, he was ready to mount her. She had never actually seen him in the darkness.

Her finger reached out of its own accord, and traced the path of the red-haired man's erection. Was it possible that it might become that large? If so, it certainly hadn't felt quite that grand. She pressed her fingers against her lips and stood there debating with herself.

Should she turn another page?

Knowledge should never be shunned, especially in areas in which she was ignorant. Over the next quarter hour she managed to educate herself quite well.

The book was a collection of some thirty paintings, each one more fascinating than the last. Toward the end of the book the paintings changed. Instead of one man there were two, one often featured touching the other admiringly.

One of the last pictures was the most shocking of all. A man was featured kneeling at the feet of a young man, his mouth open, his tongue just about to touch the other man's erection. Both men's faces wore a look of utter bliss.

"My great-uncle collected such things," Moncrief said from behind her.

She jumped so much that she dropped the book on top of the case and for a horrified second thought its weight was going to shatter the glass.

"I didn't hear you," she said, quickly closing the book. Her voice was shaking, but so were her hands. She lifted the case, replaced the book, and shut the case again. Only then did she turn to face Moncrief.

"He has other books in his collection. Japanese *shunga,* featuring women as well."

"Indeed?"

He came to her side, and lifted the top of the case, retrieving the volume she'd so hurriedly replaced.

"Did you find this interesting?" he asked, turning to a random picture of a naked man with a shield and sword beside him on the ground. He stood, with his back half-turned, his pose one that would still allow a glimpse of his erection. His back was muscled all over, his buttocks solid and defined, his arms stretched over his head.

Except, of course, that a certain part of him didn't look the least relaxed.

She closed her eyes rather than look at the next illustration he'd turned to, this one of two men reclining on a stone bench, each one's head at the other's feet. Both men had their hands outstretched, their fingers brushing the other's erection. The look of pleasure on their faces was so vibrant that she was certain she could recall the image even with her eyes closed.

"Does that really feel so wonderful?" she asked.

For a moment there was silence in the room, interrupted only by the sputtering of the oil lamp. Catherine was horrified that she'd voiced the question. And Moncrief? She glanced at him to find him smiling at her. Not a pleased smile, as if she'd done something of which he approved. Or even a forced smile, such as he'd worn the night of the disastrous dinner. This smile was altogether different. He looked more amused at himself than at her.

"I can assure you it does."

For a moment she was utterly shocked, enough to open her eyes wide and stare at him.

The moments ticked by, measured by a flush on his cheeks. "I prefer my partners to be women."

"A woman could do that?"

She reached out and fumbled with the pages until she found the picture she sought. She poked at the illustration with one finger. "And that?" she asked, amazed.

Moncrief looked down at the image of the young man being mouthed by another, and his smile grew. "Yes," he said, "and that."

She stared at the painting, stunned. "But why would anyone *want* to?"

His laughter startled her. He replaced the book in the case and gently turned her so that she was facing the stairs. "Passion is a like a drug, Catherine," he said, bending low to speak the words next to her ear. "When you're immersed in it, you want to touch your partner in all ways; you want to bring them pleasure in every conceivable fashion."

The thought that someone had done that to him, had touched him exactly that way was so disconcerting that Catherine was speechless.

"I hope, with all my heart, that you feel that kind of passion one day."

She glanced at him before descending the stairs. His smile had disappeared, and the look in his eyes challenged her to understand it.

She turned away and left him then, escaping from the library as if demons chased her.

Chapter 12

Catherine awoke from a troubled sleep an hour before dawn, and rather than summoning Mary, took one of the serviceable dresses she'd brought from Colstin Hall and dressed. Moncrief was not in the room, and she was grateful for his absence.

He'd been acting oddly ever since he'd found her in the library last night.

All during dinner, he'd worn a strange smile, and later in the parlor, he'd not stopped watching her. While she couldn't help but recall the illustrations she'd seen, her cheeks flushed for hours with the memory.

She busied herself with tasks relating to Colstin Hall until the sun was up and the morning well advanced. She was on her way to giving the letters she'd written to her steward to Wallace to post when she heard Juliana's voice raised in anger.

"What is it that I hear about you ordering Munson to open the southern fields? And increasing the output at the distillery? You should have consulted me first, Moncrief."

To continue with her chore meant she would have to cross in front of the open door. But she didn't want to see Moncrief at the moment. Nor did she want to encounter Juliana, so Catherine remained in the hall, a reluctant eavesdropper.

"I see no reason to do so," Moncrief said calmly.

"While you were playing war, I was managing Balidonough on my own."

"Not wisely, however, Juliana."

Catherine could just imagine what kind of look Juliana was giving him.

"In a short time, Moncrief, you have undone all of the cost-cutting measures that I have put into place at Balidonough. We're going to spend a fortune, and what will we have to show for it?"

"A better quality of life, madam? A grateful staff? People who want to work at Balidonough rather than those who are simply here by necessity? I do not intend for Balidonough to be a penal colony for the poor, Juliana. We've always had loyal and dedicated people serving us."

"But the money!"

"Yes, the money. Of which we have plenty. More than a hundred people could spend in their lifetimes. Why do you save it with such assiduousness, Juliana?"

"Because otherwise it may not be there when you have need of it."

"Or because you have other uses for it? Did you think it escaped my notice that your friends are Jacobites, Juliana? I won't allow Balidonough to be used to fuel idiotic dreams from the past any more than my father did."

"Your father was killed because of his disloyalty. Do you want the same thing to happen to you?"

Silence stretched between them, and Catherine took a step backwards. Should she retreat to the parlor once more?

"What do you know, Juliana?"

"You know as well as I that he was set upon by thieves when he was abroad."

"Were they really thieves? Or Jacobites?"

Silence again, and this time, Catherine wanted desperately to peer into the room.

"I've given orders for my solicitor to inspect the ledgers, Juliana. I sincerely hope that I will not find that you've funded any cause other than Balidonough."

"You've become too English in all these years, Moncrief. You've forgotten your heritage."

"I'm trying to preserve it, Juliana, while you would give it away to fools with glory in their veins."

A moment later, Juliana stormed out of the room, not even glancing in Catherine's direction. She would have tiptoed past the door except for one thing. Moncrief was standing there looking at her.

"She's very angry at you."

He stepped aside, and she entered the room. He placed one palm flat on the wood of the door and leaned against it as if to prevent Juliana from returning. He studied his hand and not her when he spoke, which was just as well. She wanted a respite from that intense gaze of his.

"She lives in the past. I don't."

"Have you become too English?"

"Perhaps I'm both English and Scot. I've always believed, even before joining the regiment, that the Pretender's rebellion was a poorly executed selfish act. In that, I concurred with my father. But I've never forgotten who I was or where I came from."

She'd never met anyone like Moncrief, so supremely himself that his confidence showed in everything he said or did.

"Are Juliana's sympathies dangerous?"

"Only costly." He turned and smiled at her. "Juliana's

friends are all descendants of those who supported the rebellion. No doubt they get together and lament the old days."

"Then why not send her away from Balidonough?"

"It's better to know what an enemy is doing than to be left in ignorance. I would much rather have Juliana close to me than somewhere else fomenting rebellion in the name of Balidonough."

"You're very patient with her."

Moncrief shrugged. "I can understand her discomfiture. Her rank has changed, her position of power. Life is different for Juliana, a fact that I suspect she does not quite comprehend as yet."

"Life is different for me as well," Catherine said.

He walked toward the windows and stood there looking out at the view. The morning sun spilled into the room bathing him in radiance. Light and dark. Brightness and shadow.

"I suspect your life is no different at all," Moncrief said. "I think you have brought your grief with you like a turtle houses his own home on his back. The only thing that has changed for you, Catherine, is the location of your mourning, not the intensity of it. I see your grief growing as each day passes. Harry is dead, and death did not make him a saint, yet you almost pray to him as if he's become your Almighty."

She pressed her hand to the base of her neck; her other hand rested at her waist. His attack was unexpected.

"I think that's an unfair accusation, Moncrief. I've taken my duties to heart. I have met with Cook, I've supervised the making of new clothes for the servants. I am in the process of doing a complete inventory of all the stored furniture at Balidonough."

"All very admirable, and all duties Glynneth could do. What about the duties of a duchess? My duchess? Perhaps I should write you a letter to explain what I'm talk-ing about. Perhaps you'll hold it as sacred as you do Harry's. Or do you think I don't know that you sleep with them?"

She moved to the fireplace, wishing her curiosity had not led to this confrontation.

"Or perhaps I wouldn't read it at all," she said, hurt and angry. "But do write me a letter, Moncrief, because at least I could wad it up and toss it in the rubbish."

He turned from the window and folded his arms and studied her. A ghost of a smile played around his lips, and she wondered if he had manipulated her into this trap of words.

"Why do you not give your new life a chance, Catherine?"

She fingered the statue of the shepherdess on the man-tel, concentrating on the tiny flowers arranged in the bas-ket she held. Slowly, she turned and forced herself to face him. "I feel as if everything I was or had been is gone. My home, my family, my servants. My husband."

"You have a new home and a new husband."

"Yes, I do."

"Could you not summon a modicum of enthusiasm on my behalf, madam? I agree that it is not an ideal situation, yet it could be much worse. I could be a pauper, someone out to steal your funds. I could be a despot. And I'm not that, even though I am beginning to understand how despotic a man can become under certain situations."

"Are you referring to the bedroom? I am a widow, sir, not a virgin. I am accustomed to a man's needs."

"Are you?"

"I do not like your tone," she said, drawing herself up. Even though her face felt warm, and her chest tight, she didn't look away.

"You are no longer a widow, madam. Call yourself

duchess. Or wife." A beat of silence stretched between them as he studied her black dress.

He was a supremely arrogant man, every inch a duke. How strange that at this moment she had a flash of memory as he'd been when she'd first met him, attired in his Highland Regimental uniform. He'd been kind then, she remembered, and almost charming, nothing like he was right now.

He stood straight and tall as if he were still a soldier, at least in bearing. His shoulders were broad, almost too broad for the severity of his coat. And should his trousers be that tight? Her eyes jerked up to find his gaze still on her, his face severe and utterly devoid of emotion, except, of course, for the fact that one corner of his lip was upturned. Had he realized her thoughts?

He was entirely too handsome a man, and seemingly aware of it, as if he had no modesty at all.

"It was not my decision to marry you, Moncrief. And while I understand the honor that drove you to doing such a foolish gesture, it does not remove the fact that I am an unwilling bride."

For a long while, he didn't respond. Finally, he said, "Keep your letters, and your self hallow and inviolate, dear wife. Keep your memories until they begin to fade as all memories do in time." He strode toward her, reached out one hand, and cupped her cheek, allowing his thumb to trace her chin. "It is a pity, however, that you choose death over life with such alacrity. I could show you the joy of passion. Or is that what you're afraid of? Strange, I never thought you a coward, Catherine."

"Is a woman allowed no loyalty?" she asked.

"Is it loyalty that keeps you so chaste? Then I pity you, Catherine. Harry Dunnan was not worth your loyalty."

She closed her eyes, willing him away. His hands were rough, his fingers callused. But he was gentle in their use, smoothing them over her face and spearing them in the hair at her temples. Curious, she had never thought herself affected by touch, nor had she ever noted that a questing finger along the rim of her ear caused her to shiver.

She was defenseless against his tender onslaught. And perhaps that's what he wanted, to remind her that he was alive and Harry was not. If so, she was only human, and being human, turned her face against his palm, an encouraging gesture that she instantly regretted. His thumbs spread from her nose across her cheeks and down, as if he measured her face for a sculpture in his mind.

"I can't stop thinking of you staring at that book, Catherine. I want your gaze on me, not on those other men."

Shocked, she opened her eyes and stared at him.

Then he was gone from the room, as if she'd imagined him. She took a few deep breaths to steady herself. He had done that on purpose, and she hated him for it. Or perhaps herself, that she was so desperate for a little warmth and the touch of another person that she would crave it from Moncrief.

Resolutely, she squared her shoulders and went about her tasks, determined not to think of him.

Chapter 13

There were four keeps at Balidonough, but only one was used to store furniture. The others were filled with instruments of war or trunks filled with letters and books that had not been able to fit in the library. In the first week she was at Balidonough, Catherine had explored the circular tower facing west, the only keep restored as it might have looked two hundred years ago.

The lower part of the keep had been a dismal place since no windows existed on the first floor. The earthen floor smelled sour and musty, so she had quickly taken the steps built into the wall up to the second floor.

The floor was constructed of wood and had evidently been replaced over the years. A series of steps led her to the crenellated roof. From here she could see the whole of Balidonough's land, as far as the eye could see. How foolish she had been to think that Colstin Hall was a prosperous estate. When compared to the Lymond heritage, it was a tiny property.

This keep was constructed just like the others, but the door was more solid, having been reinforced with iron bars. She opened it with the key Glynneth had given her, surprised that the door opened easily. The hinges must have recently been oiled.

She lit a candle against the darkness, and was pleased to see that someone had cleared a path through the accumulated furniture to the steps beyond. She was halfway up the curved stairs when a figure brushed by her, pushing her so violently that she found herself tumbling down the stairs. The candle fell to the ground, mercifully missing the furniture and extinguishing itself against the dirt floor. A moment later she heard the door slam closed, and she was left in the darkness.

Catherine pressed her hands against the stones and eased into a sitting position. The only thing that had saved her falling the whole length of the stairs had been the curved wall.

She sat on the step and wrapped both hands around her throbbing ankle. Flexing her toes worsened the pain, and she uttered an unladylike curse below her breath, some combination of words she'd overheard one of the stable-boys use, and had always secretly wanted to say.

The door opened suddenly, and a shaft of light penetrated the darkness.

"Catherine?"

She winced at the sound of Moncrief's voice.

"How did you know I was here?" she said, looking down at him from the stair. He was the last person she wanted to see, the sting of their last conversation too fresh in her mind.

"I was looking for you, Catherine."

"To apologize for your churlishness?"

"Perhaps. Would you accept my apology?"

"Not if you have to ask before it's tendered, Moncrief."

She frowned at him. "Please go away, Moncrief. I really don't need you here."

"Why do I not believe you?"

"I don't know, and at this particular moment I don't care. Go away."

A swift glance and he bounded up the stairs two at a time. "What have you done?" he asked.

"What do you mean what have I done? I haven't taken any laudanum, if that's what you mean. I was simply inspecting the keep when someone brushed by me and nearly pushed me off the steps." She truly wished he would go away. Granted, her ankle hurt like blazes at the moment, but all she needed was a few moments, then she could navigate the stairs.

"Is this something you should have been doing? Where is Glynneth?"

She crossed her arms and tried to ignore both him and the pain in her ankle. "She asked for the day off, and I gave it to her."

He sat back on his heels and studied her. "You're very generous with the servants."

"So are you," she said, matching his frown with one of her own. "Peter thinks the world of you, and Wallace follows you around as if you're God."

She did wish he wouldn't look at her so intently. Sometimes she felt as though he examined her, as if he were not quite certain of who she was.

"You're still angry with me."

"I congratulate you on your perception, Moncrief. Go away."

"What's wrong with your ankle? Why are you rubbing it?"

She moved her hand. "Go away."

"Are you going to be so stubborn as to refuse help? It's obvious you've hurt yourself."

"I am not so addled by drugs that I can't figure that out."

"But perhaps you're blinded by anger."

"I know of no one else at Balidonough who has more of a right at this moment. Go away. How many times must I tell you?" She frowned at him, which had the opposite effect on him. He smiled.

"You're the one person at Balidonough, besides Juliana, who doesn't give a whit for my consequence."

"Am I supposed to be flattered that you've compared me to Juliana?"

He bent down and scooped her up in his arms effortlessly. She let out a tiny sound of surprise and tried not to look over the side of the stairs.

"We could sit here all day trading barbs, but I want to get somewhere to look at that ankle."

"You needn't carry me."

"Surely you didn't think I would let you walk with an injured ankle?"

"It's just that I've never been carried in such a way before."

She might have felt very cosseted being carried in such a way, if the person doing so was anyone but Moncrief.

He strode through the keep and bent below the lintel to emerge into the cold, sunny day. The wind that blew around the keep made her grateful for her cloak.

She closed her eyes, bent back her head, and felt the sun on her closed lids. One hand rested against Moncrief's coated chest, the other trailed up to curve around the back of his neck.

When he abruptly stopped, she opened her eyes to look up at him. She didn't realize that his deep blue eyes had a touch of black to them. She was so close that she could see each tiny fleck of color.

His head bent and for one breathless moment she

thought that he was going to kiss her, but he drew back at the last moment.

"You needn't carry me, you know."

He looked down at her. "Shall I set you on your feet, then?" He began to lower her, and she frowned at him, then shook her head reluctantly.

"No."

"Is it so difficult to accept my assistance, Catherine?"

"I have done nothing but accept your assistance, Moncrief, from the very day we met. It seems our relationship is off balance."

"You can care for me when I'm ill, then. I will expect a tray in my bed and a compress for my head."

"I cannot imagine you ever being ill," she said, half-smiling.

"I am human, Catherine," he said in a clipped voice. "Not a god."

She found it very difficult to think with him so close. And for a blessed score of moments, simply didn't. She laid her cheek against his chest and felt the booming of his heart. He was so tall and strong and capable that it would be easy to allow his strength to overcome hers.

In a sense, that's exactly what she had done with the laudanum.

She wouldn't replace the drug with another form of helplessness.

She wished he would put her down now, and she would make her own way back to her room. A cold water compress and putting her foot up on a pillow for a few hours would ease the discomfort. If that didn't work, she would wrap a bandage around her ankle so the swelling wouldn't increase.

Moncrief turned to the right and walked directly toward the gatehouse wall. There, half-hidden behind a tall bush, was an ironbound door, one she'd never before seen.

"Where does this lead?" she asked, as he ducked his head and then turned sideways to enter.

"To the dungeon. From there to a secret passage."

"A secret passage?"

"Balidonough has had a long, tumultuous past. There were times when my family had to have an escape route. It was judged wise to keep the passages in good working order. It's shorter this way."

Soon they were in the cold cellar, a place used to store some of the foodstuffs and casks of wine. This room was truly cold but free of the dampness usually associated with rooms below ground. A set of stairs led to the kitchen, but Moncrief avoided them, and instead walked straight to a wall of tall shelves filled with an assortment of bags and barrels.

"I'm going to put you down for a moment."

He lowered her and she stood pressed against him, balancing on her uninjured ankle. He reached over and placed his hands flat against the wall behind the shelves.

"What are you looking for?"

"A certain brick. When I was a child I had to climb up on the shelves in order to reach it. Here it is."

Catherine heard a groaning sound as Moncrief pressed his shoulder against the bricks. Suddenly, the whole of the wall moved inward. Once more he picked her up and this time she was so bemused that she didn't say a word in protest. The corridor was pitch-black, but he acted as if he knew exactly where to go.

"How can you see anything?" she asked, straining to see something through the blackness.

"I haunted these passages when I was a boy. I know every twist and turn."

"Does everyone know about the passages?"

"The eldest son is supposed to know," he said. "In order to protect the family."

"Yet you knew."

"I was a precocious child," he said, and it sounded as if he were smiling. "I was determined to discover everything kept secret."

In the gallery it had occurred to her that Moncrief had been a lonely child. Now she was certain of it.

"Did you have no playmates?"

He didn't answer for a moment, and she wondered if he was going to respond at all. "My brothers were much older than I, and had their own pursuits. The last thing they wanted was a younger brother following them."

"Were you a happy child?"

"I think I was. I was alone most of the time, but I managed to occupy myself."

"So you had no childhood companions?"

"I didn't say that. The cook at the time had a boy, and we played together, and there was Hortensia, of course."

"Hortensia? You knew each other as children?"

"Juliana and her sister were neighbors."

Before she could frame the question, he answered it. "Juliana was a bit more tolerable as a child. She was older and had already been promised to Colin. As for me, my tutor kept me busy most of the time. I remember occasions when he was gone or ill and I felt heady with my freedom." There was a pause, and she wondered if he was remembering the boy he'd been.

"When Dermott died, I found myself trying to escape my father's attention as much as possible. Luckily, Colin had come into his majority by then, and he and my father traveled a great deal."

"And your mother?" They had reached a landing now.

"She died when I was two." Silence again. "I remember being cosseted by a succession of nurses, all of whom spoiled me. I was a very pampered young man, or so my father would say."

"I don't think I would have liked your father," she said.

He chuckled, a sound that seemed to change the atmosphere in the passageway, bringing a certain warmth and comfort to the shadows. They didn't seem as gloomy now as much as shielding. "I'm not certain I liked him, either."

He was climbing stairs now, and she pressed her hand against his chest. "Wouldn't it be easier if you put me down?"

"Can you walk?"

"I'm certain I could with your help."

"I'd prefer to carry you."

He stopped for a moment, and she wondered if he was trying to get his bearings in the dark. But she heard another scraping sound, then he turned and pressed his back against the wall. A screech preceded the wall moving, and light spilled into the passage.

She breathed deeply of fresh air, then realized they were in the ducal chambers.

Sunlight streamed into the room through the open windows, and for a moment she was blinded by the sudden brightness. Moncrief momentarily hesitated before striding to his bed, gently placing her on the end, and kneeling before her.

"I'm all right," she reassured him. "Truly."

Without any thought to decorum, he lifted the hem of her dress. She leaned forward and pulled it down, and he simply lifted it again.

Without even asking her, he began to unfasten her shoe. A stab of pain so sharp it took her breath away kept her from objecting. But a moment later, when his hand trailed up her leg, she slapped at it.

"Moncrief! What are you doing?" She tried to pull away, but he kept his hand where it was.

"How do you think to treat a broken ankle *and* retain

your propriety, Catherine? One or the other must be forgotten."

If she didn't know better, she would have thought he planned this. There was a wicked twinkle in his eye, and her admonishing look did nothing to banish it.

But what he said was the truth, wasn't it? She could either ignore her ankle or the fact that he was sitting much too close, with his hand flat against her calf, his fingers trailing across her knee.

Her leg didn't hurt, merely her ankle, and it was beginning to ache abominably.

"Do you actually think it's broken?"

"I have no way of seeing until your stocking is removed."

She flushed, thinking that surely there could be a way to do it with greater decorum.

"You'll have to turn away," she said.

"No."

"No?"

"I am your husband, madam, a fact that you've consistently tried to ignore. However, the law recognizes it, the whole of Colstin Hall recognizes it, and now all of Balidonough recognizes it."

He was an intractable man. However, she could be as stubborn.

"Very well," she said, and pulled up her skirt with as much dignity as she could muster.

Instead of being gentlemanly and looking away, he looked fascinated by her actions, and the mischievous glint in his eyes didn't lessen as she reached her garter and slowly slipped it below her knee and down her leg.

She almost slapped his hand away when he grabbed it from her fingers and slid it over her foot but then she realized he was doing so to ease it over her swelling ankle.

Slowly, she began to roll down her white cotton stockings, wishing he would look away. Then, as before, he took over the chore for her at her knee. But this time, he allowed his fingers to drift down her leg in a long, slow caress. As her stocking reached her ankle, he glanced up at her, and for a long, mesmerizing moment, her gaze was captured by his.

Look away. Look away. Look away. However much she commanded herself, she couldn't. Something in his look compelled her to study it. Or perhaps it was because his pose reminded her of the book she'd discovered the night before. A warmth traveled up her chest to her cheeks.

She was no virgin, but at this moment she felt unknowing, and too innocent.

"I don't think it's broken," she said, feeling as if her throat were constricted.

She closed her eyes, breaking the bond between them.

"Please, Moncrief," she whispered, and she felt his fingers move on her ankle again. His fingers gently caressed her toes, examined her foot with tender fingers.

"I don't think it's broken," she said again.

Once again he didn't respond.

Slowly, he elevated her foot, his hands warm on her heel. A few probing touches brought about a gasp of pain, and she clamped her lips shut.

"Have I hurt you?" he asked.

She opened her eyes. "It would simply be foolish to complain about something you're doing to assist me."

He studied her for a moment, then concentrated once again on her foot.

"We need to wrap your ankle," he said. "Whether it's broken or simply sprained, the treatment is the same."

She nodded.

"Would you like something for the pain?"

"And have you accuse me of being addicted to laudanum? No."

He didn't respond to her taunt, and for a moment she was almost disappointed.

"One of my relatives had gout. I'm sure we have a pair of crutches somewhere in the attic."

"Everything else is there," she said, having more than a passing acquaintance with the attics of Balidonough.

"My family has always had a sense of the future. My grandfather seven times removed walked these halls, no doubt thinking of me and my brothers. Plans were made for us before our great-grandfathers were ever born." He glanced at her. "Just as I must plan for my grandchildren."

The conversation had taken a delicate turn, and it had so innocently begun. She looked down at her ankle. "The pain is not all that great. I'm sure if I remain off my foot, it will heal shortly."

"Tell me about the accident."

She glanced up him, surprised.

"Someone brushed by me. They had evidently been on the second floor when I entered."

"Did you see who it was?"

She shook her head.

He moved to the head of the bed and turned down the counterpane. "Why don't you rest while I gather up something to wrap your ankle."

"I'm really not tired," she said, facing forward.

Suddenly, he was there again and scooping her up in his arms. He carried her to the head of the bed and sat her down against a pillow. A glint of a memory made her frown. "You've done that before," she said.

"The night you nearly died."

"You didn't exaggerate, Moncrief? Was I truly that ill?"

"Why would I exaggerate? So that I would have an opportunity to marry a woman who chooses to forget it at every opportunity?"

She looked away. "I didn't mean to die," she said slowly. "True, life had become unbearable, but I don't think I wanted to die."

"Are you certain?"

"Yes," she said. "I am." She glanced up at him. "Nor did I take too much laudanum by choice."

He surprised her by bending down and kissing her lightly on the lips before leaving her. She watched him walk toward the door and decided that no one could be as confusing as Moncrief deliberately.

She had been an only child, comfortable with being alone. Only since Harry's death had she begun to rely on other people, and probably too much.

Being dependent upon Moncrief was a disconcerting feeling.

Her ankle was rapidly swelling, and she wondered if she should go in search of some bandages. Before she could even attempt it, Moncrief returned to the room followed by two maids. One was carrying a tray and the other an ornately carved wooden chest with an arched top and a brass lock. After placing their burdens on the table beside the bed, they both curtsied nervously to Moncrief, who paid them not one whit of attention.

She mouthed a soft, "Thank you," to the maids, one of whom hurriedly closed the door behind her.

"The least you could do is notice when people serve you."

"They hate it when I notice them," he said, not glancing at her. "They'd prefer to remain invisible, at least to me."

He sat on the edge of the bed. "This is not Colstin Hall, Catherine. People aren't used to seeing you in all sorts of roles. At Balidonough they expect certain things of their dukes, and I try to oblige them."

"Such as?"

"A certain distance, for one. If I called any of them by

their first names, they'd faint first and complain to Glynneth or Wallace as soon as they awoke." He began to unroll a length of linen bandage, rolled ahead of time for just such a use as this.

"And the other things they expect of you?"

"To be the same as I was yesterday. Balidonough has been here for centuries and almost demands a constancy of behavior."

"Do you serve the castle, or does the castle serve you?"

He didn't answer, only gently elevated her ankle and continued to wrap it with the sure and certain touch of someone who had done this many times before.

"Now you will tell me," she said, forcing a smile, "that you have acted as a medical practitioner to your troops."

"I did what was necessary at the time," he said, his attention still on her ankle. He was like that, focused and determined. Suddenly, she wondered if she were up to the task of being married to Moncrief.

His touch was gentle, more so than she expected, and when he finished and tied off the bandage neatly to the side, she was impressed by the results of his handiwork. The bandage was tight, but she didn't complain, knowing that it was better to be as snug as she could bear.

"Thank you, Moncrief."

He slid a pillow below her calf so that her ankle was elevated, and stood.

"It should feel better in a little while."

"It feels better now."

After opening the ornately carved wooden chest, he withdrew something that looked like a twig, together with a small, round ceramic dish. He inserted the twig into the dish and then lit it with the tinder. He allowed it to flare for a moment, then blew out the flame. Immediately, the room was filled with an exotic scent.

"Incense," he said. "Something to relax you, without being an opiate. It has no addictive properties."

"What would you consider your most onerous faults, Moncrief? Other than refusing to believe me about the laudanum?"

He smiled at her, an expression so lacking in mockery and filled with such gentleness that she was unable to form another sentence.

"I meant no insult, Catherine. I know that you don't want to take anything for the pain, just as I know that your ankle must be hurting you. My most onerous faults, however, are ones that you've no doubt already witnessed." He closed the chest and moved it to the top of the dresser and did the same with the tray containing the bandages and scissors. "I feel responsible for those under my care."

"That could be considered an asset."

"Except that my idea of caring for them and theirs sometimes come into conflict. I'm not always right, yet I have to convince myself of that fact occasionally."

"It has not escaped my attention that you are sometimes arrogant, Moncrief. Not to mention stubborn."

When he came back to the bed, he sat at the end of it, careful not to dislodge her ankle. Gently, he covered her foot with a small blanket.

"I have been trained all my life to anticipate the worst, and to plan against it. Therefore, I sometimes forget to anticipate the best."

"So you are not an optimist by nature."

"Perhaps. But neither am I dour. Also, I will admit to being tenacious. Even when I have the most limited chance of success, I will grasp it and hold on. Such an attitude is an asset in battle, but it has a tendency to annoy other people."

The fact that he was admitting to his own weaknesses surprised her. So, too, was the reemergence of that twinkle in his eyes.

"Are those your only flaws?"

He shook his head. "My major ones. The others I'd prefer you discover as time passed." He reached over and took one of her hands, placing it between his. "I intend to make this a real marriage between us, Catherine, given enough time and our joint willingness."

She didn't know how to answer him, but then it seemed as if he didn't expect an answer. "Be angry at me if you will, be furious if you must, but don't hide what you feel. Perhaps one day the emotions between us will turn to softer ones, but I doubt we will ever be indifferent to each other."

"And sadness, Moncrief? What about sadness?"

"You've had your share of it, I think. Or will you wallow in it long after you should have healed?"

"Have you never lost someone, Moncrief?"

He hesitated for a moment before speaking again. "A woman I loved."

She wanted, suddenly, to ask questions about this unknown woman, but she didn't. Instead, she breached their fragile truce by asking a favor of him.

"Would you fetch one of my letters, please?"

For a moment, she expected him to refuse, but he surprised her by standing and moving to Harry's trunk at the foot of the bed.

"Which one?"

She had taken to rereading them in chronological order. "The one on the top, please."

He bent over the trunk and pulled the letter free of its ribbon, closed the trunk, and returned to her side, handing it to her. He didn't speak, but neither did he look pleased at his chore.

"Will you sleep with it pressed to your bosom?"

"Does it matter to you if I do?"

"More than you know."

Silence stretched between them as she fought the urge to ask why. Finally, she placed the letter on the bed beside her, content to have it nearby. She would read it later.

"Thank you for your kindness."

He only nodded before leaving the room.

Chapter 14

Moncrief left the ducal chambers before he ravished his wife. He nodded to a footman standing in the corridor and vowed to lessen the presence of the servants, especially in this wing.

Descending the staircase, he heard Wallace's voice first, then the others. Four voices were raised, hardly the behavior he expected at Balidonough's front entrance. At the foot of the staircase he found himself face-to-face with the vicar. An unlikely guest and, if the truth be told, an unwelcome one, especially now.

He forced a smile to his face and extended his hand in greeting. The vicar immediately fawned and bowed so low Moncrief thought he'd never be able to straighten again.

"Your Grace," the older man said. "I beg that you will forgive this intrusion, especially with no notice to you, sir, and your staff." He sent a heated glance toward Wallace. "But it is prompted by the greatest concern, Your Grace."

"We are her family, sir," a woman said, pushing herself to the front. "Her only kin in this harsh world."

Behind her stood a tall man with silvery blond hair. The man's appearance instantly told him who the couple was. Harry would have looked the same in thirty years.

"Mr. and Mrs. Dunnan?" Moncrief asked, cutting through the vicar's stammering introductions.

"Indeed we are, Your Grace," the woman said. "It is our intention to see dearest Catherine. The vicar informed us that she has wed you, and we are here to see for ourselves that she is pleased with her lot." She pressed a handkerchief to the corner of one dry eye. "I cannot believe that she is ready to desert poor Harry."

Poor Harry, who had been dead these past months. Moncrief was heartily tired of poor, dead Harry.

However, he inclined his head and motioned to Wallace. "Send for Glynneth," he said in an aside, "and inform her that two chambers need to be readied for our guests."

Wallace nodded and bowed himself out of the group. Moncrief turned his attention back to the vicar and Harry's parents.

"Catherine has suffered an accident, so perhaps we can schedule your reunion for later this evening. At dinner, perhaps?"

"An accident?"

He turned to Mrs. Dunnan. "She has injured her ankle."

"I want to see her."

He forced an amenable smile to his face. "She's resting. You will, of course, be my guests for a few days?" Since no inn was nearby, he had little choice in the matter but to extend hospitality he didn't want to give.

A murmur of assent from the vicar and the Dunnans solidified Moncrief's dread.

He saw Wallace out of the corner of his eye, followed by a smiling Glynneth. The moment she saw him, her faced changed. Gone was the hint of her smile and in its place a sober expression. She stood off to the side, coming forward only when he gestured to her.

"My housekeeper will show you to your rooms." A quick questioning glance toward Glynneth and her answering nod assured him there were two guest chambers in readiness.

He had thought to order a tray for Catherine, but that had been changed with the vicar's arrival. He should've known that the man would not let Catherine go so easily. She had proven to be a generous asset to Thomas McLeod's congregation. Why, however, hadn't Moncrief heard of Dunnan's parents in all this time?

He watched as the group climbed the staircase, Mrs. Dunnan still in possession of her handkerchief. If the night ahead proved anything like this short meeting, he would be regaled with Harry stories. All the while, he would need to guard his responses, just as he did when thinking of Catherine's devotion to her dead husband and his letters.

Moncrief wanted to tell her that she mourned the wrong man. But she was so immersed in the pleasure of her grief that she couldn't see anything else.

Perhaps he had had the right idea after all, and should simply write her a letter.

My dearest lonely wife, look up from tracing your hands across words I wrote a lifetime ago. Hear me breathe, see me move toward you, touch my hand, my chest, my face. Embrace me. Laugh with me, tell me the stories of your days. Give to me what hides in your heart.

He wondered if she would ever come to his bed. Perhaps he could show her with his hands and his lips what he couldn't say with words.

He retreated to his library, sending for Glynneth after their guests were established in their rooms.

Balidonough's new housekeeper entered his library after a resounding knock. He studied her as she walked toward the desk. She didn't look the least bit circumspect. In fact, she looked more the lady of the manor than one of its servants.

He couldn't imagine why Catherine considered her a friend, not when it was patently clear that she didn't have Catherine's best interest at heart, only her own.

"Where have you put them?" he asked, making no effort whatsoever at polite conversation. Had it been his previous housekeeper, he would have spent a few moments inquiring as to her health, and that of her widowed sister. Glynneth was an entirely different situation. He didn't like the woman, and he saw no reason to lie about it.

"In the west wing, Your Grace. The Blue Room and the Lady's Suite."

He nodded. The Blue Room overlooked Balidonough's chapel and was an apt place for the vicar. The Lady's Suite was nearby and was a comfortable choice for Mr. and Mrs. Dunnan.

"I don't know your surname," he said.

"Rowan, Your Grace."

"Thank you, Mrs. Rowan. You've chosen well."

Instead of turning and leaving the room, she hesitated.

She clasped her hands together and addressed him. "I appreciate the fact that you have allowed me to keep this position, Your Grace."

"It was my wife's choice, Mrs. Rowan. Not mine."

She didn't flinch beneath his honesty.

"But you could have as easily revoked her decision."

He nodded, and she left the room. What Glynneth didn't know was that he would have done anything for Catherine, including allowing her to promote the pig farmer as Keeper of the Silver.

Moncrief sat in his library until after sundown, performing those duties that came with being Duke of Lymond. He had decisions to make, and orders to give, all of which needed to be conveyed either to his steward or to his solicitor. The chiming of the clock was the only reminder that he had other duties as well. No one came to his door, no one questioned his delay. Even Peter, who had once been responsible for seeing that Moncrief was where he needed to be when he needed to be there, chose not to interrupt the duke.

Finally, his work done, he strode up the stairs and into his apartment, half-expecting Catherine to be dressed for dinner. Instead, she was asleep, curved around the pillows, one arm draped over them, the other below the counterpane.

He stood at the end of the bed and watched her, thinking that she looked too voluptuous to be in his bed alone. Her curves pressed against the material of her clothing, reminding him of firelit limbs and a body so beautiful that memories of it had never left his mind.

Every night he wanted her, and every morning he desired her, and the pain of it was so constant that he had almost become used to it.

"Catherine," he said, not truly wishing to wake her, but knowing he must. Damn the vicar and Harry's parents while he was at it.

He walked around the bed, bent over her, breathing her name against her ear.

"Catherine," he whispered again, and she slowly roused, blinking a few times, then turning her head as she began to stretch. All movements ceased as she opened her eyes wide, their faces but a few inches apart. In that instant when she went from sleepy pleasure to recognition and wariness, he saw just how great a journey lay between them.

"We have guests," he said, stepping back.

"Who?"

"The vicar and Harry's parents."

She looked surprised. "Why are they here?"

"Evidently, they're curious about your well-being. They want to know that you're here at your own instigation. That I didn't drug you senseless in order to marry you."

"They never had much concern for my well-being at Colstin Hall," she said. "Why now?"

"Perhaps they missed you only after you left. It's a common occurrence. People often don't realize what they have until it's no longer there."

He removed his stock and moved to the bureau. One of the prerequisites of being Duke of Lymond was the fact that he didn't have to wait to be served. The water was hot in the pitcher, the towels had recently been replaced, a piece of fruit and a plate filled with cheeses had been placed atop the bureau to tide him over until dinner. Living at Balidonough was a far cry from the days when he and Peter huddled, nearly freezing, in a makeshift tent with only salted meat as their one meal for the day.

Moncrief washed his face and hands and began to dress for dinner. He removed his jacket, then his shirt, wondering if Catherine was watching. Was she as curious about him as she had been about the book she'd found? Soon he was bare to the waist, and he turned to face her, daring her in his thoughts not to watch him, not to be aware of him as a man.

She was sitting up against the headboard, fingers pressed against her lips, her eyes wide.

He removed his trousers in front of her, and divested himself of his undergarments. If anything, her eyes grew wider. He turned and poured the rest of the hot water into the basin, leisurely bathing himself, all the while intent upon her in the mirror.

She didn't look away.

He turned to face her again, this time drying himself. He took care not to hide any part of his body from her gaze. When his erection began to grow in an expected response to her fascination, he didn't hide that either.

"How would you rank me if I were an illustration?" he asked, keeping his voice steady and disinterested. He dried himself slowly, wondering if she knew that her attention was fixed on the actions of his right hand. He was fully engorged now, aching with desire. But he'd had practice in unrequited lust, since he'd been sleeping nude next to a woman who expressed little interest in that fact for the last two weeks.

Catherine looked dazed.

He walked to the side of the bed and gripped her hand, pulling it to him. Her fingers were hot and damp against his flesh.

"I'm human, Catherine. Not a monster, not a myth. Only a man."

Her hand flattened against his erection.

Where was it written that men were the seducers? He felt less like the instigator of this sweet scene than a lamb led bleating and dumbly happy to the slaughter. Catherine stared at him, her eyes wide as he hardened even further at her touch.

Restraint was a natural circumstance for him. So much so that while his mind urged completion of this long-held fantasy, his body remained immobile. He had never wanted to love her so much or counseled himself against it so fervently.

Slowly, he stepped back and moved away to stand before the armoire.

"Shall I fetch Mary to assist you in dressing?"

She still didn't answer.

"Or shall I do the honors?"

She shook her head from side to side slowly.

He pulled on his dressing gown and jerked on the bell rope. When the footman appeared a moment later, he summoned her maid. Before she could protest, he scooped her up in his arms and carried her to her vanity.

"I don't want you hurting yourself," he said, breathing the words against her ear. She shivered, keeping her attention on her hands resting on the vanity's edge. "Is there anything I can get for you?"

Finally, she spoke, "I'd prefer a little privacy, Moncrief. That's all."

He straightened and moved to his dresser. He brushed his hair with a pair of silver-backed brushes, then selected the clothing he would wear to dinner. He'd not used a valet since Catherine had begun to share his room, and prior to that he'd had to do for himself. But he no longer polished his own boots, although he inspected them well when they were returned by a footman.

A tap on the door signaled the arrival of the maid. Mary curtsied, too low as usual, and he realized that she wouldn't feel comfortable until he was out of the room.

He inclined his head to Catherine, but she wasn't paying any attention, evidently immersed in the study of her own fingers. He bid her farewell and closed the door.

Instantly, the atmosphere in her room altered, became less turbulent and at the same time, paradoxically, less comforting.

Catherine turned and studied the closed door. Only then did she release the breath she'd been holding.

"Your Grace?"

She looked up to face Mary's concerned look. "I'm fine, Mary. Truly."

Was it a sin to lie for a good reason? She was certain it was, just as she was certain that such a lie didn't rank high on the lexicon of her other, more onerous, sins.

As she readied herself for the dinner and the reunion with her former in-laws, Moncrief still remained in her mind. Why had he undressed in front of her? He must know how favorably he compared to the lithographs in that daring book she'd found. He was not as muscled as the Roman soldier, but his buttocks had been more shapely, his erection larger than that of the red-haired man.

Why had he made her touch him?

She stared down at her fingers, still feeling the heat and the hardness of his erection. Her fingers had wanted to curve around it, measure its girth, stroke it from its nest of hair. Pet it.

"Are you feeling well, Your Grace?" Mary asked. Her eyes met those of the young maid in the mirror. "You look flushed. You're not coming down with a fever, are you?"

Catherine shook her head. Not unless the fever was Moncrief, and that was entirely possible.

What sort of man had she married? Although she had never seen him on horseback, she would wager that he was a master horseman. Did he gamble like Harry? She could not envision him spending his money unwisely. And as a commander of men had he been fair and just, and stern when it was necessary?

And as a lover?

Her thoughts stopped abruptly as she censored herself.

He had asked her how she ranked him among the illustrations she'd seen. What would he have thought if she'd told him the truth? Moncrief was more beautiful than any of the illustrations she'd seen. Instead, he reminded her of the statues she'd seen in the garden. Entirely shocking, but beautiful renditions of male beauty. At least the statues had had a fig leaf or two to hide their most intimate assets. It would have taken a veritable branch of fig leaves to cover Moncrief.

She had heard of lascivious women, females who could not control their basic impulses. Every village had a woman whose reputation was soiled, whose less-than-sterling past could dictate the tenor of her future. But Catherine had never, until this moment, thought she might be like one of them.

She stared at herself in the mirror and realized why Mary had thought her becoming ill. Her eyes were gleaming too brightly, and her lips looked swollen. The flush extended over her entire face, not just her cheeks. There were other changes as well that blessedly did not show on the surface, such as the tightening of her breasts and the floating feeling in her stomach.

Did lust feel this way?

Mary had dressed her hair in a flattering style, something with ringlets gathered at the back instead of at the sides. She looked young and vibrant and alive, and instead of a widow, she looked the picture of a bride. Someone eager for night so her wifely duties could begin.

Dear heavens, was she so pagan as to lust after a man because of how he looked naked? Evidently so, because she could not rid herself of the image of Moncrief standing there indolently drying himself. Nor could she forget the touch of him as if her fingers bore the shape of him still.

Abruptly, she stood, turning and thanking Mary for her assistance.

"It's time I greeted our guests."

"But a few more pins, Your Grace—"

"Are not necessary."

Catherine took one foolish step on her injured ankle. A gasp of pain had her abruptly sitting once more.

"I'll call His Grace," the maid said, bowing herself out of the room.

Catherine held up one hand as if to forestall her before realizing there was no other way down the stairs, unless the footmen created a chair of linked arms for her. However, anything might be preferable to Moncrief holding her in her arms.

But that was, nonetheless, how she descended the steps to greet her former in-laws.

Chapter 15

"You will grow tired of carrying me about, Moncrief," she said, as they descended the stairs.

"Only after the first year or so," he said, easily navigating the landing and down the steps.

She glanced at him, then away. It wasn't a good idea to stare too closely into Moncrief's eyes. A woman might get lost in the deep blueness of them.

"I give you leave to carry me the next time I'm injured," he said with a small smile.

"I should need two footmen for certain."

"Perhaps they could carry me about in a barrow, with my legs and arms hanging over the side. When someone asks me what I am doing, I shall simply say that I am losing my consequence, in order to even the circumstances."

She had never joked with Moncrief before, and it was a heady experience. How long had it been since she had laughed? Much too long.

He hesitated at the door of the parlor, and they shared

a look before she turned the handle and Moncrief strode inside.

Juliana was the closest to the door. At their entrance, she looked as if she wished to say something scathing. Ever since the dinner party, however, she'd been restrained in her comments to Catherine. She was not unlike a small child who, having tested his boundaries, is content enough for the moment to remain within them.

"My dear girl, what has happened to you?" Mrs. Dunnan stood in the middle of the parlor, pressing her handkerchief to her mouth. "What tragedy has befallen you, my dearest girl?"

"Nothing but a foolish accident," Catherine said, as Moncrief set her down on the settee. She smiled at him, but the expression that began as a politeness lengthened as her gaze was caught by his.

She heard someone speak, and turned away with difficulty only to be hugged by Mrs. Dunnan, so tightly that Catherine felt as if she were being strangled.

"It has been so very long."

At least five months since they had come to Colstin Hall. At least that long since they'd inquired as to her health or sent word about their own.

She gently pulled away and greeted Mr. Dunnan, who had always been her favorite of Harry's parents.

Moncrief moved away, but she noticed he didn't go far, only to the fireplace located a few feet to her right. His attention was split between the Dunnans and the vicar, his look one that was so easily interpreted that she wanted to caution him that he might wish to be more controlled in his aversion.

When he glanced toward her, she felt the warmth deepen on her cheeks.

"I'm sorry," she said to Mrs. Dunnan, "but what was it you asked me?"

"Your new sister-in-law was commenting upon the footmen," Mrs. Dunnan said almost apologetically.

Catherine waved her hand in the air as if to give Juliana leave to continue with her ceaseless carping. She was the most frugal woman Catherine had ever known. What she didn't realize was that an estate the size of Bali-donough needed to be maintained on a daily basis to prevent even more costly expenditures later. Even Catherine knew that from her stewardship of Colstin Hall, minis-cule in comparison to the castle.

"I was saying," Juliana said, affronted, "that we have too many footmen and maids. I saw one of those girls giggling with one of the footmen the other day. If they were truly busy, they would have no time for such foolish pursuits."

"Perhaps we could discuss it in the morning," Mon-crief said, effectively quelling a subject which was not appropriate before guests. Juliana subsided against her chair, frowning.

Catherine looked at her former mother-in-law. "How was your journey?" The village where she and her husband lived was a short distance away, less than an hour of coach travel at the most.

"Quite pleasant," Mrs. Dunnan responded. "The day was so favorable that we made time to go and place flowers on dear Harry's grave."

Moncrief moved restlessly. Catherine glanced at him, then away.

"As I was saying to Hortensia the other day," Juliana interjected, "there is absolutely no sense in having more than three gardeners. After all, we are entering the winter season, and the gardens are dormant. I cannot see employing servants simply for them to sit around and eat our food, putting their feet up, and enjoying the day."

"His grave was so lovely," Mrs. Dunnan said. "It seems so hard to believe that he's been gone all these many months. Less than a year." She then looked pointedly at Catherine's lavender dress.

Catherine wanted to halt the other woman's reminiscences, since it didn't seem quite proper to wax poetic about Harry in front of Moncrief. However, once Mrs. Dunnan began speaking of her son, nothing seemed to deflect her course.

"I remember how utterly splendid he looked in his regimentals." She sighed and dabbed at the corners of her eyes with a handkerchief. "So handsome a young man. Cut down in his prime."

"Did he have consumption?" Hortensia asked, leaning closer. "I myself have a certain weakness of the lungs. My cough grows deeper in the winter even though I take several herbs and potions. I have half a mind to visit the goodwife in the village to see if she can prepare a poultice for my chest."

Mrs. Dunnan looked nonplussed for a moment. She wadded her handkerchief in one fist and turned to Hortensia. "He was a soldier, a brave hero."

Catherine studied the floor.

"My son deserved to be mourned for longer than a few months."

She glanced up to find Mrs. Dunnan staring at her.

"More money," Juliana said. "More good money after bad, I say."

Catherine smiled at Hortensia. "Would you mind summoning one of the servants to build up the fire? I find that I'm a little chilled."

"You'll have us all destitute within the year," Juliana grumbled. "A little discomfort will strengthen your character."

"I fail to see how chilblains will make me stronger."

"You never used to be such a spendthrift when you were married to Harry."

Moncrief only raised his eyebrow at her, a supremely irritating gesture that had Catherine frowning at him.

"What shall I do, Juliana?" Hortensia asked in that tiny little bird voice of hers.

Catherine refrained from rolling her eyes only by the greatest of wills. What she truly wanted to do was banish them all from the room, but she only smiled, and said, "Ring for a servant, Hortensia." She turned and looked directly at Juliana, almost daring her to countermand her request.

The older woman only sniffed and muttered something about profligacy.

Catherine pressed two fingers to her temples and wondered if the headache that was brewing was going to be as fierce as she feared. She knew better than to mention it for fear Hortensia would recommend all sorts of dubious remedies. Mrs. Dunnan looked as if she were crying again because no one wished to talk about Harry. Juliana, on the other hand, still appeared angry. All the while, Moncrief was wearing that half smile, an impenetrable expression that she couldn't decipher.

If she were truly addicted to laudanum, tonight she would partake of it.

Moncrief was in a surly mood, and he knew it, which kept him silent.

As he had feared, Harry's parents lost no time in singing his praises. Catherine was unresponsive to most of the comments, and unless a question was directed at her, nearly silent.

Every time he saw glimpses of the woman he had come to know through her letters, she retreated back into a shell as if terrified to reveal more of herself. He was beginning to believe that there were two Catherines. One he loved because of her honesty, her wit, and her forthright way of viewing the world, but the other one, a pale shadow who spoke, moved, and responded as if she were only half-alive confused him.

Wallace appeared with a small silver tray of Balidonough whiskey and served it to his male guests. Moncrief was amused to note that the vicar had evidently not eschewed those mortal pleasures in favor of God's love. He picked up the crystal tumbler appreciatively, holding it up to the light before sipping it with relish. Mr. Dunnan was more circumspect, but evidently enjoyed the whiskey as well.

"Very good, Wallace," he said, applauding his new majordomo's initiative as the young man bowed in front of him.

Wallace tried very hard to stifle his smile, but it would have been like hiding the sun behind a wisp of cloud.

After Wallace left the room, Mr. Dunnan turned to Moncrief. "Have you known our Catherine long?"

Moncrief debated for a moment before answering. The tone of this inquisition would be set by his first answer. "Not long," he said easily. "And you? Did you know her a long time before she and Harry married?"

He glanced over at Catherine, who was studying the floor with great concentration.

"Only a few months, I confess. It was a love match. Her father was a very prosperous landowner and Catherine his only child. Consequently," he said, sending a fond smile in Catherine's direction, "she had her choice of bridegrooms."

"He would have refused her no one, I think," the vicar replied. "Although I didn't know the man myself." He sent a sorrowful look toward his glass. "The poor man died before I came to Colstin Hall."

"But you are correct, vicar," Mr. Dunnan said. "The man could deny her nothing. When she decided she wanted Harry, the marriage was made, and they lived as happily as any two people ever have."

"Were you surprised when he joined the regiment?" Moncrief asked, deliberately not looking at Catherine. Nor did he remind them that this glorious union had lasted an entire month before Harry departed Scotland with all possible haste.

Dunnan looked surprised by the question.

"Catherine's father was a dear and giving man." He took another large sip of his whiskey and made an appreciative sound deep in his throat. "Harry did not have the temperament to be a farmer, so the man generously made him a gift of a commission."

"Moncrief was Harry's commanding officer," Catherine said. The comment was said almost in the nature of a goad, but when Moncrief glanced at her, she was still studying the floor intently.

"Were you, indeed, Your Grace?"

"I was only recently released from my commission," Moncrief said. "My brother had died, and I inherited my title."

"Was my son a good soldier?" Mr. Dunnan asked.

Once again Fate maneuvered Moncrief into the position of praising Harry. But he couldn't very well tell the man who looked at him so expectedly and proudly, that the hero, the son, he mourned had been a despicable human being.

"A very fine soldier, indeed," he said, finishing his whiskey in one gulp.

"Did he mention me at all, Your Grace?" Mrs. Dunnan's voice was hopeful. Moncrief was all too aware of that tone. He'd heard it whenever he'd visited a dead soldier's home, and read it in the letters he'd received from parents and loved ones.

"He had a great fondness for his parents," Moncrief said. "Indeed, for everyone he left behind in Scotland."

There, if liars went to hell, he would be leading the procession.

Dunnan looked down into his whiskey, twirling the glass around in his hands. "Which makes it all the more strange, Your Grace, that Catherine would wed so quickly."

"It is an advantageous alliance," Moncrief said, referring obliquely to his title.

Dunnan looked around a room at all the trinkets accumulated over the centuries for the sole purpose of impressing guests at Balidonough. "I can see that, Your Grace," he said slowly. He glanced at Catherine. "But she was devastated by Harry's death. And gave no mention of you."

Moncrief exchanged a glance with the vicar, who had evidently maintained some shred of decency and not divulged the tale of his wedding, candlelit and surreptitious.

"I can assure you that Catherine is a beloved bride," he said, trapped in the position of not telling a lie after all. "I adore her." He turned his empty glass one way or another, watching a droplet of whiskey roll around the bottom.

When the room remained silent, he unwisely glanced at Catherine to find her staring at him. "In that, Harry and I are alike," he said softly.

A half lie, then. Harry loved no one but himself, but again, that was not a comment he could make to a father who was so intent on enshrining his son's memory.

"He was a fine young man," Mrs. Dunnan said. "A kind and a handsome young man who would have warmed any mother's heart. I shall never forget him, even though others have." She didn't look in Catherine's direction, but there was little doubt about whom she spoke.

Moncrief put down his glass and forced a smile to his face. "Regrettably, life is for the living. We can mourn those who have passed, madam, but if we live for them, it's the same as dying."

Mrs. Dunnan's eyes widened, but she said nothing, no doubt unsure of how to respond to being censured by a duke.

Catherine looked away, her flush replaced by a sudden pallor. Good. He wanted to disturb her, wanted to shake her from her widow's weeds and her soft air of constant mourning. He wanted to press her up against the wall and feel every curve of her body, and gauge how it fit against his. He wanted her to feel how hard he grew whenever she smiled in a certain way or brushed against him accidentally, unknowing. Or when she put her arm around his neck and sighed against his chest as he carried her.

He had never, to his knowledge, hinted at his feelings for her, but some part of him wanted to make a declaration, to strip her of the ignorance that surrounded her.

I want you for my wife now and always. I want you in my bed, and I will be content with only a portion of the devotion you've lavished on Harry.

She would no doubt be shocked or clench her hands together and back away slowly as one would from a madman.

When Wallace announced dinner in that newly self-important tone of his, Catherine allowed Moncrief to assist her into the dining room. She insisted upon walking, so he merely wrapped his arm around her waist and allowed her to lean on him so that she needn't put any weight on her bad ankle.

They were pressed so close together, however, that he couldn't help but feel her hip, the brush of her arm, the curve of one impudent breast. If he bent his head just so, he could smell the scent she used and place a quick, surreptitious, kiss on the nape of her neck.

Instead, he did nothing but meet her gaze, and curse Harry to damnation in his mind.

Chapter 16

The wind fought the building, roaring around the ramparts of Balidonough as if it were in the midst of a fierce winter battle, striving for dominance against stone and mortar that had stood for centuries. Catherine could hear the fire spit and hiss in response to the muted roar of an angry wind. The night itself seemed viciously indignant, not a setting to induce peaceful sleep.

Catherine and Moncrief lay in bed together, each staring up at the ceiling. Catherine couldn't help but wonder what he was thinking about, but that was such an intimate question that she couldn't voice it.

"How long will they be remaining with us?" Moncrief asked in the silence. She was relieved to know his thoughts were on their guests and not her.

"I don't know," Catherine said. "Surely not long. It's less than an hour's journey back to their home, not a vast distance."

"I have a suspicion, however, that travel time will have no bearing on the length of their stay."

She turned her head to see his shadow. "I fervently hope you're not correct."

If he was right, she was disheartened. Mrs. Dunnan had a way of making her feel inadequate, and together she and Juliana could make her life at Balidonough miserable. Unless, of course, she busied herself with everyday tasks. But with her ankle, that was going to be impossible. Not impossible, merely inconvenient. She would learn how to walk on the crutches tomorrow, and surely her ankle would get better with each passing day. All she needed to do was to take care on the stairs.

"Did you see Mrs. Dunnan often when you were married to Harry?"

"No," she said, recalling those early days of her marriage. "I can't help but wonder now if Harry forbid her to come to Colstin Hall. I only saw them infrequently. In fact, the last time I saw her was at Harry's funeral."

For a long time neither spoke, and she couldn't help but wonder if Moncrief had fallen asleep.

But then he turned toward her.

"The past can be a burdensome thing, Catherine," he said softly. "Shall we call a truce and pretend, at least, that it does not exist for either of us?"

To pretend that Harry had never been alive? To expunge him from her heart? No Colstin Hall? No memories of her father? No bittersweet recollections of a happy childhood?

"Who should I be," she asked him finally, "if I cannot be myself?"

"Whoever you might wish to be."

"When I was a child, my father was forever calling me a princess. I thought I was one, and that he was a benevolent king who had given up his castle for a small home next to the woods."

"You have a castle here at Balidonough."

"Are you the prince?"

"Why not a king as well?"

She smiled at Moncrief's arrogance even in this playful pretense.

"Very well," she said, "you shall be a powerful king. You've united all the kingdoms and here you reign."

"Then I must have a queen, not simply a princess."

"No," she countered, "princesses have golden hair and ride unicorns. Queens are more serious, like Juliana."

His laughter made her smile.

"There, you've destroyed my illusion with just one name."

"So I did. Then shall we imagine another place? Although I can't imagine a more enchanted castle than Balidonough."

"You like it here?"

"I do," she said, surprised to find it true. "It inspires awe, don't you agree? I haven't yet explored all the rooms, but what I've seen is amazing. If we ever grew tired of this wing, we could choose to settle in the east wing. And there is a marvelous conservatory on the second floor that I discovered a few days ago. All it needs is a little care."

"I'm told my mother loved Balidonough," he said, then added a few moments later, "I'm the one who has destroyed the illusion this time."

She turned toward him. "That's all right. Tell me about her."

"I don't remember anything," he said. "My recollections are secondhand, from my brothers. They told me about her laugh, and said everyone who met her went away charmed. Colin said her hands were always cool and smelled of lilac."

After a few moments of silence, Catherine spoke. "I don't remember my mother, either. My father always told me she was beautiful. And I think she must have been. But, then, he said the same about me," she added, smiling into the darkness.

"But you are."

She rolled onto her back to stare up at the ceiling, wishing he hadn't said such a thing.

"Surely you know that," he said.

She turned her head to look at him. He had risen up on his elbow and was a blur in the darkness, a looming dark shadow that was, somehow, reassuring.

"I am not beautiful," she countered. "But I thank you for the compliment all the same."

"Are you being foolish? I never thought you to be the type to solicit compliments."

"I am not."

"Your eyes are so deeply brown they're almost black. Your nose is perfect; your mouth is full and shapely. Even in repose your face is lovely, but when you smile you're the picture of joy."

"My appearance cannot compare to yours," she said, embarrassed.

He laughed. "Now who's being a flatterer?"

"Surely you see the way the maids look at you when you pass? Even Cook seems to be enamored of you. Why else would she always be sending a tray of tarts to you? If you ate everything she made for you, you'd be as large as a stoat."

"I doubt they see me as a man, Catherine, but simply their duke."

It was her turn to laugh. "You are either very modest, Moncrief, or foolish."

"I doubt I am either," he said stiffly.

She realized in that moment that he was embarrassed, and his discomfiture was another side to him, one she found utterly charming.

"You have a very soft side to you, Moncrief, one that I suspect you do not show to others easily."

He didn't answer her, and for a moment she wondered if she'd gone too far. Had their intimacy, only moments old, been endangered by her frankness?

"I have revealed more to you, Catherine, than to anyone. I wonder why you cannot see it."

She heard him turn again and knew that his back was to her, his repudiation sudden and surprisingly painful. She clutched the sheet with both hands and wished she knew what to say. Finally, the words came to her, and she spoke them, praying they were the right ones. "I want to be your friend, Moncrief. Can we not have that between us?"

"We have so much more than that, Catherine. The pity of it is that you don't realize it."

"I don't understand."

He didn't turn. "I know."

She placed her hand on his shoulder and felt him tense. "It is not wise to touch me at the moment, Catherine."

Slowly, she withdrew her hand, telling herself that she did so in order not to tempt Fate. It was not cowardice that kept her still and silent and wakeful on the other side of the bed.

When he turned to his back, she half expected him to speak, but he didn't. Finally, she pretended sleep to hide her hurt.

"Your breasts sway sometimes when you walk," he said sometime later.

She kept her breath even, a more difficult task than she'd considered, since she could barely breathe at all.

"I've begun to watch for it. I wonder if it's because

Mary doesn't lace your corset tightly. If so, I must commend her. I want to put my hands on the sides of them and feel them against my palms. It has become my abiding curiosity of late."

Her breath hitched, and with great difficulty she kept up the rhythm of a sleeper.

"The other day you were wearing a new dress. Something in that infernal lavender, but the bodice was lower. I had to keep myself from plunging my hand inside and teasing your nipples to hardness."

She didn't move, too afraid to let him know that she was awake and privy to his licentious thoughts. That he had been thinking about her, that he had watched her like that was disconcerting.

"I can't help but remember the night I bathed you."

She closed her eyes tightly as if to banish the sound of his voice. But despite her wishes she had a flash of memory of the warmth of the fire, the sensuous abandon she felt as the laudanum warmed every part of her.

"Hell is remembering that you are my wife, and knowing all too well what you look like and being forced to sleep next to you without being able to touch you."

He sat up and lit the candle on the bedside table. "You can open your eyes, Catherine. I know you're not asleep."

Resolutely, she blinked open her eyes. "How did you know?"

"Sleepers rarely blush," he said.

Catherine turned to find him standing there naked just as he had been this afternoon.

She swiftly clamped a hand over her eyes, but he was still imprinted on her lids. He was wearing neither a dressing gown nor underclothes. His shoulders were wide, his chest broad, and his legs long and lean.

She heard the sound of him moving and allowed herself to peek behind her hand. He had turned and was bending for his dressing gown. Dear Lord, he had muscles even on his backside.

Her hands slithered down to cup her nose as she stared. She had been unable to stop thinking about him all evening. Now he gave her time for a more leisurely inspection.

"Do you never wear a nightshirt?"

"No, never."

"Is it entirely healthy to sleep naked?" She had never seen a man as gloriously fit as Moncrief.

"Have you never slept without a nightgown?" he asked. She shook her head.

"Perhaps you should." He pulled on his dressing gown. "I would give half my fortune to know what you're thinking right at this moment."

No one had ever thought to ask her such a question. For a moment, she was more startled by his curiosity than by her thoughts. But when her eyes traveled slowly up his form to meet his gaze, she felt her blush intensify.

"Is it necessary that I tell you?"

"I do not command your thoughts, Catherine."

She was not that much a ninny that she would have confessed to him that he was quite the most beautiful specimen of man she'd ever seen. She pushed away the thought—disloyal as it was—that he was taller and broader than Harry. Dearest Harry had not been so . . . firm.

But she was no coward either, and as the minutes stretched between them, she took his unspoken dare. "I was thinking that you must be very active to be so fit."

He stood with his hands at his sides, the dressing gown open, simply regarding her. She wanted to tell him to tie the belt at least, to overlap the material, perhaps. Or turn, if those actions were beyond him. Had he no modesty?

An imp of a thought whispered that he was so beautifully formed that it was a shame for him to be covered.

Finally, blessedly, he did tighten the belt, obscuring his most impressive attributes. Not, however, before his penis had begun to lengthen and harden.

"Does it always do that?" she asked, staring at the tent forming in the front of his dressing gown.

"I do not command it, either."

He turned his back to her, and she had the feeling that he was embarrassed. With Moncrief, it was difficult to be certain.

"I will ask Juliana to move from the Duchess's Chamber in the morning. We needn't share a bed any longer."

He didn't give her time to respond, merely opened the door and immediately shut it behind him.

What about his time limit? What about her wifely duties? Had the arrival of Harry's parents done what her mourning had not?

She sat up and frowned at the door. Would she ever understand Moncrief?

Chapter 17

⌒～◌◌～⌒

The next week was dismal. Worse than dismal, in fact, with as many different difficulties as Catherine could imagine all compressed into one seven-day period.

She learned how to get around on crutches and did so with determination but not much grace. She wasn't fast enough, despite her practice, to escape Mrs. Dunnan. The woman insisted upon following her around to the extent that not one single room was a haven, except, of course, Moncrief's library. Mrs. Dunnan dare not invade that sanctuary, but neither did Catherine. Ever since that last night they'd shared a bed, he'd been very cordial but very distant.

Perhaps it was better that way, but she couldn't dismiss the niggling sense of sadness that trailed after her. This time, however, it had nothing to do with Harry.

Added to her wretchedness was the fact that Juliana evidently suspected she was spending money, and consequently either watched Catherine closely herself, or sent Hortensia to follow her about. Catherine felt more and more like a mother duck with a bevy of ducklings tagging along behind her, some more surreptitiously than others.

To make things worse, Hortensia had developed a rash, the cause of which was either the lavender water Catherine suggested the laundry maids use to rinse the sheets, or the salve someone had given Hortensia to ease her aching knees, or something she'd eaten. She would not cease telling anyone not fast enough to escape about the pustules that covered her body. The last time she'd done so, Catherine had grabbed her crutches and limped away, only to find Hortensia following her.

Catherine had moved into the Duchess's Chamber to find that the room was as daunting in its way as the Duke's Chamber. The bed jutted out into the middle of the room, shielded by a noxious-looking drapery in a shade of green Catherine had never before seen. In fact, everything was green, from the floor covering to the tapestry behind the bed. Even in daylight the room was dim, as if seen through a murky pond, and the bed was entirely too large.

All in all, it was a very disturbing week, and it was no wonder that she was at her wit's end come Saturday. She ordered a hot and relaxing bath and even that was interrupted by Juliana complaining about the time it took two of the maids and two of the footmen to fill the tub, and the cost of the bath salts she had used, and the twice-milled soap from France.

So on this night, exactly a week after the Dunnans had arrived with the vicar, she was annoyed, tired, and feeling entirely inhospitable.

The men had rejoined them from their time of smoking cigars and drinking their after-dinner whiskey. The air of conviviality among the three was annoying, to say the least. The vicar had not, as he was wont to do with her, brought up one single scripture in the time he'd been at

Balidonough. He didn't seem entirely like the vicar at all, but a portly replica of himself, a man who insisted upon being called Thomas, and one who spent entirely too much time smiling. He and Moncrief seem to get along well, as did Mr. Dunnan.

The ladies were not nearly as amenable.

Hortensia sat, as she usually did, to the right of Juliana. She had retrieved her needlepoint and now sat demure as a mouse. But Catherine knew Hortensia listened avidly to any conversation around her, and she didn't doubt that the older woman was the source of much of the servants' gossip about the family.

"I do think it's very pleasant in here, Catherine." Hortensia smiled timidly at her.

"It's too warm. We're burning too much coal."

Catherine didn't bother responding to Juliana.

Mrs. Dunnan took a chair by the fire. "I think we should indulge in creature comforts as long as possible. Who knows how long we have before Death himself visits us?"

"I agree," Hortensia said, turning and facing the older woman. "One never knows how long one has to live." She placed her needlework on her lap and devoted her entire attention to Mrs. Dunnan.

Mrs. Dunnan shot Catherine a look, one that managed to be both accusatory and pitiful. "My dearest son died too young. He had the whole of his life before him. He might have been a father if he survived. I can see his children in my mind." She began to weep into her handkerchief. "But I shall never see them in the flesh now."

Moncrief poured himself more whiskey and sat back in his chair contemplating it.

Mr. Dunnan and the vicar were discussing the weather. The clouds promised snow, and Catherine fervently hoped the weather would hold since icy roads would be an excuse for the Dunnans to remain at Balidonough. As for the vicar, shouldn't he be missing his church, and shouldn't his congregation be missing him?

"What was that wonderful beef dish we had at dinner?" Hortensia asked. "It was very tasty. And that sauce was so rich that I can still taste it now."

"It contained too much cream, and the beef was too expensive."

Catherine sighed. "I will not charge you for the dinner, Juliana."

In the silence that reigned over the next few moments, Catherine had ample opportunity to chastise herself for her rudeness. The fact was, however, that she didn't feel the least remorseful about what she'd said. Instead, she fixed a stare on Juliana that dared her to comment. Mrs. Dunnan looked down at her hands, an identical pose to the one Hortensia had instantaneously assumed.

"I don't know what's come over you, Catherine," Mrs. Dunnan whispered. "You were never so rude when you were married to Harry. He would have been mortified at your behavior."

Catherine kept silent, but only for a moment. "I cannot remember a time when Harry was alive that you were so solicitous of his well-being."

Mr. Dunnan stood, moving toward his wife as if to protect her.

"In fact, I do not believe I have ever seen you at Colstin Hall since Harry died," she said, unable to halt her own words. It was as if some demon inside her was speaking despite her will. She looked helplessly at Moncrief but he, that fiend, was smiling.

The vicar strode forward, one hand outstretched as if to physically place a hand over her mouth. But she ignored him.

"I'm sorry to be so outspoken, but it is nothing more

than any of you have subjected me to over this past week. I have been regaled with tale after tale after tale of Harry as if he were an angel." She heard Moncrief mutter something beside her and vowed to ask him what he said later. For now, she was facing a group of people who were staring at her as if she'd lost her mind.

"Hortensia," she said, addressing her comments to that woman, "I beg of you, do not tell me another tale of woe. I do not want to hear of your lumbago or your arthritis, or any disease of the blood you suspect you might have. And please, I beg of you. I do not want to hear of your rash.

"Juliana, I have had enough of your eternal carping. I suggest you take up residence in a nunnery and give up all your worldly goods and spend each day in prayer. The vicar can no doubt help you find a place that needs your talents in thrift."

Juliana blessedly did not say anything in response, merely fixed a look of such animosity on her that might, at any other time, singe her to the floor. At this particular moment, however, Catherine was too angry with the whole lot of them.

Everyone but Mr. Dunnan. Poor man, he had done nothing but accompany his wife to Balidonough.

"Mr. Dunnan," she said softly, "do you not think it is time you and your wife go home?"

He looked rather shamefaced at her words, but remained silent, only placing his hand on his wife's shoulder as if to restrain her.

"Catherine," Moncrief said softly in remonstration.

She glanced over at Moncrief. He was still smiling, but his eyes looked wary now. He should count himself fortunate that she only sent him an annoyed look before leaving the room.

Catherine made it up the stairs and to her room with some difficulty and Wallace's help. The young man held her left elbow while she gripped the banister and took one halting step after another. All in all, it was easier to have Moncrief carry her, but she would die before admitting that.

She thanked Wallace and closed the door behind her with relief. If Moncrief knew what was good for him, he would avoid her this evening. She was in no mood for smoldering glances or confusing conversation. She wanted to be left alone, not to think on her sins as the vicar might suggest, but to simply be free of thoughts. Tonight she didn't even want Harry's letters.

She was heartily tired of everyone, living or dead.

A timid knock made her sigh with exasperation. She made it back to the door and opened it only to find Mary standing there.

"Wallace told me you had retired, Your Grace. I was wondering if you needed help with your gown."

Of course she did, and how foolish of her not to have thought of it. She opened the door to the maid. "If you would just unfasten me in the back, please Mary, that will be all."

She turned to allow Mary to unlace her.

"What about your hair, Your Grace?"

"I'll brush it myself," she said.

"If you're certain, Your Grace."

"I am not good company right now. I am, in fact, likely to snap at anyone who is unfortunate enough to cross my path."

"Should I arm myself with one of the shields from the Great Hall?"

Catherine closed her eyes and let out a sigh. "Moncrief, go away."

"You have a penchant for telling me that, Catherine."

"You have a penchant for ignoring me."

"Perhaps if you gave me another type of order?"

"I feel compelled, in this instance, to repeat the one I already gave you. Go away."

Mary made a small sound behind her, and Catherine gritted her teeth. She had never before spoken to him in such a way in front of the servants, but it could not be helped.

"That will be all, Mary," he said kindly, and the young maid escaped through the door faster than lightning.

"I take it you are still annoyed?"

"Tonight is not a good night for any kind of confrontation."

"Why should we confront each other? I thought we had become friends, if nothing else."

"Friends? Do friends glower at each other the way you do at me?" She whirled, forgetting about her ankle, and let out of gasp of pain.

He came to her side, but she pointed one arm imperiously at him, a forefinger digging into his chest. "Stay where you are, Moncrief. I can deal quite well with such a simple injury. I need no cosseting, and I certainly don't need you to pick me up and carry me somewhere. Just leave me alone."

His smile slipped a little, and his eyes grew harder. She might have realized what his next words would be if she had been paying more attention to his mood rather than to her own.

"What are you going to do, Catherine? Retire to your bed with one of Harry's letters?"

She pressed her fingers over her eyes and wished him away. But Moncrief was a stubborn, intractable, obtuse, annoying man who never left when she wanted him gone.

"Leave Harry out of this," she said, annoyed with everyone who had mentioned his name in the last week. It was one thing to mourn her husband, quite enough to hear his praises sung at least a thousand times by his mother.

"I'm surprised you haven't asked for me to unearth his coffin and have it buried here at Balidonough. Better yet, why not inter him in the chapel? That way you can go and visit him every day without having to expose yourself to the elements."

When she didn't respond, he continued, his tone leaving no doubt of his anger. "Shall we have a ceremony? Unearth the bastard, and have him laid out on the dining room table? All of you can wail and gnash your teeth and rend your garments for the hallowed Harry."

She should have told him, perhaps, that she was as heartily tired of hearing Harry's name as he was, but something about that last comment made her glance at him curiously.

"You didn't like Harry, did you?"

When he simply stood there, his intense blue eyes unreadable, she knew she was right.

She moved a few feet away, drawing closer to the fire. Moncrief, she was grateful to note, remained where he was.

"If you disliked him so much, why did you call upon me? Wasn't that carrying your sense of duty a bit far?"

Moncrief didn't answer.

"Peter didn't like Harry either. Why?"

"There wasn't much about Harry to like," Moncrief said, before turning and striding toward his door.

"You can't leave now," she said. "You can't simply say something like that and then just leave."

"Can't I?"

"I never took you for a coward, Moncrief."

He stopped where he was, his back rigid.

"Why didn't you like Harry?"

"Don't ask me, Catherine, unless you're prepared to hear the answer."

She balanced herself against the mantel, holding on to

it with one hand and the crutch with the other, as if it were a weapon that she needed to protect her right at this moment. A premonition, as strident as Juliana's voice, warned her that she shouldn't ask him, shouldn't listen. They had gone too far, however, to stop now.

"Tell me." To soften the edge of the demand she added, "Please."

He turned and faced her, his face carefully wiped of any expression. "He was a womanizer, a liar, and he enjoyed killing."

She held on to the crutch so tightly that she could feel the wood soften in her grip.

"If he hadn't been at war, I'm sure he would have murdered someone sooner or later. He had a bloodlust that was unnatural. Harry never took a man prisoner when he could just as easily kill him."

"A womanizer?"

Moncrief looked straight at her, his face somber. "He bedded half of Quebec. If a woman wasn't willing, it really didn't matter to Harry."

At her silence, he continued. "He never told the truth when a lie could suffice."

"How did he die?" She wasn't the least surprised that the words came slowly. She was surprised that she could speak at all.

Instead of answering, he turned his head and stared out the window, retreating into silence with such alacrity that she couldn't help but wonder if it was a place of refuge for him.

"Why did you come to see me? Duty? Guilt?"

He still didn't speak.

"Did you kill him? Was your hatred of him so great that you killed him?"

Could a heart stop? She felt as if hers had while she waited for him to answer her.

Finally, he spoke. "I didn't like him, but I didn't kill him."

"How did he die?"

"He was shot by his lover's husband. In the man's bed."

Silence ticked between them, measured by the absurdly loud sound from the mantel clock. Why had she never before noticed how annoying it was?

"Thank you," she said, finally.

He studied her, and for the length of his perusal, she stood upright and tall forgetting about the pain in her ankle or the pain in her heart. What was important at this moment was her dignity. Somehow, it was vital that she face down Moncrief with all the resolve she had.

"You don't believe me."

She couldn't. If she did, her entire life had been a lie, or at least the best and most precious parts of it.

"I should not have spoken."

She shook her head, the effort nearly beyond her.

His blue eyes were softened by concern. The moments slowed as she wanted to shout for him not to reveal the depth of his compassion, because it proved his words true. As the silence lengthened she felt as if it were a signal, ending something, like the last tick of a failing clock or a final lamp being extinguished.

Her chest hurt, and felt heavy, as if an hour or two of unwept tears lay there waiting.

Moncrief had to go, and now. Her composure was tenuous and not long-lived.

"Please leave," she said, trying to couch the request is politely as possible. It was not, after all, his fault that she simply wanted to die at this moment.

"I don't want to leave you alone."

"But you must."

He strode to her side and cupped her face. "I should not have said anything."

"Why did you not, before?" she asked, looking up at him. She felt only pain seeing the kindness in his eyes. "How foolish I must seem to you."

"Why is it foolish to love someone? Regardless of Harry's sins, you loved him."

She pulled away and faced the fire. In this room, Juliana's thriftiness had not won out. Catherine had a fire lit against the winter chill, but right now it was unable to warm the cold she felt inside.

"May I tell you something strange?" His hand on her shoulder was a comfort and encouragement enough to continue. "I fell in love with Harry through his letters."

His hand moved, his fingers stroking the back of her neck softly, so softly it elicited a chill. But she didn't tell him to cease. Her connection to the world seemed to be from that single touch. If he moved away, she would lose herself in a maelstrom of pain and regret.

"I loved what he wrote, and the depth of his thoughts, and his ideas. I could read his descriptions of North America and Quebec over and over again and it felt as if I was there beside him. I realized that I didn't know him well when he went off to join the regiment, you see. But I grew to know and love him through his letters."

She glanced over her shoulder at him. His hand had fallen to rest at his side. She turned and touched his arm, needing that connection.

"That's why I hold them in such high esteem. Because they are Harry to me. I sought his counsel when things became difficult at Colstin Hall, and he never once failed to offer me good advice. I told him things that I had never told another living soul, and I thought he treated those confidences as if they were treasures."

"A man is more than what he writes. Words are only a measurement of minutes, a way of holding a thought, a question."

She looked up at him. "But how could he have been both thoughtful and horrid? How can you love someone you don't even know?"

He didn't answer her. What could he have said, after all?

"Please," she said, exhaling deeply. "Please go."

She heard the door close behind her and wanted to call him back again. She'd never felt so desperately alone.

Chapter 18

Moncrief stood at the window, his fist clenched, knuckles pressing hard against the pane. Without too much effort, he could have shattered the glass. What would that prove? That there were other things in the world as brittle as his mood, perhaps?

She'd fallen in love with a man through his letters, a bittersweet revelation that was surprisingly painful.

I am your ghost, Catherine. Words he should have said. Words that would have also been profoundly unwise. She needed time between her disillusion and the realization that love waited for her, patient and unceasing. Or perhaps not so patient.

He heard the door open and didn't bother to turn, since he'd been waiting for her. He probably would've done exactly what she was going to do now. Upon reflection, she'd decided not to believe him. Harry would remain a gilded saint, and Moncrief the usurper.

"You didn't lie to me, did you, Moncrief?"

He didn't turn, speaking to his night darkened reflection instead. "No, I didn't lie."

"Did he love her? The woman he died with?"

He closed his eyes, unprepared for that question. What a fool he'd been. Of course she would want to know.

"I don't know," he said, then recalled the conversation he and Harry had at Pointe Levis.

They were sitting on a hill waiting for darkness when they would, along with the whole of the regiment, ascend the sheer cliffs surrounding Quebec. Major General Wolfe's audacious plan might very well lead to his death, but Moncrief had faced that thought on more than one occasion.

"Did you ever think to find yourself on the other side of the world, Colonel?" Dunnan asked, playing with a few pebbles at his side.

"I go where the regiment goes."

"Shame I didn't refuse when I was offered my commission. But then, it was a solution to a few problems I was having."

Moncrief turned his head and looked toward Dunnan.

"Do you regret joining the regiment?"

Harry laughed. "No, it's been a fine adventure. But I sometimes miss home." A moment passed in silence, then Dunnan spoke again. "Do you believe in love, Colonel?"

"I suppose I do, why?" Moncrief said, feeling his way through the words as if dodging cannon fire.

Harry turned to face him. "A sentimental emotion, love." A pause, then he spoke again. "I find myself in love, Colonel, and it's a colossal jest." He smiled. "I'd never thought to feel this way, you know, I miss her more every damn day. I can't quite fathom it myself."

Moncrief hadn't answered, and a few moments later, they had parted company. He hadn't seen Captain Dunnan until after the victory celebration.

But that was not the sort of conversation one could relate to a wife and especially not to a widow.

"I don't know," he repeated, wishing he could give her more than that.

How vulnerable she looked at this moment, how young and untouched.

"Did he really treat his horses badly?"

"Where did you hear that? Peter?"

She nodded.

"Harry didn't care for anything or anyone quite as much as he cared for Harry."

Do not question me further. Thankfully, she didn't. She turned and walked toward her door.

"You must have pitied me a great deal to make me your wife."

He whirled and stared at her. "I did not marry you for pity's sake."

"Why did you marry me, Moncrief?"

For love, but she wouldn't have understood that answer.

"Must I justify my actions, Catherine?"

"So speaks the duke."

"You are a duchess, and tonight, in the parlor, you were as arrogant as one."

He thought he saw the ghost of a smile on her lips and was glad for it.

She stood in the doorway and lifted her eyes to the ceiling. "Moncrief, I feel like such a fool."

"You should not," he said, wishing he could do something more to ease her pain.

"Can love just die?"

"Sometimes time helps," he said, resorting to platitudes.

"What about the woman you loved, Moncrief? Have you ever gotten over her?"

No. I never shall.

The room was rife with secrets, almost pulsating with

them. Thankfully, she didn't pursue the subject, and he was left with silence.

He did something, then, that he didn't expect of himself. He went to her and placed his arms around her stiff shoulders. His fingers smoothed over her black wrapper, his hands running from the rounding of her shoulders to the violin curve of her back, a delectable and seductive undulation of feminine flesh, awash in a cloud of warm scent.

He didn't think himself steeped in either probity or prayer although he tried to live a life defined by some moral tenets. But Moncrief found himself oddly moved standing here with Catherine in his arms, as if God had granted him his most secret wish.

His hands linked at the small of her back, a light restraint in case she wished to move away. But for long moments she remained there, her head buried in that place between his neck and shoulder, her breath warm against his throat.

A rhythm began to erupt softly between them, something fed from trembles and barely admitted insecurities. They swayed together as if brushed by a gentle wind, both holding on to the other.

The touch of her body against his was not so much spark to tinder as it was water to parched soil, a gentle rain of feeling that nourished him at the deepest level. He pulled her even closer, the heat and touch of her too much to resist.

He should tell her now that Harry never penned those letters to her. Perhaps she would understand if he told her how it had happened, his vast loneliness, the temptation of her words. Before he could say the words, she stepped back, brushing her hair from her face. Her eyes were red from wept tears, the tip of her nose pink.

"Good night, Moncrief."

"Good night, Catherine." He dropped his arms and stepped back. *Stay.* But he remained silent and simply watched her when she left the room.

Catherine made her way carefully to the small bench at the end of the bed and studied Harry's trunk.

She remembered the day at Colstin Hall when it had finally arrived, weeks after word of Harry's death. Unpacking it had taken hours, because she'd wept over every single item, tokens of a life too short. She had thought then that there should have been more, some indication of his interests: books and copies of her letters, maps, a ledger, a journal, his favorite inkhorn. Now she knew that the nearly empty trunk was an indication of Harry's character.

Slowly, she bent down and turned the key in the lock, pushing open the lid so that it rested against the end of the bed. In the top tray she'd put the letters he'd written her, storing them carefully by week and month so that she would have a chronological trail of their correspondence.

Harry had never loved her. His letters had been foolishness, a way to placate the heiress at home. The thoughts circulated in her mind, but her heart found it so difficult to believe that the man who'd written these letters could have been so perfidious.

If he stood before her, what would Harry say to such an accusation? Would he give her that grin of his and call her name in Gaelic as he sometimes did? Or would he stand there solemn and handsome, the way he looked the day he left for the regiment?

She stood and walked to the fire with a handful of letters in each hand. One by one she consigned each to the flames, remembering the contents after so many weeks and months of having read them again and again and again.

Would she ever be able to forget? Or forgive?

My dearest Catherine,

One of my friends died today and I am finding it difficult to salute death with the insouciance I normally greet it. We have been fortunate in this campaign to lose only two men. One was by way of an accident, and the other was from illness. Daniel, however, was killed by a musket ball from a French camp. I didn't see his assailant and it would not have mattered in any event who his killer had been.

If anything should happen to me, my dearest, please remember that in the twilight of my mind I thought of you. With my last breath I smiled, thinking of you, your words, your wit, the essence of Catherine. Somewhere, I will be protesting God's decision. Then, when brought before St. Peter, I will give him your name as the reason I am loath to leave my life.

She folded the letter once and once again before tossing it into the fire, watching as it burned. When Harry had died, it wasn't with thoughts of her on his mind. Instead, he had been loving another man's wife.

How could there be two Harrys? One she loved, and the other a man she could not admire or respect?

Her conscience reminded her that it had been this way from the beginning.

Harry had charmed her with his wit, with his determined pursuit of her. Until he'd come into her life, she'd lived a solitary existence, alone with her father, involved with life at Colstin Hall. She'd been captivated by Harry, exhilarated by the attention he'd shown her.

But he'd never been happy at her home, never been content with sharing her life. Even before they'd been married a month, she'd sensed it, seen the look of yearning in his eyes.

She hadn't been that sorry to see Harry leave, not with the strain of taking care of her father, and the added responsibilities of the farms. A sin, the vicar had called it, her inability to accept the man she'd married.

When Harry's letters had come, she'd felt released, as if she'd been given a reprieve from her guilt. The man who wrote her had been different, somehow, more caring, more sincere. She felt as if she'd truly not known him until their correspondence.

But he'd only written her lies, hadn't he?

Her tears fell onto the letters, but this time it wasn't loss or loneliness or grief or pain that caused them, but something infinitely more selfish. She wept for her illusions, for loving when it was not returned, for being unwise enough to give her heart so completely to someone who didn't deserve it.

Now she wasn't so much a sinner as a fool.

She walked back to the trunk and continued systematically throwing every single letter in the fire. When there was nothing but ashes left, she closed the lid of the trunk. Perhaps she'd give it to the Dunnans. Harry's mother could make a shrine of its contents, or consign it to the stables for all she cared.

Anything but let it remain in her sight, a reminder of what never was.

Chapter 19

The next morning, Catherine sat at the vanity staring at her reflection while Mary attempted to do something with the tangles in her hair.

There were dark circles beneath her eyes, a testament to her nearly sleepless night. But her appearance didn't matter as much today as her actions. First, she needed to apologize to her guests for her tirade the night before. Secondly, she would have to find a way to get through this day and the day after, and the day after that and for as long as God decreed she would live.

Since she had sent the maid away, the fireplace was still filled with ashes, the only indication that Harry's letters had ever existed. That, and her memory of them.

What had Moncrief said? *A man is more than what he writes. Words are only a measurement of minutes, a way of holding a thought, a question.*

Who had Harry been, then, if not his words? She realized she would never know.

A knock disturbed her reverie, and she turned toward the door as Mary opened it. Glynneth entered the room, her usually unexpressive face showing traces of worry.

"Did you know your guests were leaving?"

"Yes," Catherine said. If they had been alone, she might have said more, but after last night, Catherine had decided it was better to act a little more circumspect.

"They seem to be in a great deal of hurry."

Catherine only nodded.

She let Mary finish with her hair, then stood and grabbed her crutches. Only one good thing had transpired over the last few days, and that was the fact that her ankle felt much better. A day or two more and she was certain to be able to walk without assistance.

Glynneth assisted her by holding the crutches as they descended the steps and standing in front of her so that she could place her left hand on her shoulder for support while she clutched the banister with her right.

Mr. Dunnan and his wife were clustered in the foyer, along with Juliana and Hortensia. The vicar was standing to the side speaking with Moncrief. Catherine deliberately looked away from both men. She didn't want to be lectured by the vicar about charity, and she didn't quite know how to act around Moncrief.

He had been angry when discussing Harry. She'd seen his fists clench and the muscle in his cheek tighten, which only happened when he was biting back his words. And he had been kind. She could still remember standing within his embrace, a wordless comfort that had made her feel less lonely, less foolish.

Moncrief, whom she'd once pictured as a villain, had become her knight and Harry, the devil. Catherine felt as if she'd been placed inside a ball and spun downhill. Whenever she was certain which way was up, she was tossed around again.

I didn't marry you for pity's sake.

Then why had he married her?

As she walked slowly toward the group, they disbanded, Mr. and Mrs. Dunnan walking through the front door Wallace opened. She and the young man exchanged a glance and a smile that Catherine knew wasn't entirely proper. But she didn't reprimand him, since it was the first friendly greeting she'd been given since coming downstairs.

When she glanced at Juliana, the other woman turned away. Hortensia sniffled into her handkerchief and mumbled something in response. Catherine stepped out into the bright winter morning, finding that the air was as chilly as the atmosphere she had just left.

She would have been a hypocrite to pretend to be sorry to see their guests go, especially since she'd suggested that it was time for them to leave. But she did regret her rudeness, and the hurt she caused other people.

Had she gone daft last night?

Perhaps. Or perhaps she'd simply been pushed to the edge of the barrier that keeps people from being rude to each other. She had seen that line called politeness or good breeding or any other term, and gleefully, and childishly, stepped over it. There was no excuse for her behavior, and now the only thing she could do was remain polite during the leave-taking.

"I trust you will have a safe and enjoyable journey," said Catherine, clutching her shawl closer to her.

Mr. Dunnan nodded, but Mrs. Dunnan would not look at her. Knowing what she did now, Catherine could only feel pity. Of the two of them, Mrs. Dunnan's dedication to Harry was greater than hers.

"Forgive me," she said, stretching out her hands. But she wasn't surprised when Mrs. Dunnan took a step away rather than touch her.

Perhaps it was better their relationship ended here.

They were bound to grow apart with time, but instead, Catherine's words, and Moncrief's revelations, had severed their tenuous bond.

She smiled at Mr. Dunnan in farewell and turned to find Moncrief standing there.

"Cook has prepared a meal for your journey," he said, signaling to Wallace. The young man carried a basket to the coach and placed it inside on the floor.

"Thank you for your generosity," Mr. Dunnan said, pointedly speaking only to Moncrief, his gratitude echoed by his wife.

"And for your hospitality," she said.

Moncrief nodded, every inch the duke.

The vicar was in animated conversation with Glynneth. Whatever he was saying did not appear to meet with her approval because she shook her head several times. No doubt he had declared that Catherine was going to perdition because of her behavior of last night. Or perhaps he was soliciting another donation to his church.

Catherine was grateful Moncrief now handled her money. Let the vicar go to Moncrief for a solicitation. She doubted he'd be as generous as Catherine had been over the years.

Finally, Glynneth turned and walked into Balidonough, leaving the vicar to say his farewells to Catherine and Moncrief.

"Have a safe and quick journey," Moncrief said, walking with the vicar to the coach, thereby preventing him from speaking to Catherine. He looked displeased, but he mounted the steps and allowed Moncrief to close the door.

Juliana and Hortensia said their farewells and went back inside the castle. Moncrief returned to her side.

"Thank you. I don't know what I would have done if he'd begun to lecture me."

"After last night, I doubt he would have been brave enough to do so," he said, teasing her. She managed a smile in return.

For a few moments, she and Moncrief stood watching as the coach slowly moved down the gravel drive. Catherine knew she would probably never see the Dunnans again.

Why had they come? To assure themselves of her health and well-being, or somehow to ensure that Harry's memory would not fade in her mind? If they only knew how very much she wished it would, and quickly.

She felt a touch on her shoulder. Moncrief had a habit doing that, allowing his finger to stray to the back of her neck, touching her where her skin was exposed.

Today she wore black, and she wanted to apologize for it, but her wardrobe held nothing else. Her two lavender dresses were more suited for evening. She would go to the seamstress this morning and request additional day wear, something in blue, perhaps, or another bright color.

His hand flattened against her back, trailing from her neck to her waist in a slow up-and-down movement that was somehow comforting.

In a strange way, she felt as if this was the first day she'd ever spent at Balidonough. The dawn had seemed sharper this morning, a knife's edge of orange and red upon the horizon. The air was cold and clear. Even the sensation of Moncrief touching her felt more real, as if she had experienced but never consciously accepted it before now.

"I was rude to them," she said, watching the coach until it became a small dot on the drive. Balidonough was such a huge estate that it would be some time before they drove through the main gate. Before that occurred, she would lose sight of the carriage.

"Yes, you were. But people are rarely perfect, Catherine."

He never offered her platitudes or lies, for that matter.

"Still, it was not well-done of me." She turned toward him and placed her hand flat against his chest to his obvious surprise. She didn't touch him often, but she needed to at this moment.

She could feel the bulge of muscle below the fine wool of his coat. Today he was attired in dark blue and it only brought out the brilliance of his eyes. A woman could stare into Moncrief's eyes and lose herself. Instead, Catherine studied the gravel at her feet.

He pressed his hand down on hers, warming her.

"We should go in," he said. "You're getting chilled."

She nodded and adjusted the crutches beneath her arms. "I am getting so much better with this, which is a pity because I doubt I'll need them in a day or so."

"How does your ankle feel?"

She stuck out her foot for him to see. Her ankle was not nearly as discolored, and the swelling had gone down considerably.

"Should you not have it wrapped?"

"Perhaps," she admitted. "But I was in such a hurry to get downstairs that I didn't think about it."

There were both staring at her foot when she heard the noise. Moncrief looked up, then swore violently. In the next instant, he had launched himself at her and thrown her to the ground. He was on top of her, shielding her with his body when the mortar and bricks tumbled around them. Clouds of dust transformed the air to a white cocoon. Catherine hid her face against Moncrief's coat, the two of them holding on to each other until the low, rumbling sound above them gradually faded.

She began coughing, and he eased off of her, brushing away the worst of the dust from her face.

"Are you all right?"

She nodded, reaching up and threading her fingers

through his white hair. Her hand rested against his fore-head in an almost tender gesture until she realized what she was doing.

"And you?"

"Better than I expected," he said, looking over his shoulder at the roof.

One of the lions that guarded Balidonough was gone. Instead, the stone fragment was now embedded in the gravel, not far from where they'd stood only moments earlier.

Catherine looked at Moncrief in horror. "It would've killed us both," she managed to say between coughs.

He stood and brushed himself of the worst of the dust. She expected him to give her a hand so that she could rise, but he bent down and scooped her up in his arms as he had so many times in the last few days. She looped her arms around his neck and closed her eyes.

"You really needn't carry me," she said, whispering against his ear.

"I'll put you down as soon as you stop trembling."

"I don't think that's just me."

"A brush with death has a deleterious effect on me."

The door was opening, and Wallace was at their side, his words as unintelligible as Glynneth's a few moments later. Catherine held on to Moncrief's neck and ignored them both.

Instead of climbing the stairs to their chambers, Moncrief walked into his library, turning and addressing Wallace before closing the door behind them.

"What did you say to him?" she asked, as he sat her down on one of the leather chairs.

"That no one should be allowed on the roof until I inspect it."

"You can't think of going up there, Moncrief. Wouldn't it be dangerous?"

"No more so than having part of the roof fall."

"Why did it fall? Is the castle in that much disrepair?"

"Perhaps not," he said, walking to the sideboard. "It could as easily have been deliberate." He poured two glasses of whiskey and returned to her side.

"Do you truly think so?"

She took the tumbler he handed her.

"Good Balidonough whiskey."

"I've never had any."

"I think you'll find it a remarkable restorative."

Catherine took one sip of it and thought that she would never be able speak again. Her throat was rimmed with fire.

"You've changed the subject," she said, when her eyes stopped watering. "Do you think someone meant to harm us?"

"Not us," he said. "You."

Her eyes widened as she stared at him. "Why me?"

"We've never yet found the person who knocked you down in the keep."

"I didn't know you were looking."

"Do you think I would allow my wife to be injured without investigating it?"

"That was simply an accident," she said.

He looked dubious. "Until I investigate further, I don't believe a stone lion falling from the roof is an accident."

"You could be in danger as well, Moncrief. Who would inherit the title if you perished?"

The word was not easily said. In fact, the idea of Moncrief dying was entirely unthinkable. He was such a force, so much himself that it was impossible to think of a world in which he didn't exist.

She gripped the tumbler so tightly she was surprised it didn't shatter, but the multifaceted crystal only produced a pattern on the heel of her hand.

"A second cousin inherits, a man I've met only once. He is a sober gentleman, who spends most of his time cataloging his library."

"He would enjoy the library here."

"I don't intend to allow him the pleasure."

"No, but you might, if you insist on going up to the roof."

"I'll be careful."

She eyed him, thinking that he looked entirely too confident to be climbing the steeply pitched roofs of Balidonough. A little fear wouldn't be amiss. Fear kept people safe.

"Do you promise, Moncrief?"

"If I do, may I elicit a promise from you as well?"

She nodded cautiously.

"Remain in the public rooms. Don't explore Balidonough unless there are at least two people with you."

"You really do think the lion's falling wasn't an accident."

He didn't answer.

"And if it wasn't?"

"I'm going to interview the staff, regardless, something I should have done right after the incident in the keep."

"May I be present?"

"It should be a tedious task, but you're welcome to join me."

"Very well," she said, standing and limping to the door. Her crutches were still in the courtyard unless Wallace had brought them inside. "I will go and wrap my ankle and join you back here in, what, an hour?"

His smile had an edge to it, one that prompted her to add, "If you survive the roof, that is."

"Dare I hope that you have a modicum of worry about me, madam?"

"If you fall and break your foolish head, Moncrief, I will inherit all your money. Or does the family fortune go with the title?"

Moncrief's smile dimmed somewhat. "It does. Except for a widow's portion. A very substantial amount."

"Then do take care on the roof," she said. "Unless you wish to make me an heiress twice over."

Chapter 20

The part of the roof Moncrief wanted to inspect was only accessible through the smaller of Balidonough's attics. He took Peter with him. Both he and Catherine trusted people from their pasts. In her case, Glynneth, and in his Peter.

He'd not been up here since he was a boy, intent on exploring every inch of Balidonough. He had not obtained permission, but it was one of the few occasions in which his father had not learned of his misadventures and, consequently, had not punished him either.

"Wallace has had a great deal of the furniture moved, sir. We've been shuffling it back and forth so Glynneth and Her Grace could look it over."

"Let's hope they made this section a little easier to navigate," Moncrief said, squeezing past a bureau and what looked to be another bed of ducal dimensions.

Moncrief wondered if his ancestors had been like Juliana, thrifty to the extreme. If so, he was the exception.

The money in Balidonough's coffers should be spent on not only protecting the past, such as repairing the crumbling curtain wall, and the west wing foundations in need of repair, but on easing the conditions of the present, like providing a decent place for the servants to live and fires in the fireplaces.

Nor was he going to spend Balidonough's fortune to fuel a foolish dream. Funding the Jacobite cause was not only ridiculous but a century too late.

The attics in this section were built as baffles; one opened into the other. By the time he and Peter reached the end of it, below the edge of the roof, dust was thick in the air.

The trapdoor on the ceiling might have been inaccessible except for one thing—furniture was neatly stacked in a pyramid below it.

"Looks like someone was already up there, sir," Peter said, holding the lantern higher.

"It does." Moncrief climbed up on the large bureau that formed the base of the structure. "When we get downstairs, remind me to ask Wallace who he sent up here."

He reached the top of the structure and easily pushed open the trapdoor. The hinges didn't squeak, and the opening was large enough for him to pull himself through. The door led to a small cupola, shielded from the rain and the sun. An ideal place for someone to wait patiently until his victim was standing below in the courtyard.

A dozen stone lions marched across the front part of the roof, an ornamentation added to Balidonough during the last century. A previous duke, no doubt, had thought them regal and imposing. Now they looked mostly sad, discolored from the elements and stained from bird droppings. Less than an arm's length away was an empty spot where one of the weathered lions had sat. Beside it were several gouge marks in the roof, proof enough that it hadn't fallen accidentally.

Someone wanted them injured, or killed.

He lowered himself, shut the door, and dismounted.

"So it was done on purpose," Peter said, correctly interpreting his look. "But who, sir?"

"Who indeed?" He gave Peter a set of instructions before returning to the library, where he would interview the servants.

As a backdrop, the chamber was a perfect representation of the grandeur of Balidonough. If the room didn't awe the people he would soon interrogate, then his position should. Not only was he Duke of Lymond, but the title carried with it the responsibility of acting as sheriff. As such, he could convene a court wherever or whenever he saw fit. The only true check to the abundance of his inherited power was the essence of his character.

He leaned back in the chair and stared at the vista of Balidonough spread out before him. A weak winter sun bathed the faded grass and sparkled on the surface of the river. Winter had always been a time of sadness to him, as if the world stopped and reflected upon the year just passed. If he did the same, he would laud himself for some decisions and fervently ask forgiveness from a merciful God for the others.

In which category would he place his marriage? A foolish act, but one he could not regret. Especially after last night. *I fell in love with Harry through his letters*. Of a certainty, his life would have been so much simpler if he had just been honest from the beginning. But he had dug a hole so deep for himself he despaired of ever being able to climb free of it.

It would be easier to confess his duplicity if she felt something for him. Gratitude? For destroying her illusions? Until he'd come into her life, she'd made a hero of Harry. For saving her life? She still had no idea how close she'd come to death. For making her a duchess? She was already an heiress and Colstin Hall a prosperous estate. Granted, Balidonough was larger, and her responsibilities greater, but she never seemed awed by her new title or by the castle itself. Friendship? All well and good, perhaps, but the last emotion he felt in her presence was that of friendship.

He wanted her. He wanted her in his arms, in his bed, and in his heart, in an old and dusty place that had been carved just for her. She'd created the spot herself, with her wit and her charm from her letters, and in her person. These last weeks at Balidonough had been both heaven and hell, and he was tired of living in the limbo of his own uncertainty.

She wore a perfume that reminded him of rain-filled spring mornings, and she had a habit of placing her hand on the back of her neck and lifting her hair, a gesture that drove him mad. He wanted to replace her hand with his, and kiss her on the neck, encircling her throat until she tilted her head back and waited, impatiently, for his kiss.

He'd kissed his own wife only twice, and he couldn't forget the promise of it.

Through these last weeks, innocent as a virgin, she smiled at him and came close to flirting. If challenged, she would deny it, he was certain. But her brown eyes peeping out from beneath her bonnet or a wisp of curl when she was formally dressed for the evening were as enticing as any he'd ever seen.

A woman shouldn't look so alluring in mourning. Black suited her, a perfect shade for the creaminess of her skin, calling attention to the curves and hollows of her breasts, and leading him to think of other places he would have given half his fortune to touch.

He had managed to be celibate in the regiment for quite some time. This was a similar exercise. But in the Fusiliers, he'd been surrounded by men, not a beautiful woman who had no idea of her desirability. Or of his desire, for that matter.

Only a day had passed since he'd told her the truth about Harry. Only a day. It was too soon to expect more, to wish for more from her. Not too soon, however, to imagine it.

For a few moments, he indulged in a fantasy of longing. When she entered the room, he would place her on his lap, and if she protested, he would simply silence her with a kiss. One hand would trail below her skirts, not to test the swelling of her ankle but to measure the long line of her shapely legs. He would place his hand gently on her knee and allow his fingers to explore higher, perhaps to test the holding power of a garter before rolling down her stockings.

Even the idea of her stockings was giving him an erection.

Catherine entered the library on that thought, causing him to sit up. A gentleman would have stood at her arrival, but then a gentleman wouldn't have found it difficult to do so right at this moment.

He made a mental note to spur the seamstresses on to finish her wardrobe with a monetary reward. But perhaps he should drop a hint as well that the bodice of any future dresses should be made little differently. They shouldn't be quite so tight.

There was entirely too much woman for the dress.

Or perhaps he wouldn't say anything at all, because he so enjoyed the sight. This morning she'd worn a shawl, but now she didn't. He was absolutely certain she'd dispensed with it on purpose. Her breasts were lifted high, almost as if they were an offering, and he, a pagan god, was more than willing to touch them, to measure them, and to gauge the suitability of the sacrifice.

He was losing his mind.

A result, no doubt, of restless nights in which he couldn't sleep, in which he paced the length and breadth of his chamber, only to stop and glower at her closed door. Unrequited desire was a painful experience. In the last few weeks he had taken more horseback rides, and cold baths, than in all the months he'd spent in Quebec. He ached for war, some reason actually to be belligerent. He wanted to fight someone or destroy something or otherwise act as aggressive as he felt.

A pity Juliana was being so amiable of late.

At that moment, Catherine smiled at him with virtue pasted on her face. He should warn her that it was not wise to goad a hungry beast.

She sat in the chair opposite him and he was grateful for the distance and the depth of his desk between them. At the same time, he wanted her close to him so that he could smell her perfume or reach out to touch her hand. Small impersonal, almost friendly, touches that would keep the raging beast at bay.

He stood and moved the other chair next to his and invited her to sit there. She gave him a quizzical look, but otherwise did not demur, coming to sit beside him with a gentle grace that he found unsettling.

"Are you warm enough?"

"I seem to have left my shawl somewhere."

He pulled on the bell rope behind the desk and immediately Wallace was at the door.

"Yes, Your Grace?"

"See if you can find Her Grace's shawl. If you can't, fetch her another."

"I don't have another," Catherine said softly.

"Then find one."

After Wallace had closed the door, he turned to her. "I know you came to the marriage with your own money, Catherine. More than enough to furnish your own wardrobe. What do you mean, you don't have another shawl?"

"My wardrobe has not been my primary concern of late, Moncrief." She frowned at him. "And before you accuse me of being addicted to laudanum, it was not that."

"Then what was it?"

"Planning the next season's clothing didn't seem important, when I missed Harry so much. But I thank you for your concern."

"I'm your husband, madam, and it is not necessary to thank me so often, as if any kindness I offer you is a surprise. Do you want to know what I found on the roof?"

She gave him a crooked smile. "Of course I do. Every time the wind blew hard I worried it might pitch you to the grass."

He wanted to kiss her just then, for no special reason than she'd smiled at him. Instead, he said, "The lion fell because it had been dislodged from the parapet."

"Deliberately?"

"Deliberately."

She shivered and once again he wished she had her shawl. He stood and removed his jacket, placing it over her shoulders.

"I'm not cold. At least not on the outside. But I am horrified at the thought that someone might have wanted us hurt or killed."

She caught his glance and smiled softly. "Very well, if not us, then me. But why me? As Juliana is fond of saying, I am only a farmer's daughter. The only change to my life of late has been my marriage to you. Perhaps the second cousin should be investigated a little further."

"Or perhaps I should have an heir at all possible speed."

He watched as her cheeks pinkened and wondered if he had embarrassed her with such frankness.

"I'm going to call the servants in one by one," he told her, changing the subject to spare her any further embarrassment. "We'll see if they know anything at all. Shall we begin with Glynneth?"

"Do you think she would have anything to do with this?"

Of all the people at Balidonough, he thought Glynneth might bear watching the most, but he kept that thought to himself.

"She might have seen something."

She nodded.

He summoned Wallace again, and when the young man entered, handed him a list of names. "Call them in one by one. When one leaves, send in the next."

In a few moments Glynneth stood in front of them, dressed in her dark blue housekeeper's uniform. Her golden hair was tucked beneath a small lace-trimmed cap, and she wore a blue apron, spotless as usual.

"Your Grace." She stood with hands clasped and head slightly bowed. Her gaze was on the desk, not on Moncrief, a pose that managed to convey respect and independence at the same time.

At her waist was a large ring of keys that had once belonged to the Duchess of Lymond. Over the years, however, Balidonough had become too large for one person to manage, and the duties of chatelaine had been entrusted to the housekeeper and her staff.

"Did you hear about the accident this morning?"

Glynneth looked confused. "Of course, Your Grace. The lion fell from the roof."

"Did you see anyone approach the attics?"

"No, but I am not on the third floor often." She hesitated. "You're saying it wasn't an accident."

"Where were you this morning? After your conversation with the vicar concluded?"

She stared at him, startled at the accusation. "You can't think I would do such a thing?"

"Someone did, Glynneth, and I intend to find out who."

She looked away, but nevertheless answered him. "I spoke with the vicar before he left, then I went directly to the kitchens. Cook can attest to my presence there for most of the morning."

He dismissed her, and she left without another word.

"We've insulted her."

He glanced at Catherine, but didn't comment.

After Glynneth, the rest of the household staff entered the library one by one. Cook looked terrified, and he was quick to reassure her that she had done nothing wrong.

"All we want to know is what you might have seen."

He saw Catherine hide her smile, since at the moment Cook's apron was pressed against her face.

"I haven't seen anything, Your Grace," she said tearfully. "Not a blessed thing. I swear on St. Hegrid's grave."

He wasn't entirely certain who St. Hegrid was, but now was not the time to ask. A few more moments of reassurance, and she was composed enough to leave the room. Wallace opened the door for two of the housemaids.

They didn't weep, which was a welcome change, but they did stare at him with wide eyes as if he were some sort of monster they'd been threatened with as children. He counted six curtsies before he excused them, certain they knew nothing.

Fifty-three servants later, he turned to Catherine. "We have only have Juliana and Hortensia left to interview."

"Do you think that wise?"

"They were in the house at the time, and with Juliana's

Jacobite sentiments, I wouldn't be surprised at anything she'd do."

He rang for Wallace and sent for his sister-in-law.

The door opened a few moments later, and Juliana strode into the room, her narrow face contorted in an obvious effort to restrain her temper. She took a seat in the lone chair in front of the desk

This afternoon her face paint was less heavily applied. He wondered if anyone had ever had the courage to tell her instead of enhancing her appearance, the concoctions she used only drew attention away from the fact that she was still a lovely woman. Dissatisfaction, however, pulled down the edges of her mouth and her frown was an almost constant expression.

Hortensia had followed her into the room and not finding a convenient chair, simply stood behind her sister.

When Juliana turned her glare in Catherine's direction, Moncrief placed his hand on his wife's, an unspoken gesture of reassurance. Juliana might be a force to reckon with, but she wasn't someone to fear.

The gesture startled Catherine into glancing at him. He didn't return her look, instead concentrated on the paper in front of him. He had asked the servants three questions: Had they witnessed any activity near the roof, had they seen anything suspicious at Balidonough, and did they know of any reason why someone would try to harm a member of the family.

Every single one of them had answered negatively.

The questions he would pose to Juliana would be somewhat different.

"I don't understand why we've been summoned here as if we're servants, Moncrief," Juliana began.

He held up one hand to halt her tirade. "Let me explain it to you in as concise a way as possible. Someone has attempted to harm my wife or myself, someone who currently resides at Balidonough. You are being questioned because you've left no doubt of your feelings for either of us."

"I do not have to sit here and listen to this." Juliana rose from the chair.

"Yes," Moncrief said, "you do. At least you do if you wish to continue to live at Balidonough. If not, the gate-keeper's cottage can be made into a suitable living space for you and Hortensia."

"Then command it to be done, Moncrief. Because I will not listen to such scurrilous accusations against my character." She took one step closer to the desk. "I do not like you, Moncrief. You are a spendthrift. You have sided with the English all these years. You have even fought at their side. But you are blood, and for that reason I have been willing to overlook your grievous faults. But this, Moncrief, is too much."

"I will have the cottage readied for you. Please ensure that your move from Balidonough is accomplished within the week."

Juliana actually looked taken aback, as if he had called her bluff.

"It will be done within the day." She turned and stormed through the door, calling for her sister as she left.

Hortensia, however, did not move.

"I beg of you, Moncrief," she said softly, taking the chair Juliana had left. "Do not make me move with her." She clasped her hands together on her lap. "I know Juliana has not treated either of you with good grace. But I would gladly become a servant in your house rather than live in the gatehouse with Juliana."

Hortensia looked as though she might weep, and he fervently hoped she would not. He almost issued a dictate that if she did cry, he would change his mind and send her after Juliana.

"You are welcome to remain at Balidonough, Hortensia," he said, hoping that Juliana's absence would have a salutary effect on her sister.

She did cry then, holding her handkerchief to her face to muffle her tears. When she left, he exchanged a glance with Catherine. "Why do you have that look on your face?"

"I am forbidden to thank you, I believe. But I can't help but think that was a kind gesture on your part."

"I cannot imagine a grimmer fate than being forced to live with Juliana in a small cottage."

"Do you think she'll stay there?"

"She doesn't have a choice. Besides, it will serve as a backdrop for her martyrdom. This way she can tell her friends how much she's suffering for the cause."

Interviewing the remainder of the staff was much easier than the meeting with Juliana. As they began interviewing the stableboys, however, Moncrief began losing any hope that someone might have seen something.

After the last of them was excused, Catherine turned to him. "Do you think we'll find a witness?"

"I'm coming to the conclusion that everyone at Balidonough is blind."

He stood up and walked to the other side of the room, standing in front of the windows. The afternoon sun gleamed on the surface of the river, turning it gold. In the distance he could see the forest surrounding Balidonough. Once it had been used as a defense, but the need for that had diminished over the years. Now they sold some of the wood, and allowed hunting in the larger section.

Catherine no doubt thought that he was entranced with the view, but at the moment he was formulating a confession.

I wrote the letters to you, Catherine. I was lonely and the temptation too great.

But before he could speak, she stood. "I will be in your room tonight, Moncrief. I will come to your chambers as befitting my place as your wife."

Startled, he turned to face her.

"You have been patient enough."

Tell her. But if he did, he knew she wouldn't come to him. He was no saint nor wholly sinner, but a man torn between his goodness and his need.

"Why now?"

"For an heir? Because it's time? Your month is up, Moncrief, and I no longer have a reason to mourn. Until tonight," she said, and quitted the room, leaving him with the vague, dissatisfying, feeling of guilt tinged with anticipation.

Chapter 21

Worrying about a task did not make it easier. A coward avoided the difficult. The brave faced a situation directly and did what must be done.

Catherine stood in front of the connecting door attired in a new nightgown and wrapper. Thankfully, it was neither overtly revealing nor entirely concealing. She had found it at the end of her bed after returning to her chambers this evening. A card indicated it was delivered from the seamstress at the orders of the duke.

At the orders of the duke. She was here at the orders of the duke. Everything at Balidonough happened because, ultimately, Moncrief wished it done.

How had this situation ever begun? How had she ever found herself married to a duke, and Moncrief of all people?

Perhaps she should consider herself fortunate to have married such an attractive man, one both young and wealthy. His character gave her no reason to fear him. In fact, he cared for those in his keeping, was concerned about Balidonough, and was often compassionate although not overtly empathetic. He was, as he had said, Moncrief.

Would he be like Colin? She'd overheard Juliana's complaints often enough to know that Harry had not been the only husband guilty of adultery.

How did one ask a husband if he intended to be faithful?

And why wasn't fidelity an issue of any importance to men?

Would Moncrief be faithful?

Catherine took a deep breath and raised her fist to knock on the door. She was no coward, and the act had been quickly done with Harry. She enjoyed the moments afterward when Harry lay beside her before he left for his own chamber.

Twenty minutes, perhaps an hour at the most, and she would be back in her room. After that, they need not discuss the matter anymore. She would visit Moncrief a few times a month and keep her part of the bargain as his wife.

All she had to do was begin.

Her soft tap on the door received no response.

Again she knocked, and this time she heard his voice. She pressed down on the handle and pushed in the door and entered his chamber.

Moncrief was standing at the end of the bed, dressed in a long dark blue dressing gown, the silk molding to his body and leaving no question that he was naked beneath it.

Was he going to reveal himself as he had before? If so, she was quite prepared for the sight.

"Do you come in a gesture of sacrifice, Catherine?"

"No," she said, surprised at the question.

"Then why?"

"Because it's time. Because you've been patient as I asked."

"Do you think you know me any better now than on the day we married?"

"I think I know myself better," she answered honestly. "As to you, I doubt anyone will ever know you completely, Moncrief, unless you allow them to do so."

"Would it surprise you to know that you probably hold that honor more than any other person?"

The surge of pleasure she felt was wholly unexpected. "Yes," she said. "It would."

"Where is Harry?"

She blinked at him, startled at the question. "Harry?"

"Is he in your heart, or your mind at this precise moment?"

She was uncertain how to respond.

"Do you think of your wedding night with Harry?"

"I hadn't, until this moment." Perhaps that was a statement she shouldn't have made, because he frowned at her.

"Don't bring him into this room."

"I had thought of him." She played with the ring on her left hand, turning it over until only the gold showed, and then once again until all the jewels were revealed. "Is it your intention to be faithful to me, Moncrief? I must have your promise on it."

He didn't answer her, only slowly walked toward her, like a predator might stalk its prey. She remained where she was, an act of courage more difficult with each step Moncrief took.

"Why should I ever choose another woman when there is you, Catherine?"

There, another surge of pleasure.

"Do I have your promise?"

"Did I not do so in our vows?"

"I don't remember our wedding. But I will remember tonight."

"I promise." He reached out and placed his hands over hers, the act one strangely ancient, as if he swore fealty to her. "I promise to be faithful to you, Catherine."

She nodded, satisfied. Moncrief would never break his promise; his honor would not allow him to do so.

She waited for him to disrobe or enter the bed. He did neither, only stood in front of her looking calm and relaxed while she felt just the opposite.

"Your gown is lovely. Blue is a color that suits you."

"Thank you. I like it as well."

Reaching behind her, he slowly closed the door. The latch made a very loud click, and she jumped at the sound.

"It's a lovely evening."

"Yes, it is. But cold."

"If it were warmer, I would open the windows. Unless, of course, you ascribe to the notion that the night air is dangerous for the health."

"No, unless one is in Edinburgh or Inverness."

"I didn't know you were so well traveled."

"My father bought cattle stock in Edinburgh. We had friends in Inverness."

Moncrief reached out and slowly unbuttoned two of the top buttons of her wrapper. She bent her head and watched him.

"My father was a little old-fashioned. He was disturbed that Scotland had been so easily assimilated into Britain. I think he wanted things to always be as they were."

"Things change. Circumstances alter."

"Yes."

She moved away from him, to sit at the bench at the end of his bed. Now that she was in his chamber, the three steps up to the mattress was a momentous and nearly impossible journey. Although she'd slept with him for weeks, this night would be different.

"Where would you like to travel if given the opportunity?"

Must they talk? She simply wanted the bedding done, then they could converse.

"I've always wanted to travel aboard ship."

The answer evidently surprised him.

"I have never been on a ship, but I've seen them along the coast. They look like magnificent things with their sails furled and the wind guiding them."

"And the destination?"

"It doesn't matter," she said.

"Then I shall try to grant your wish."

"Truly?"

"Absolutely. I have no other obligations than my wife and Balidonough."

"Balidonough is a great responsibility. Your wife is not so much of one."

He sat on the bench beside her.

"I do wish you wouldn't do that."

"Do what?"

"Look at me so intently." She studied the tapestry on the far wall, wondering why she'd never noticed that the maiden pictured there looked suitably terrified. Catherine couldn't help but wonder if she, too, was about to go to her husband's bed. "You look at me as if you're focusing directly and intently on me."

"Would it bother you if I told you I was?"

"Yes."

"But you can hold me in thrall with a smile."

"It's not necessary to flatter me. I'm quite resigned to this night."

"Are you?"

"Yes." She stood, wishing that the portraits had been moved to the dining room. The previous dukes all seemed to be looking at her, a dozen pair of eyes gleaming with satisfaction.

Moncrief's smile had disappeared, and his gaze was, if anything, more intense than before.

"You look both beautiful and terrified, Catherine, standing there in your blue gown. You look entirely too young and virginal."

"I am not neither."

"I think, perhaps, you are, and you simply don't know it."

She drew herself up and frowned at him. But before she could comment, he stood and walked toward her.

"You didn't use the crutches. How is your ankle?"

"Fine," she said, her voice too tremulous. "At least for short distances."

He bent and scooped her up in his arms, ignoring her sigh of exasperation.

"The passages are cold at night, and you're barefoot."

"Passages?"

He didn't answer, but walked toward the wall containing the hidden door. Once again, he pushed against something, this time a wall sconce. A painting slowly moved inward.

"The journey will not be a short one and I don't want you hurting."

"Are you taking me to the keep?"

He stopped and glanced down at her, the shadows softening his smile. "We'll have to explore this imagination of yours, Catherine. We're going to one of the guest chambers. Anyplace but here." He glanced behind her, his gaze encompassing the portraits of the Dukes of Lymond. "I've often thought of redecorating this suite. Perhaps my ancestors should be relegated to another chamber."

"Do they look at you, too?"

"With more than a little jealousy. But let them get their own brides."

She smiled and leaned her cheek against his chest.

The wall closed behind them, darkness obscuring her vision. Moncrief, however, didn't hesitate, striding through the passage as if he could see.

"How do you know where we are?"

"I count the doorways." A few feet later, he stopped. "There's a slight rise at the threshold of each door. This is the first of the west wing guest rooms."

"You must have spent a great deal of time exploring as a child."

He chuckled.

"There's an adage about eavesdroppers not hearing the best of themselves. Unfortunately, I was often in that position. My father never learned that his punishments were rarely a surprise. I had ample opportunity to anticipate them."

"Were you punished often?"

She could envision Moncrief only too well, a lonely little boy with a pugnacious attitude and air of bravado about him.

"Often enough to make me dread my father, but not often enough to enforce some lessons. Time has done that better than my father could."

She wanted to know what lessons time had enforced, but he stopped and reached up on the wall. Slowly, an entrance opened, and he walked into a room that looked brighter somehow. Then Catherine realized the effect was caused by all the white dust sheets covering the furniture.

Moncrief moved unerringly to a chair, where he set her down. She immediately stood and watched him turn and devote himself to building a fire.

"I didn't know a duke was adept at such chores."

"Remember, I wasn't born into the role. I had to do for myself for fourteen years, and the experience prepared me well for living as a normal man." He turned to glance at her, the firelight behind him. "But not necessarily as a duke."

"You've done well at both, I think, Moncrief."

"Is it your aim to charm me to bed, Catherine? It isn't necessary, you know."

"Is that what I'm doing?"

He stood. "Don't look so stricken. I was teasing you." He reached her side and touched her face with his fingertips, stroking a path across her cheek. "Lovemaking shouldn't be a dour thing, Catherine, but should be entered into for joy, for the passion of it, in friendliness. Perhaps for comfort, or simply to ease an unbearable ache. It should not be done with excess piety and words like honor and duty and obligation."

She could hardly speak, her heart was beating so hard. "The vicar says that all women are punished by God for having licentious thoughts. Do you think it's true?"

"I don't. But the important thing is whether you believe it or not."

"I haven't had many licentious thoughts."

"Then you're safe from the wrath of the vicar." He smiled, and she felt captivated, so much so that when he placed his hand on the back of her neck and pulled her gently forward, she didn't feel any fear.

But she kept her eyes open until the last moment, until his lips touched hers. Then all thought simply stopped as he kissed her.

Her senses were caught up with how his lips felt against hers, the brush of his breath against her cheek. He tilted his head just a little, and she followed his lead, the kiss deepening. She felt his thumb brush against her hairline, and her hands, kept clasped in front of her, loosened of their own accord and sought Moncrief. She placed the tips of her fingers against the skin at his throat, feeling his heat.

She sighed, and his mouth coaxed hers open wider, his tongue touching the center of her bottom lip. Her senses were too acute. She could smell Moncrief's soap, feel the curious warmth of his silk dressing gown, feel the beating of his heart.

He moved his mouth, ending the kiss. But he didn't go far, only enough to embrace her, his chin resting against her temple. His breath was harsh, his heart beat as frantically as hers, and something audaciously large and hard pressed against her hip.

Slowly, Moncrief led her to the side of the bed. This mattress was not as high as that in the ducal chamber. Here there were only two steps. She climbed up, sat on the bed, and faced him.

"Do you remember me once telling you that you were beautiful?"

"Yes. Have you changed your mind?"

The fire had caught, the flames were growing brighter, casting an orange glow to the room. He was arresting in fire and shadow, his eyes seeming dark and slumberous, his lips curved in a faint smile. He reached out and traced a path from her shoulder to her hand, and she wondered if he could feel her tremble.

"No, if anything, you're more beautiful than before."

"Who is being charming now?"

"I'm not in the mood for charm," he said, enfolding his arms around her. "I'm too hungry."

A shaft of something that felt like pure flame arced through her, stealing her breath.

She was adrift in sensation and he'd done nothing but hold her, touching her with gentleness and the shivery stroke of a fingertip on her arm, hesitating in the juncture

of her elbow, testing there as if pleading permission to go
farther.

She loved the texture of his skin, the softness of a
man's face newly shaven, whiskers tamed, yet hidden for
only hours. Her temple was pressed against his cheek, her
chin shelved on his collarbone.

Her fingers reached up and stirred the hair at his nape,
where it curled softly.

Loving had not been something she'd missed. She'd
wanted to be held more than anything else. Yet she'd
never before felt this exultation. This sense of being lifted
above and out of herself was so odd and different that it
was strangely frightening.

Right at this moment, she only wanted to feel. She
didn't want to think, or reason, or rationalize.

"Moncrief," she said.

"What?" A gentle whisper with a note of teasing in his
voice.

"Nothing." Just Moncrief. He seemed to understand
because he pulled her closer, kissed her cheek in an infinitely tender gesture.

His touch was like the delicate filament of a spider's
web sliding along her skin, prickling nerve endings. With
one finger, he tipped up her chin, traced the line of her
throat, back up to her nose and over to her ear, a triangle
of flesh delineated with precision. She licked her lips,
unprepared for the softness of this, the tenderness of his
restraint.

"Catherine?"

She turned her head, swerving away from lips tracing
the line of her jaw, memorizing each placement of bone,
each line of muscle.

"Are you sure this is what you want?"

Another demonstration of Moncrief's honor. She nodded, almost overwhelmed by him.

His kiss was soft, barely discernible, and when she reached out for him, hands on his shoulders, he pulled back.

"You're trembling, Catherine."

"It could be the cold."

"Or fear. Don't be afraid."

She didn't respond.

He slowly bent forward and kissed her again, gently and persuasively urging her lips apart. Long moments later, he drew back.

"There, your lips are warmer."

She nodded.

"I'm going to take my dressing gown off now and get into bed with you. Is that acceptable?"

She nodded again. But where a more circumspect woman might have looked away, she was intent upon watching him. He shrugged off the silk garment with one movement and turned to throw it to a nearby shrouded chair.

His thighs were smooth, his calves heavily developed. Muscles arched across his back below his shoulder blades. Her eyes traveled to his hips and buttocks, so firm and perfect in shape that she had a shocking urge to cup them in her hands.

When he turned to face her, her face was flaming, but more at her own wishes than his nakedness.

"I would like to see you naked now."

"You would?" Her voice came out in a squeak. "Is it entirely necessary?"

"It's customary."

She had never been naked with Harry, but that confession didn't seem at all proper for this moment.

Moncrief circled the bed and sat on the other side. She was facing away from him now and grateful for the respite.

"You have a beautiful body, Catherine. The sight of you naked has been one that I've not been able to banish from my mind."

The flush that swept through her now was oddly comprised of both hot and cold sensations.

"Is that why you married me?" she asked, turning to him. He was sprawled against the pillows, his arms behind his head, so indolently nude that he could have posed as a satyr at that moment. Her thoughts slipped and then re-formed. "Because you saw me naked?"

Instead of answering her, he reached over and pulled her to him, then rolled with her so that she lay half beneath him as he bent his head and whispered against her lips. "Partly, perhaps. Or it could have been that I lusted for you immediately and had to have you in my bed."

She was stripped of words, pressed against him as she was. His erection lay nestled between her thighs and if she moved just so, he would be inside her. He bent his head and kissed her.

A moment later he moved away, and she was oddly disappointed.

"Aren't you going to do the rest? Are you only going to kiss me?"

"Don't you like kissing?" he asked, reaching out and stroking her bottom lip with the tip of his finger.

"I do," she said, a strange confession, since she'd never particularly liked it before. "Would you like to kiss me again?"

His lips were infinitely skilled, his breath hinted of spices. There was nothing to do but match him kiss for kiss, a simple battle joined for the sport of it. She smiled just for a second until he held her tighter, angled his head for a more thorough invasion, sent his tongue darting into the recesses of her mouth, tasting her warmth and her receptivity.

Wasn't it strange that a mouth could feel so much? That lips could tingle? Her skin was as tactile, sending messages of excitement to her brain. She pressed her lips to his neck, feeling the pulse beneath her lips beat as strongly and as rapidly as her own. Her tongue darted out, tasted the salt of his skin, felt him shudder in response.

His hands were at her shoulders, pushing back her wrapper, and skimming it down her arms. His gentleness was somehow too slow, too careful of her. She wanted to urge him to hurry, but instead she remained silent, trapped within a web of sensation.

His warm palm flattened on her nipple, a gentle touch despite the insistence of it. She arched against him, feeling the heat of her own flesh as her nipple lengthened, silently imploring a deeper contact.

This time, she pulled his head down for a kiss. Moments later, his head was on the pillow beside hers, his forehead buried in the down, his lips resting against her earlobe.

He was breathing as hard as she was, a circumstance that delighted her.

Suddenly, he drew back and looked at her.

"What is it, Moncrief?"

"Harry was a fool."

The comment was so unexpected that she could only stare at him.

"Why the hell would that idiot ever look at another woman when you were his wife?"

He sat up and pulled her into a sitting position, then very calmly grabbed her nightgown and ripped it from neckline to hem.

"I hesitate to think what you might have done if it had been black," she said, staring at him.

His laughter was as unexpected as his next words.

"Damn it, Catherine," he said. "Don't you know enough to let a man be angry?"

"Are you angry? If so, Moncrief, perhaps we should wait for another night to do this."

"I am not angry with you, Catherine. At myself possibly, at circumstance. Never at you. Besides, I'm afraid a delay is impossible," he said firmly. He laid her back among the pillows and looked into her face. "I would never survive it."

When she would have covered herself with her hands, he grabbed her wrists.

"You have the most beautiful body I've ever seen, Catherine. Your torso is long, and there is an unbroken line of beauty from your shoulders to your ankles. Everything about you is supple and curved and as graceful as a Grecian statue. You're the epitome of all things female."

Her eyes closed.

"Do I embarrass you?"

"Yes," she whispered.

"I can't think of anyone who should be less embarrassed than you. There is not a mark on your body, not a defect, not a blemish. You are as perfect as Eve."

Her eyes flew open to meet his gaze. "Now you are being sacrilegious, and the vicar would lecture you for such a thing."

"Then he can add it to the list of my numerous sins. But the vicar has no place here."

His fingertips trailed across her rib cage. Not quite a caress, only a bare whisper of a touch. She closed her eyes against the gentleness of his hand stroking upward to cup a breast, then fall away.

Touch me. A command she uttered deep in her mind. She arched toward him, a wordless entreaty he obeyed. Cupping her breast in his hand, he stroked the waiting nipple just once.

As if in apology for his teasing, he gently squeezed her

breast, then lowered his head. Catherine felt as if a life-time elapsed until she felt his tongue on her nipple. A moan escaped her, and she bit her lip as he moved to the other breast.

She placed her hand at the back of his head, pressed him forward in wordless encouragement. A small, nearly soundless moan escaped her as he drew her nipple fully into his mouth, flicking it with his tongue.

Exploring fingers brushed against her closed eyes, counted the eyelashes, sank into the hair at her temple. And all the time he touched her, he said nothing. Silence, except for their breathing, as if they labored at loving.

She shivered when he touched her, warmed when he palmed her. His lips replaced his fingers, as he began an exploration of her more fierce than before, more domi-neering. The inside of her elbow, her knees, her stomach, were all gently stroked. She opened her legs slightly, aching for him to touch her there. He seemed to know, because he threaded his fingers through her hair at the apex at her thighs but didn't go deeper.

"Please." A damning word, a licentious thought.

He cupped her, fingers pressing against her as if to as-suage her sudden need. One finger entered her, pressing hard in one long stroke that had her almost lifting off the bed. His thumb danced in a circular motion, inciting a re-sponse from deep inside. Her body moistened, readied for him.

"You are so soft, so wet," he whispered against her ear. A lover's conversation, one between only the two of them.

He was trembling, as was she.

Her breath escaped her in a rush and she gripped his arms with both hands. "Moncrief." His name had become a plea, a word to express so many feelings.

His thumb rested against her, boring softly down, then

slowly, achingly slowly, around one swollen, sensitive spot.

She buried her head against his shoulder, biting her lip to keep the sounds restrained. Her legs widened, and she arched against him. Her hands reached up to wrap around his neck as she kissed him. Passion was only a word she'd read. What she felt at this moment was something so alien that she wanted to stop time to study it.

He traced the outer lips with his fingertips, then inserted two fingers inside her just hard enough for her to need more. He curled up his fingers, stroking deep and rhythmically.

His lips and teeth were devoted to her breasts, his hand to teasing her to torment. She was heating up from inside, her skin drawn and tight and too hot.

He rolled with her over the mountain created by the heavy coverlet. His knees on either side of her legs, his forearms bracketed on either side of her head, he lowered himself so that he was only inches from her body, warming her.

Only his erection touched her now, engorged, heavy, hard, it brushed the curls between her legs in a teasing dance as old as time.

For long moments he remained that way, his body a brazier of heat, keeping the chill of the room from her skin.

Her body was beginning to hum, as if a bee were trapped inside, fighting for freedom. It was like nothing she'd ever felt, like no experience she'd ever had. Catherine wanted to move, her undulations instinctive, necessary, as ancient as the act they would soon share. She remained still, instead, holding all these trapped feelings together to experience them more fully.

He bent his head, his lips touched her throat before moving to the curve of her shoulder. Just that, and no more. She reached up and kissed him, and felt him smile against her lips.

His kiss became more carnal as his hands roamed over her body. She did the same, feeling his muscles, the brush of hair on his chest, the powerfully built shoulders and chest.

Time both raced and slowed, measured not by minutes but by touches: his fingers moving her hair aside, thumb resting in the well at the base of her throat, cupping her breasts and stroking the sensitive flesh of her areoles. Over and over he returned his hands to her skin, as if reacquainting himself with her form. Catherine closed her eyes, her hands resting on his shoulders and, selfishly, simply *felt*.

He leaned over her to take her breast in his mouth, the soft hair on his chest brushing across her other breast, the nipple so acutely sensitive that she shivered.

Then he rose up and knelt between her legs, studying her. She wanted to cover herself with her hands, anything but be exposed to such an intense regard. But he shook his head when she would have done so, leaned forward and gripped her wrists, placing a tender kiss on the inside of each.

"I want to remember you as you are now, Catherine, bathed by the firelight, your breasts wet with my kisses."

Should he be doing that? Talking to her as if this was a conversation they were having at dinner? Surrounding her with the deep sound of his voice, his words improper and vastly arousing?

She licked her lips and his face changed, becoming more severe. He leaned forward and mirrored her action, their tongue dueling just beyond lips. She sighed as she closed her eyes, hearing him murmur something before deepening the kiss.

He speared his hands in her hair and held the heels of his palms against her cheeks. His fingers slid through her hair and rested behind her ears, toyed with the lobes, then dusted over her collarbone to her shoulders. She arched upward, wanting them on her breasts again, but he traced an invisible path down to her fingers.

He held her hand in one of his, cupping and studying it as if he'd never before seen a hand. Time slowed as he took one shuddering breath after another, then gently kissed the palm in a gesture that felt somehow reverent.

All he said was her name, his voice deeply resonant. "Catherine."

He raised himself over her again. Catherine was adrift in a river, not a gentle meandering current, but one strewn with waterfalls and churning water, boulder-filled. She clenched her hands hard on his shoulders but he didn't invade, did not urge himself within the wet and willing cocoon of her body. He remained, like a dark and slumberous cloud over her, dominating without touching.

She rose up, imploring, impatient, her nipples brushing against his chest, her knees cushioning his. She felt him, gently insistent, aroused and hot, against her and widened her legs. He did not, however, take advantage of her artless invitation, nor did he move from his position, other than to bend his head and trace her lips with a tender tongue.

His delicate touch was no more substantial than that of a ghost, a friendly, lustful spirit lightly touching a corporeal body.

She could not breathe, could not open her lungs far enough or deep enough for the air she needed to inhale. There was a pounding in her head, and her body, that demanded she pay attention to it, a thrumming that screamed for release.

His fingers found her again, touched her in demand and desire. None of his actions were designed to dominate. He sought to appease, to extend a finger and gently coax her where he wished, a destination she suspected was as alien to her as the darkness of the passageways.

Her eyes opened wide, and she moaned once before

clamping her lips shut on the sound. As her hips arched off the bed, Moncrief lowered himself and kissed her deeply. Her chest was rising and falling with the effort to breathe, her heart was beating like a thunderous drum, and her fingers tingled.

He seized her wrists and held them with one hand, and with his other guided himself into her. Catherine closed her eyes, wanting to experience every second of his entry. The tip of his penis touched her outer lips, and she arched her back impatiently.

"Please."

"Anything you wish, anything you want." Slowly, he entered her, moaning as he did so.

He sank farther until he was completely filling her. He rested a moment to give her a chance to adjust to his size. Her hips rocked forward, her legs spread wider, her core of heat invited, entranced, beckoned. He slid against her, a gentle movement, an infinitesimal distance that made Catherine shiver, not out of shyness this time, or fear, but a quivering of nerve, and muscle, and skin measuring need and building desperation.

His rhythm was slow, relentless. She bucked against him. Gradually, his speed increased until he was pressing her into the mattress and she was clinging to him in protest as he withdrew.

He gripped her by the hips and pulled her onto him.

He pulled out of her and she gasped, an open mouth expression of loss and wonder and surprise. He bent and trapped her breasts between his hands, scraping his teeth along the edge of both nipples, creating fire with his sucking mouth, branding her with an emotion she'd never before felt.

She was making sounds, Catherine knew, little noises betraying her body's surprise and jubilation. She no longer cared. When he slid inside her again, she sighed, a long-awaited sound of welcome. This steadfast invasion was like torture without pain. She felt stretched and waiting, a pulse beat deep inside her body like a drum ticking off the limits of her endurance. She wanted movement, friction, an easing of the building tension.

"Oh, sweet Catherine. Soon." He slowed, further teasing her.

It was the promise of sunlight in the depths of a darkened cave. She wanted the brightness, needed the sun, but he only bent to capture a hard nipple into his mouth, grazing it with tender teeth, sucking at it. It was not enough, even when he kissed her, mouth to mouth, tongue to tongue. She ravaged his mouth, realizing that he kissed the way he spoke, kisses the texture of warm honey, the flavor of Moncrief, intrusive, occasionally demanding, enticing.

His lips moved to nuzzle in the soft, damp tendrils of hair at her temple. "Catherine."

He began to move faster then, and she nearly screamed, the feeling making her hold tight to him, nature and instinct writhing her hips forward to cradle him on his withdrawal, entice him on his return.

Catherine bit her lip and wrapped her arms around Moncrief's neck. Her hands shook, her feet tingled, her nipples were hard, painful points, and a flush of heat raced through her body.

He reached down and teased her with his fingers, urging her to explode with him an instant later. When she did, her vision darkened, and for long moments the world simply ceased.

Moncrief gathered her close, kissing her eyelids and smoothed his hand across her face down to her throat. For long moments they lay entwined, Moncrief making no effort to move.

She traced the curves of muscle down his arm to his palm. There was nothing soft about him, yet his touch was so tender she felt as if she were melting with it.

His chest brushed her breasts, tantalized them with the gentle abrasion of hair, teased them with a soft side-to-side movement. Her hands skimmed impatiently against the skin of his back, her fingertips gently smoothing against his sweat-sheened skin.

She had known passion before, but never like this. Nothing had prepared her for what she'd just experienced, as if she'd wandered into a world she'd heard about but never seen.

Slowly, she turned her head and looked at Moncrief. His eyes were closed, his breath quick, his heart still beat strongly against her breast.

A feeling of sadness suddenly came over her, a sensation so strong that she blinked back tears. Yet she didn't mourn Harry at this moment, or even her previous life. She grieved, instead, for what she might have felt at this moment if Moncrief had loved her.

He turned his head, and before he could speak, she kissed him. Wrapping her arms around him, she kissed him again, then again to keep him silent, and then once more because she liked his kisses, and a few more because her lips were warming and her heart beating rapidly again.

Catherine awoke and stretched and then, as she had for several days, tested the pain in her ankle. It didn't hurt. Nothing hurt. In fact, she felt glorious. She stretched, her hands going under the pillows.

Only to encounter a male elbow.

Moncrief.

Her hand spread wide, fingers splayed to touch his arm gently before retreating slowly back to her side.

She turned her head to look at him.

Moncrief was a sorcerer. He'd made her forget everything—the place, the chilled room, the fumbling embarrassment she'd felt. She closed her eyes, wondering if she were indeed lost to lust to think of such things in the bright light of day. Dawn had come and gone and sunlight was stealing in between the curtains. Yet she was still having night thoughts.

Dear heavens, she'd screamed. Thank Providence that Moncrief had thought to procure a guest room in an unused wing. Still, had anyone heard her? She eased the pillow from behind her head and placed it over her face.

Perhaps she should simply claim fatigue and stay in her chamber all day. That would give the servants something to discuss, wouldn't it? They'd think that Moncrief had hurt her while the very opposite was true.

Where had he learned some of those things he'd done? He'd kissed her in places she was entirely certain were not normally kissed. Not, however, that she wouldn't care to have it done again. The sensations had been, well, addictive.

She peeked out from behind the pillow and focused on the ceiling. Plaster cherubs cavorted in the corners, stringing a ribbon around the chamber. They seemed to ridicule her with their smiles.

Very well, the whole night had been glorious.

She remembered the first time she'd sampled Balidonough whiskey. The whiskey had burned only her throat. Moncrief had made her whole body feel on fire.

She pushed the pillow back and looked at him. Moncrief slept deeply, his whole being seeming to focus on rest. His eyelids didn't flicker, and he looked so blissfully peaceful that she wondered if he had any sins or flaws resting on his conscience.

Although she had always thought him an arresting men, now she recognized that he was truly handsome. He lay half on his side, curled toward her, one arm curved beneath the pillow, the other resting on his hip.

She wanted to reach out and place her hand on his chest, thread her fingers through the soft hair there, but doing so would probably wake him. She was not yet ready to greet him.

Instead, she closed her eyes and enjoyed the softness of the morning, the quiet in the room, and a feeling of lassitude that came not from a good night's rest as much as Moncrief's skill.

He had taught her so much in only hours.

Could it be possible that she was in lust with her husband? Husband. He was her husband, and she had the right to sleep next to him every night of her life if she chose. There would be no whispers about her doing so, except perhaps the maids wondering at her eagerness for the end of day. But she could return tonight if she wished, and he would think her merely attempting to be an accommodating wife.

She felt him stir and considered feigning sleep before chastising herself for being foolish. She turned her head and opened her eyes to find him watching her.

"Good morning," he said softly.

She smiled in reply, feeling tongue-tied and absurdly embarrassed. She'd screamed and otherwise acted as foolish as a virgin.

But he did not seem to think so, not with his answering smile and that wicked gleam in his eyes.

"It doesn't seem fair."

"What doesn't seem fair?" he asked, reaching out his hand to brush back her hair from her face.

"That you are so handsome first thing in the morning."

"Am I? An entire coterie of Balidonough's servants has been here to make me look presentable for you."

She raised up on one elbow to survey him. "They did a spurious job. I can't see any evidence of their handiwork. Besides, Moncrief, you have no need of servants."

He only smiled, and she realized he was embarrassed by her words. She should have felt, perhaps, a surge of power, but all she felt was tenderness, an oddity in itself. The night before had not lent itself to soft emotions.

She placed her hand flat on his chest and threaded her fingers through the springy hair there. He gripped her wrist with one hand and gently brought it up to his mouth to plant a kiss against her palm.

"I have a meeting with Juliana, but I can gladly postpone it," he offered in a low voice. "My wife comes first."

She felt her cheeks warm.

"Wouldn't it be decadent to lie abed in the middle of the day?"

"It's expected of a newly married couple. Or I could always claim ducal privilege."

What sort of power did he have over her that he could suggest such a thing and she'd give it consideration? The idea of making love to Moncrief again was an exciting one. To do so in the middle of the day, however, might be tempting even her newfound licentiousness.

Before she could change her mind, she sat on the edge of the bed and reached for his dressing gown. She wanted to escape to her chamber before any more temptation was laid before her.

He raised up on his elbow and watched her, his smile broadening. "If you take my dressing gown, what will I wear?"

"You give me no choice, Moncrief. You destroyed my gown."

"You should sleep naked from now on, Catherine."

If the seamstress couldn't make her another gown, she'd be forced to do that. Or sleep in her ugly black gowns. But she didn't think that Moncrief would tolerate that.

"A sheet, perhaps? Or you can simply take the passageway back to your chamber."

He glanced up at the ceiling. "I can always walk back to my room naked."

"You wouldn't," she said, shocked.

She could very well imagine what all the young maids would be doing as he strode down the hall: looking through their fingers at him, memorizing the shape of him.

"We would never get any work out of the maids from that moment on, Moncrief. They'd be lusting after you."

He only smiled. The silence stretched between them as she realized he was capable of doing something so brazen. Nor would it bother him. He was so perfectly made and so completely comfortable with himself that nudity wasn't important.

Just like the men in those illustrations.

"There's only one woman I want lusting after me, Catherine."

The sheet had fallen to his waist, and she wondered if he was erect, if that was the reason for his wicked, almost promising, grin.

The deed had been quickly done with Harry. It had been nothing like this moment, with Moncrief singeing her skin with his gaze, with her imagining all sorts of scenes, and her body responding in ways she had felt before but only when surfacing from particularly troubling dreams.

"If you give me but a moment, I will send your dressing gown back with Wallace."

"I think it would be quicker if I took the passageway. Can I carry you back to your chamber, duchess?"

She could imagine being in Moncrief's arms, naked.

"My ankle doesn't hurt this morning. I think I'll walk."

He pulled the covers back to expose his glorious erection. She glanced away before she was tempted to reach out her fingers and stroke its length. She hadn't touched him the night before, and now she wanted to almost desperately.

"If you think that's the best solution."

"I do," she said, and escaped the room before her own desires overcame her.

Catherine walked back to her chamber in Moncrief's dressing gown, holding her head up high as if it were an everyday activity she was performing. Several young maids polishing the brass of the door handles glanced at her as she passed, but she didn't hear their giggles until she reached her room.

She pressed on the handle and stepped into the room quickly, placing her back against the closed door. Looking up at the ceiling, she sighed, and wondered if she should summon Wallace after all. But Moncrief's voice speaking to a footman in the next room made that errand unnecessary.

Catherine clutched the silk of the garment to her and went to sit at the vanity. Staring back at her in the mirror was a woman with flushed cheeks and swollen lips, whose hair was mussed and whose eyes still reflected the passion of the night before. A heavy pulse beat between her legs, as if her body were somehow summoning Moncrief, as if she needed only the thought of him to feel desire.

She laid her head down on her arms, wondering how she could wait until night fell again. Her hand cupped her own breast beneath the silk, and the sensation was one she wanted to share with him. How was she to get through her duties today feeling this way?

She felt both weak with pleasure and hungry for it.

If she had known that bedding Moncrief would cause such feelings, she wouldn't have fought it with such intensity.

She raised her head and looked in the mirror, feeling like a foolish, foolish woman.

Chapter 22

Life at Balidonough assumed a normal pattern, at least on the surface.

The cleaning of the castle continued. Once the maids were finished with one wing, they began on the original one again. Catherine couldn't conceive of Balidonough ever being so filled with people that it would feel crowded. In fact, there were times during the day that she saw no one at all except for an industrious maid or a bored footman.

Balidonough was filled to the brim with those items Moncrief's ancestors had collected over the centuries. Most of her time was spent cataloging all the various furniture, china, tapestries, and paintings. Catherine took pleasure in the restoration of several valuable pieces of furniture from the attics. She had them repaired by the castle's carpenter before being stained and polished. She wished she knew of someone to consult about the tapestries, as well as someone knowledgeable about several Chinese vases she suspected were priceless.

If nothing else, she would be known by future generations for her neat handwriting and the journals that were being filled with list after list of Balidonough's treasures.

Their conversations at dinner were lively enough, with Hortensia, Moncrief, and herself in attendance. They discussed all manner of things, some of them no doubt disapproved of in polite society. She was learning, however, that Moncrief made the rules rather than following them. Catherine did not doubt that anyone welcome to their home would realize that within the first two minutes of his arrival.

He treated the servants as if they were troops under his command, expecting a great deal from them but willing to treat them fairly in return. Yet the distance he maintained from people, even Peter, indicated that he was familiar with being in charge and not uncomfortable with an aura of aloofness.

Moncrief instituted a rule that the footmen were not to stand at attention five deep down the hallway like marionette soldiers. Instead, only a pair of men were to remain at the end of each corridor unless summoned by a guest or family member. They were released from duty at ten at night and were not expected to appear before eight in the morning. He gave similar orders that the maids were not to be on duty past nine, and not to be on the main floors until seven. Even at Colstin Hall, the servants worked longer hours.

Hortensia had questioned him one night about his leniency toward the servants.

"Do you not think it a bad thing to set such a precedent, Moncrief? After all, none of the other estates allow their servants such latitude."

"Why should I demand more of a man than I need?

We're not at war. Balidonough will suffer no hardship if a man spends an hour less at work."

Catherine couldn't help but wonder how his childhood memories of his father's autocracy or his service as a colonel had molded him into the man he was today. Both no doubt had a place in making him Moncrief, just as her childhood and her marriage to Harry had altered her to become the woman she was now.

Whoever she had become. Whoever Catherine, Duchess of Lymond, was. A confused woman, certainly. But feeling that way was to be expected around Moncrief.

He'd awakened something in her, long dormant or never used. Moncrief had always been honest about his need and his desire. She found such forthrightness both startling and amazingly exciting.

She discovered her days were less disturbing if she was busy. She didn't want to think about her relationship with Moncrief, complicated as it was. During the day, they were perfectly amenable to each other, courteous and polite, the epitome of ducal restraint.

At night, they were wild.

During the last month, Catherine was very much afraid that the wildness would begin to seep over into the days as well. When he wasn't around, she found herself thinking of him. What was he doing? Where was he? When would he return?

When he was near her, she couldn't seem to stop touching him. She'd find a way to brush his lapel, or put her hand on his sleeve, or be close in some way. She hadn't moved from her place at the table and sometimes during dinner he would reach to his right and place his finger on her hand. Such a simple thing but it stole her breath.

After dinner, she would sit in the same room and feel his eyes on her. She would put down her book or her needlework and look over at him to see that expression in his eyes. She'd come to understand what it meant. Now she knew that it was caused by hunger, the type that races through the blood and causes an ache, a feeling almost like pain if it wasn't satisfied. From the moment he looked at her, she would feel it as well.

Too many nights they'd left Hortensia alone in the parlor, no doubt confused as to their rapid departure.

Moncrief had become her obsession.

Today, she found herself rising from her desk in the ducal suite too often and going to the window to see if she could catch sight of him. Finally, she did see him, striding across the frosty grass, attired in his greatcoat against the chill of the day.

He was, no doubt, on his way to the distillery, where he was modernizing the building, or to talk to Munson or tour the home farms. Moncrief had a thousand errands, a hundred duties, and he was diligent in every one of them, including enthralling her.

She placed her fingers on the glass, obscuring the sight of him. Then, because she couldn't bear it any longer, she dropped her hand and watched him until he was out of sight.

An unbearable sadness crept over her, a feeling that mimicked her grief for Harry. She pushed it away, unwilling to think about what it might mean.

One night she had studied his hand, as if to discern the magic of it, but it was an ordinary hand, just like his eyes were like any other eyes. There was no reason why his touch should make her shiver so, or that his look would cause a flush of heat to warm her body. But what made him different was the force of his personality, the strength of his character, a dozen attributes that separated him from other men.

I am Moncrief.

She could remember the exact moment he'd said that, could recall the exact tone of his voice, so ducal and authoritative.

A touch of color caught her eye, and she saw Hortensia bundled against the cold and picking her way across the frozen ground on her way to visit Juliana. Despite the weather she made a daily pilgrimage to the gatekeeper's cottage, although Juliana never visited her in return.

Members of a family, however, were to be valued despite their personalities. Neither she nor Moncrief had a large family, and Catherine was acutely aware of Juliana's absence at dinner. But even when she'd sent an invitation with Hortensia, Juliana had refused to attend.

"She doesn't feel welcome here," Hortensia said, attempting to explain her sister.

Hortensia, however, had blossomed in Juliana's absence. She didn't discuss her health incessantly, and a bloom of color on her cheeks made her look more vibrant and healthy. Also, she'd gained weight, and the resultant curves were very attractive.

The older woman reminded Catherine of a widow in the village not far from Colstin Hall. Moira Campbell had been widowed for a decade, each successive year of her loneliness brought about a change in her temperament. She became more and more surly around people, more judgmental, more apt to make quick pronouncements and condemn wayward behavior. What she saw as incorrigible behavior, however, was often nothing more then the exuberance of youth.

The greatest change in the widow Campbell's demeanor came about every third month when the peddler stopped by the village and stayed a few days. Her smiles, rarely in existence until that time, broadened, her demeanor changed, and her step grew livelier. The peddler was an old man with a hunched back and a weathered, wrinkled face. Love hadn't changed the widow but attention had, and she responded to it like a flower would the sun.

The peddler was an expert in deciphering what people wanted and giving it to them. His skill translated also to seeing the needs of the human heart. He had evidently discerned what the others in the village had not, that the widow was not so much angry at the world as she was acutely lonely.

Catherine couldn't help but wonder if Juliana's departure had changed Hortensia, or if there was a peddler in the other woman's life.

Now Catherine resolutely turned away from the window and left the suite, her destination Moncrief's library. She nodded to the footmen aligned along the wall like soldiers, and not one of them nodded back or otherwise pretended to see her. Such was Moncrief's doing, of course.

She descended the graceful stairs slowly, still cautious of her ankle even though weeks had passed since she'd used her crutches. The foyer was empty, Wallace no doubt about on his duties. Only one young maid was in sight, and the girl curtsied at Catherine, then went back to polishing the glass in one of the windows.

With Moncrief gone, it felt as if Balidonough had lost its heart. The strumming energy she felt when he was striding about, intent on one task or another, was oddly lacking.

He evidently loved his home and tended it with the dedication of a doting father. Farms in the outlying regions had been left fallow for too many years, and he was determined to make them produce. He had given orders that the stables were to be renovated as well and had put Peter in charge.

In a surprising move, he'd called her into his library just a few days earlier, to announce that he had invested her funds in a way that would no doubt prove wise over the future.

"But you have control over my money, Moncrief," she'd said. "You needn't show this to me."

"On the contrary, Catherine. It's your money now. Use it for what you wish, or save it for our children."

She'd left him, not revealing how much that one word had shocked her. Children. A child. She pressed her hand against her waist and wondered if their passion would result in a child soon.

She'd always wanted a child, but after Harry died, she'd put those thoughts away, and grieved for the loss of those unborn children.

What would it be like to bear Moncrief's child? He would be solicitous of her, she knew, simply because everything he did was performed with care and concern. She imagined that he had been a great commander of men, and all the ladies with whom he had been involved had no doubt loved him.

She halted, stunned by the thought. She was not in love with Moncrief. True, she admired him, and perhaps respected him. He touched her and she shivered with desire, but that was not love. No, she was not in love with him.

Instead of continuing on to the library, she turned and walked into the Ladies' Parlor. Here, the windows faced the front of Balidonough, and she wouldn't be tempted to stand and watch for Moncrief as she had upstairs.

The upholstery in the Ladies' Parlor was yellow with sprigs of flowers, a perfect counterpart to the dark wood of the tables and mantelpiece. If the day had been sunny, the room would have been bright and cheery. But it was overcast now and cold even though someone had wisely lit a fire.

One advantage to Juliana's living in the gatekeeper's cottage—no one complained at the cost of anything, and everyone was a great deal more comfortable as a consequence.

Catherine closed the sliding doors and went to sit beside the fire.

From here she could see the view of the front gardens. But they held no appeal at the moment. Instead, she leaned her head back against the chair and closed her eyes. The mantel clock ticked the moments as she grappled with her thoughts.

Her life had been so much easier when she had been married to Harry. How innocent and naïve she'd been. She had loved him unreservedly, believing him to be kind and gentle, a man of character and honor.

When he died, she had grieved deeply, but her mourning had been untainted by the truth.

Only after coming to Balidonough had everything she'd known to be true been questioned and proven false. First Harry and now her own nature.

She lusted after her own husband. There, the crux of her confusion.

Over the last few weeks, she'd become a raving beast, a creature who thought only of pleasure. Her nipples tightened painfully when Moncrief would look at her in a certain way, and she warmed all over with the thought of him entering the room.

He'd taken her against a wall one day, and she'd gloried in it. When it was done, she'd straightened her skirts and placed her hands on his chest for support, unable to speak for the sensations running through her. Outwardly, they looked demure enough if a servant happened upon them. But she'd felt his seed in her, and the thrumming aftermath of intense pleasure hadn't faded for an hour or more.

If she looked in the mirror now, she knew what she'd see: sparkling eyes, glistening lips, and fiery red cheeks.

She felt restless and unsettled, and her limbs felt weak, but they weren't, of course. A deep tingling raced through her body, spread outward to her fingers and toes. Her eyelids were weighted, her mouth too full, her breath too tight, and a pulse beat heavily between her legs to signal her body's craving.

A moan emerged from deep in her throat, and she wasn't entirely certain if it was a sound of despair or longing. She clenched the chair arms with both hands. Anyone looking at her would think that she was resting, that she was decorous and ladylike. They would never know that she was becoming heated with desire from only the memory of him.

Nor did he leave her after taking his pleasure. Sometimes, he'd even question her, shocking her with his frankness.

"Did you like that?" he'd ask, and she would nod, burying her face against his shoulder.

"I like to touch you there. You are so responsive."

She would kiss him on the throat in a bid to silence him. His comments embarrassed her, because she was not used to such things, but she suspected she could become quite comfortable with telling him exactly what she liked, and how.

Moncrief lost control from time to time, and it was when she touched him or kissed him in certain places. She felt an incredible power that fed on her desire and even strengthened it. In passion they were equals.

She had never had that type of partnership before. Nor had she imagined that such equality could exist. But in the Duke's Chamber, he became simply Moncrief and she was Catherine. Titles, rank, birth, and even the past didn't seem to matter.

Sometimes, they spoke of mundane things and they would laugh over a petty annoyance, or a story the other told. A laugh would lead to a kiss, and Moncrief's kisses always led to her desire.

She wanted him now. There, another truth she told herself. She wanted his kisses now, wanted his hands on her.

If she were as brazen as she felt, she'd go in search of him and demand that he perform his husbandly duties. She did not have such courage.

Or did she?

The clock's ticking was louder, as if reminding her that it was just noon.

The distillery was not accessible to her because of an old superstition that stated the presence of a woman could sour a good mash and turn a fine ale to bitter dregs. She'd never been inside the building. But the workers wouldn't be there either. They'd be taking their midday meal.

She stood, walked to the pocket doors, and opened them. Her body felt flushed, her thoughts solely on Moncrief.

He heard a sound and looked up to see Catherine standing there, attired in one of her new dresses, and nothing more than a shawl. The bitter cold had seeped through his greatcoat, and he could imagine how frozen she felt.

"What you doing here, Catherine?"

"I'm not supposed to be here, am I?"

"Have you come to sour the mash?"

"No," she said, smiling. "Will I shock the workmen?"

"Most of them have left for their noon meal."

He studied the copper kettle for a few moments, then carefully turned the long wooden handle to the left until it was pointing up. He stepped back, and the steam volume immediately decreased.

"I didn't know that you knew anything about making whiskey."

"Every member of the family learns," he said. "From the time we were little boys, we had to learn the business. Whiskey, after all, has been more profitable than marrying heiresses."

She didn't respond.

"Did you need me, Catherine?"

"Yes," she said.

She turned and watched him as he walked to the door and turned the key in the lock before facing her again.

"If I were a proper woman, I would demand that you release me at once."

"You are a duchess," he reminded her.

"I have a journal to complete, an inventory to finish."

He nodded.

"Menus to approve."

"Yet you came here without a proper coat just when you knew we'd be alone."

"Yes."

"Have you come to be a temptation to my duties?"

"I hope so."

She was still perfectly dressed, and he was properly attired. But they might have been naked for the hunger in their gazes.

"It's afternoon."

"It is."

"There are hours and hours until nightfall."

"I agree."

"And hours and hours until bedtime."

"That too."

"How will I last, Moncrief?"

"Can I assist you?" he asked.

"If you'll try, I'd be very grateful."

"You must come closer."

She walked slowly toward him, allowing her shawl to drop. Perhaps it landed on the floor or on one of the numerous barrels but she didn't seem to care. He reached out and took her hand, placing a kiss on each knuckle.

"Where do you hurt?"

"Here." She traced her finger around her breast.

He rubbed his palms back and forth over her bodice. She grabbed one hand and placed it over a protuberant nipple. "There."

His fingers pinched it gently, and she closed her eyes on a sigh.

With one hand, he gathered up her skirts, a finger trailing up her stockings to rest in the curls at the jointure of her legs. His finger traced along the outer lips, unsurprised to find her wet for him.

"You thought me drugged before, but you are my opium, Moncrief. Can I take too much of you?"

"No," he said, inserting one finger into her.

She made a sound deep in her throat, and he added another finger.

"It's not enough," she complained.

"I know," he said gently, beginning a rhythm. Two fingers were gently sliding in and out of her, his thumb beginning a rotating motion.

"I need more, Moncrief. I need you."

"Now you know how I feel about you."

She reached up and pulled the lace fichu from her neck. And then, still not removing her gaze from his, slowly began to unlace the front of her dress.

"I should undress you, Catherine. It looks as if you need my lips on your breasts."

"Yes, please." Her brown eyes were lambent, the pupils large. Desire was there in her eyes, in the fullness of her lips.

He smiled with the glee of an errant schoolboy aided and abetted in his debauchery by a beautiful and amply endowed wild girl.

Her skin was the softest silk, her blush caused either by anticipation or embarrassment, he could not be sure. He fervently hoped it was not the latter, because he could not have spared her now. He reached out with a hand that shook a little despite its gladness, buried it in the mane that was her auburn hair, stroking through the heavy tresses and lifting them to his nose.

"You smell of lilacs," he murmured, and she made a sound of agreement deep in her throat.

He finished unlacing her.

He pulled back, and studied her. Her eyes were luminous, her lips pink from his kisses, open, slightly moist. It was the first time in his experienced life he'd ever felt desire and sweetness melded together.

His palm slid up her rib cage to the fullness of a breast, cupped it, felt the smooth globe of its perfection, its tip tightly drawn and needy. They were equals, evenly matched in need at this moment. Her nipple puckered in invitation; he soothed it with a small kiss, a gesture accompanied by a hiss of Catherine's breath, a short, abortive sound of awareness.

Her breasts lured him, their creamy softness a pillow for his tongue, their jutting nipples tender and defenseless, an easy conquest given his determination. He held her captive by that touch, her nipple hot in his mouth, ringed by lips not willing to surrender their prize. He sucked her hard, a demand for both surrender and succor. Catherine's response was to moan softly, helplessly.

She reached up with both hands and looped her arms around his neck and pulled his head down for a kiss. She made a sound, and he smiled, knowing the power of their kiss. Kissing Catherine was like disappearing inside himself, as if he were experiencing all the sensations of his body from a different place.

A jerky little breath escaped her, a sound of such distress that he smiled, softly. He felt the same.

When the kiss was done, he pulled back.

"Shall I enter you now?"

"Please. Please."

He unbuttoned his trousers and pushed them down. But before he could enter her, she pushed him away, surprising him. He watched as she knelt, staring at his body. With one tentative hand, she reached out and touched him, one finger sliding down his erection as if to measure its length.

She licked her lips, and he almost spilled his seed then and there.

"Catherine," he warned, but she only shook her head, empress of the moment.

He was hard, but at the touch of her finger, he'd grown even harder.

Moncrief slowed his breathing, to allow her time to explore, time to satisfy her curiosity. But when she bent forward, and he felt the warmth of her breath, he moaned aloud.

She brushed her cheek against his penis, then her mouth, as if acquainting him with her touch. Her tongue lashed out, and she licked the crown. He shuddered, and she smiled.

When he would have put his hands on her shoulders, she only moved back, a warning not to do so again.

He dropped his hands to his side and she tongued him once more, this time an excruciatingly slow touch from base to tip.

"Catherine."

She concentrated on her task, reaching out and holding him steady while her lips rounded and her mouth opened. Then he was inside, the sensations so exquisite that he tilted back his head and closed his eyes.

His hips moved of their own accord, and his breathing

accelerated, but she kept up the same slow exploratory rhythm, licking first the crown, then the sides, finally placing the head in her mouth like a treat.

She moaned, and the sound of it against his penis was too acute.

"If you keep on, I will not be able to satisfy you."

"Then you will have to do so with your fingers, Moncrief. Or your mouth." She began the soft licking rhythm again. "I know why people want to do this," she added, speaking against his erection. "It feels unbelievably wonderful."

"Catherine."

"It's all right, Moncrief." She tormented him by taking him into the warm wetness of her mouth again. This time, however, she increased how much of him she took inside, until he was certain he was going to explode.

She reached up and gripped his hips, urging the rhythm to begin. At that moment, he knew what she wanted and what he couldn't prevent.

"Catherine," he said roughly.

She made a sound of assent deep in her throat, her lips pressing against him as she slid him in and out of her mouth.

He stepped back, freeing himself, and bent to her, nearly throwing her across an empty barrel. He lifted her skirts and entered her from behind. The barrel rolled a little, and he reached out his hands to steady it, and then slid slowly inside her. Her nails gripped the barrel so tightly that he wondered if she would get splinters, a question he forgot when he was rooted deep in her, his welcome eased by her incredible heat.

She made a little sound at the back of her throat, something like a whimper, a muted murmur so provocative and feminine that it aroused both a protective impulse and one to dominate.

He slammed hard against her, driving into her with a ferocity unlike him. She was sobbing now, insistent sounds that ground at his composure, ate away at the remnants of his restraint.

He felt her explode around him, her gasps transformed into a low moan, her convulsions shattering to become tight little shudders in the channel that surrounded him, grabbed him with greedy tremors, inviting him to surrender, Nature's plea.

He didn't last long, the combination of her teasing mouth and her hot welcome didn't encourage restraint.

But he heard her sounds of pleasure before his world darkened.

Chapter 23

A week later, dawn found Moncrief awake.

He lay with his arms behind his head staring up at the ceiling. As the minutes passed, he watched as each successive portrait of an ancestor was illuminated by the golden fingers of the sun. Surprisingly, he rarely noticed any of them lately. They were simply ornamentation, something unimportant to be ignored in the face of more pressing matters.

Sometime in the night, Catherine had moved closer to him. Her hair brushed his side, her soft breathing warm against his skin.

He turned and faced her, watching as she slept.

If a man could choose one memory to hold with him for eternity, this one would be his.

There were many things about his life he could not change: the distance between him and his father, the fact he had never reconciled with Colin, his duplicity about Harry's letters and a dozen other, less important, sins. But he had been given an opportunity to change the future when he didn't think it possible.

He had known of Catherine's intellect, her wit, her determination, and her obstinacy. He'd been enthralled by the strength of her character, by her beauty, by her dedication to each task she assumed, and her compassion. Yet he'd never thought that her passion might be the equal of his. She was always responsive, the most exciting lover he'd ever known.

Somewhere in his life, he had done something correct, or God was rewarding him now for future deeds performed.

He was, at the moment, supremely happy, blessed by what life implicitly promised him. At his side was a woman who might come to love him one day for who he was and not solely for what he could make her feel. But even that journey was proving to be an exciting one.

He leaned over and kissed her, and she sighed, then moved, settling on the other side of the bed.

He smiled and left the bed, caring for his morning needs.

Once dressed, he stood at the door to the balcony. Ice covered the ornamentation, and the far trees, making Balidonough appear like an enchanted castle in the midst of a magical winter kingdom.

The wind coming from the north was chilly, but for the first time in years he didn't detest winter. There would be no need to find quarters in some overcrowded European city. Nor would he ever again have to crouch near a sputtering fire in the wilderness, praying for spring and war.

Instead, Balidonough was his haven; the outer walls keeping all who lived here sheltered from the worst of the winds. Winter was a time of peace and solace, for planning and respite.

As a child he could remember his father standing on

the balcony just beyond the door, overlooking Balido-nough. His father had never looked as if he were uncertain, or unsure of his role. Instead, the man appeared to know exactly what he'd wanted and how he wanted it to be achieved. It was that same aspect of his character that had allowed him to refuse to join the '45. He and several other high-ranking Scottish nobles had stoutly refused to support Prince Charles's assertion that his father was the logical heir to the Scottish throne. Instead, they remained aloof, neither aligning themselves with the English nor the Scots, but playing a very difficult game somewhere in between.

Because of his father's decision, Balidonough had been left intact after the rebellion. Not for the first time, Moncrief wondered if that's why his father had acted as he had. Another question that would never be answered.

The morning sky was a mix of yellows and blues and greens, the bright orange disk of the sun still demure on the horizon.

Today he would take Catherine on a tour of the home farms, perhaps solicit her advice about some changes he was making. After all, she'd managed Colstin Hall for years during her father's illness, and it had been a prosperous estate.

He glanced to the left of the driveway, his attention caught by a movement.

In the dawnlight, he saw Glynneth attired in her traveling cloak and carrying a basket, walking swiftly down the drive. This was not a woman on a morning stroll, but someone with an obvious destination in mind.

"It's a glorious day, isn't it?" Catherine said from behind him.

He turned to find her attired in nothing but a sheet.

"You'll catch cold," he chided her, walking back to where she stood.

He wrapped his arms around her, and she gripped him around the waist, tipping her head back and smiling up at him.

"What were you thinking about with such a fierce glower on your face, Moncrief?" she teased. "The morning is too beautiful to have such a dour Scots look."

"I was wondering where Glynneth was going."

"Glynneth?" She looked past him to the figure growing smaller on the drive.

"She seems intent on an errand."

"It's her day off," Catherine said, shrugging.

He turned and walked her back to the bed. "You need a dressing gown. Remind me to the tell the seamstress."

"I believe she is working on an entire wardrobe for me, Moncrief. I beg of you, do not give the woman one more chore. I have been fitted until I could scream. Besides, I do not need you to tell her what I need. I'm perfectly capable of doing so on my own."

"Yes, but then you would make it sturdy and warm, while I have other plans entirely."

"You would make it transparent," she said, smiling. She reached out and touched him through his trousers. "What is good for the duke is only fair play for the duchess."

He laughed.

When she sat back on the bed and pulled the sheet around her, he debated joining her for a moment. But another problem still invaded his mind.

"Where does she go on her day off?"

Catherine gave him a quizzical look. "I don't know. Why?"

He shook his head, unwilling to say more.

"No, Moncrief," she said firmly. "You will not do that."

"Do what?" he asked, even though he knew full well that he was being less than candid with her.

"Retreat into silence. What do your suspect poor Glynneth of now?"

"Poor Glynneth?"

"She was newly widowed when she came to me, and I think she grieves still."

"I can't help but remember when I first met you."

"A meeting I still cannot remember," she said.

"Someone must have known how much laudanum you were taking, and my guess is that Glynneth was aware of it."

"Are you accusing Glynneth of trying to hurt me? I have never heard of anything so ridiculous, Moncrief. She would not have. She was my companion for nearly a year. She could have harmed me at any time if she wished."

"Like poison you with laudanum? Perhaps make you so addicted to it that you didn't know when you were taking too much?"

"I didn't try to die, Moncrief."

"I know."

"You know?"

He smiled as she began to frown at him. "Let's say that I've revised my opinion. I don't think you meant to take too much, but I don't think it was an accident, either."

She looked stunned. "Have you always suspected her?" He nodded.

"And that's why, of course, you barely speak to her."

"Does she have any family?"

"No. It was one of the reasons I hired her. She and I were similar in circumstance. Alone in the world."

"Has she any friends nearby?"

He walked to the window. Glynneth was barely visible.

"I don't think so. She never mentions them."

"Then why is she heading for the crossroads and the coach? Where's she going with a basket?"

Perhaps it wasn't his concern, but anything to do with Catherine was of interest to him. Nor had he quite forgiven Glynneth for her lack of care of his wife. There was the matter of the laudanum.

"You're going to follow her, aren't you?"

He turned, surprised. Had she learned him so well that she could divine his thoughts?

"I am," he said, staring after Glynneth.

"Mrs. McClaren says that you have been a very good boy lately," Glynneth said, ruffling her son's hair. He looked so much like his father that her heart felt as if it were being squeezed by a fist.

He didn't say anything. Instead, he concentrated on the tarts she'd brought him from Balidonough.

"He's a smart one, he is," Mrs. McClaren said from the doorway. "The schoolteacher in the village said he'd be glad to teach him, private like."

"When it's time, I'll bring some books from Balidonough for his lessons." She ruffled Robbie's hair again. "He's growing so fast, every time I see him, there's another change."

Mrs. McClaren nodded.

He had learned to walk and had said his first word without her being there. She told herself that at least he was safe and protected, and with people who loved him. She had been able to give him that, at least.

"More," Robbie said, thrusting a hand at her.

She smiled and shook her head. "Not until after dinner." She bent and kissed the top of his head. He looked as if he would have liked to indulge in a tantrum, but one look toward Mrs. McClaren had him changing his mind.

Glynneth stood and walked toward the kitchen, where Mrs. McClaren was making a soup. The day had been a blustery one, and she wore her coat, still chilled from the long walk to the crossroads. Perhaps one day, she could even take one of the carriages from Balidonough.

As her position stabilized, so would her power. The only detriment was Moncrief himself. He didn't like her, and she knew why. They each held secrets, but not from each other. She knew who he was, and she suspected he knew of her secret horror.

How foolish of Catherine not to know how much her new husband adored her. But there were other things Catherine did not realize as well, and Glynneth would just as soon she remained in ignorance of those facts.

"It's a cold day all right," Mrs. McClaren said. "And hardly fit for travel."

"I don't have to be back until tomorrow," Glynneth said, unfastening her cloak.

"Well, that's a blessing then. Sit down and have something hot to eat."

She liked Mrs. McClaren; the woman reminded her of her own mother. Not for the first time, Glynneth wondered if her life would have changed if her mother had still been alive when Robbie was born.

Her mother might have softened her father's stance, made him feel something for his grandson. As it was, her father had never been in Robbie's company, and chose not to acknowledge him.

"Where is Mr. McClaren?" Glynneth asked.

"Off hunting. The man is fixed on a rabbit stew. Go and get me a rabbit then, I told him." She grinned at Glynneth, who smiled in return.

The McClaren house was in a secluded area, surrounded by woods. They had few neighbors, which would be a drawback when Robbie was old enough to want a childhood companion. But for now, the privacy was perfect for her. Her arrival and departure weren't noticed, and no one asked questions as to her identity.

A lesson from her father, that she was so circumspect even when there was no need.

"You'll not shame me, Glynneth. Have you no idea of what gossip will do to a man in my position?"

She'd always found it sad that he thought more of his position than of her.

Over the next hour, Glynneth and Mrs. McClaren sat and talked, mostly of Robbie, who sat on his mother's lap and shared her soup. When they didn't talk of the little boy, they discussed Mrs. McClaren's arthritis. Occasionally, the sound of shots in the distance interrupted their conversation. The older woman would always nod in satisfaction, proud of her husband's prowess as a hunter.

Moncrief didn't find it difficult to follow Glynneth. The only inconvenience was having to slow his horse and wait several times rather than overtake the coach. An hour later, the coach stopped at another crossroads and Glynneth and another woman dismounted. The driver handed down her basket, and Glynneth walked toward him.

For a moment, Moncrief was afraid she would see him, but she suddenly veered to the left, and walked into the woods. He gave her a few moments before he followed, urging his horse through the fallen leaves. A few minutes later he realized he'd lost her trail.

The forest simply grew together, without any vestige of a path. He dismounted, tying the reins of his horse to a tree and following on foot. A few minutes later he was in the middle of a thicket. In the distance was a house, smoke billowing from its chimney.

He stood there for some time, waiting for her to come back outside. When it was clear this was to be a lengthy visit, he went back to his horse, found a patch of green for him to graze, and settled back against the trunk of a tree, still watching the house.

If he'd brought a companion, he needn't be so diligent, but he didn't want to explain this errand to anyone. Nor did he want word of it to get back to Glynneth. Even Peter had a habit of being voluble now that he was no longer a colonel's aide.

A twig snapped, and he turned, to face the barrel of a musket. Before he could explain his presence, before he could say a word, the gun exploded.

And then nothing.

"You were followed."

Glynneth turned at the sound of Mr. McClaren's voice. The older man stood in the doorway clutching his musket with one hand, the other braced on the doorframe.

"At first I thought he was a poacher, but he was dressed too well."

"Did you shoot him, Simon?" Mrs. McClaren asked.

"I did. He was on my land."

Glynneth stood, a sickening feeling overwhelming her. No one knew she was here. As usual, she'd been very careful leaving Balidonough, making certain that no one followed.

"Show me," Glynneth said.

A moment later she stood over Moncrief's prone body, fighting back her nausea.

She knelt and put her fingers against his neck to feel his pulse. Thank God he was still alive.

"You have to take him back to Balidonough."

Mr. McClaren shook his head.

"He's a duke, Mr. McClaren. Do you think he won't be missed? People will come looking for him. What are you going to do, let him bleed to death in your woods?"

"They'll say I tried to kill him."

She wanted to knock something against his head. "You shot him!"

"He was on my property."

"Say it was an accident."

He still looked mulish, but she had no other choice. Moncrief had to be taken home and tended to immediately. The only other option was to bring him inside the McClaren's home and hope that he recovered quickly. When she mentioned as much to McClaren, he paled.

"I'll take him back," he said, "but I won't be blamed for his own damn foolishness."

"He won't blame you," she said, knowing it was the truth. Instead, Moncrief would find some way to lay his injury at her feet. He had disliked her from the first, perhaps rightly so.

She knew, in that moment, that more had changed than Moncrief being injured.

She helped Mr. McClaren load Moncrief into the back of a wagon, borrowing a coverlet and pillow in order to make him more comfortable.

Her prayer was simple and fervent. Help him survive until he reached Balidonough.

Chapter 24

Moncrief hadn't returned home by gloaming, and Catherine was worried. He would have sent word if he was going to be delayed. That was the kind of man he was, considerate of others.

Three times she asked Wallace if any news had come, and three times, the majordomo shook his head.

Had he dressed warmly enough? Would he stay the night at an inn? Silly questions, to forestall herself from asking the one that truly mannered: Where was he?

Another question demanded an answer. Was Glynneth guilty of trying to harm her?

As much as she tried, she couldn't remember a time when Glynneth had been angry with her. Or an occasion when she had been anything but pleasant. Their relationship of companion and employer had altered over the months as they had become friends. At least, she'd thought they'd been friends.

Had she been as guilty of poor judgment in Glynneth's case as she had been in Harry's?

As the hours wore on, her concern sharpened. She tried to calm herself with the thought that Moncrief was more than capable of protecting himself. Besides, Scotland was no longer a heathenish place. This was not, after all, the border country, and there were no raids for cattle to bother them. Balidonough was too far south of the Highlands to be concerned with any lingering barbarity from that quarter.

Catherine paced in Moncrief's library until darkness came, then, too restless to eat or remain in the parlor with Hortensia, headed for the entranceway, uncaring if the servants knew she was concerned. Let them consider her besotted with the man. Perhaps she was.

Wallace stopped her at the front door of Balidonough.

"Your Grace," he said gently.

She blinked at him before realizing he was holding out her cloak.

"It is cold outside, Your Grace."

She nodded, and allowed him to help her on with the garment.

"Shall I send a footman with a lantern?"

"Yes, please," she said, almost reduced to tears by his kindness.

Juliana would have said that he was merely doing what any conscientious servant would have done. But she saw the look in Wallace's eyes and wanted to thank him for it.

Evidently, she wasn't the only one who was worried about Moncrief's absence.

"Do you think we should send a search party out looking for him, Wallace?"

He considered it for a moment, and then shook his head. "If he is not back by morning, Your Grace, I would. But perhaps he has only been delayed. His horse might have become lame, or lost a shoe."

She nodded in acceptance of his words and his unspoken optimism that Moncrief was all right and had merely been detained. Why, then, did she have a feeling that something was desperately wrong? The answer came swiftly to her. The reason she was expecting the worst was because the worst had already happened to her once.

Before Harry's death, she'd never believed that he would die. Now she was well aware that Fate often visited the unwary.

Dear God, how could she live if something had happened to Moncrief?

That question caught her unawares. She opened the door and left Balidonough before Wallace could summon a footman. Standing in the darkness in front of the castle, she looked up at the bright pattern of stars in the chilled night.

Moncrief was unlike Harry the way the sun is unlike a candle. True, they had both been in the Fusiliers, both had served in North America. They were both men. Beyond that, however, there were no similarities.

A footman finally joined her, clad in a gray coat that reminded her of Moncrief's. Had he worn it this morning? Surely he had, the weather had been cold and dismal with fog.

She took a few steps down the gravel drive, then a few more, beginning to pace with lengthening strides through the promenade of trees. The leaves were thick on the gravel, muffling her steps as she repeated her journey over and over and over.

Activity was what she needed, activity to banish the thought that something had happened. She would exhaust herself with pacing. Or begin to run, perhaps, through the corridors of Balidonough like a madwoman.

No. She stopped and shook her head.

Moncrief would come riding in any moment and be

amused at her concern. And then, once he realized how terrified she was, he would dismount and hold her close.

She began to walk down the drive, the footman following at a sedate distance, careful not to interrupt her reverie. She'd grown accustomed, at Balidonough, to the constant presence of servants, and she barely noticed him.

Moncrief come home. If you do, I promise not to be so worried again. But come now so no one shall know how hysterical I'm becoming. I am very calm on the outside, but I am replaying the moment I opened the letter and read the news of Harry's death.

Who will write to tell me you're gone?

"Please," she said, looking up at the stars, uncaring that the footman could hear her prayer. "Please God, please guard, and guide, and protect him, and keep him safe, and free from harm."

A faint mist began to fall as if God himself wept.

She was chilled to the bone, but not from the weather. Her thoughts froze her. She kept walking because she couldn't keep still.

A quarter hour later, she heard a sound at the end of the drive.

She walked through the gravel and told the footman to remain behind. She wanted to greet Moncrief on her own.

"Where have you been?" she would say in wifely annoyance.

Or perhaps she wouldn't say anything all, just be pleased that he had returned home at last.

But it wasn't Moncrief after all, but a farm wagon driven by a heavily cloaked stranger.

The footman stepped in front of her, holding out the lantern.

"You there! If you're on your way to Balidonough, deliveries are to the rear. The next road."

"I've got a delivery, all right," the man said, his bulldoglike face turning toward the rear of the wagon. "But it's the Duke of Lymond I'm bringing home, and I hope to God he's still alive."

Catherine raced to the end of the wagon. Before anyone could stop her or comment on the impropriety of the Duchess of Lymond clambering about a farm wagon, she was at Moncrief's side brushing the hay away from his face. He was covered with a quilt, but it was soaked through with his blood.

Inside, she was shaking, but she cradled his head on her lap and smoothed back his hair with trembling fingers.

"Drive slowly to Balidonough," she told the wagon driver. "Get help," she said to the footman, and watched the lantern bob as he raced down the drive.

The journey seemed endless, but finally the wagon pulled into the drive and halted in front of Balidonough's tall oak doors. A phalanx of footmen stood there, their faces mirroring almost identical expressions of worry. Someone had procured a door, and they held it at the end of the wagon bed for a makeshift stretcher while four footmen climbed up beside her.

Wallace stood outside the wagon and leaned over the side, pressing his hand to her shoulder. "Your Grace," he said gently. "Let them take him."

She nodded, tenderly placing Moncrief's head on the hay and moving into the corner out of the way.

"Be careful with him," she said, a command that was hardly necessary.

Once he was lying on the door, looking too much as if he rested on his bier, they carefully carried him up the stairs and to the Duke's Chamber.

"Have we someone practiced in healing at Balidonough?" she asked Wallace.

"One of the house maids has a mother in the village who's always treated our worst injuries," he said.

"Send for her," Catherine said as she followed the footmen upstairs.

Moncrief's blood was on her. She glanced down at herself and felt a frisson of horror at the sight. Someone had injured him, and she would demand the knowledge from the wagon driver.

And one other person.

"Send Glynneth to me the moment she returns," she called over the banister.

She didn't stay to see Wallace's response, intent, instead, on reaching Moncrief's side.

The footmen gently settled Moncrief into the bed, and his valet leaned over to remove his boots. Catherine sat on the edge of the bed and peeled back the bloody shirt.

Someone had shot him.

She wanted to scream. Instead, she asked for a bandage. A square of folded linen was handed to her, and she pressed it against the still bleeding wound.

"He looks to have lost a bit of blood," an older woman said, startling her.

Catherine turned to find a stranger standing there. She smiled, showing several gaps in her teeth.

"I'm Annie," she said, "and I've come to make him better. Unless, of course, you wish to do the task yourself."

Deep wrinkles radiated from the corners of her eyes all the way down to her lips, as if her entire face had been scrunched up and then released by a celestial sculptor. The woman was no taller than the middle of Catherine's chest, but what she lacked in height she made up in force of personality. She folded her arms and tapped her foot on the wooden floor, her lips arranged in a wry smile that held, in Catherine's mind, a tint of contempt about it.

"Well? Are you going to let him bleed to death, which

it looks like he's halfway to doing? Or are you going to move aside so I can treat him?"

"This is the healer you spoke about?" she asked Wallace, who stood in the doorway.

"Yes, Your Grace. She was here tending to one of the maids."

"The poor girl burned herself yesterday. But I don't suppose you'd be knowing anything about that?"

When Catherine shook her head, Annie sighed loudly and nodded. "I didn't think so. You type of people never seem to notice what's below your noses. Or your stairs."

"Are you going to insult me or assist my husband?"

"I've a mind to do both," the woman said surprisingly. "But I suppose I should assist your husband first."

Catherine stood aside and watched as Annie cut away the shirt and gave instructions that Moncrief be stripped of his other clothing. One of the maids went to fetch some boiling water, another Annie's bag, left behind in the kitchen. The third obeyed instructions to gather some herbs from the kitchen garden. Even Catherine was put to a task.

"Sit over there," Annie said, pointing to the opposite side of the bed. "Hold his hand. He'll come to soon enough, and I think looking at your pretty face would give him more comfort than seeing mine."

Catherine did as she was told, pulling up a chair and placing her elbows on the mattress, gently holding Moncrief's left hand between hers.

"What are you going to do?"

When the woman didn't answer her, she asked again, more forcefully. She would've stood between Annie and Moncrief if the old woman hadn't spoken, determined to protect him even from those who said they had his interests at heart. She was uncertain of Annie's skill and didn't want her practicing on Moncrief.

"Don't tell me you're the weepy type," Annie said. "I cannot abide weak aristocrats."

"I'm not an aristocrat. I'm a farmer's daughter."

"Then you shouldn't be so squeamish."

"What are you going to do?" she asked for the third time. "And don't change the subject by insulting me again."

"I'm going to remove the bullet in his shoulder," Annie said, retrieving a long and ominous-looking pair of tweezers from the bag the maid had brought to her side. "Since he's not yet conscious, I can't give him anything for the pain. It's going to hurt like the devil. Let's see how much help you can be, farmer's daughter."

Catherine had nursed her father in his final days, had sat at his bedside as he lay dying. Numerous times she'd been called upon to help others or assist in a birthing, but she had never truly felt as useless as she did now, gently holding Moncrief's hand and wishing to spare him from the pain that would surely come.

Annie sprinkled something on his wound, a yellow, foul-smelling powder.

"What is that?"

"Are you going to ask me questions or let me do my work?" She ignored Catherine then, and spoke to one of the maids. "Hold the candle closer." The young girl raised the taper so that Annie had better light for her task.

Catherine was tempted to close her eyes, but she kept her gaze fixed on Moncrief's face. At the first exploration of Annie's tweezers, his eyes flew open.

"It's all right, Moncrief," Catherine said. "I'm here."

His hand tightened on hers, and she wondered if he'd comprehended what she'd said. Had her words given him any comfort at all?

She ran her hand up his arm, from his wrist to the inside of his elbow in a gesture that probably gave her more comfort than it did him. His skin felt so cool, unlike him. He was normally so warm, his skin heated.

The footmen and the valet finished undressing him, and she swept the blanket up to his waist.

Annie gave her a crooked grin. "He doesn't have anything new, farmer's daughter. I've seen it before."

Catherine only frowned in response, certain that she'd never met a more obnoxious woman. Even Juliana was more pleasant.

Annie returned to her task. Moncrief's eyes remained closed, and Catherine rested her cheek against his knuckles and prayed that it would be over soon. A lesser man might have cried aloud. Moncrief, however, remained silent, the only sign of his pain the tightening of his hand on hers.

"I was worried about you," she said, talking to him as if they sat in the parlor. He opened his eyes and looked at her, his gaze clouded.

He tried to say something, but she touched her finger to his lips.

"You're here now, and that's all that matters."

He closed his eyes again, just as Annie stood, clutching a fragment of metal in her long tweezers. "I have it."

Moncrief was ashen, and growing colder. She pulled another blanket up to his stomach.

"Do you want to sew him closed yourself?"

The idea of inflicting injury on Moncrief was more than she could bear.

"No. Finish it."

"I'm not a seamstress," Annie said. "He'll no doubt have a scar." She retrieved a threaded needle from her pack and began to stitch Moncrief's injury closed as if he were no more than a shirt to be mended.

Catherine looked away, and when Annie said something to ridicule her squeamishness, she didn't deny it. His pain felt as if it were her pain, an empathy she didn't question. But she never let go of his hand and occasionally stroked his arm with her fingers, feeling it necessary to touch him, to reassure him she was there, and to assure herself that he was safe.

Peter was suddenly at the door, pushing through the maids and footmen congregated there. He'd been given command of the stables in the last month, and she hadn't seen him often. When she had, he and Moncrief had been in conversation. Sometimes they had laughed together in the courtyard, and the sound of it had buoyed her spirits. Moncrief had sounded younger, no older than Peter himself.

Now he thrust a leather case toward Catherine.

"There's a powder in there we used on all bullet wounds," he said. "It worked in Quebec, Your Grace. It would work here."

She opened the case and found a selection of small apothecary jars, each one labeled in a bold and distinctive handwriting.

"It's the one called bullet powder, Your Grace. The colonel marked it himself."

She withdrew the jar and handed it to Annie.

The healer waved a hand dismissively. "If you've a mind to use that, do so. But if you do, you can bandage him yourself."

Catherine turned to Wallace. "Escort this woman from Balidonough," she said. "Is there no other person with medical skill in the whole of Balidonough? No one we can send for, someone a little gentler and more compassionate?"

Wallace flushed. "I will attempt to find one, Your Grace."

Catherine nodded. "See that you do so, Wallace." She glanced at Annie, who was scowling at her. "I will not have you near my husband."

"You'll call me again, farmer's daughter. I may not come."

Catherine stood and waited until the woman had made it through the room and out the door.

She turned to the servants who were still congregating at the end of the bed.

"Thank you for your concern, but it would be better to give Moncrief some privacy now."

A young maid turned at the door and curtsied, glancing back at Moncrief. "He's not just the Duke of Lymond, Your Grace," she said, dabbing at her eyes with her apron. "He's our duke."

Catherine nodded, understanding.

"I promise I will keep you informed of his condition." Finally, they left, until she and Peter were alone with Moncrief.

She went to the right side of the bed and leaned over Moncrief. The wound was stitched haphazardly, just as Annie had threatened, but it looked clean.

"I'm to sprinkle it on the wound?" she asked Peter.

He came and stood beside her. "Yes, Your Grace, liberally. Then bandage the wound." He withdrew a rolled bandage from the back of the leather case and handed it to her.

Gently, so as not to cause him any more discomfort, Catherine used the bullet powder and rolled the bandage around his shoulder and upper arm before carefully tying it off.

"I wish we could give him something for the pain," she said. "But I have no laudanum."

"I doubt he'd take it, Your Grace. He never did the other times he was wounded."

"Other times?"

She'd never seen scars on Moncrief, but then she'd never looked for any, either, being so overwhelmed by the sheer beauty of the man.

Peter only nodded, no doubt taking pity on her ignorance. "His leg, Your Grace, and he took a musket ball to the chest. We didn't think he'd live through that one."

Catherine pulled the sheet up beneath Moncrief's neck and covered him with the blanket. He was beginning to tremble, but she had seen other people do that in the aftermath of an injury.

She sat on the side of the bed and watched him for some time, feeling inadequate and helpless. Finally, she held his hand, brushing her fingers across the top of it.

"I'll be leaving you now, Your Grace," Peter said. "Is there anything I can fetch for you?"

She wanted a friendly voice, a hug, a tender reassurance that Moncrief was going to be well, that he would survive this wound and that infection would not lessen his chances of doing so. She wanted answers to her questions. Who had shot her husband? Where was Glynneth?

But it was all too obvious that the young man standing at the door and smelling of the stables knew no more than she and was not capable of offering comfort. Strength, yes. Loyalty, of a certainty. But the only person who could offer the comfort she required was Moncrief.

"Thank you, Peter," she said. "I don't need anything." But before the young man left, she spoke again. "Thank you for your loyalty," she added. Moncrief prized loyalty.

He hesitated, as if wondering whether or not to speak. "He inspires it, Your Grace," he said, and slowly closed the door behind him.

If he bowed to her, she didn't notice it. She wasn't impressed with the trappings of being a duchess. Except, her conscience whispered, when power accompanied the position. Not one person had argued with her when she had banished Annie. Instead, they had looked awed at the signs of her temper. But she couldn't help but wonder as she sat there if the woman they obeyed was the duchess or the wife?

Someone had built up the fire before leaving, and she was grateful for the warmth. Still, the room had a chill that made her cover Moncrief with another blanket.

The night was too quiet, Moncrief's stentorian breathing the only sound. She watched him until she was certain that he rested comfortably. Only then did she stand and walk to the windows, gazing out at the darkness surrounding Balidonough.

Her prayer was unspoken, out of deference to Moncrief's sleep. Instead of the vicar's pompous and somewhat arduous prayers to the Almighty, hers was plain and uncomplicated.

Heal him. Make him well and strong and vibrant. Take anything you want from me in payment.

She could hear Moncrief's laughter in her mind, and almost feel his arms around her. Only a wish, one so desperate that she wanted it to be true.

The night was eerily reminiscent of when they had married, at least according to details from Moncrief and Glynneth. Had Moncrief maintained a vigil as she did now, wondering if she would live or die?

She closed the curtains and walked back to the bed, staring down at him. He was too pale, almost ashen. She bent over him and placed her hand on his forehead to find it cool.

He had given more than she in this marriage. He had given her his name, his patience, and his great wealth. He had made her his duchess. He had taught her passion and delighted in her response.

What had she given in return? Nothing.

Uncomfortable with the tenor of her thoughts, she sat,

reaching over to smooth Moncrief's cheek. His eyes opened at her gesture, her heart aching at the look of pain in his eyes.

"Would you drink some whiskey? It might ease the pain."

"A barrel of it," he whispered, and tried to smile.

He reached out and touched her arm, and she placed her own hand over his. He closed his eyes again.

"How did I get home?"

"A man brought you in a wagon," she said, describing what had happened.

His eyes opened again, his gaze fixed on her.

"Tell Peter to keep him here. I think he's the man who shot me."

"Where do you think you'll be going?" Mrs. McClaren asked her.

Glynneth held on to Robert's hand, an overstuffed valise in the other, and faced the woman who had been kind to her from the moment they'd met.

"Mr. McClaren isn't back yet, which means that something has gone wrong. I can't bring disaster down on top of your heads," she said. "It's better if Robert and I go away."

"He could have broken a wheel, gotten lost, a hundred explanations."

She shook her head. "No, something else has happened. I know it."

"You can't think I'd let you out in the cold," Mrs. McClaren said, reaching down to pick up the small boy. "Not my little Robbie. Where will you go?"

"I have a place," Glynneth said.

Mrs. McClaren didn't move, swaying back and forth with Robbie in her arms, a more than adequate barrier to the door. "What place?"

More than once she'd wanted to tell her story to the older woman, and no more so than now.

"I'm going home."

"Will they take you in?"

Glynneth thought of her father, the man who had been so intolerant of her until the last few months. He'd sought her out on his own, even going so far as to say that he had missed her. He'd wanted to mend their estrangement, he'd said, and had asked after Robbie from time to time. Very well, now would be the time to test his words and his newfound affection.

"Yes," she said firmly. "I am certain of it." Then, because of the fondness she felt for Mrs. McClaren, she left her with a warning. "The duke will come back here," she said.

"What shall I tell him?"

"Do not lie to him," Glynneth said. "He has a way of discerning the truth even in the most improbable situations." He had seen through her early on, and had realized that she'd felt a confusing mixture of hatred and friendship for Catherine.

"Why leave, Glynneth? You've done nothing wrong."

Yes, I have. But they were not words she could tell Mrs. McClaren. The other woman finally surrendered Robbie, and Glynneth took him in her arms. She picked up the valise again, and before she could change her mind, walked from the house where she had known such peace and safety.

Perhaps it was time everything came out in the open, but she was not so brave as to tell Moncrief herself.

Chapter 25

Twice more during the night, Catherine treated Moncrief's wound, and each time she did it looked the same. There were no red streaks emanating from it, no swelling that might presage another worry, that of infection. For all her cantankerous words, Annie had treated the wound properly, or perhaps Moncrief's bullet powder had simply done its job.

Occasionally, Moncrief would rouse, his eyes at first hazy, then slowly recognizing her. In the middle of the night he woke again, and when she would have given him a little more whiskey to ease the pain, he pushed the glass away and struggled to sit up.

She pressed him back against the pillow. "You will not get up," she said sternly. "You've been wounded, and you've lost a great deal of blood."

"What a pity that I managed to escape Quebec only to be shot at home in Scotland." He looked disgusted, and

317

she smoothed her hand over the scowl between his brows. "Where is the driver?"

"Downstairs, being interrogated by Peter. But I will not discuss that with you now. Instead, tell me how you feel?"

"As if he'd run over me in that wagon," Moncrief said, smiling. "But it's no worse than I've had before."

She folded her hands primly and tried very hard not to frown at him. "Peter tells me you were wounded before," she said, feeling somehow as if she should have known.

He waved his good hand in the air in an obvious attempt to make light of it. "Every soldier is injured sooner or later. I managed to be in the wrong place twice."

"You have to take better care of yourself, Moncrief."

"If I promise, may I get something to eat?"

She stood and went to the bellpull located beside the bed and gave it a sharp tug. In less than a minute, a footman entered the room.

"Your Grace," he said, bowing toward Moncrief.

Catherine frowned at him, then realized that as long as Moncrief was in the room, his staff would always defer to him. She might as well have been invisible.

"Fetch His Grace a bowl of broth, and have Cook also prepare a strong herbal tea."

She heard Moncrief's sound of disgust and smothered her smile. "You will not have any solid food yet," she said over her shoulder at him.

"Add a custard to that," Moncrief told the footman, "and I'll double your wages."

"Do so, and I'll have you pulling weeds tomorrow," Catherine threatened.

The footman looked from one to the other as if doubting what he should do.

"Very well," she said, sighing. "I don't suppose a custard can hurt you all that much." She nodded at the footman who looked relieved. "Do not, I beg you, take the duke's words to heart. He is no doubt feverish."

"I'm feeling quite well," he said to the young footman as he turned to leave. "I'll double your wages regardless."

As the door closed behind him, Moncrief glanced at Catherine. "They were, no doubt, paid lamentably by Juliana. We should review all their salaries."

She nodded, wondering what kind of man could be lying wounded in his own bed and be concerned with what his servants were paid. A different one, certainly, from any she'd previously known.

"Tell me what happened," she said, "while we're waiting for your broth."

"And custard. Don't forget the custard."

She only shook her head at him.

He lay there bare-chested, one shoulder wrapped in bandages, his hair askew, a lock of it falling in the middle of his forehead. An utterly charming smile revealed lines at the corners of his eyes. There was something altogether wicked about the look in those eyes, however.

Catherine returned to sit at the side of his bed. He stretched out his hand to her, and she slid hers along the sheet until their fingers touched. How illustrative of their relationship. Here he was, in his sickbed, recovering from a wound, and she was so demented or perverted that all she could think about was that the touch of his fingers brought magic even to her hand.

She had fallen to the depths of depravity, especially since she wanted to lean over and kiss him gently on the lips.

"How does your arm feel?" she asked, to get her mind off the subject of kisses.

"Sore." He tried to flex his arm but grimaced at the effort. When he attempted to sit up, she pushed him back down on the pillow again, smiling at his foolishness.

A knock on the door preceded a startling procession of

footmen and maids. One of them carried Moncrief's napkin, another a glass of wine she had not ordered but about which she didn't comment. A third offered him a pitcher of hot water, a fourth a basin. Each of them made obeisance to Moncrief, and each of them was the bearer of something entirely inconsequential and unnecessary.

At least ten people filed into the room, all looking delighted that their duke was half–propped up in bed, his color returned to normal and his smile firmly in place. A few of the maids, however, were staring a little too long and hard toward his waist, where the sheet abruptly stopped and more of Moncrief began.

Catherine stood and walked to the open door, a none-too-subtle encouragement for them to leave.

Moncrief only grinned at her when she closed the door firmly behind them.

She sat and watched him devour the custard first, then the broth. He looked around the tray as if expecting more food to appear. Perhaps tomorrow he could have something more substantial.

"You should continue to rest."

"Only if you join me in this bed. What sort of a gentleman would I be if I allowed you to sleep on a chair?"

"It's nearly dawn," she told him.

He looked surprised.

"Your staff has been lurking outside your door for most of the night. They were worried about you."

"Have you been awake all this time as well, Catherine?"

"I'm your wife," she said. "Why wouldn't I care for you?"

"If you are as good a nurse as you claim, you would know to humor a patient. Come and join me."

"I would shock Peter, not to mention Wallace."

"I trust our servants will ignore us." He looked the consummate duke with one eyebrow raised.

She nodded, unable to keep from smiling. She was just relieved he was feeling better, that was all. She was not entertaining any notion of getting into his sickbed with him.

But when he pointedly glanced at the door, she stood and turned the key in the lock. When she returned to the bed he moved to one side slowly so that she could lie beside him.

"I'll have to remove my clothing," she said softly.

"Of course," he said, smiling. "Shall I turn my head?"

"You won't," she said, knowing him only too well.

"I've been wounded."

"And you need to be humored."

"Yes, please."

One candle was lit upon the mantel, the better to allow him to sleep. The light in the room, however, was still too great to disrobe in front of him. When she glanced at the candle, however, he shook his head.

"You wouldn't deprive a wounded man of such a treat, Catherine?"

She slipped off her shoes, feeling wicked and depraved. Perhaps that was the price she paid for being Moncrief's wife and his partner in loving.

Her skin felt flushed and tingling, but she very carefully raised her skirts and removed her garters, rolling down her stockings as slowly as her impatience would allow.

"You have beautiful legs," he said. "I thought so from the first moment I saw you. But, then, all of you is beautiful."

She felt the warmth rise from the core of her to spread up over her chest to her cheeks. Slowly, she unlaced her dress, grateful that it was easily done without a maid's help.

"I thought you'd dispensed with all those ugly black dresses."

She hesitated, then told him the truth. "It felt appropriate to wear it when you were missing."

He didn't say anything for a moment, and when he did

his voice was hoarse. "Come and join me, Catherine."

Once the dress was dispensed with, she stood in front of him attired in nothing but her stays and shift. Slowly she unlaced her wood and leather stays and placed them on a chair. Her shift was heavily embroidered with multi-colored thistles, but wrinkled where the stays had been, and she smoothed the garment with her fingers before turning back to him.

She would have entered the bed then, but he shook his head again, still smiling.

"Almost, Catherine. But you have to remove your shift."

"May I blow out the candle?"

He shook his head.

She gripped the hem of her shift and pulled it upward, until her head was through the garment. For a moment she held it in front of her before tossing it to a nearby chair.

A more modest woman would probably have covered herself immediately, but she couldn't help remember that night when she'd first seen him. He'd simply stood before her with his hands at his sides, allowing her to look her fill. She did the same now, feeling a curious sort of pride when his gaze traveled up, then down her body.

His smile had disappeared and so had the mischievous glint in his eyes.

"I remember how you looked that first night," he said softly. "You were the most beautiful creature I've ever seen. I kept thinking that you must be a statue come to life because your body was so perfect."

"And now?"

He glanced at her, a smile easing the somberness of his face. "Are you soliciting compliments, Catherine?"

She was embarrassed at the accusation because that's exactly what she was doing.

Slowly, she walked toward the bed, climbing the steps and sitting with her back to him. "I don't remember anything of that night. Even after all this time, I can't remember."

"Perhaps it's a good thing you don't. I was lecturing myself the whole time. I told myself I should not consider the fact that you were naked. Instead, you needed my assistance, not my lust."

His comment was so close to her own thoughts of late that she smiled.

"Take your hair down, Catherine."

She reached up and removed the pins that held her hair, letting it fall below her shoulders. She threaded her fingers through it.

"It will get tangled."

"I'll comb it for you."

"With one hand?"

"You might be surprised at all the tasks I can accomplish with only one hand."

She felt her face burn, imagining exactly what he could do.

His hand was on her back, tracing a line from shoulder to waist. She shivered, then raised her legs until she was lying on the bed beside him, facing him. He surprised her by covering her with the sheet. She could feel his breath on her arm, but he didn't say anything. Nor did he move away or closer to her.

He was watching her, a small smile playing on his lips. "You act as if we're strangers, Catherine."

Not strangers. Too close in some ways. He held her mood in the palm of his hand and could alter it with a smile.

Moncrief reached below the sheet and cupped her breast with his hand, his thumb brushing over the nipple. "You are so responsive to my touch, Catherine."

She allowed her eyes to flutter shut, wishing he wasn't injured. If he wasn't, she would kiss him or place her hands on him in a dozen or so places he liked. But all she could do was lie there and let his words fall over her like heated rain.

"I remember how your nipples taste against my tongue. Or how slick you are when I enter you."

Her skin felt as if it was burning.

"Do you remember the day in the distillery? When you put me in your mouth?"

She nodded, finding it difficult to breathe.

"I've had to force myself not to think of that memory. It inflames me too much. I want to seek you out wherever you are and bury myself in you."

Now she truly couldn't speak.

Their faces were only inches apart. He was lying on his good arm, his bandage appearing over the sheet.

She touched him there, with the most gentle of touches, thinking that if the man who'd shot him had been a better marksman, he wouldn't be with her now.

Her hand flattened against his chest, fingers splayed. Slowly, as if she explored him for the very first time, her fingers traveled down his chest, stopping at his abdomen and tracing the shape of his erection.

"You should be resting."

"I am," he said, smiling. "You're doing all the work. I'm only enduring the torture."

Such a silly word for what he must be feeling if he was like her, inflamed with need, almost in pain from it.

Neither moved, and the air below the sheet grew heavy and heated with desire. Her blood felt like warmed oil, but he didn't move to kiss her. Nor did she, trapped in a hazy seduction. She was content to allow him to tease her softly and gently, with whispered words and the most delicate touches.

He moved closer, placing his hand flat against her back, pulling her close until her cheek was against his chest. For the first time in what felt like a very long time, she was at peace, feeling safe and secure.

At last she fell asleep, her last thought a startling one—Moncrief was not only an exciting lover, he was a tender one, almost as if he felt more for her than desire.

Chapter 26

Catherine placed the apothecary jar back in the case, glancing at the label as she did so. The writing appeared vaguely familiar. She didn't think she'd ever seen Moncrief's penmanship before. Strangely, the script reminded her of Harry's writing.

She'd changed Moncrief's dressing and used the bullet powder, and now he was insisting upon getting up and dressing. Throwing her hands up in defeat, she summoned his valet and Peter as well.

"I'll return in a few moments," she said to Peter, unwilling to divulge her errand or that curiosity was propelling her to do something altogether foolish.

She descended the stairs and nodded to Wallace, who was looking stern and official in his new black suit. He bowed in return, the young man with the laughing eyes buried behind the majordomo's flat gaze and tight mouth.

Everything had changed since Moncrief had been brought home wounded.

"He slept well," she said, "and is insisting upon rising and dressing."

Wallace's face eased somewhat. "That's good to hear, Your Grace."

"I doubt I'll be able to keep him in his room, Wallace. But he will not leave Balidonough."

They shared a complicit glance. "As you wish, Your Grace. I'll pass the word to the staff."

"Thank them for their loyalty, Wallace."

"I will, Your Grace," he said, his words accompanied by another bow.

"Has Glynneth returned?"

He only shook his head.

Catherine left him then, entering the library, pausing at the door to allow her eyes to become accustomed to the sunlight streaming in through the windows. In Moncrief's chamber, she had closed all the curtains and extinguished the candles, the better to allow him to rest.

She took the two steps down into the rotunda and sat at the desk that dominated the space.

Why had the driver of the wagon shot him?

Where was Glynneth?

There were too many questions to be answered, which was why she was here. Why did Moncrief's writing seem so familiar to her?

She opened his top left drawer to find a selection of quills and two inkhorns tightly capped. One held a brown ink, the other black. The top right desk drawer held a selection of paper.

Moncrief's correspondence from his solicitor was in the second drawer, and a variety of journals and ledgers were neatly aligned in the third. She would not invade his privacy by reading his letters, but she did open a few pages only to glance at his signature. His M was a swooping letter but neatly restrained. The other letters looked similar to the writing on the apothecary jar.

She closed the drawer and sat back against the leather chair. From here the entire expanse of the library was visible, all except a few nooks and crannies on the second level. Here, Moncrief could sit and look out over the inner courtyard of Balidonough, could see the rolling hills and woods that bordered his land, could trace the path of the river. He was king of this particular domain, a duke with princely arrogance.

Harry's writing shouldn't be similar to Moncrief's. There, the thought that she was trying desperately hard to ignore. They were educated differently, came from two different backgrounds. One was a merchant's son and the other the son of a duke. One was regrettably lacking in character while the other was the epitome of nobility and honor.

Dear God, what was she thinking?

One drawer was left, and she gazed at it for a moment before placing her hand on the pull. The fact that it was locked didn't surprise her. She fumbled around inside the knee well for the latch, but there was none. Finally, she found a small keyhole that must be the locking mechanism. She had a choice—simply to ignore the matter and return to Moncrief's side, or to find the key.

She turned in the chair and glanced at a small porcelain jar on the shelf. Her father had had a habit of keeping important items in odd containers. Had Moncrief hidden the key in plain sight?

If the drawer was locked, there was a reason for it. She should not invade his privacy in such a blatant way. But she looked inside the jar anyway, to find nothing. The curious little brass monkey statue posed with a removable hat was likewise as empty. A small carved chest opened to reveal a wonderful scent and something that looked like incense. Just as she despaired of locating the key, she found it in the bottom of a magnificent red Chinese urn sitting on its own pedestal in the corner.

She slipped the key into the lock and turned it slowly, telling herself that there was still time to repent of her curiosity. Besides, she might well be disappointed in what she found in this locked drawer.

An instant later, she realized she couldn't do it. Catherine turned the key again, testing the drawer to ensure that it was still locked. Instead, it slid open at a touch, and she stared at the contents, horrified that she'd accidentally invaded his privacy. She slammed it shut, only to realize, a second later, what she'd seen.

Slowly, she pulled out the drawer again. The drawer was empty except for a collection of letters, tied together with a leather string. She knew the handwriting on these only too well. She'd written them herself.

In loneliness, in despair, in times of joy and uncertainty, she'd written Harry of her hopes and dreams, of her irritations, and her accomplishments. She'd avidly read the letters he'd written her in return, gradually coming to love the author of such poetic and lovely words.

What was Moncrief doing with them?

Her father whirled and marched toward the fireplace, only to turn and advance on her again. "Is he dead?"

"I'm certain he is not," Glynneth said. "You would have heard, I think. Catherine still admires you."

"No thanks to you," he said, scowling at her. His normally round and cherubic face was flushed, and he wore such a look of rage that any member of his congregation would be shocked. Contrary to their belief, the vicar was not a man of genial temperament. Or at least, he'd never been so around her. Being his daughter had never been an easy task, but never more so than now.

"You can't stay here."

She held Robbie's hand too tightly; her son squirmed to get away. She bent down to comfort him. "I have nowhere else to go, Father," she said, straightening again.

"You should have thought of that earlier."

"No, Father. I think Robbie and I will stay here," she said.

"And what do I tell my congregation?"

"Tell them whatever you wish. Or should I tell my own tale? About how you tried to kill Catherine with laudanum? Or how you tried to kill both of them at Balidonough?"

For a moment father and daughter stared at each other. Then the vicar smiled, such a charming expression that anyone else might have been taken aback. But she knew him well, and knew that his smiles were often used to disarm. Therefore, Glynneth prepared herself for his next words.

"I did it for you."

"You did it for me. Surely you don't expect me to believe that?"

"Who is Catherine's heir?"

She frowned at him. "She doesn't have one. She's the last of her family."

"Not true, daughter. She was married to Harry, and Harry has a son."

She felt a frisson of horror. "Robbie."

"He is Harry's son, is he not?"

She nodded. She'd never kept her lover's identity a secret from him. In fact, she'd begged to marry him, but her father considered Harry a wastrel and a fool.

"If she dies, the courts would look kindly on the fact that Robbie is his only child. Everything could become Robbie's."

"I will not profit over the death of another, especially in the case of murder."

"Are you certain? You would never have to work for other people again, Glynneth. Never take their orders. Robbie would be a gentleman."

"What kind of man serves God and himself with such greed? Or do you pretend that you don't want part of Robbie's inheritance?"

"It's a moot point, is it not?" he asked. "She's married to Moncrief now." He flicked a finger at one cuff, before straightening the lace. "He's made her a gift of her inheritance."

"How do you know that?"

"You'd be surprised what servants will say. Especially those who can read. A paper left here or there can be fodder for all sorts of gossip."

"Especially if you've paid for it."

He smiled. "A judicious investment, my dear."

He was too pleased with himself. She finally understood. "If Catherine dies, her fortune reverts to her heirs."

"Robbie," the vicar said, smiling.

She studied him, wondering which, of the two of them, was the more loathsome creature—him, for being a man of God and yet so immersed in greed that it made him want to kill another person, or herself, that she had not told Moncrief or Catherine her suspicions about her father.

Evidently, he'd interpreted her silence as an assent. "Perhaps I'll call upon them, ensure myself of Moncrief's well-being or help him along the path to heaven itself. If he predeceases her, Catherine, finding herself a widow again, would naturally become despondent. Think of all that incredible wealth, Glynneth."

"Which you would have to administer for your grandson's sake," she said, fully understanding the depth of his greed.

At his silence, she felt a sickening lurch of fear. "What are you going to do?"

"Something," he said. "Anything. God does not pay as well as you might imagine, Glynneth."

Catherine sat at Moncrief's desk, her hands folded together in front of her. When the door opened, she turned, unsurprised to see him standing there.

"You're not supposed to leave your room."

"By whose dictates?"

She sighed. "I would be foolish to expect you to obey anyone's orders, Moncrief. How did you do so in the regiment?"

"I occasionally chafed against the restrictions."

She only shook her head.

"What is it?" he asked her, frowning. "You look pale, Catherine. Are you ill?"

"No, Moncrief, I'm not ill."

He came forward and stood beside her until she was forced to turn her head and look up at him. He was dressed so perfectly that it almost hurt to look at him. He was a portrait made alive, a duke in all his superiority and power. His dark blue breeches were topped with a matching coat, and a heavily embroidered waistcoat. He wore white stockings, and black shoes with gold buckles. Even his buttons were gold, heavily incised with his family's crest.

His arm was carefully supported in a triangle of white silk that looked to be a cravat pressed into service as a sling.

"You're certain you're not ill?"

"Very certain," she said, standing. She moved aside so that he could sit behind the desk.

She wandered to the edge of the rotunda, mounted the steps and stood staring at the shelves aligned in perfect order, filled with thousands upon thousands of volumes. More than a lifetime of learning was stored there.

His hand was suddenly on her shoulders, and she flinched from the touch. He turned her in his arms and studied her face as she raised her eyes.

"Tell me. What is it?"

Catherine only shook her head, so stunned by the revelation that had come to her that she still couldn't speak of it.

"Truly, there's nothing wrong," she said. In fact, she wasn't altogether certain she lied. She wasn't angry. Nor did she feel betrayed. She was simply confused.

"I need to talk to the wagon driver. Do you want to be here?"

"Of course."

Catherine knew him well enough by now to know that when he was fixed on a point, he wouldn't budge from it. She wouldn't be so foolish to ask him to rest or even to delay his interrogation.

Peter entered the room a few minutes later and looked from Moncrief to her. Had he sensed the tension in the air? Unspoken words hung between the two of them. Moncrief, however, was wise enough not to question her further.

What could she possibly say?

My dearest Catherine,

You will probably not receive this until spring. The river is frozen and the snow is thick upon the ground. I used to believe that the winters in Scotland where harsh, but this barren landscape is empty except for snowdrifts, and trees laden with icy branches.

Perhaps it is because we are soldiers and missing our loved ones, but nothing about Quebec appears hospitable. We do not venture far from the city in our patrols, since there are French who would like to boast of our capture or worse.

She could almost feel his loneliness through his words, but by the time she had received his letter, he was already dead.

Or was he?

"The man, McClaren, admits to shooting you, Your Grace. Shall I call the sheriff?"

"I am the sheriff," Moncrief said.

"Throw him in the dungeon." Catherine turned and faced Peter.

"Such a bloodthirsty woman," Moncrief said, smiling.

"I have no compassion for the man who nearly ended your life." When she glanced at him, he winked at her, a gesture that was so out of keeping with Moncrief's demeanor that she was startled.

The man was brought into the room, his wrists bound in front of him with a rope. One ugly gash sliced through his cheek, and his left eye was swelling. Evidently, some of Moncrief's staff felt the same way she did.

McClaren was older, but not infirm. His arms were thick, as was his chest, and he stood in front of them with a belligerent look on his face as if he dared any of them to strike him again.

"Release him." Moncrief's command had all of them glancing at him.

He sat behind the desk and surveyed the prisoner, evidently oblivious to their looks of disbelief.

"What have you to say for yourself?"

The man who faced him remained silent.

His hat had been stripped from him, revealing long, graying hair. Yet for all his maturity, the look in his eyes was young and angry.

"You shot me?"

"I did, and I'd do it again. You were on my land, and I've no liking for poachers."

Moncrief let that pass and asked another question. "Do you know Glynneth Rowan?"

The man remained silent. Peter shoved him in the arm, making him stumble forward.

"I'll not say whether I know her or not. And you can strike me all day, and my story'll not change."

"She commands great loyalty from you, then," Moncrief said, nodding. "What I want to know is why you shot me? The real story, and not the tale you dreamed up about a poacher."

The other man remained mute.

"Was it because I was coming too close to learning her secret?"

Catherine glanced at him.

McClaren still didn't speak, but the look in his eyes was now wary.

"How long have you cared for her child?"

"Since he was born," the man said.

Catherine sat abruptly on the chair beside the desk.

"How did you know?"

Moncrief didn't answer her, only addressed another comment to the man. "My quarrel is not with a child. Nor with Glynneth."

"Then why did you follow her? I saw you."

Moncrief glanced at Catherine. "Because I believe she knows who injured my wife."

McClaren's gaze slid to Catherine. She returned his look steadily, torn between anger at him and at Moncrief.

"He's like a son to me," McClaren finally said, looking at Moncrief once more. "Or a grandson. Either way, he's just a little boy. Barely more than a baby. She told me that people might come, asking. It was my decision to shoot you. And I'm a better marksman than you think. If I'd wanted to kill you, you would be dead."

Moncrief only nodded.

"I'm going to let you go," he said. "Because you brought me home."

"I wouldn't have," McClaren said. "It was Glynneth's idea. She didn't want you dying."

Moncrief smiled. "For that I thank her. And you."

When Peter and Wallace escorted the man from the room, Catherine turned to Moncrief. "How did you know that Glynneth had a child?"

"A guess," he said. "She never missed one of her days off, so it was an important destination. What's more important than a child? Cook said that she always asked her to provide a treat before she left, something she packed in a small basket. In addition, the maids who cleaned her room said that she was always knitting something, a pair of socks, a small sweater."

"But she never said a word," she said, shaking her head. "Never."

He didn't answer her, but studied her almost speculatively, almost as if they were strangers, certainly not two people who had lain in each other's arms for hours.

"You may learn some difficult things in the next few days, Catherine. Are you prepared for that?"

She was uncertain how to answer that, since she already suspected the most difficult truth of all.

"Do you mean that Glynneth meant me harm?"

He nodded.

She would not have believed it a few days ago. But

then, she would not have believed that Moncrief was the man who'd written her all those beautiful letters, or been the author of words that had touched her heart.

"She was a widow," Catherine said. "Like me. I suppose it's why I hired her."

"What about her references?"

"She worked for a family in Inverness, and one outside the city. They'd both written a glowing recommendation for her."

"Did you never write them?"

She shook her head. "There was no reason to."

He glanced down at his desk, aligned two of his quills, readjusted the edge of his blotter.

"You disapprove?"

He glanced over at her. "I think it would have been wiser to examine her references."

"I didn't feel it necessary."

"You're offended."

"A little."

"Would it offend you further if I asked for the name of her employers?"

She stared at him, truly annoyed. "I haven't an idea, Moncrief. That was well over a year ago."

"And you didn't keep the letters?"

"I don't have them with me, no."

"Are they at Colstin Hall?"

"Yes. Do you want to send Peter for them?"

"I think it would be best, don't you? The more we know about Glynneth, the better."

She didn't answer.

"What is it, Catherine?" he asked, placing his hand atop hers. His hand was so warm, and she could feel the booming of his heart through his shirt. "You're upset with me, and it's more than Glynneth or my health. What is it?"

Ask him about the letters. But she didn't. Instead, she

raised her head and looked him, feeling helpless, confused, and more than a little cowardly.

He bent forward and kissed her.

"You should be in bed," she said when the kiss was done. "You were shot two days ago."

He didn't answer, only kissed her again until the blood in her veins felt like heated honey.

"I think you'll find I heal quickly." He kissed her again.

Before she could protest, he led her back to the desk.

"Step up," he said, motioning her to the chair.

She looked at him questioningly, but he only shook his head. She placed one foot on the chair and he helped her sit on the desk, right in the middle of his leather-trimmed blotter.

"Moncrief—" she began, only to have her words smothered by another kiss.

"I heal *very* quickly."

He stood between her knees, and fumbled with the buttons of his breeches.

"Moncrief," she said again, shocked.

"I'm a wounded man, Catherine. I need some comfort."

She shook her head at him, half-amused, half-horrified. "On your desk, Moncrief?"

"Would you prefer the floor?" He nuzzled her neck, placing a ring of kisses up to the back of her ear. She shivered. His good hand traveled up her skirt to rest between her thighs.

"Although I think my balance might be off. You could always ride me, though."

She'd done that before, and found the position fascinating. Nothing like being taken on his desk.

He stood closer, pulling her to the edge of the desk.

Sighing in surrender, she braced her knees on either side of his hips and crossed her feet behind him, welcoming him with a sigh when he entered her. She was bent back against the desk, the inkhorn her pillow, but he removed it carefully and swept his hand across the desk impatiently clearing it of any other objects.

She laughed, and he smiled, both ruefully aware of their impatience.

He would have ripped open her dress if she'd not been able to loosen her laces.

Moncrief cupped her breasts and placed a kiss upon each tight nipple, all the while surging backwards and then fully into her. She closed her eyes at the sensation of being so beautifully filled and wondered if someone could die of passion.

The thought that he was overdoing slipped from her mind as he pumped once, twice, a thousand times into her. He kissed her again, and she spiraled into it, feeling as if each part of her body were molten hot. A tiny spark a pleasure traveled from the core of her outward, touching her fingertips and toes. She began to tremble, small, insistent tremors traveling up her legs and arms as she felt herself erupt.

She awoke to hear Moncrief calling her name. With some difficulty, she opened her eyes at the sound of her name to find Moncrief looking at her in some concern.

"Why are you crying?"

"I didn't know I was," she said, touching her face with her fingers.

"Did I hurt you?"

She cupped her hand against his cheek and smiled up at him. "No. And you? How is your shoulder?"

"If it pains me, the sensation has faded beneath pleasure."

A few minutes later, she placed her hand on his good shoulder, and he helped her sit up.

He held her against him for a moment.

"Catherine," he said gently.

She raised her head to look at him. There was no smile on his face now, and the glint of wickedness was gone from his eyes. Something altogether disturbing in his gaze, something solemn and important, made her look away.

He tilted up her chin with one finger and placed the softest kiss upon her lips before helping her down from the desk. He held her there for a moment, wrapping his arms around her and kissing her on the forehead.

"Will you tell me now?"

The question was surprising. So, too, was her sudden wish to weep again.

Lust was no longer an acceptable substitute for love, and wasn't that a surprising thought.

Chapter 27

〜♘〜

"Yes, Moncrief," she said. "Something is wrong." But she didn't speak, only licked her lips and looked down at the floor. Finally, she looked back at him. "Why do you have my letters in your desk drawer? My letters to Harry. Why do you have them?"

"Should I ask how you know I have them?"

"I looked." She didn't appear the least apologetic, and he decided that now was not the time to broach the issue of his privacy.

"I debated sending them back to you," he said. "But I took them out of Harry's trunk at the last moment."

"Why?"

These past weeks had been an idyll, a time for him, a time he'd known he'd have to pay for eventually. Now might well be the time.

The longer he knew Catherine, the more certain Moncrief was that he had underestimated her. The woman of the letters neither kissed with abandon nor laughed with glee. She was, for the most part, a somber and lonely soul, who had touched something in his heart. This woman, this enchantress with her mussed hair and her swollen lips and her eyes flashing fire at him was a greater challenge and a more earthbound delight.

Now was the time to tell her of his deception, but he didn't want to destroy what they were creating between themselves. Their relationship was gossamer thin and so fragile that a stiff wind might rip it apart.

He gave her the truth, only not the full measure of it. "Because I didn't think Harry deserved you."

"And you kept them."

"I did," he said, almost daring her to question him further.

She held up her hand in a gesture that strangely mimicked one of his. "When you send Peter to Colstin Hall, will you ask him to fetch something for me?"

"We can go there ourselves if you wish."

"There's no need," she said, turning to leave. Her shoulders were straight, her whole bearing stiff.

She hesitated, and he wondered if she waited for him to offer an apology for his actions, or perhaps a further explanation. He did neither.

"I'll send Peter. If he leaves now, he should be back by tonight."

"My important documents are in my father's library," she said. "In a strongbox in the second cabinet from the door. I'll also need the box in his desk."

"I'll convey that to Peter."

She only nodded in reply. The woman who'd laughed with him, who'd loved him with abandon only minutes ago had disappeared, and in her place was a pensive stranger.

Had finding the letters altered her feelings for him? Not an encouragement for the truth.

As he watched Catherine leave, Moncrief couldn't help but wonder what she would do if he imprisoned her in the keep. He would set up a boudoir at the top of the winding stairs and refuse to let her leave until she confessed that she loved him.

It was an idea that had merit.

"You're right, daughter," the vicar said, entering the house and removing his scarf and greatcoat. He handed both to the maid who stood waiting, then dismissed her with a waggle of his fingers. "Moncrief is vigorously alive at Balidonough. Whoever shot him did a poor job of it, I'm thinking."

Relief flowed through Glynneth at his words, but it was short-lived at best.

"How do you know?"

"The servants at Colstin Hall still need counseling, my dear girl. You'd be surprised how much wickedness flourishes in a master's absence. The cook is disturbed about the downstairs maid, who's been seeing too much of the groom. I spoke with all of them this evening. One of the men from Balidonough had been sent to fetch some of Catherine's belongings. Naturally, he talked of the new duchess and the duke."

Her father had such a look of unholy glee on his face that she was worried.

"What are you planning?"

The vicar considered her for a moment and shook his head. "I don't think I will divulge anything to you, my dear. You have a habit of ruining my very best plans. It was you, was it not, who poured out Catherine's oatmeal posset at every occasion?"

Startled, she stared at him. "How did you know that?"

"A very simple deduction. Catherine would have died

weeks earlier if she'd taken it. What I don't understand is why you feel compelled to protect her. She was your lover's wife."

She glanced down at the wooden horse a neighbor had carved for Robbie. Her son had a habit of leaving it everywhere. Twice she'd nearly stepped on it. Now she placed it on the table in a standing position, ready for him to play with it when he awoke from his nap.

Catherine had unstintingly offered her friendship. Glynneth had been prepared to hate the woman who had married Harry and instead had only pitied her.

She'd never known Harry, not truly.

"Leave her alone, Father," she said. "Leave both of them alone. We'll make do."

He waved his fingers in the air much as he had dismissed the maid. "Do not bother your head about it, daughter. I will do what has to be done."

Peter returned that evening with the strongboxes from Colstin Hall. Instead of leaving them in the library, the former aide brought them to her chamber. Catherine thanked him and sat for a few long moments staring at them on the vanity.

The first of the two boxes wasn't large, but it was heavy, the bottom being layered with coins. She'd kept incidental papers here, and she retrieved Glynneth's references without too much difficulty and placed them aside for Moncrief.

The other box was larger since it had been crafted only for the storage of important papers. Here was the deed to Colstin Hall, the survey of her land, a copy of her parents' marriage lines, and Harry's will.

She opened it with the key she kept with her, and pushed back the top. Finally, she found what she was looking for, the papers Harry had signed before leaving Scotland.

She'd often wondered why her father had been so generous with his new son-in-law, why he'd purchased an expensive commission for a man he barely knew. Had he known of Harry's gambling habits and his infidelity?

With one hand, she held the apothecary jar, the other smoothed out Harry's will.

Harry wrote with a great flourish, his letters swooping and taking up too much of the page as if needing to call attention to his name. Moncrief's writing, on the other hand, was not as large, but the characters were easily read and stronger somehow.

If she hadn't burned all the letters, she would have known earlier. But now, staring down at Harry's signature, she realized she'd never seen it before this moment.

How curious that she didn't seem to be able to breathe. She sat encapsulated in a narrow little bubble of time. Nothing felt real at the moment. She wrapped her hands around the small jar and pressed it to her chest, as if doing so would ease her breathing.

My dearest Catherine, I miss you so.

There are days when I wake and feel your hand on mine, your fingers lingering just for an instant before dawn arrives. I feel as if you are bidding me farewell from my dream. I remember when you said that you hated the darkness. I have begun to crave it, because sleep brings me closer to you. But perhaps I exaggerate. I feel close as well when I am writing to you. I am free to express my inner thoughts selfishly, I fear, because I have you as a captive audience.

Thank you all for your prayers for me and my men.

*Any soldier can use the prayer of a lovely woman.
Tell your vicar, however, that you need not share your
time with him. I am certain you are part angel.*

She had shared her soul with him. She had confessed every deep and hidden secret with him. She had adored him.

Why would Moncrief have written her?

Because Harry couldn't be bothered. Because he was bedding other women. Because she was lovesick and heartbroken and insisted upon writing a man who no doubt looked upon her frequent letters as an imposition and an unwelcome reminder that he was married.

She folded her arms on the vanity and buried her face in them.

Was she such a pathetic creature that he'd taken pity on her?

Catherine forced her hand open, placing the jar on top of her vanity. Her fingers hurt from clenching it so tightly. Slowly, she spread her hands open and placed them palms down on her lap. She was trembling and altogether unprepared for the knock on the door.

For a heart lurching moment, she wondered if it was Moncrief, but then she heard Wallace's voice.

"Your Grace!"

She opened the door to find him stripped down to his shirt and breeches. "Your Grace, the keep is on fire." He peered over her shoulder into the room.

"Moncrief isn't here, Wallace. Perhaps he's at the distillery." She didn't doubt that he would be there, or somewhere else he shouldn't be. Instead, he should be resting, recuperating from a gunshot wound. But "should" was not a word to be used around Moncrief.

"Yes, Your Grace."

He bowed himself away from her, intent upon finding Moncrief.

Catherine stood and walked to the window. Yellow flames shot from the top of the round, turreted structure, the fire evidently fueled by the stacked furniture stored inside.

No moon shone in the sky; the night was clear and cold. The yellow-and-orange flames of the fire and the resultant smoke obscured the canopy of stars.

Catherine pressed her hands against the glass, feeling the bitter cold against her palms, horrified at the sight of the keep burning. The wooden floors would be the first to go, then all the furniture, paintings, and trunks stacked on the first floor.

When she finally saw Moncrief cross the courtyard attired in nothing more than his shirt and trousers, she left the room, racing down the steps. Wallace was gone, but she grabbed her cloak and a servant's greatcoat and made her way to the fire.

Moncrief was already organizing the men into two groups, each of them acting as a brigade of sorts, conveying buckets to the flaming keep. She wanted to shout at Moncrief to be careful, the revelations of only moments ago somehow fading in importance to his safety.

"You shouldn't be here," he said, coming to her side.

"Nor should you." She handed him the greatcoat and helped him don it over his sling. "You must not tax yourself."

His smile was crooked and thoroughly charming. "I told you I heal quickly."

She shook her head at him, then stared at the fire. "I never took a full inventory of the keep. Heaven only knows how many precious treasures are being destroyed."

"If they were that precious, they wouldn't have been stored in the keep."

She glanced at him. How like him to put the loss into perspective.

He smoothed a hand over his hair, leaving a soot mark on his forehead. She wiped it away with her fingers, a gesture that surprised both of them.

"Forgive me," she said, unable to explain that she needed to touch him, or convey in some way how she felt about him. All the conflicting emotions she'd felt earlier surged through her.

All those months she had grieved for a man who had never been, only to find, tonight, that he'd been resurrected right before her eyes. She remembered so many things that he'd said that brought his letters to mind, so many hints that might have proven his true identity.

At first, she had been so wrapped up in her despair that she had not seen it. Recently, however she had been so immersed in delight and passion and even lust that she had ignored the signs as well.

What a gift God had given her, to love a man of such promise and ability.

But did he love her in return? Or had he only felt sorry for the widow and before that, the wife?

"Go back inside."

"Can I not do anything?"

"Arrange for Cook to make a meal and something hot to drink. It looks as though we'll be here all night."

She nodded, then brushed an ember from her cheek. But it wasn't hot. She glanced up at the sky.

"It's snowing."

The heavy flakes were mixing with the smoke, creating a strange combination of gray snow.

"Get inside." He gripped her cloak in one hand and pulled her close. "I don't want to have to worry about you as well."

Catherine only nodded again, prevented from asking the questions she needed to ask by the circumstances and the too-interested bystanders. Hortensia was there with only a shawl to warm her. Standing close, and in animated conversation was Wallace. She nodded from time to time, but didn't speak. Cook was there along with her helpers, and a battalion of maids were standing to the side.

She made her way back to Balidonough, intent on Moncrief's task, glancing back at the fiery keep from time to time.

"A most forbidding welcome," a voice said.

She turned to see a man standing in the shadows.

"Vicar?"

"My dear, have I startled you? It was not my intent."

He came forward, and she realized he'd disappeared into the shadows because of the dark greatcoat he was wearing.

"What are you doing here, vicar?"

"I've come with news from Glynneth."

"Glynneth?"

They walked toward Balidonough together, him falling into step beside her.

"Where is she? Where has she been all this time? Why has she not returned to Balidonough?"

"Perhaps I might prevail upon you to offer me something warm to drink before I begin to answer all your questions? Some of your famous Balidonough whiskey would not be amiss, I think."

Most of the staff of Balidonough was in the courtyard. She took the vicar into the Red Parlor, a familiar place since they had often retired there after dinner when he'd visited with the Dunnans.

She motioned toward the sideboard as she sat on the settee in front of the fire. Someone, blessedly, had kept it burning. The snow was still blanketing the ground, and from her vantage point it looked beautifully peaceful. Except that Moncrief was out in it, fighting a fire.

"Serve yourself some whiskey, vicar."

"And may I serve you as well, my dear? I would feel somewhat awkward partaking of your generosity alone."

"A small whiskey, then."

He had his back to her and was taking an inordinately long time to serve them both. She wanted to ask him if there was a spot on the glass that had offended him, or if he was praying over the whiskey, but she didn't voice either thought. The last time she'd seen him, he'd been leaving Balidonough because of her rudeness.

Instead of saying anything, she merely took the glass from him and motioned to the settee beside her.

"What about Glynneth?" she asked, taking a small sip of whiskey.

Although everyone at Balidonough was justifiably proud of the distillery and drank their whiskey often, Catherine had not yet developed a taste for it. However, she couldn't remember it ever tasting this bitter.

"Glynneth is well," he said.

Catherine took another sip, then set it down on the table between them.

"She's returned to Kirkulben."

She sat back against the cushions and looked at him. "I'm surprised. I didn't know that she had friends there. In fact, I thought the opposite."

"She has no friends. But she does have family." He looked down at the floor, then back at her, a small boy confessing a large misdeed. He took off his spectacles, rubbed them briskly with the edge of his waistcoat, and replaced them. "She is my daughter."

Chapter 28

Catherine leaned forward, grabbed the glass, and took another sip. This time the taste was not so bitter. Instead, it was sweet. She would have to ask Moncrief if he'd made some adjustment to the distilling process.

When she sat back it was to find that her balance was slightly off. She bumped her elbow against the arm of the settee, nearly spilling the remainder of the whiskey.

One hand went up to press between her brows and ease the tingling there. She blinked at the vicar, and he smiled back at her. A very calm smile, as if he understood everything that was suddenly happening to her.

"You are her father," Catherine said, finding her lips suddenly dry. Her tongue felt too large for her mouth.

"I am. It's not something I mentioned in the past. After all, she has an illegitimate child. But I'm sure you know that already."

She nodded.

"Did you know that Harry was the father?"

The glass slipped from her numbed fingers and fell onto her lap, pooling the liquid. She watched as the whiskey seeped into the pale blue fabric, ruining it. Moncrief would be unhappy. He really liked this dress.

Glynneth. The vicar was talking about Glynneth and Harry.

"Did Harry know?"

"Of course he did, my child. But there is nothing he could do. You know his family. They have no money, certainly not enough to please a man like Harry. He needed to marry an heiress. You."

She nodded, remembering tales of Harry's gambling. The Dunnans would never have been able to support Harry's losses.

"So he introduced himself to your father, then to you. One thing led to another as things do, and you found yourself besotted with him."

"I was in love." She had to enunciate her words carefully. Was she getting tipsy? She had never been tipsy before. Is this what it felt like?

"Of course you were, my dear. All young women were in love with Harry."

"Why are you telling me this?"

Instead of answering her, he stood. "I think you need to rest now, don't you?"

His voice was so soft, she almost leaned into it. It sounded as if it must be a cloud, billowy and restful.

She found herself moving, but she couldn't feel her feet. She looked down to make sure she wasn't floating, but no, her shoes were touching the shiny wooden floor. She meant to mention it to the vicar but before she could, the thought simply slipped through her mind. He was walking her upstairs. Wallace still wasn't at his post. No doubt he was fighting the fire.

"Everyone is there but me," she said, suddenly feeling uncomfortably warm. "I should be outside as well."

"You need to rest."

"Yes. But there's a fire."

"Yes, I know. A pity that all those lovely things had to burn."

She glanced at him but before she could formulate a question, it simply slipped away.

"I've had too much whiskey. Forgive me."

"You haven't really. Have you forgotten the taste of laudanum, my dear? This time I've given you enough to ensure you sleep. Long and forever."

Catherine felt her heart begin to slow, her limbs grow heavier. Each inch they traveled down the corridor was a mile.

"The Duke's Chamber is this way, is it not, my dear? I must admit I didn't have the time to explore during my last visit to Balidonough. Perhaps at your funeral I will have the opportunity to look around."

She glanced at him, wondering why she didn't feel the least bit intimidated by such a word: funeral. Funeral. It seemed have no meaning at all but sounded only like a strange grouping of syllables strung together. But even that thought was too difficult to maintain for long.

Suddenly she was in her chamber. No, not hers. Moncrief's. But then, she rarely spent any time in hers lately. She slept with him, always touching him in some way.

He laughed about her cold feet.

She couldn't even feel her feet.

All the past dukes looked down at her disapprovingly, as if she had no place in this room all by herself, that her only position was as Moncrief's consort. Otherwise, she was unknown, unliked, and unwelcome.

The vicar led her to a small desk in the corner and

placed a quill in her hand. It fell from her numbed fingers and he patiently replaced it.

"I want you to write something, my dear." His voice was so kind, but then he'd always been kind to her.

"I want you to tell Moncrief that you would like to die now."

But it was so far from what she truly felt that she could only grip the quill with trembling fingers.

"I don't," she said, forcing the last bit of lucidity from the haze that had become her mind. "I want to sleep."

"I know, my dear, but you must write the letter first."

She wanted to ask how he knew what she was thinking. Did he have the power to define her thoughts, did God give him that ability along with his calling? But then she realized she was speaking aloud because she could feel her lips move. Puzzled, she placed two fingers against her lips to silence her thoughts.

She dropped the quill and it made a blot on the paper he'd put before her. A sound escaped her, an inarticulate protest. She was incapable of speech, her mind becoming more and more numb as the seconds ticked by.

He placed the quill once again in her fingers. She wanted to apologize, but his swearing confused her.

She couldn't write to Moncrief and tell him she wanted to die. She wanted, very much, to live. The quill dropped again, and she leaned over to pick it up from the floor and fell to her knees.

He swore again, and suddenly he was walking her to the ducal bed. Moncrief had often done the same, but there would be no passion in this night, but only a sickening kind of horror that would accompany her death.

She understood that much.

The vicar wanted her to die.

He laid her down and covered her with a blanket. She wanted to ask if he was going to pray over her, but she couldn't say the words. She wanted him gone. If she was going to die she would do so without a witness. Perhaps she could say something in the silence of the room, words that would linger on long after she died, thoughts that Moncrief would hear when he entered the room.

She wanted him to know that she hadn't planned any of this, that it was as much horror for her as it would be for him. Would he mourn her? Please God, don't let him mourn her as she had Harry. She would not wish grief or despair on anyone, especially not the man she loved.

She heard a key in the lock and realized the vicar had locked the door to the hall.

"I'll just lock the door, shall I? Until such time as you've gone to sleep, my dear. By that time, the fire will be out, and I'll be gone."

And she would be dead.

She forced open her eyes, and the ceiling whirled above her.

He stood at the connecting door to her room. "I'll lock this one as well. You mustn't call for help, my dear. That would ruin all my plans."

Then, just as she was certain he would leave her, he pulled the bell rope free, the embroidered length of it falling in a puddle to the floor.

She heard the sound of a door close, and waited. Only then did Catherine rise from the bed, stumble to the wall, and half slump against it. Above her head was the sconce Moncrief had turned to release the secret door.

Please, let me survive. She reached up only to find that she couldn't touch the bottom of it.

The laudanum was sapping her strength, but she was not going to die, not without a struggle and not without using the very last drop of her energy. She edged against the wall, and stood on tiptoe before reaching up again. This time, her fingertips brushed against the bronze circle welded to the bottom of the sconce. But she couldn't pull on it hard enough.

She kept blinking to clear her vision, but a gauzy white haze obscured her sight. The fireplace was on the other side of the room, and she made her way toward it, her steps slow and unbalanced. Once, she nearly fell over the ottoman arranged in front of a chair, but steadied herself. When she reached the fireplace tools, she gripped the poker and, holding it like a scepter, made her way back to the sconce.

The laudanum slowed her movements, made it difficult to aim with the poker or hook it into the circle. Perspiration dotted her forehead and she felt nauseated but she didn't give up.

Moncrief.

His name was a lodestone, a beacon through the mist that was beginning to cloud her mind. She wouldn't succumb because of Moncrief. He had saved her before, but this time she would have to save herself.

The next try she hooked the circle with the end of the poker. She wrapped her hands around the brass handle and used the weight of her body to pull it downward. Slowly, the door opened with a creak, so loud that she wondered if the vicar could hear the sound.

Please don't let him come in. Please, let him have left Balidonough.

She entered the dark passage and closed the door with her shoulder.

Moncrief.

She placed both hands on the walls and stumbled forward, trying to get her bearings. She couldn't feel her feet, didn't know how many doors she passed. There should be stairs, but she felt as if she walked the length of Balidonough and could not locate them. At one point, she stopped and turned, certain she should have turned left instead of right. But finally she noticed a pool of darkness

ahead of her. The stairs. Slowly, she descended them, trip-
ping on the next to the last step and landing heavily on her
knees.

She was not going to die here. Swaying, she tried to
stand, fighting back the surge of nausea. The smell of
onions sickened her, and she was violently ill. Laudanum
always made her sick.

The smell of onions. She was in the cool room.

She reached up with both hands, praying that the handle to the door was not too high to reach. But she found it
on her third try and turned it. The groan of the opening
door was the sweetest sound she'd ever heard.

The cool room was filled with food, all stored for the
winter. Bags and barrels filled with all sorts of grains and
oats. Meat hung overhead, salted and cured.

A faint glow from the fire penetrated the staircase
leading to the kitchen. She doubted she could manage
the steps, so she turned to the left and traced her hands
over the bricks until she found the door to the courtyard.

This one was more difficult to open, but she persisted,
pushing on it until she tumbled out into the night, lying
on her back in the open air, snow falling down upon her
face like soft, chilled feathers.

She could sleep now.

Her stomach rolled again, and once more she was ill.
On her hands and knees with her head hanging between
her arms, she summoned all her flagging strength to stand.

Moncrief.

She finally stood, then began to walk toward the keep,
her gait lurching, her mind on him. As she grew closer to
the keep, the air grew warmer, smoky. Catherine fell
again, choking in the thick air.

Juliana was suddenly there, her face devoid of makeup,
her cloak shielding only a printed wrapper.

"Will you get up, Catherine. You're the Duchess of Lymond, and as such must comport yourself with greater dignity. No matter the provocation."

"Moncrief."

"I will summon him, you silly chit. But first, you really must rise. You're causing a scene."

The blur surrounding her was suddenly peopled with faces.

"Catherine!"

She felt Moncrief's arms around her. "Vicar." Another word she forced herself to speak.

Suddenly, she was in his arms, moving toward Balidonough. Snow fell on her eyelids, a chilled benediction. She was out of energy. Her hands would not work; she could only slap them against his chest. Her lips were numb, and she suspected it wasn't the cold as much as the effect of the poison the vicar had given her.

"Please save me," she said, certain that the words did not come out correctly. Moncrief must know that above all, she had tried. She had tried, not to die, but to live. To remain with him, to love him—he must know.

Please, let me live.

Catherine awoke to find herself in the Duchess's Chamber. Annie sat in the corner, dozing. When she attempted to lift herself up on one elbow, a male hand gently pushed her back against the pillow.

"I didn't see you there," she whispered, as Moncrief came into focus.

He looked terrible, as if he'd not slept for a week. His eyes were reddened, and a growth of beard obscured the sharp angles of his chin. She stretched out her fingers and touched his face.

"I don't know why," Annie grumbled. "He's been beside you for this last week. The most obnoxious man in the entire world, farmer's daughter. I should have left the bullet in him."

Moncrief sent her a look that would have terrified any other woman, but Annie was oblivious to it.

"I thought I banished you from Balidonough," Catherine said weakly.

"You did, farmer's daughter. And I un-banished myself." She grinned, revealing the gaps in her smile. "It's a good thing, too. You would have died if I hadn't been here."

Catherine glanced at Moncrief for confirmation. He only nodded.

"How?"

"I made you sick. I've never seen anyone lose the contents of their stomach so often and so long. You reminded me of a cow I had once, when she was poisoned with spiritweed."

For a healer, she was an insufferable creature.

Moncrief must have shared that thought because his eyes suddenly twinkled.

"The vicar tried to kill me."

"I know. As sheriff, I took the liberty of sending Wallace, Peter, and a number of footmen after him. He is now resting, not so comfortably, in Edinburgh."

"You have your own regiment, Moncrief."

"I do. Some of them are more able than the soldiers I commanded."

"Do you miss being colonel?"

"Not a whit," he said. "I'd much rather be duke. But for the sake of my modesty, perhaps I should not admit such a thing."

What else would he admit?

He bent his head and kissed her softly, gently.

Suddenly, she realized it no longer mattered. None of it did. All that mattered was that she was alive, and so was he. They could reason out the future when it came.

Chapter 29

A week later, Catherine left Moncrief sleeping, intent upon her errand. If she were quick about it, she would be back by noon. He would, of course, be angry with her, but he would simply have to be angry.

The vicar had been taken to Edinburgh for trial, but no one had mentioned what would happen to Glynneth. Catherine was determined to ensure that her former companion was cared for and that she didn't suffer for anything.

She entered the coach, Peter palpable in his disapproval. She managed to ignore him for the most part, concentrating ostensibly on the view, but mostly on the upcoming confrontation with her former companion, and with Moncrief on her return.

At Colstin Hall even winter seemed to be a gentle season. The icy crust on the ground was being blanketed by a soft snow. The weak rays of the morning sun, diffused by a gray sky, struck the manor house, sparkling the windows and lighting the path.

She was welcomed back to Colstin Hall as if the two months away had been a year. She greeted the cook and the assorted maids, and nodded to the majordomo and two footmen in attendance. Colstin Hall was a prosperous manor home, but their staff numbered less than a fifth of what was employed at Balidonough. Because of the size of the home itself, Colstin Hall maintained a coziness lacking at the castle.

At Balidonough, there were hints of war in every place she looked, shields and claymores and banners hanging in mute praise for Moncrief's ancestors' warlike nature. But here in this manor house, there was nothing to remind her of the past.

The sixteen years that separated them from the war with England might have been three hundred, so untouched was Colstin Hall. The world was turning more English, like it or not, and her home seemed to epitomize the change.

But she much preferred Balidonough, because Moncrief was there.

Catherine sent word to her solicitor and remained at the house long enough for her business to be transacted. Only then did she enter the coach again, her destination not Balidonough but the vicar's home.

Peter opened the coach door and helped her descend once more. For a moment, she looked at the small cottage, wondering if she was up to this meeting. Resolutely, she knocked on the door. Moments later, Glynneth answered.

A kerchief covered her golden blond hair and an apron the front of her dark blue dress. Her eyes looked shadowed as if she hadn't slept for days.

They stood looking at each other before Glynneth spoke. "You know."

"Are you talking about your father? Yes, I know he tried to kill me. Did you?"

Glynneth looked startled by such a frontal assault.

She stepped back and wordlessly invited Catherine into the small, warm cottage.

A little boy sat playing with a wooden horse on the rug in front of the fire. He looked so much like Harry that Catherine waited for the pain to come. When it didn't, she only smiled, grateful.

"You gave Harry a son."

"Yes."

"Did you try to harm me, Glynneth?" Catherine asked softly. "Did you give me the laudanum?"

Glynneth took a deep breath and faced her. "I suspected what he was doing, and I stopped him when I could. But I think he put it in your food a few times."

"Why didn't you tell me?"

"You wouldn't have believed me."

Catherine nodded, unable to argue. That time in her life was still cloudy, still a blur.

"I loved him, you know."

"I thought I did as well," Catherine said, giving her the gift of truth in reward for Glynneth's own honesty.

"That's the difference between us, Catherine. I loved him regardless of his faults, while you found a reason not to love him because of them."

Catherine loosened her scarf and wound it from around her head. Now was not the time to discuss Harry's character.

"What are you going to do now?"

"Find someone to care for Robbie. Find another position," Glynneth said. "Find another place to live. A new vicar will be here in a month."

"Come back to Balidonough," Catherine said. "You were an excellent housekeeper, Glynneth, and we might be friends again."

"What would Moncrief say?"

Catherine smiled. "I am the Duchess of Lymond. In this matter, Moncrief has no say."

Glynneth glanced toward her son. "And Robbie?"

"Bring him with you. There are plenty of children at Balidonough."

She withdrew the document from inside her cloak and handed it to Glynneth. "When he's old enough, Colstin Hall will be his."

Glynneth didn't say a word, but she blinked back tears as she read the agreement Catherine had devised, handing over the deed to Colstin Hall to Robbie on his twenty-first birthday.

Glynneth studied the floor. After a few moments, she finally looked at Catherine.

"What I have to tell you may cause you to rescind your offer. I came to Colstin Hall because I wanted to see the woman who had married Harry. I wanted to hate you, and maybe I did, a little. But I realized that you hadn't known Harry, not truly, and I never wanted you to be hurt."

Catherine nodded, believing her.

"Harry would never have written you. He wasn't that kind of man."

A gulf existed between them at that moment and probably always would. Not because she and Glynneth had loved the same man. But because Glynneth was willing to settle for what Harry had given her instead of wanting more.

"You loved someone who never really existed," Glynneth added.

"That's where you're wrong," Catherine said, beginning to smile. "He's very real."

Very real, and very much her love.

Moncrief rang for one of the servants. When the footman peered into the room, he scowled at him.

"Where is Wallace?"

"Moving furniture, Your Grace."

"Moving furniture? Haven't we anyone else to do that chore?"

The footman's face reddened. "I believe he's assisting Miss Hortensia, Your Grace."

Moncrief leaned back in his chair and surveyed the footman, restraining his comments only by the greatest of wills.

He'd seen Hortensia being comforted by Wallace on the night of the fire. He wasn't a fool, he'd seen the looks exchanged between them. He hadn't told anyone of what he'd found in the keep after the rubble from the fire had been cleared out. A bedframe, fully assembled, a bedstead, and a melted silver candlestick.

Hortensia had come to Moncrief a few days ago, and confessed that it was she who had been so panicked at the thought of discovery that she'd raced down the keep stairs. She'd not meant to injure Catherine. While Catherine had been intent on performing an inventory, Hortensia had been waiting for her lover. She hadn't mentioned the man, but it hadn't taken all that much deductive ability to discern who it was. Wallace was some years younger than Hortensia, but relationships such as theirs were not as uncommon as society would like to believe.

"Is Peter back yet?"

"No, Your Grace."

The footman seemed to back up without moving, as if hesitant for the next question. Moncrief asked it anyway.

"And my wife? There's no word?"

She'd been gone from their bed when he awoke this morning, with a short note delivered by this same footman that she had urgent business at Colstin Hall.

He couldn't remember being as angry at anyone in his entire life.

The footman might be wise to be slinking away.

"Give this to the duchess the moment she returns," he said.

The footman stretched his arm forward, careful to keep a distance between himself and Moncrief. He gripped the heavily carved box and stepped back again.

"Yes, Your Grace. Shall I wait for an answer?"

Moncrief should have ignored that idiotic question, but he said, "I believe I'll see my wife soon, unless you are privy to some knowledge that has heretofore escaped me."

The footman paled, and Moncrief excused him with a wave of his hand.

Was she coming back? Or would she choose to remain at Colstin Hall? They'd spoken of her health, of the vicar's trial, of other consequential things this past week, but not, perhaps, the most important.

His love. Their marriage.

"The duke isn't going to be happy, Your Grace." Peter looked toward Balidonough with a frown.

Night was approaching, the sunset glowing richly pink and orange, bathing the world with celebratory colors. A tint of it touched the window of the coach, drifted shyly onto the leather sill, and brushed coyly against Catherine's hand.

She'd thought to be home by noon, but she and Glynneth had sat and talked of Harry, of life, of the future. She'd been charmed by Robbie, and made a fast friend of the little boy by giving him a sweetmeat she'd brought in her reticule for him.

"No doubt Moncrief will be very annoyed," she said, pulling her gloves on tighter. "It's just as well, Peter. I'm not too happy with him."

Now that Glynneth was taken care of, she would have to have that conversation with Moncrief.

Peter only glanced at her, surprised.

On the way into Balidonough, however, she heard her name called in a hoarse voice.

She turned to discover a nearly frozen footman standing there, hopping on one foot, then the other, to keep warm.

"Your Grace," he said, holding out a carved box. "I'm to give this to you the minute you arrive."

She took the heavy object from the footman. She remembered it well from Moncrief's library. She'd even looked inside it for the key to his desk.

Her letters were neatly tied and resting on the bottom of the box.

She slammed the lid shut and brushed by the footman. "For heaven's sake, come inside. I'm sure Moncrief didn't mean you to freeze to death," she said, glancing over her shoulder at him.

The look of fear on the man's face wasn't the least reassuring.

"Where is Moncrief, Wallace?"

"In his library, Your Grace. I'm to let him know the minute you return."

So, the confrontation was going to be a little earlier than she expected.

"Have the candles lit in the chapel, Wallace." He gave the order and the frozen footman walked jerkily down the east wing.

She turned to Wallace. "Tell Moncrief I'll join him shortly," she said.

Wallace looked as reluctant to face Moncrief as the footman had been fearful of him.

She sighed, thinking it was going to be a difficult confrontation, indeed.

The chapel was located on the exact opposite side of Balidonough from Moncrief's office. The structure was connected by a narrow walkway to the main part of the castle. In many respects, it was a miniature Gothic building with buttresses and a soaring arched roof. There were eight panels of glass which, in the daylight, bathed the worshiper in a variety of colors as if celebrating both the penitent and God Himself.

Tonight however, the young footman had lit the altar candles. Each day they were trimmed so they remained the exact height no matter how quickly each burned. The flickering flames illuminated the gold of the altar plates, the candlesticks, and cast shadows upon the antique ivory altarpiece.

If God truly resided in places created for Him, then the God of Balidonough was prosperous and well-favored.

As she sat on one of the heavily carved and well-padded pews, Catherine couldn't help but wonder what type of prayers had been uttered here over the generations. Wealth does not make a person immune from heartache or pain or despair. In many ways, however, it had probably isolated the inhabitants of Balidonough.

Even her modest wealth had done that. People had not so much talked with her as they did to her, in response to a question or comment or a pleasantry. She was, for the most part, alone even before Harry died. Perhaps that is why she had treasured their correspondence so, coming to look upon it as the companionship she lacked.

She picked up the box she'd placed on the pew and opened it again, withdrawing the letters she'd written him. Only then did she see that another letter lay at the bottom, one written in a handwriting she recognized only too well.

Catherine placed the other letters beside her along with the box and stared at Moncrief's letter for a few moments, almost afraid to open it. He would never be hurtful; that was not his way. But he might reveal some things that her heart was not quite ready to learn.

Resolutely, she slid her finger beneath the seal and un-folded the one-page letter. This one was smaller in script than most of his letters to her, as if he had more say and less time in which to do it.

My dearest Catherine, it began. Her heart surged at those words. Strangely, it felt like a shaft of light entered the chapel and pierced right through her.

> *I give these back to you under duress, because while they were originated by you, they have come to give me great comfort. When I was alone in North America, I found they were my lifeline to all things I valued most highly in the world. I read and reread them until I memorized them. I fell in love with the woman who wrote them. That, dearest Catherine, was my greatest mistake.*

Her hands trembled on the letter and she took a deep breath before continuing.

> *These last months in your presence have proven to me how limited your letters truly were. They could not convey your laughter, or the sparkle in your eyes when you are amused. They have no way of demon-strating your kindness, or even revealing your irri-tation, your habit of expressing your annoyance with a roll of your eyes or a look.*
>
> *I fell in love with your words until I fell in love with you.*

His signature was different, and after a moment she smiled.

She folded the letter very carefully and put it in the bottom of the box, then put the box on her lap and ex-tended her arms around it. Catherine took one of the letters from the stack at her side and opened it. How strange that she could remember every single letter he had written her, but she had not recalled her own words to him.

My dearest,

The other day I saw a robin, a pretty little bird, surrounded by sparrows. I wondered why I felt such compassion for him and then realized he was alone of his kind. While the robin had a lovely plumage and was a more attractive bird, the sparrows were a community.

   How silly I am to envy the sparrows.

She smiled as she remembered those words and the morning when she'd written them. She'd been sad and missing him acutely.

Catherine began to read aloud in the chapel as she had often done when finishing a letter to him, to ensure the words didn't sound too maudlin or pitying.

I worry for you so, in the wilds of North America. I cannot think the winters there easily spent. I ache in our chamber when the wind grows wild and the storms come, thinking of you suffering in that desolate place. I have procured a map, and marked the continent in my mind, wondering where you are in that vast and strange country.

Moncrief's voice took up her words, repeating them verbatim as he entered the chapel. " 'Keep yourself safe for me. Forbid yourself, I implore you, the opportunity of being a hero.' "

She carefully folded the letter and put it, and the box, aside. He came to stand in front of her, extending his hands to her. Slowly, she placed hers in his and he drew her up.

" 'Tell yourself, instead,' " he continued, " 'that you must return home, whole, and safe to me.' "

"Dearest Moncrief." She tried to blink away her tears, but they still escaped her eyes to fall unchecked on her cheeks.

"I wrote you those letters, Catherine, not Harry."

"I know."

One aristocratic eyebrow rose. "You know?"

"The writing on the medicine bottles was the same as the letters."

He studied her for a moment, then shook his head as if he chastised himself. "I thought you weren't coming back."

"How could you think that?"

He reached out and touched her cheeks with his fingers, wiping away her tears.

"Welcome home, Catherine."

In that moment, she knew the words were true. Home was where Moncrief was.

"Stay with me. Forever. I love you."

She was so overwhelmed by him, by the look in his eyes, that she couldn't speak. Love warmed his expression and reached between them in an unspoken arc.

"I love you, too, Moncrief."

"A sentence that might have been crafted in granite with a blunt stylus, for all the endless time it took to be uttered."

She lifted her hand and placed it against his cheek, feeling an absurd tenderness for this so powerful and arrogant of men. "Dearest Moncrief."

He bent forward and kissed her, and the world was lost to both of them.

One of the candles sputtered. A flaw in the making of

it, perhaps. A touch of water in the wax. Or perhaps it was simply the effect of four hundred years of prayers still lingering in this hallowed place—prayers that had just been gloriously and lovingly answered.

*It's time to crank up the Summer heat
with these releases coming in June
from Avon Romance!*

Marry the Man Today by Linda Needham

An Avon Romantic Treasure

The very last thing lovely Elizabeth Dunaway plans to do is marry! Determined to liberate the women of Britain, Elizabeth opens a private Ladies Club, scandalizing every male in Victorian London. Of course, Ross Carrington, the Earl of Blakestone isn't like most other men. Ross sets out to tame her rebellious spirit, but soon finds that he's met his match!

Running on Empty by Lynn Montana

An Avon Contemporary Romance

Josie Mayne is on the verge of accepting a bad marriage proposal when her ex Pardee reappears. He needs Josie in an incarnation she's left behind, as his former partner in a bounty hunting business, to help him rescue his kidnapped son. Torn between her crazy old life and a promising new one, Josie takes one last plunge—headfirst into passion with her old flame . . .

Beyond Temptation by Mary Reed McCall

An Avon Romance

Lady Margaret Newcomb is a disgraced daughter of a powerful English earl. Sir Richard de Cantor is a highly skilled warrior of the Templar Brotherhood. Though of different backgrounds, in truth they have both been battered by the world, and only the acceptance—and love—of each other can save them from dangers afoot in this time of battle . . .

The Runaway Heiress by Brenda Hiatt

An Avon Romance

Dina Moore lives under the watchful eye of her bullying brother, Silas, until she learns he has a financial interest in seeing her remain unwed. Never a passive victim, she runs away in the hopes of marrying a kind stranger. Instead, she finds roguish Grant Turpin, and their marriage of convenience turns quickly into a marriage of passion . . .

REL 0505

Avon Romantic Treasures

*Unforgettable, enthralling love stories,
sparkling with passion and adventure
from Romance's bestselling authors*

Avon Romances—
the best in exceptional authors and unforgettable novels!